'Grippy and twisty, this one will keep you guessing' Mel McGrath

'A unique vibe that makes it stand out, and also a truly twisty yet believable tale with memorable characters and a cleverly woven atmospheric narrative' Liz Loves Books

'Filled with jaw-dropping revelations, I had no idea where the book was heading and I was certainly surprised as I followed this twisty rollercoaster journey' Off-the-Shelf Books

'Throughout much of the story, readers will feel like Lynn, off balance as certainties evaporate, but they'll be relieved when she finally stops being a victim and goes on the attack ... an expert piece of contrivance' *Publishers Weekly*

'An addictive thriller with a damaged and relatable heroine at its centre, *The Old You* is an original novel that is both shocking and touching' *Foreword Reviews*

'Tantalising, irresistible and extremely satisfying novel. I loved it and will be shouting about it for a long long time!' Random Things through My Letterbox

'Compelling. Dark. Mysterious' Ronnie Turner

'A tale of manipulation, deception, secrets and lies ... it's a total triumph' Short Book and Scribes

'Domestic Noir with a little *je ne sais quoi*! Sit back and enjoy the read folks, this one is a cracker!' Chapter in My Life

'It's an intriguing account of a marriage full of secrets and lies but with a sinister undertone that slowly drags you under until you're completely immersed in the menacing atmosphere' My Chestnut Reading Tree

'An excellent psychological thriller and one of the best books I have read so far this year' Donna's Book Blog

'Filled with anxiety, understated danger, and delivered with well-timed surprises and finesse. Fans of Clare Macintosh and B.A. Paris should add to their must-read list' Murder and Moore

'Fantastically clever and has certainly raised the game in the world of domestic noir' My Bookish Blogspot

'Intensely suspenseful and gripping tale that kept me guessing until the end' Novel Deelights

'A real page-turner; the characterisation is stunning and there are some really ingenious and original twists' Hooked from Page One

'The plot is compelling and keeps the readers on their toes. It's a psychological thriller that will leave your mind reeling and your heart craving for more from the author' Book Worldliness

'This is such a wondrous blend of poignant reflection, dark-rooted secrets and cunning deception with a tense and twisted heart-thumping conclusion' Jen Meds Book Reviews

'Vivid characters, cleverly plotted' Where the Reader Grows

'An absolute cracker' Me and My Books

'Original and compelling' The Shelf of Unread Books

'A truly excellent and well-written story that will leave you gasping and desperate to read everything Louise Voss has ever written!' Broadbean's Books

'A gripping story full of twists and turns. It will grab you by the neck and won't let you go until the very end' A Lover of Books

'Louise has crafted a completely different but intriguing read that really got under my skin. An absolutely incredible read' Katie's Book Cave

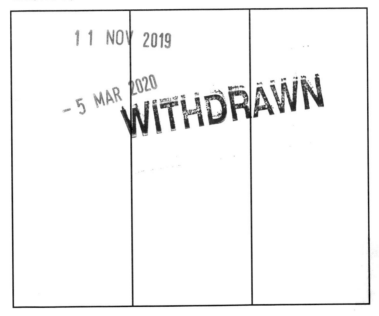

'A skilfully crafted masterclass in writing and I loved being so confidently led through the beautifully woven and elaborate plot' Hair Past a Freckle

'A superb read and seriously the best domestic thriller I have read this year. Unnerving, compelling and just phenomenal' Crime Book Junkie

'Tense, chilling and cleverly plotted' Bloomin' Brilliant Books

'Gripping plot, well-rounded (and unreliable) characters, twists, turns and revelations – all along the way rather than just at the end' Crime Squad

'Haunting, intense, and riveting' Book after Blog

'Voss has written a page-turner with strong character development and compelling emotional resonance' Crime by the Book

'Tense, propulsive, compelling, Louise Voss has created a spellbinding tale of deceit, lies and betrayal that had my brain whirling and my attention focussed throughout' Live and Deadly

PRAISE FOR LOUISE VOSS

'Storytelling at its best' *Now*

'Compelling stuff' *Heat*

'It is Louise Voss's voice that you remember at the end: contemporary, female, authentic' *Independent*

'An exhilarating ride' *New Woman*

'Strong characters, a meaty plot and a satisfyingly unexpected twist' *Woman and Home*

'It's brilliant ... Funny, smart, believable, honest, moving ... a lovely book' Phill Jupitus

'My favourite book this year. A beautifully written story which I didn't want to end' Cerys Matthews

The Last Stage

ABOUT THE AUTHOR

Over her nineteen-year writing career, Louise Voss has had twelve novels published and has sold more than 350,000 copies. Her six solo titles and the six co-written with Mark Edwards are a combination of psychological thrillers, police procedurals and contemporary fiction. Her last book, *The Old You*, was a number-one bestseller in ebook. Louise has an MA (Dist) in Creative Writing and also works as a literary consultant and mentor for writers at www.thewritingcoach. co.uk and as a crime fiction coach. She lives in south-west London and is a proud member of two female crime-writing collectives, The Slice Girls and Killer Women.

Follow Louise on Twitter *@LouiseVoss1*.

The Last Stage

Louise Voss

ORENDA BOOKS

Orenda Books
16 Carson Road
West Dulwich
London SE21 8HU
www.orendabooks.co.uk

First published in the United Kingdom by Orenda Books 2019
Copyright © Louise Voss 2019

A catalogue record for this book is available from the British Library.

ISBN 978-1-912374-87-8
eISBN 978-1-912374-88-5

Typeset in Garamond by MacGuru Ltd
Printed and bound by CPI Group (UK) Ltd, Croydon CR0 4YY

For sales and distribution, please contact *info@orendabooks.co.uk*

This one's for Adrian, with love.

Prologue
1995

At first, you think you're imagining it. An old house, but new to you, one whose soft grunts and shifts you're still becoming acclimatised to; of course there'll be the occasional rumble in the radiators or protest from a floorboard. It's a big house, a proud Georgian beast of a house, bought with the collective pocket money of more than a million teenagers.

But why would a floorboard creak, without a foot putting pressure on it, at three in the morning, and loud enough to wake you from a deep sleep?

Wide awake now, everything tensed, listening so hard it hurts. Nothing. You switch on the bedside lamp, leap out of bed and lunge for the key in the lock, turn it silently. Thank God for the lock on the door.

Then a soft noise on the other side of the door: half swallow, half gulp.

Then the sight of the slow dip of the door handle as someone turns it...

1
2017
Meredith

'Meredith Vincent, you're a hard woman to track down,' said an accented voice Meredith vaguely recognised as belonging to someone she disliked.

'Who is this?'

A laugh. A smoker's cough. She thought, *Ah no, not him. Please say it's not* him.

His next words confirmed it: 'It's Iain McKinnon from Big World.'

Meredith couldn't speak. 'The Pointless I', she and her fellow band-members used to call him, a play on the unnecessary vowel in his first name as well as his capabilities as a marketing manager.

'Merry, are you there?'

'Don't call me that. It's not my name,' she managed.

'Sorry, *Meredith*. Long time, no speak, hey?'

She had forgotten how affected his South African accent sounded. Why did he even still *have* an accent? He'd lived here since before apartheid was abolished.

'How did you get my number?'

He laughed again. 'It wasn't easy, hey. I had to get a private detective on the case!'

He pronounced it *ditictive*.

'You did *what*?'

'Yah. It took him a good few weeks. Hiding in plain sight, you are. We thought you'd left the country! In a million years I'd never have thought you, of all people, would end up working in a *shop*. I mean, it's not like you need the money!'

'I'm the manager,' Meredith said, immediately hating herself for it. She did not have to justify herself to Iain McKinnon, the lecherous creep. He represented everything that she had eventually come to loathe and detest about the music industry, with his fake, smarmy smiles and assumption that every woman wanted to rip off his clothes ... And when he discovered that she didn't, he'd threatened her.

'You know where I work?' She felt as if the walls of her living room were folding in on her, one at a time, bang, bang, bang, bang, squashing her beneath them.

'I know where you work, I know your address and home phone number, I know where you buy your groceries, where your brother lives ... the detective guy was top notch. Cost an arm and a leg,' he said proudly, as if she should be congratulating him instead of feeling that it wasn't just her room that had collapsed, but her whole world.

She had been found, by a man she wouldn't trust further than she could throw.

He seemed to read her mind: 'Merry, I'm not the guy I was back then, I swear. Obviously you know I never had anything to do with ... what happened to you ... I was just a pushy bastard who wouldn't take no for an answer.'

'You blackmailed me, Iain.' Nausea bubbled in her gut.

He coughed. 'Well, I think that's too strong a word ... I just suggested that it might not be a good thing for it to be made public knowledge...'

She noted that he knew exactly what she was referring to.

'It's sad,' she said, her hands shaking, 'when I think how worried I was back then. I thought I had to do what you said. But I was naïve if I thought you had my best interests at heart. Because if it had been this big scandal – which I don't think it would've been anyway; so what if I was sleeping with a woman? – you thought it would have harmed you as well. You were our label manager. If Big World hadn't re-signed us because I was in a relationship with a woman, you'd have lost your most successful act.'

She was trying to act blasé, but in truth she was worried – more than worried. Not about him, not anymore, but because she'd been unearthed. Dug up like a hibernating mole, blinking and afraid. Neither she nor the police had ever been able to prove that what had happened to her back then was connected to him – to his blackmailing her – but it would forever be linked with him in her memory.

'Actually, no biggie,' he said airily. 'It wasn't like I was on commission. They'd have just assigned me to another band. But that's not the point. I shouldn't have got involved in that way. I was ... wrong.'

The last word was extruded with difficulty, as if he had speech constipation.

'Is that why you're ringing me now? What do you want?'

She would have to move. Leave the country, start again.

'Right, so, I have something *amazing* to tell you! You gonna be so psyched. Are you still in touch with the other guys?'

'If you mean Cohen, then no. They hate me, if you remember.'

Meredith had read enough bitter interviews with her former band members over the years to know this was true. After her sudden and inexplicable defection in ninety-five they had laid low for a while, then employed a short-lived series of alternate female lead singers, none of whom had set the charts alight for them. They'd eventually disbanded a couple of years later. She knew she'd hurt them, personally as well as professionally – they had been such good friends – but she hadn't ever dared contact any of them again, or even try to explain, for fear of discovery.

He made a 'pffft' noise. 'Ah, that's all in the past!'

The man was unbelievable.

'Iain, it's *all* in the past. I don't know what you want from me, but if it's anything to do with the band, the answer is a definite "no way". I don't care what it is.'

'We should meet for a drink, so I can explain it better.'

'Not happening.'

'Don't be like that! Don't you want to make half a million quid this year?'

'No.'

He laughed. 'Come off it! I don't believe you. That's what you'd get for a reunion. Only has to be three weeks, headlining one of those retro eighties tours. The promoters are desperate to have Cohen top the bill, how about that! You don't even have to leave the UK.'

'Iain, I'm hanging up now, and if you ever contact me again, I'm going to report you to the police for harassing me.'

'Wait! You can't. I mean, you can't want to say no to that, surely?' He tried another tack. 'Even if you don't need the money, you must have charities you support. Think what they could do with five hundred grand!'

He found me, he found me, he found me. The panicky voice inside her head swelled, drowning out his words, and she only heard 'charities you support'. It took all her effort to keep her tone low and calm.

'So, you're suggesting I quit the job I love, get in a tour bus with a load of blokes who hate me for ruining their careers, stand on a stage in black PVC – when I'm over fifty – and not even keep the money? Plus, have the world's press looking for all the skeletons in my cupboards, demanding to know why I quit in the first place. Are you off your head? I mean, you of all people should know why I'd never in a million years contemplate it, not for all the money in the world.'

'What do you mean, me of all people?'

She tried not to snap at him. 'You *know*, Iain. You know what happened to me: why I left the band the first time. You talked to me right before—'

'Yah, and the police talked to *me*! Grilled me for hours, they did. Where was I? Who was I with? What was I doing? Yadda yadda.'

She maintained a stony silence. She couldn't just hang up and block him, it was too risky. He knew where she lived now, and he didn't give up easily. Everything was ruined.

'What do *you* want, Meredith?'

Perhaps it was because his voice suddenly softened, or perhaps it was the directness of the question – one she asked herself a lot but that nobody else ever had, not even Pete – but her throat tightened, and for a moment she couldn't speak.

She tried to deflect it: 'Right now, I want you to go away and swear you won't tell anybody where I live or what I do.'

'No ... I mean, what do you want out of your life? You don't have a husband – or wife – or kids. How do you want people to remember you?'

'Well, it's sure as hell not by having a comeback on some shitty eighties reunion tour.'

Iain sighed, and she could tell he'd lost patience. 'Right. I'm trying to help, Meredith. I thought you'd be interested, hey. It could change your life for the better. But never mind. I'll text you my number in case you have a change of heart.'

I'll delete it straight away, she thought. *And then change my own number.* 'Swear you won't tell anyone where I am,' she begged.

He promised, but she didn't believe him.

When the call was finally over, Meredith sat down slowly in the big wingback chair overlooking the garden. Two blackbirds pecked at the early blackcurrants beginning to ripen on the bush outside the window. She watched the cat, Gavin, unsuccessfully stalking them, weaving around the budding canes.

She believed she had – eventually – got what she wanted from her life. A home, a job she liked, friends, and over the years a gradual lessening of the excruciating fear and paranoia. But Iain's call made her realise that in an instant she could be right back to where she'd been, twenty-two years ago, and it was a place she never, ever wanted to revisit.

2

One Year Later
Meredith

The security camera's lens had been poked out, and it had been twisted off its perch above the till, leaving it hanging limply, a useless append-age. But it was a while before Meredith noticed it, her horrified gaze being first drawn to the shelf of Minstead House-branded pottery, now at a forty-five-degree angle, its contents in a smashed pile on the shop floor. Plates, mugs, tea sets, each with its own delicate line-drawn silhouette of Minstead House, now all in a jumble of shards. Who would do this?

She scanned the rest of the shelves, taking a hasty mental inventory of the shop's stock, but nothing actually seemed to be missing, not even the more expensive jewellery in the glass display case. No money had been taken. They always cashed up and put it in the safe when they closed the shop at night; the safe, hidden behind a painting, was still locked and untampered-with. So strange that there was no sign of a break-in. Someone must have had access to the keys.

Footsteps coming up the stairs. The door handle slowly turning. A heavy black boot through the locked bedroom door. Warm urine tickling my thigh as the panel splinters and shatters and I wait, paralysed.

Stop. Focus. Call security.

'George, it's me, Meredith. The shop's been broken into, but nothing seems to have been taken, just some stuff smashed and the security camera broken.'

'Hey, love, don't sound so upset ... I'll call the police and check the exterior CCTV. Leonard didn't mention anything, useless old bugger. Get the kettle on and I'll be over in two minutes.'

Leonard was night security at the house, and was older than some of the antique furniture. He and George had a decade-long simmering feud as to which of them was the more efficient – or as everyone else had long ago decided, the least useless. Nobody could understand why the Earl kept them on. He must have promised them both jobs for life, preferring for his own reasons to update the security technology rather than the technicians themselves. Ralph, as estates manager, was always grumbling about both of them.

Meredith sat down behind the counter, still feeling shaken and a bit nauseous. She gulped in air, then picked up the internal phone again.

'Hi, Ralph. Some shit's broken into the shop and smashed it up a bit, but nothing seems to be missing. George is calling the police.'

'What? Good grief. I'll be right down,' he said immediately, and she felt a tiny bit better. There were people who cared, about her and the shop. People she could ring and who would come, even though they didn't know what had happened to her before.

There'd been nobody I could ring that night and nobody to come.

Ralph arrived before George, panting slightly from sprinting down the stairs in the main house and across the wide cobbled courtyard. Through the plate-glass window, Meredith saw him just about avoid crashing into the iron racks of pot plants for sale outside the shop door, such was his haste. He came in and walked straight over to the counter, almost knocking down a hat stand draped with hand-dyed silk scarves, and gave Meredith a huge avuncular hug, wrapping his arms around her and pressing her face into his barrel chest so she could barely breathe.

'Well, this is all a bit shit, isn't it? Who the hell would do this and not even bother to nick anything? Are you sure nothing's gone?'

He sounded jovial, but Meredith, once she'd extricated herself from his embrace, could see from his eyes that he was worried. Despite the combined age of its security guards, Minstead House had never been burgled before.

'I'll have to have a word with the Earl,' he said, his voice now sombre, and she knew he meant about Leonard.

'Maybe Horace is back,' she said, turning her back to him as she went to make tea. Horace was the house's once-active poltergeist. She wasn't joking – she did hope it was him. The thought of a ghost was a lot less unnerving than a human intruder.

Horace had been a regular spectral visitor in the chapel a few years before. Leonard would lock up at night with the only key then come in the following morning to find the furniture rearranged and candles laid out in serried rows on the flagstone floor. The Earl had eventually had an exorcism conducted, which had got rid of the entity. They'd christened it Horace, after the spurned lover of the house's original owner, Lady Wilmington – the most likely candidate to want to hang around, causing trouble.

'No sign of a break-in, stuff randomly smashed,' Meredith said. 'Sounds like Horace's MO, doesn't it?'

'Mmm,' said Ralph, who had always been convinced that there was no Horace, that Leonard had done it himself for the attention. Meredith disagreed though. Leonard could be a bit of an old drama queen, but he wasn't a fantasist, as far as she could tell. And she'd heard enough stories about ghosts from reliable sources to believe in them, even without first-hand experience. 'Well, the CCTV should show who came in out of hours, so I don't think we're going to need Sherlock Holmes's expertise to figure out who the culprit is.'

George arrived next, knocking a pile of hairy blankets crooked with his hip as he bustled in. Meredith had to sit on her hands to stop herself immediately going over to the shelf to straighten them. She couldn't even look at the broken china.

'Police are on their way,' he said, self-importantly.

'Nothing's been taken,' she told him. 'Maybe we should tell them not to even bother. What if the shelf just collapsed?'

'Oh no,' George said, looking shocked. 'It can't have done. That bracket's clearly been tampered with. And the camera! That's not an accident. I mean, look.'

She didn't want to look. She didn't want to talk to the police. Police made her itchy with panic. Police brought back memories she didn't want to think about. She'd had enough of police to last a lifetime.

But in the end, though, it was OK. A slope-shouldered PC who couldn't pronounce his R's turned up and took some photos and notes. Scratched his head about how the intruder got in, and why they'd bother. Asked her if anything else 'unusual' had happened.

Meredith looked at Ralph and raised her eyebrows. He was the only one who knew about the flowers. She hadn't told him; he'd seen them. He nodded, briefly.

'Well ... I didn't think anything of it, but there have been a few things. Last week, for example...'

'Yes?' The PC poised his pencil over his pad.

In fact, there had been more than a few things, on and off, in the year since Iain's call, but they were so small, Meredith hadn't bothered to mention them. If she did, she'd need to admit *why* they worried her. And anyway, it was all just tiny stuff: far easier to dismiss as nothing – as her own paranoia: the unopened can of green paint left in her front garden – a visitor could have dumped it there. The bathtub full of cold water she came home from work to find one day – she must have run it herself that morning and forgotten. Things moved around in her living room – must have been her. The fact that she woke up every night screaming and covered in sweat was nothing to do with it, she insisted to herself.

Nothing to worry about. Nobody else apart from Pete had keys to her house. Everything else, apart from her anxiety levels, had remained the same, at least for the next few months. She had kept her head down, carried on working in the shop.

The eighties revival tour happened, without Cohen. Nobody came for her. To her knowledge there had been nothing in the papers, and no reporters had come to the shop.

'I live on the estate, in a cottage just past the greenhouses. It's about five minutes' walk from here. Last week, when I arrived home I saw that ... it's probably nothing ... but someone had cut the heads off all my dahlias. I've got my own little fenced-off garden in front of the house, but anybody could walk in – to the garden, obviously, not the house. Visitors pass it all the time when they're walking round the grounds. I just thought it was weird. They were definitely beheaded intentionally; clean cuts, with scissors or secateurs, and the heads were just left lying in the flowerbed, about twenty of them. Every single flower had been cut.'

She felt sick, as if it was only real now that she had admitted it.

'I see. That is a bit weird,' agreed the PC, scribbling furiously.

George bristled. 'Why didn't you tell me? You should have reported it!'

'Because, like I said, I just assumed it was a visitor with anger issues, or one of the gardeners having a bad day. Or even a kid, messing around.'

'That's vandalism, that is!'

'Well, in the grand scheme of things I didn't think it was a major crime.'

Not a major crime, no ... but another of those little things that were probably just coincidence. They had to be.

It had been well over twenty years since she'd left the band, and during that time – until Iain's phone call the year before – Meredith's paranoia had subsided to a dull roar; most days, anyway. Sometimes, though, she was almost puzzled why nobody ever recognised her, but simultaneously relieved. As Pete always said, though, it was about the context. When she'd been in the band, she'd had black backcombed hair and jumped around stages in black PVC, shrieking into microphones. Now she had short blondish hair, wore Boden dresses and sold beribboned packs of honeycomb brittle and overpriced Minstead House merchandise to Japanese tourists, most of whom were far too young to remember her.

The day of the break-in dragged by without further incident, but Meredith couldn't settle to anything. It was a big relief when the time came to flip the sign on the door to 'closed', and set off through the grounds towards her cottage.

On the far side of the ha-ha, she felt calmed by the sight of the Surrey Hills rising up in the distance, stolid layers of hazy shadow thickening as the sun slid down behind them. It was a balmy June evening and the rolling lawns, a vibrant green after a week of rain, smelled fresh and new as she headed past Lady Wilmington's grave, planted in solitary state in the middle of a separate grassed area, flanked at the back by box hedges with marble statues in front of them. Lady W had planned it all herself before her death, leaving sketches showing exactly where in the shadow of the house she wanted to be buried, and which statues would be her marble guardians for eternity.

Coming through the archway from the vegetable garden, the sight of her little Victorian cottage's bottle-green shutters, turreted gables, Gothic-arched front door and barley-sugar-twist chimney pots reassured her even more.

It had just been an accident. No sign of a break-in, nothing stolen. One of the cleaners had probably done it and been too embarrassed to admit it.

She opened the wooden gate and walked up the path. Coming home always felt like she was meeting a friend, she loved her cottage so much. Built in 1879, at the same time as the house, gatehouse and other outbuildings (including the stables, which now housed the shop), historically it had been the residence of generations of gardeners – she was the first non-gardener resident. The Earl had let her rent it since the current head gardener started having children, and his wife wanted to live somewhere less isolated.

Pete always questioned the logic behind living in such a secluded place. 'You're lonely,' he'd say, bluntly, and she always denied it – because, when she was with him, she never did feel lonely. And the rest of the time, it wasn't loneliness as such; it was paranoia. She only really felt safe once she was sequestered away in her cottage.

As she put the key in the door, she glanced at the bare dahlia plants, their severed heads now brown and rotting into the earth underneath. She had a momentary wobble, then dismissed it again.

Beheaded dahlias and some smashed china didn't have anything to do with what had gone on before. She was sure of it.

3
Graeme

'How's your week been? I brought you some Marlboros...'

Silence. As Graeme slides the cigarettes towards her, he looks nervously across the table at his beloved, whose arms are folded and brows knitted. The black circles beneath her eyes are spreading, the puffy darkness like dual bruises. Catherine ignores the gift.

'Have I done something to upset you ... angel?'

The 'angel' is rushed out on fast, feathery breaths, fearing it will be swatted away. A nerve ticks in Catherine's doughy cheek, pulsing irritation.

'You look sad,' says Graeme, trying again, when what he really wants to say is, *How can you be sad when we're together? You are the love of my life, the apple of my eye, the yin to my yang.*

He has no idea what yins or yangs actually are. Something to do with seesaws perhaps?

The expression on Catherine's face is not so much sadness – it's more bitterness, but all the same, Graeme supposes, it must be hard for his love, watching him walking in and out each week when Catherine herself isn't allowed to walk anywhere outside of the perimeter fences. Yet. Surely the fact that he visits religiously counts for something? Maybe Catherine doesn't love him. Maybe these decades of devotion are all a waste of time; maybe their plans and dreams will never come to fruition.

But ... they're getting closer. Catherine's been good as gold for years – not a foot wrong. And she knows that Graeme would do anything for her.

Anything.

So why can't she be a bit *nicer* to him?

Just when Graeme is starting to feel the prickly heat of rejection and paranoia, Catherine raises her head, the effort visible. She reaches across the table and takes his calloused hand.

'Tell me about our house.' Finally, she gazes into Graeme's eyes, and he feels relief flood through him.

He smiles. 'It's going to be a cottage, with so much whitewash on the walls that when the sun comes out, it blinds you. We'll have yellow roses growing up the front walls on either side of the porch – it'll have one of them little pointy porches with its own roof. We won't have thatch though – the roofs will be all tiles. I looked into it. You have to renew thatch about every ten years and it costs thousands. Fifteen thou at least, and then you have to get extra insurance and that.'

'Not thatched then,' Catherine agrees, staring intently. Her eyes are brown, with a hazel rim to the irises that Graeme finds hypnotic. Catherine's thumb begins stroking the web of skin between Graeme's own thumb and forefinger, and his voice trembles.

'Veg patch in the back garden with everything in it – not just the boring stuff like carrots and tomatoes. We'll have rhubarb and parsnips and that posh, pointy green stuff, what's it called?'

Catherine looks blank.

'You know. It sticks up through the ground, all of a sudden.'

'I have no idea what you're talking about.' She looks bored and Graeme panics. He's lost her, which in his experience can be disastrous.

The word comes to him: 'Asparagus! You have it in fancy restaurants with butter and that.'

'Right.'

'And ... and there'll be dark wood floorboards all through the upstairs. One of them baths with the metal feet that look like animal paws.'

Graeme has an interior-design magazine that he nicked from the doctor's waiting room. It's from two years ago and the front cover is missing, but he reads it religiously, holding it like a comfort blanket whenever it seems impossible to think that he and Catherine will ever be together again, that Catherine will ever be released. God knows where they are going to get the money to afford this cottage with its flowers and veg patch and polished floors. Even Graeme realises it's a far cry from the grim shared flat he's been living in since his own release. He tucks the magazine in the middle of a pile of bodybuilding magazines by his bed, because every time he gets back from visiting Catherine, something else has been nicked by either the dead-eyed smack addict or the malodorous shoplifter he has to share with. He's never even set foot in a place like the dream home of his imagination.

'Claw-foot tub.'

'That's the fella. And a big white sink. Fresh flowers in every room.'

'From our own garden.'

'Yeah, definitely.'

'Gym in a shed outside so me doing weights don't bother you.'

'Too right. And ... nice, non-nosy neighbours.'

Graeme laughs. 'We can't arrange *that* beforehand!'

'Yes we can,' Catherine argues. 'We'll just be careful. But what if we see our dream house but the neighbours are horrible?'

Graeme frowns, giving this some thought. 'We'll vet them first. We won't let anybody horrible stand in the way of our happiness. And if they do ... then they'll regret it, won't they?'

Catherine laughs again, looks at her watch then stands up. 'You'd better go. It's *Cash In the Attic* soon and I want to watch it. See you next week. Ta for the fags.'

Graeme feels stricken. He opens his arms for a hug, but Catherine is already waddling away.

4

Meredith

It was after the third mug of Jack Daniels that it all went weird. A moment of sheer madness, the sort when you're thinking, *Oh no, what am I doing? I need to stop right now*, but are unable to stop, driven by an almost ghoulish compulsion to see it through to the bitter end, despite the background awareness of the potential consequences.

Ralph was just *there*, kneeling in front of her in his office. Pissed as a fart, but still a very sexy man – tall and broad and reassuring. More than that, he was sympathetic and – unexpectedly – so flattering and comforting that, in that moment, her body completely disobeyed her brain and conscience, and she was overcome with a great wave of pheromones and whisky-fuelled lust and emotion.

Ralph, her friend and boss. Worse: Ralph, her friend's husband.

For the first hour everything had been on solid ground. She would have laughed derisively if someone had told her what was about to happen. At work, she was just Meredith From the Shop – solid, reliable Meredith.

At first they had discussed work stuff, albeit in slightly slurred voices. Ralph was rambling on about a newly hired gardener who had apparently lied at interview and therefore got the job under false pretences. Meredith wasn't really paying attention. She still felt horribly disturbed by the break-in at the shop the day before, and by having to talk to the police.

If only Ralph hadn't changed the subject and asked what was bothering her. If they hadn't veered into personal problems territory, it would never have happened.

It wasn't unusual for Ralph to take an interest in her private life, although they had previously only discussed it when Paula was there too. Meredith's hapless love life was a well-worn topic that, both Ralph and Paula laughed, they enjoyed vicariously. So she pretended this was what was bothering her now. She couldn't risk articulating her fears; it would have made her sound paranoid.

'That bloke Gary dumped me at the weekend, after three weeks. I just have no luck with men at all,' she pronounced weakly. She'd gone on a few dates with Gary off Tinder, and yes, as dates went, she thought he had potentially been someone she could possibly stand to look at in the morning, maybe even more than once; but Gary had clearly thought otherwise. Perhaps her ambivalence about the whole mating business had slowly leached through her carefully cultivated persona, like armpit sweat through silk.

'Gary's an idiot, then. You're a huge catch,' Ralph had said staunchly, propelling himself across the room on his office chair and grabbing the bottle of Jack from the top of the filing cabinet. He scooted back with it and replenished his mug. It smelled so good as he poured.

'Yeah, right.' She drained her own mug – her second, at that point; she remembered wondering how many he'd had – and Ralph immediately topped her up.

'Do you know what he said to me? He said, "I'm just not attracted to you enough."' She gave a hollow laugh. When she thought about it, though, she had already forgotten what Gary's face looked like.

'Then he tried to make it better by saying "It's not that I don't fancy you at *all*, because I kind of do. Just not enough. I'm sorry."'

'What a bastard.' Ralph's words were slurring a lot more than Meredith's.

It had stung a bit, if she was honest, that particular rejection. Perhaps it was because she had felt that Gary and she actually did have the chance at a connection. Once or twice, in more optimistic moments, she had let herself think that he might even be 'the one'. He'd seemed OK – kind, funny, solvent, age-appropriate, sensible, liberal. Nice house, cute dog, matching socks. Four dates, lots of laughs and kisses that started off enthusiastically but – and she hadn't noticed it at the time – lost commitment as time went on, like a hurricane that gradually blows itself out. Then, finally, his sad words of realisation.

'He's not a bastard. That was the problem,' she said. 'I'm obviously a terrible kisser. Or I'm just too old and ugly.'

Ralph had laughed, thinking she was joking. 'Obviously!' he chuckled drunkenly. 'I mean, look at you!'

'I'm serious, Ralph.' Unexpectedly, she got the tingling in her nostrils that preceded tears and inwardly berated herself. It was almost certainly Jack Daniels-induced. She really didn't give a shit about Gary, only what he had briefly represented: the chance of a partner, someone to cuddle up on the sofa with, plan holidays with.

Always look at what you have, she reminded herself, not what you're missing. Although that was more difficult after three mugs of whisky.

Two decades ago, when her band won a BRIT Award for their third million-selling single, she'd have been as horrified as Iain had sounded in that phone call last year to know that this was where she would end up. And now she had talked herself into teariness over a rejection, after four dates, by a guy in his fifties who wore bicycle clips and played bridge.

But she knew that Gary wasn't the real reason for her distress.

'You aren't remotely ugly,' Ralph finally said, about two minutes past appropriate.

'I mean, I think I've lost my looks since I was younger, but I'd never have said I was ugly.' Meredith forgot that Gary actually hadn't ever used that word. 'My eyes are too close together, I'm too old and I have too many crow's feet, but really?'

'I'm sure it's nothing to do with that. You're a stunner, even for a woman your age. Especially for a woman your age. Maybe you've got bad breath? Paula's always telling me that I have.'

'That's not particularly helpful,' she said grumpily.

'Come here, I'll check. I'm your friend. I'm allowed to tell you these things.'

She started to laugh as Ralph hauled himself out of his chair and lumbered towards her, steadying himself on the edge of his desk on the way.

'No! Go away!'

He crouched down with difficulty and gently took her chin in his hand, laughing too. 'Breathe!' he commanded.

'Stop it!' She wriggled away, feeling that moment of euphoric drunkenness where life seems suspended in happiness, like an insect in amber.

Ralph always cheered her up. When the three of them got together on the wine, horseplay and a lot of giggling weren't unusual. Ralph and Paula's son, Jackson, now twenty, had witnessed this a couple of times, much to his disgust and opprobrium. This, however, was the first time it had happened without Paula there to be the third corner of the triangle.

Ralph was still squatting at her feet. She had always thought what nice eyes he had – kind, green, and surprisingly clear for a man of his age and prodigious alcohol intake. And despite the undertone of JD, he smelled amazing.

He stopped chuckling and put his palm heavily on her knee as if to haul himself back up. Then he paused. 'For what it's worth, Meredith, I think you're gorgeous. Honestly. I always have.'

'Thanks,' she said, smiling. It was the tender affection in Ralph's voice that made her lean slowly towards him and rest her cheek on the side of his striped shirt. His shoulder felt reassuringly meaty and warm, and she felt his arms encircle her, his chin digging gently into her neck. At that moment he felt like a dad, and her instant response wasn't remotely sexual.

'You smell fantastic,' she muttered, just stating a fact, but he must have construed it in a different way because he pulled away and kissed her on the lips, so lightly at first that she saw it only as a gesture of affection. She responded…

… And that was the point of no return.

There was always a point of no return.

A minute later they were kissing, properly, and it was lovely. He no longer remotely felt like her dad. He was a really good kisser, just the right amount of pressure and tongue action, and his hands began to roam around her body, rubbing her back at first, then along her thighs, and up over her breasts, where they stayed, squeezing gently until she felt a corresponding thrill between her legs. She wanted to stop but found herself pressing closer to him, sliding out of the chair and onto her knees so that their torsos were pressed tightly together.

'I want you,' he murmured, and in the heat of the moment it didn't seem ridiculous or at all inappropriate. She just nodded, kissing him again. 'I always have. Can we go back to the cottage?'

Meredith hesitated, reality creeping in for a moment. She didn't want to sleep with Ralph in her bed or on her sofa. Somehow that felt worse than anything that happened here. Like calories in food not counting when it was eaten from someone else's plate.

'I can't wait that long. And someone might see us walking over there,' she said. 'One of the gardeners might be working late.'

'Do you want to?' His hand was inside her bra, rolling her nipple between his fingers.

She nodded again.

'You know what else I've always wanted to do,' he whispered.

'What?'

'Have sex in the Gilt Room.'

'Ralph! You dirty bugger. With me, or just anybody?' She couldn't help laughing. The Gilt Room was as it sounded – the house's formal drawing room on the ground floor, a chandelier the size of a baby elephant in the centre and the walls and ceilings entirely covered in ornate gold leaf. 'There's CCTV in there; we can't.'

'Let's go and have a look,' he said, dragging her to her feet and handing her the bottle of Jack. 'With you, of course, in answer to your question,' he added, as Meredith took a swig, grinning at his answer. They had dispensed with the formality of mugs.

'Surely you know where all the CCTV is? You're estates manager!' she reminded him, feeling naughty and rebellious. 'And if there is a camera in there, deal's off.'

Meredith was fairly sure there would be a camera. The room was stuffed with valuable vases, oil paintings and *objets d'art*. But as Ralph said, they didn't have CCTV in every room. She started visualising where they might do it. On the rug? Best not on the rickety old brocade sofa; that was an original piece from when Lady Wilmington lived here. That would be hard to explain, if they broke it.

They adjusted their clothing and Ralph finished the bottle, putting it back in his desk drawer, and then they walked down the back stairs together from the converted servants' quarters. He squeezed Meredith's arse on the way. 'No cameras down here,' he said cheerfully.

She thought later that it was strange she hadn't come to her senses in the brief hiatus, while they tried, like teenagers, to find somewhere exciting and forbidden to shag. But, she supposed, she was so aroused by then that *not* doing it didn't feel like an option anymore.

They reached the ground floor and cautiously emerged through the *Staff Only* door into the public areas of the house. It was still and quiet.

'Where's Leonard?' she whispered.

'His shift doesn't start till nine-thirty,' Ralph whispered back. 'And George is over at the stables this evening. He told me earlier he was going to go and change all the lightbulbs in there because Fred's on holiday. I think we're alone.'

Had he planned this? Meredith doubted it. He was too pissed. But he was right about Fred the handyman being on holiday.

He did seem very aware of the timings ... but she soon stopped thinking about it. They were in the long, dark corridor leading to the Gilt Room, four vast six-foot-tall Chinese vases acting as sentries as they passed by.

'Dammit, look,' Ralph said, jerking his head up towards the doorway. The small shiny black dome was affixed to the ornate ceiling just inside the room; a CCTV camera. 'Kind of spoils it, doesn't it?'

Meredith didn't know if he was talking about the architecture or the moment.

'Follow me,' he added. 'I have a plan B.' She laughed and did as he said. This was crazy, but it was fun.

Why had she not been thinking of Paula? she later thought. It wouldn't have seemed so much like fun then. But she felt possessed, overtaken, wild with abandon.

She followed him through the public areas of the house towards the back entrance. At the last moment he dragged her in through a wide door.

'Ralph, oh no, not the disabled loo!' she protested, but he pushed her up against the mirror and kissed her again as he reached over and flipped up the handle to lock them in.

Her fingers went to his zip as if they were obeying someone else's command.

5

Meredith

Dear God, thought Meredith. *Why did I do that? Why? What the hell was I thinking? And with* Ralph?

She was regretting this even before Ralph withdrew from her with a sticky swoosh. He turned, yanked up his trousers and leaned over the sink, his shoulders heaving. For a moment she thought he was being sick. She felt the same, wondering how she would ever be able to face Paula again. But then she realised he was just getting his breath back. In the mirror his reflected face looked a dull purple, like liver.

'Let's go for a walk,' he panted as Meredith retrieved her knickers from the floor. 'Spot of fresh air in order, I think.'

They slipped out of the side door of the house, and Meredith gulped down lungfuls of the summer-evening air. It always felt incredible after the musty scent of the house – furniture polish and decades of visitors' discarded skin cells. Outside smelled of lilac and roses.

Ralph was giggling like a schoolboy, giddy with the thrill of their naughtiness, but Meredith already felt numb and horrified. She'd never even thought about kissing Ralph!

She liked him enormously, of course – it was impossible not to – but it had come as a complete surprise when he'd told her he'd always wanted her. That had probably been the whisky talking, though. He'd likely have said the same thing to Mumblin' Mo or Ceri, if they'd been sitting in front of him half an hour ago.

Ralph was singing to himself as they strolled across the primrose-studded lawn. He tried to take Meredith's hand, but she politely pulled away. 'Someone might see,' she said. 'One of the gardeners, or someone.'

Ralph laughed drunkenly. 'Little Miss Worried!'

She tried to turn in the direction of the rose gardens, so she could head back to her cottage and have a shower, but Ralph had other ideas. He suddenly took her hand again, and pulled her through a copse of lilac bushes. 'Have you ever been in the ice house?'

'No, I haven't.'

He was already dragging her down the steps to the abandoned Victorian cellar standing alone and half buried in the grounds, which used to cater for the house's refrigeration needs.

'Why isn't it locked?' Meredith was sure it was usually padlocked; visitors weren't allowed inside. But there was no padlock tonight; the wooden arch-shaped door cut into the small hillock was ajar. She was curious. She had always wondered what it was like in there. From the outside it resembled a hobbit house.

'It ought to be. The surveyor was in earlier. We're planning some renovations, making sure it's sound, then perhaps we'll open it up to the public – or at least reconstruct it with some plastic blocks of ice, and the punters can peer in. He'll get the report back to me next week. Don't want to do it if it costs a bomb, though.'

He took out his phone and switched on the torch function, pulling the door fully open. 'Not a whole lot to see, but interesting, isn't it?'

'Um...' Meredith stepped cautiously inside. It was cold and dank, and smelled of damp stone and raw earth – how she imagined the depths of a well would be. Gooseflesh swept up over her arms and shoulders and back down her chest as the door swung shut behind them. He was right, there wasn't a lot to see, just gracefully curved brickwork, like in a wine cellar. It went much further back than she would have thought, though.

'Room for a lot of ice in here,' she commented.

Ralph wrapped his arms affectionately round her neck from behind, blinding her with his torch. Meredith pushed his hand away, mostly to deflect the torch beam. 'Gerroff!' she said, trying to pretend they were back to normal, that he hadn't just had his penis inside her. Sparring buddies, mates.

He turned her round and tried to kiss her again. She responded, but half-heartedly this time. 'Ralph,' she said, wriggling free. She didn't want to hurt his feelings. 'We should never have done this. I feel terrible about Paula. She's my friend. Your wife!'

A flash of guilt passed over his features, but then he gave an airy wave of the hand, the one holding his phone, making the torch's white light strobe round the cellar. 'Don't,' he said. 'She'll never know. And she's no saint herself, so you don't need to feel all that bad.'

'Really? She's never mentioned any indiscretions to me.' Meredith was genuinely surprised. Paula didn't seem the straying sort, any more than Ralph did.

But then Ralph had just fucked her.

'Anyway,' she said decisively. 'I'm going to go home now, and we will never speak of this again. OK?'

'OK dear heart. One more kiss first ... please?'

She did kiss him again. One for the road, as it were. It was a tender, lingering kiss that, weirdly, spoke more of their friendship than of their illicit sexual congress. She was very fond of Ralph, she realised afresh.

'I don't want this to ruin our friendship,' she said, breaking off the kiss and raising her hand to stroke his face with her fingers. But he sneezed, suddenly and explosively, and as they both turned their heads away, the sharp edge of her ring caught him under the eye and she felt it drag down the flesh of his cheek.

'Ow! Shit!'

'Oh no. I'm so sorry. Did I get you? Is it bleeding?'

Ralph dropped the phone, torch down, and they were plunged into darkness, bar a sheet of white light at ground level. They both lunged down to get it, banging heads on the way, and started to laugh. Meredith got to it first, shining it towards him.

'Let me see.' There was a crimson teardrop sliding down his face. She pulled a tissue out of her skirt pocket and dabbed his cheek with it. 'You'll live,' she said. 'Now can we please get out of here? It's horrible!'

They emerged, blinking like moles, into the welcomingly fresh evening air. Meredith could see the twisted barley-sugar chimney pots of her cottage in the distance and had a fierce yearning to be home, running a scented bath that she could lie in with a book and a glass of wine and try to forget that she'd just been hideously disloyal to a mate.

'Right. I'm off. See you tomorrow. Don't drive home, will you? You're way over the limit. Are you going to get a cab?'

Ralph nodded, still holding the tissue to his face. 'I promise. I'm just going back in to take a few photos of the big damp patch in the cellar while it's unlocked, and those loose bricks at the back. I'm sure the surveyor did it when he was here, but it'll be good to have a few for our records.'

'OK. Have a good evening. Hope the hangover's not too bad in the morning. And that you're not scarred for life.'

Meredith set off towards her cottage as Ralph laughed and went back inside the ice house.

Walking back through the rose garden, she tried to analyse her emotions. The guilt was the worst – and she had a feeling that it hadn't yet properly sunk in. It had been so long since she'd had sex – three years? four? – that there was also, she had to admit, a whiff of relief in the mix, if only to remind her that sex wasn't all that. Not when it was with someone else's husband, anyway. It would never happen with Ralph again, she was quite sure of that. A moment of madness.

She walked through the arched gateway separating the rose garden from the kitchen gardens and felt in her pocket for her front door key.

It wasn't there. Dammit! It must have fallen out in the ice house when she pulled out that tissue for Ralph. Oh well. It was a beautiful evening, no hardship whatsoever to retrace her steps and stroll back. The bath could be postponed for ten minutes.

The sun was beginning to set over the layers of hill when she arrived back at the little grassy ramp leading down to the subterranean ice house. The hobbity door was still slightly ajar. Good, Meredith thought, as she'd had a sudden fear that Leonard on night security might have seen it flapping open and found a padlock to lock it up again; not that there was anything to steal in there. She took out her phone and activated the torch, pushing open the door ready to search the earthen floor.

Something impeded the door's smooth opening. Weird, she thought. It had been fine just now. She pushed harder. It yielded a little way, just enough for her to squeeze through, but it felt as though an object had been placed behind to block it.

It was only when she got inside that Meredith realised. It wasn't an object.

It was Ralph, lying face up on the cold, damp floor. When her torch beam, shaking wildly, found his face, he was purple and distended-looking, popped blood vessels in his cheeks forming tributaries around the scratch her ring had inflicted; his staring eyes bulging with death's outrage. She had only been gone for ten minutes at the most. How could this possibly have happened?

'Ralph!' She crouched next to him, ripping at his tie and shirt, squishing two fingers into the underside of his wrist to try and find a pulse. Nothing. 'Fuck! Ralph! Wake up!'

Meredith lifted his wrist and tried again. Still nothing. She pulled his shirt out of his trousers and ripped it open from the bottom up – he was wearing a tie and it seemed too difficult to try and loosen it from the top. Buttons bounced all over the floor as she commenced CPR, her shaking fingers interlocked as she pounded his chest and breathed into his whisky-sour mouth, pounded and breathed. She needed to call an ambulance but didn't dare stop. *Oh God, this is a nightmare.* She didn't realise she was crying till the tears splashed on her locked-together hands.

She had no idea how long she tried to revive him, just that it wasn't working. She opened the door fully to let more light in and saw that his darkened face was already settling into a kind of livid rigidity, as if preparing for rigor mortis.

'Ralph's dead, Ralph's dead, Ralph's dead,' she chanted like a mantra with every chest compression. The house had a portable defibrillator, but it was miles away, in the ticket office, which was in the gatehouse entrance across the courtyard. It would take far too long to go and get it.

She ran outside and threw up in the bushes, vomiting Jack Daniels and guilt and horror.

How was she going to explain what Ralph was doing in the ice house? Perhaps she wouldn't have to. Perhaps she could just tell the police that they'd both been working late and he had taken her down there to show her what the interior looked like, because she'd always wanted to see it. That was reasonable. She'd dropped her key – in fact, there it was, lying half under his right calf. Meredith retrieved it and stuck it back in her skirt pocket. She'd gone back for it, and found him like this. It was the truth.

But ... but ... also true were the following additional facts:

He was blind drunk.

Her DNA would be on his penis.

Her DNA would also be all over the scratch on his face, and the vomit in the bushes.

Ralph was dead.

If I tell them I was here, they might think I killed him.

She tried to stop thinking about herself and how this could affect her, but failed. It would all come out after the autopsy, that he'd recently been having sex. With her.

But how bad would it look, if she said nothing? If he'd had a heart attack and she didn't even call an ambulance? She could be up for manslaughter or something! At the very least, she'd lose her job, and if she lost her job, she'd lose the cottage. Of course she could afford to buy a new place, but this one was her home; her sanctuary.

Paula would never speak to her again, and rightly so.

Yet surely there was no point in calling an ambulance now. Meredith had seen a couple of dead bodies before – twice over the years, pensioners visiting the house had collapsed and died. She was head first aider, so both times she'd been called to try and revive them while the ambulance came. Both of them, a man and a woman, had looked less dead than Ralph did currently.

Meredith sat back on her heels, almost hyperventilating. *Are you insane?* she asked herself. Of course she should call 999, even if he was dead. She knew the drill. With shaking hands she picked up her phone, forefinger trembling over the nines.

Then she straightened up and walked away from the ice house, back towards the rose garden. He was dead. She couldn't be near him for a second longer.

As she walked, she dialled – but it wasn't three nines she pressed.

Pete answered instantly.

'Hey Sis.'

The comforting sound of his voice dissolved her, and for a moment she couldn't speak.

'Are you there? What's wrong? Has something happened?'

'Pete ... help me. I don't know what to do.' Her voice wasn't her own, a shrill of panic.

YOU DO KNOW. CALL A FUCKING AMBULANCE, NOW, her conscience yelled.

'OK, calm down. Breathe.'

Him telling her to breathe made her think about Ralph's failure to do so, and she thought she was going to pass out. She sank down on an iron bench in the rose garden, dizziness making the pastel petals blur into confetti.

Focus. Pete would help her.

'Are you hurt?'

She shook her head as if he could see her. 'No. I'm in the rose garden. I did something stupid.'

He paused and she knew, with the twin telepathy that occasionally flared between them, that he was momentarily thinking of saying something flippant, something like 'Did you burn the house down?'

'I got drunk in Ralph's office earlier. He was hammered too and he came on to me. We ended up having a quick shag in the bogs...'

If she said it fast enough, perhaps it wouldn't sound so bad. But she couldn't keep the shudder out of her voice.

'Oh, Mez, come on, it's not ideal, but worse things happen at sea...'

'It IS worse!' she wailed. 'Way worse. Now he's dead.'

'*What?*'

'I think he's had a clutcher. We went for a walk afterwards, he showed me inside the ice house – you know, that cellar in the grounds. I've never been in there before. I left him there taking photos, but dropped my front-door key. I just went back to get it and ... He's there, dead. He's either had a heart attack or someone went in and strangled him after I left. He looks all purple and puffy but then he looked like that beforehand, cos he was pissed and anyway, how unlikely is that? I mean, who would *strangle* him?'

She was gabbling.

'Slow down.'

She took a deep, gasping breath, trying to speak more slowly. 'He can't have been strangled, that's ridiculous. There's no-one even here apart from security! He must have had a heart attack. I came out of the ice house, walked home, realised I'd dropped my key, went back, and he was lying on the floor. I did CPR on him for ages, but nothing. It must have happened right after I left. I was only gone a few minutes!'

Tears flowed down her cheeks. She couldn't even remember the last time she cried.

'But what do I do? I don't know what to do! I can't call an ambulance. Nobody must know. What if they think I killed him? I accidentally scratched his face – he sneezed and my ring caught it. The police might think we were fighting!'

'Mez. You can't leave him there. Listen, don't panic. I'll come and meet you, and we'll call together. Give me ten minutes. I just need to lock up the workshop. I'll come on my bike. The van's being MOT'd.'

Meredith sniffed hard. Perhaps they wouldn't care about her DNA. No need to be suspicious from a heart attack, surely?

'The main gates'll be locked. Come in through the back gate – you know, the one near the orchard that goes to the staff car park? Code's 4989.'

'Right. Sit tight and I'll be there ASAP.'

'Thanks. I'll be at home. Love you.'

He was gone.

Meredith had been waiting for him to command her to call the emergency services, do the sensible thing – and he hadn't. Without her explaining, he understood why she was ringing him instead of 999.

She sniffed and dragged the back of her hand under her nose, concentrating on getting her breathing back to normal. She hoped – always hoped – that she was as precious to Pete as he was to her. She knew she must be fairly precious. Pete had moved from Salisbury to live near her ten years ago.

By the time she had hauled herself off the bench, across the vegetable patch and in through her front gate, she had made a decision: when Pete arrived, she would call the police.

6

Graeme

'You stink,' Catherine says, wrinkling her nose as he walks into the visitors' lounge.

She's in a bad mood – again. That's the fourth day in a row now, Graeme notes. Maybe she's going through the change. Although to be fair she'd always been moody. Just his luck, to have spent most of his miserable life in love with a moody cow.

He didn't usually think like this, but he was tired and stressed, and worried by the way she constantly badgered him.

'Been working on the van,' Graeme says. 'It broke down yesterday, and I couldn't afford to take it to the garage. Had to mend it, otherwise I wouldn't have been able to come in today.'

He pauses, waiting for Catherine to ask, but she doesn't.

'I fixed it! Myself. Just with a YouTube video. You can look up how to do anything on there, it's wicked.'

'*It's wicked*,' mimics Catherine. 'What are you, twelve?'

Graeme drops his head. Sometimes Catherine's so mean that he wonders why he bothers. He could just walk out of here and never come back, but the thought of that fills him with such panic that he feels his legs begin to jiggle and his hands tremble.

Catherine is all he has. Catherine is family, friends, partner, wife (maybe, one day, when they're both free). Catherine is his world, and there is just no point to anything without her.

Graeme remembers the first incredible months when fate shoved them onto the same path, when they both arrived at Rampton around the same time. Decades ago, back when they were both young and

Catherine had been beautiful. Before the weight had piled on them both, the gradual build-up of excess institutional carbs and the refined sugar that were one of the few pleasures in that place. At least Graeme had managed to convert his into muscle now he was out. But he had never managed to convert his love for her into anything else, a fact about which he often felt depressed.

Cheap chocolate and mutual masturbation were all they'd managed. Graeme recalled the sour but thrilling taste of Catherine's tongue in his mouth, the feel of it on his cock. There had been one bush in the grounds that all the security cameras' angles just missed, and that had been where they had rendezvoused every day, meeting behind it, next to the fence, when they were supposed to be doing their sports sessions. That was many years ago, but you didn't forget your first sexual experience. He helps keep the memories alive when he's alone on his single mattress with its yellow-grey sheet.

Clean, ironed, fresh sheets. That's what they'd have on all the beds in their cottage.

'It wasn't that easy,' he says with eyes downcast, picking at his oil-grimed fingernails. 'The alternator had gone. I had to reconnect the—'

'Yeah, yeah, aren't you clever? Anyway, more to the point...' Catherine glances towards the guard, but he's talking to another inmate, so she continues. 'How's the plan coming along? Did you get what I told you to get?'

This is the question Graeme has been dreading and one he's amazed Catherine hasn't asked sooner. He replies in a low gabble. 'I'm working on it, babe. I spoke to a bloke down the gym who says he can get one, but that was a month ago, and I ain't seen him since. You can't rush these things, he warned me it would be difficult.'

'For fuck's sake, Graeme, it's been months since we first discussed it! I'm going insane in here! Being this good isn't frickin' easy.'

'You've been dead good. Ground leave every week for, what, two years now?'

'No need to patronise me.'

'I'm not!'

Graeme wasn't. He was genuinely pleased that Catherine's behaviour had stabilised enough for her to finally have been moved to the medium-security Ashworth. He secretly hoped it was because Catherine was getting better, rather than the true reason – that it was a means to an end.

Catherine had a plan. She'd had the same plan ever since they'd first met. And every time the plan met a setback – another sentence for another crime committed to add to her now very long list of ABH, GBH, attempted murder – she never, ever associated her own actions with the consequences. Instead, the long, bony finger of her blame stayed pointing at the one oblivious person whose fault she believed it was. All of it.

Sometimes Graeme thought that if someone told Catherine this individual was responsible for world poverty and global warming Catherine would readily believe it ... He almost felt sorry for them. Catherine had always made it sound like they were a mixture of Saddam Hussein, Pol Pot and Hitler, all rolled into one.

Although he'd never dare suggest that to Catherine. She'd never speak to him again.

'So,' Catherine said impatiently, dropping her voice, 'let's have a recap of where we are. Once you've got it, we'll keep the shooter for the final showdown – if you ever finally get your bloody act together and sort it. In the meantime, you're still doing what I told you to?'

More a statement than a question. He hesitated, and she jumped down his throat: 'What's wrong with you! Why aren't you?'

'I am! I am, Cath, honest.' He told her what he'd managed to do just the other day, and was rewarded with a faint smile that lifted the corners of her mouth.

Graeme, however, *had* been stalling. It wasn't that he didn't want to get Catherine out of there – far from it – but there was always the risk that it would all go badly wrong, and instead of getting her out, he would end up back inside himself – for good this time. They wouldn't let him anywhere near Catherine. Neither of them would ever get the cottage, the dream life.

Graeme took a deep breath. 'Cath ... are you sure it's worth it? I mean, darlin', if you keep your head down they might review your case and you can get out legitimately.'

Catherine's face darkened and her eyes narrowed, reminding Graeme of a glowering cartoon villain. 'You chickening out on me?' she demanded. Her voice compressed to a terrifying hiss. 'Because if you're not with me ... you're against me.'

She didn't need to say any more.

'I'm with you, babe, all the way, I swear. I love you,' said Graeme, the words falling over themselves as they tumbled out of him. 'You know I'd do anything for you. Anything!'

'I know,' Catherine said, smugly.

7

Pete

Pete was out of breath, having cycled from his workshop to Minstead House at high speed. His shirt was clinging unpleasantly to his chest. The last few hundred metres of the driveway were up a steep hill, and then he had to cycle around to the back entrance and up the rutted gravel pathway that ran along the side of the estate up to Meredith's cottage.

Propping his bike against the iron railings boxing in her garden, he hung his helmet by its chin strap over one of the handlebars and ran up to hammer on the front door.

'Mez, it's me!'

Meredith unlocked the door, shooting back the heavy Victorian bolt to admit him into the gloomy porchway. He put his arms tight around her, resting his chin on top of her head.

'Why have you bolted the door? You're not seriously worried that someone's done this to him? Any guy his age could have a heart attack; it happens all the time.'

She didn't move except to bury her face further into his chest.

'At least you know there's nothing more you could have done. If the CPR didn't work, an ambulance crew wouldn't have revived him either.'

They rocked together. 'I'm sweaty,' he added, unnecessarily, although he knew she didn't mind. She always told him she loved his smell: tobacco and sawdust. He was a whole foot taller than her, and she pressed her face into the right side of his chest, where he could feel his heart beat against her ear. Perhaps they had been that way round in the womb.

It gave him a pang of actual, physical pain when he thought about how they had been estranged for more than ten years when they were younger, until the terrible event that at least had the corollary of bringing her back to him.

What a waste. But then, she had behaved like a complete dick. They'd made up for it since. He used to work for film studios, building sets, but when he moved to the area to be nearer Meredith ten years ago, he'd rented a workshop and shop front, and started taking commissions for tables and cabinets made of slabs of cherry or oak, inlaid with mother of pearl in intricate designs.

Last year he'd moved from his tiny cottage into a beautiful Dutch barge that Meredith insisted on buying for him. It was called the *Barton Bee* and was moored on the River Wey at a marina just on the outskirts of Minstead Village, a mile from Minstead House. Now he saw Meredith several times a week, without fail.

He often wondered if their mutual adoration was the reason they were both over fifty and single. Nobody else was ever good enough.

'I keep thinking I should've run to get the defibrillator, but it was too far away.' Meredith's voice was muffled.

She finally pushed herself away from him and stared up into his face. Hers looked ravaged, a sickly greeny-yellow with huge black shadows under her eyes, like she had the worst possible hangover.

'Maybe we still should,' she said. 'Maybe it's not too late. We need to get back there anyway. I've decided I'm going to call the police. We're going to walk back there as if we're just having an evening stroll, then I'm going to "notice" that the ice house door's open, go and investigate, scream, alert night security, et cetera, et cetera.'

'What if they look at the CCTV recordings from earlier and see that you went in together, but you came out alone?' Pete asked, doubtfully.

Meredith shook her head. 'There aren't any cameras in that part of the grounds. I'm sure there aren't. We came down from his office the back way. He didn't want the security guys to see us go in to the loo. Or risk doing it in his office, because they sometimes pop in for a chat if he's working late ... We'll just say you came to meet me and we were having a walk because it's such a nice evening.'

'OK ... but what about when the police find your DNA on him?'

Something else occurred to him, and he grimaced, pushing his sweaty hair out of his eyes. 'Um ... did you use a condom?'

Meredith hung her head, shamefaced.

'Mez! That's terrible! You should know better.'

She rolled her eyes. 'Listen, you might have sex every other day, but I haven't done it since Alasdair and I split up, and that was about four years ago! I didn't even get that far with Gary. And Ralph is – was – a sixty-year-old married man. It certainly wasn't planned, and I really doubt he's been putting it about. Risking herpes is the least of my problems. It's a good thing there's no condom – less evidence to be found.'

'Well I'm disappointed in you, sis. And I don't know what you think I get up to when I'm not with you, because I certainly haven't been at it every other day for quite some time. Promise me you will be safer in future.'

'Whatever, Pete. It's irrelevant anyway, because I am never, ever having sex again, as long as I live.'

They walked in silence back towards the ice house. Pete reached out for her hand, as he occasionally had when they were kids.

As they rounded the corner from the rose garden onto the sweeping back lawns, a cheery voice came out of nowhere, and Pete felt them both jerk with shock, as if there would be two more heart attacks in the grounds that night.

''Ello! Evening constitutional, is it?'

The owner of the voice was a portly, elderly man in some kind of dark-green uniform, carrying a huge torch, even though it was still light. He was almost as wide as he was tall, with a flat but bulbous nose that spread halfway across his face, like it was trying to escape.

Meredith dropped Pete's hand fast, but stayed pressed close to his side, hoping, he could tell, that the man hadn't noticed.

'Pete, this is Leonard, our night-security guard,' she said. 'Leonard, my twin brother, Pete. You must have just come on duty?'

Pete was impressed at how normal she made her voice sound. But then she always had been good at hiding her real feelings from the rest of the world. Too good, often.

Pete remembered Meredith telling him that Leonard had been wearing out shoe leather in the corridors of Minstead House for almost three decades. He recalled the conversation because he never understood how anyone would want to work nights for more than a couple of weeks, let alone over half his lifetime. Thirty years! Even the thought made him want to punch a wall. But then, now he was meeting the man and seeing the look of placid acceptance in his baggy eyes, it made more sense.

'Evening, Leonard. Nice to meet you.'

'I can't believe you two haven't met before!' chirped Meredith as if they were all at a cocktail party.

'Pleased to meet you,' Leonard said, tipping his cap to Pete, who bared his teeth back at him.

'Just going for a stroll. Such a lovely evening.' Pete put his arm around Meredith.

'Aah, that's sweet. I hated me sister, personally. She used to give me wedgies and Chinese burns.'

'Meredith wouldn't do that,' Pete said, squeezing her arm. 'Not unless provoked. Well, nice to meet you, Leonard. Have a good night.'

'Night, Leonard,' Meredith added.

It was only when Leonard had waddled off back in the direction of the house that Pete realised Meredith was shaking. She had to lean against him to keep herself upright.

'I need to sit down,' she whispered.

'Stay cool, Mez. You're doing great.' Pete took her hand again. 'It's good that he saw us. Where is this ice house, then?'

'Just here, behind these bushes,' Meredith said, as they reached a bank of flowering rhododendrons.

As they rounded the corner she added, loudly and brightly, presumably in case anybody was in the vicinity to overhear, 'Oh look! Someone's left the door unlocked.'

This was crazy, Pete thought. She was acting like *she'd* killed Ralph. She shouldn't just ring the police and say she'd found him; she should tell them everything. Be honest.

He was about to tell her this, but she spoke first.

'I will never forgive myself,' she said, her voice cracking.

'Mez. Stop it. It's not helping.'

'I slept with my friend's husband.'

Pete turned and grabbed her hands. He'd already changed his mind about persuading her to ring the police. She was right, it was too risky.

'Listen to me. We've all done stuff we know we shouldn't have. Don't beat yourself up about it – at least, not right now. If you want to keep your job, your reputation, and not have Paula hating you forever, you have to stop this. She's going to need you. Be there for her – that'll help make it up to her, even if she doesn't know it.'

'But that's even more hypocritical!' she wailed.

Pete shook her shoulders gently. 'It's not about you now. Your friend's husband's died. She needs you.'

Meredith sniffed hard. 'Right. Yes, you're right ... OK. Let's do this.'

She glanced nervously in the direction of the open door. To Pete, it looked like the entrance to a mausoleum, a place so dark that it would inevitably suck the breath from anyone venturing inside. He felt sick at the thought that there really was a dead body behind the door in front of them. He'd never seen one before. They stared mutely at one another, then Pete nodded towards the entrance.

'You only have to go in for a second, and I'm right here.' Something occurred to him. He put his hand on her arm and whispered close to her ear. 'We should just, er, check one thing...'

'What?'

'You said he'd either had a heart attack or been strangled, because he looked so purple, and now I can't stop thinking about it. When you "find" him, we should check his neck ... just in case...'

Meredith frowned. 'Surely nobody would kill Ralph!' she whispered back. 'I wasn't being *serious*. He always has a red face, and I opened his shirt to do CPR, so I'd have seen if there was anything wrong with his neck.' She paused. 'I was only out of the place for a couple of minutes!'

'Burglars, seeing if there was anything worth nicking?'

'Oh, come on. In the ice house? Burglars would go straight to the house!'

Pete looked through the bushes and across the empty lawns, worried that Leonard would pop up again at any minute. 'Well, we can't stay out here talking about it all day.' Meredith's face had gone green again, presumably at the prospect of examining Ralph's corpse. But she took a deep breath, swallowed hard and pushed open the ice house door.

There was nobody there.

8

Meredith

Meredith stared in disbelief at the earth floor. The only signs that Ralph had ever been there were the buttons she had ripped off his shirt to perform CPR – unnecessarily, but she hadn't been thinking straight. Some part of her brain must have been blindly assuming that someone would be arriving with the defibrillator, and had made her follow her first aid training. But of course you didn't need bare flesh to do CPR. And there had been no-one to bring a defibrillator.

Pete looked over her shoulder, his breath hot in her ear, his fingers digging into her shoulder with the shock. 'What the hell? Have you got the right place?'

'Of course I bloody well have,' she snapped. 'How many ice houses do you think there are? He's gone!'

'All right, all right,' he said, trying to placate her by rubbing the back of her neck with his thumb, but she jerked away from him, her heart pounding with fear. 'He must have just been unconscious, and woken up,' he said. 'This is good news, it means he's alive! Ring him.'

'But he was dead,' Meredith said with bewilderment, clutching the door frame to hold herself up. 'No question.'

'He can't have been. This isn't the frigging Resurrection! Ring him,' he insisted.

She took her mobile out of her pocket and scrolled to his name. 'I'm phoning a dead man,' she muttered. 'This is insane.'

'And lo! The stone was rolled away,' Pete added, without a smile.

They both held their breath as the phone rang once, twice, three times ... then the voicemail kicked in. The sound of Ralph's cheerful, booming voice instructing her to leave a message nearly broke Meredith. She killed the call and dropped to her hands and knees to pick up all the buttons scattered on the damp floor.

'Someone's moved his body.' She stared up over her shoulder at Pete, who was leaning against the doorjamb, scratching his stubble, his forehead furrowed.

'You think I'm losing my marbles, or having a breakdown or something,' she said. 'I can see it in your eyes. But I haven't made it up. What do you think these are doing here, then?'

She held out her hand to show him the four buttons she'd collected, stuck to her palm by the cold sweat she had burst out in. She peeled them off and put them in her skirt pocket. She was pretty sure there hadn't been more than four, although she kept scanning the floor in case.

'I don't, Mez, honestly. Obviously something happened, Ralph passed out, but—'

'Pete! How many times do I have to say it? He hadn't passed out; he had no pulse. HE WASN'T BREATHING AT ALL. I'd know. I've done a first-aid course once a year for the last decade ... Can we get out of here? And – look at that.'

There were marks on the earth floor leading out of the door, like something heavy had been dragged through it.

Pete shook his head. 'This is mental. Let's go back to your place and have a drink.'

They left the ice house in silence and started to cross the lawn again. Meredith concentrated on taking deep breaths and focussing on the roses as they walked through the walled garden and then the vegetable patches, trying to find equilibrium in the deep-green leaves of kale and the frilly-edged cabbages.

She had always said she would never want to live anywhere else, but now she wasn't sure if she would ever feel the same, not after this. If something really had happened to Ralph, everything would be different from then on. Until now, Meredith had always felt safer here than in a town, because nobody apart from Pete knew who she really was.

Nobody had ever recognised her, not once in the many years she'd been working at Minstead.

Over all those years she had gradually become less scared that her attacker would find her and finish what – for reasons totally unknown to anybody apart from himself – he had started that night when he took her from her London home.

These fears had waned, but they were never far from the surface. A part of her, she knew, would never stop worrying. The nightmares would never completely leave her alone – in fact they'd flared up again recently, since the break-in; the severed dahlias. It didn't take much.

And it *was* pretty isolated here – a five-minute drive to the nearest inhabited houses and, if the house was closed, apart from the security guards she was the only person on the whole fifteen-hundred-acre estate. Conversely, of course, during summer opening hours she could literally be pushing her way through the crowds of people admiring the vegetable gardens to get to her front gate.

The staff car park was just visible behind her cottage, up a small flight of stone steps.

'Let's just check if his car's still here.'

They ascended the steps. The car park was almost empty, just Meredith's car, Leonard's – and Ralph's, in the far corner. Meredith pointed at it. 'There it is. Shit. That's not a good sign.'

'Come on,' Pete said, seeing her face. 'No point in panicking till we know what's going on.'

He held out his hand and she took it gratefully.

She felt detached, as if she was looking down on herself and Pete as they walked back down the steps and opened the creaky front gate of the cottage. Of all the extraordinary, freaky things that had happened in her life, this had to be the worst.

The second worst.

She handed Pete the front-door key, not trusting herself with even the simple task of fitting it in the lock. As he jiggled it, he kept asking her over and over if she was sure Ralph really had been dead, until she felt like kicking him in the shin out of frustration and confusion, like she used to when they were kids.

'Stop it Pete! He was dead as a frigging dodo. I told you, I did CPR on him for ages – ten minutes at least. He had no pulse, before or after. I don't know how else to say it. Someone must have moved him. Just get the sodding door open.'

Stress was making her scratchy.

'All right, all right! Chill out.'

Meredith scowled at him and jammed her hands in her skirt pockets. The door finally yielded and they crowded into the cool, dark flagstoned porch. She breathed in its familiar scent of lavender wax polish, dusty old cushions, mouldy umbrellas and the permanent faint whiff of woodsmoke, desperate for the combination to soothe her.

She probed her fingers around the bottom of her left pocket for the buttons. They felt like grim trophies, pearls of teeth, and she shuddered as her fingers came in contact with them. She pulled them out and threw them out of the still-open front door, one by one, in different directions into the overflowing flowerbeds.

Pete looked at her as if she had gone crazy.

'Best to get rid of them, don't you think? Nobody's going to search the garden.'

'Hopefully not,' he said, darkly. 'Go and sit down, I'll put the kettle on.'

'Wine for me. There's a bottle in the fridge.'

She went through to the front room, kicked off her shoes and lay down on her back on the sofa, staring at the nicotine-yellow ceiling, thick wooden beams running along its length.

'We should still call the police,' she said as Pete came in with a full glass of wine for her and an open bottle of IPA for him.

'I changed my mind about wanting tea ... Well, maybe – but to say what? We don't know for sure that any crime's been committed. You're going to feel daft if he turns up tomorrow.'

Meredith sat up and swigged the wine as Pete took a tobacco tin and cigarette papers out of his jacket pocket. Something caught her eye: a dark, bulky shape she hadn't noticed in the hearth when she first came into the room. She screamed, jumping up so violently that the wine sloshed out of the glass and onto the carpet. 'Holy SHIT!'

Pete followed her horrified gaze, and when he saw what she was looking at, he made a disgusted sound in his throat. It was a huge, fat, dead brown rat, lying belly up by the grate, its yellow teeth bared in a final grimace, its thick, hairless tail stretched out behind it.

'Oh my God!' Meredith felt panic rise, a tidal wave of emotion. She was shaking so violently, her legs wouldn't hold her and she collapsed back onto the sofa. 'Someone's left it there! Someone's been in the house! Pete, get rid of it, please!'

He took her glass out of her hand and set it gently on the coffee table, while she buried her face in her palms so she no longer had to see the abominable rodent.

'Shhh, it's OK. It probably just fell down the chimney. Nobody's been in the house. It's just a coincidence.'

'Fell down the chimney? Since when does that happen? I can't cope with all this. I feel like my head's going to explode,' she said. 'The shop break-in. Flowers beheaded in my garden. Lovely Ralph is dead, and someone's moved his body. Now this fucking thing ... How can it be all coincidence? He's back, Pete. It's got to be him. What the fuck am I going to do? I'm a dead woman. It'll be me next. He's not going to let me get away this time ... Oh God, I can't even tell the police because they'll think I killed Ralph.'

Pete knelt at her feet and wrapped his arms tightly around her again. 'Shhh. Stop. Deep breaths. You're reading far too much into all this. Like I said, it's all coincidence, I'm sure it is. Nobody's after you. Nothing else is going to happen. I'm here. I won't let anything happen to you.'

'Ralph...' Meredith sobbed. 'Poor Ralph, and Paula...'

'I know... it's just horrific, and you're in shock. The rat's nothing. Nobody's been here. I'll get rid of it.'

He released her and began to roll a cigarette, his hands shaking.

'Do me one of those, would you?' Meredith asked.

Pete looked up at her, his tongue stilling as it worked along the edge of the Rizla. 'Seriously? You haven't smoked for years.'

'Whatever.'

He finished the roll-up and handed it to her, along with his lighter. As she lit it, she saw Ralph on the earth floor again, as lifeless as the rat, and nausea rose in her throat.

Paula didn't even know yet, she thought.

They moved into the kitchen so as not to have to look at the rat, and sat at the table in silence for a few minutes, smoking. Meredith usually loved the silence in her cottage, after all the visitors had left the grounds for the day, just the backdrop of birdsong and the occasional plane high overhead, but now it felt oppressive and ominous.

'Um, you don't really think it's anything to do with…?' Pete suddenly asked, his voice loud in the dusky gloom. He stubbed out his roll-up in the ashtray that Meredith reserved for him alone, and stared at her intently with his big green eyes.

Meredith knew what he was going to say and felt panic rise again even before he said it. She needed him to keep reassuring her, not to suggest she might be right when *she* suggested it. 'Oh Pete … don't even think it. I know I did, but it can't be. It was twenty-four years ago! But … all this stuff. What if he *has* found me?'

She stood up on weak legs, finishing her wine.

'Would you mind getting rid of that … thing before you go? I'm going to have a bath and take a sleeping pill. I need to sleep. God knows what tomorrow's going to bring. You don't have lights on your bike so you should go now.'

Pete laughed mirthlessly. 'Are you crazy? There is no way I'm leaving you on your own in this state … Not because I think you've got anything to fear, of course,' he added hastily. 'This is a completely different situation.'

Meredith was going to protest, but she knew she absolutely didn't want to be on her own, not tonight.

'OK,' she said, reaching down to hug him where he sat in the chair. 'I'll leave you to it. Thanks bro.'

Meredith ran a bath and lay very still in it for a long time, watching a small spider abseil from one of the ceiling beams down towards the toilet lid. It was a long way down for such a tiny creature. She thought of Pete's words. *Was* it a completely different situation? The police had never caught anyone last time – not even had any viable suspects, once they'd ruled out Iain. They'd written it off as a break-in that had gone very wrong, and that was probably what it had been. It had been almost a quarter of a century ago. Surely it couldn't have anything to do with Ralph's death now?

9

Meredith

Meredith always started her day by going into work at 8.00 a.m., an hour before she needed to, and collecting Ceri's arthritic terrier Dexter. Ceri, who was PA to both the Earl and Ralph, worked 8.00 to 4.00 and couldn't walk the dog herself, on account of her clinical obesity. Ceri was always trying to pay Meredith for the dog-walking duties and Meredith always refused. It was her routine now, and never failed to clear her head for the day ahead.

She felt a wave of nausea threaten to flood her that morning when she left the cottage and saw Ralph's car still sitting in the distant corner of the staff car park. She crunched over the gravel towards the Jag, feeling compelled to go and look at it up close. Even though she had been utterly certain that Ralph was stone dead when she ran out of the ice house to ring Pete, the only logical explanation was that he hadn't really been dead at all. He'd woken up and staggered off somewhere. They should've checked inside the car last night, she thought, hope flaring: Ralph could well be snoring on the back seat, sleeping off his funny turn and alcohol stupor.

She approached the car and peered through the window, wishing Pete hadn't already cycled off to his workshop, so that she could laugh with him at the sheer relief of seeing Ralph alive, after all that drama...

But of course it was empty, its immaculate leather seats gazing blankly back at her. Ralph wouldn't have spent the night in there anyway; she was kidding herself. He'd definitely have come and knocked on the cottage's green front door, demanding a sofa or – after the shenanigans in the disabled loo – one side of her bed.

Meredith's head began to spin, her lack of sleep and hangover combining with the disappointment of the empty seat. Not for the first time, she couldn't help wondering if this whole thing was some kind of weird revenge Ralph was wreaking – perhaps for 'making' him unfaithful to Paula? Although she had hardly forced him, she thought. The opposite. And anyway, it would've been ridiculously out of character for him to have done that.

If, for some obscure reason, he was just trying to mess with her head, she would find out soon enough – there was a heads of department meeting that morning, which Meredith, as shop manager, and Ralph, as estates manager, were both required to attend. Her gut clenched at the thought of walking into the conference room and seeing his place empty.

She wearily climbed up the backstairs, thinking of Ralph's hand on her arse on these same steps less than twelve hours earlier.

Ceri's office was next to Ralph's, and her door was always open, both literally and figuratively.

'Morning Ceri,' Meredith said, entering. Dexter yelped with delight at the sight of her, and she knelt and tousled his brindled head. Ceri was undoing a new box of Minstead House branded ballpoint pens, ready for the meeting.

'Morning Meredith! Another lovely day, isn't it!' She always said this, unless it was pissing down or snowing.

'Yeah. Anyone else in yet?'

'Not yet,' she trilled, a pile of Minstead House notebooks on the desk next to her. 'Just me, getting ready for the meeting.' She paused. 'Strange, though – Ralph's car's here. I thought he'd got in early, but there's no sign of him.'

The HOD meeting was scheduled for 9.45 a.m. in the board room next door. Ceri had already printed and carefully laid out agendas on the vast, polished oval table.

'He probably got a taxi home last night,' Meredith said carefully. 'He wasn't half putting them away at the staff lunch.'

Ceri would be devastated when she found out that Ralph was dead

– if he was – and, Meredith thought with her heart sinking further, probably out of a job too. Whoever eventually replaced Ralph probably wouldn't be so tolerant about the undelivered phone messages and the unfranked mail. Ceri loved laying stuff out neatly, but wasn't so hot on the more responsible elements of the position. But she couldn't lose her job, it would kill her.

Meredith had a feeling that the ripples of yesterday's events had only just begun to spread.

'Meredith, love, are you all right? You look terrible.' Ceri stared into her face, concern furrowing her brow.

'I'm OK,' Meredith said, turning away and clipping Dexter's lead on. 'Insomnia, that's all. It's my hormones. See you in a bit.'

Their daily circuit always took them past the bell house, up to the main gate to say hello to George, then round through the rough parkland, back into the orchard, through the trees and back up the stairs to the office, where Dexter would climb into his basket under Ceri's desk and sleep for most of the rest of the day.

'Looking a bit peaky this morning, Meredith, if you don't mind my saying,' George commented, leaning out of his sentry box as he greeted her. He was a large man, much too large for his box. When he was in there, Meredith always thought it looked like a cameraman had zoomed in on him – he filled the frame.

She hadn't wanted to see him, or anybody but Ralph, that morning, but she wanted to stick to her routine.

Just in case.

There was a splodge of something unidentifiable but disgusting-looking on the front of George's uniform. She normally would have pointed it out, peeled a wet wipe from the pack she kept in her bag and gone over to scrub it off for him, but all she could manage today was another weak protestation that she was fine.

'Late night, was it?'

'My brother came over and we drank too much wine. And I've got terrible insomnia,' she croaked.

George opened his mouth to sympathise, but his attention was taken by a coach arriving, full of Japanese tourists. George made a conspiratorial face at her, baring his small, brownish teeth.

'Shall I be nice, or shall I tell them the car park doesn't open till nine? It's only just gone eight! Reckon they're on a different time zone.'

'Be nice,' Meredith instructed, managing to make her voice sound normal – at least to her own ears. 'Just make sure they know the shop opens at ten. I don't want that lot hammering the door down in five minutes' time.'

He raised the barrier for the coach as Meredith pulled Dexter away from something by the side of the sentry box the dog was sniffing at with great interest, and they set off, back up the narrow driveway through the parkland.

It curved in a graceful arc for half a mile from the gatehouse and public car park until it reached the house itself. It was a view that still took her breath away every morning – the grandeur of the honey-coloured façade with its towers and carvings.

It often occurred to Meredith that Minstead House, somehow more so than anywhere else, was made up of millions of tiny items, not just the quotidian bricks and tiles, but great mounds of minuscule, random things, like novelty pencil-tops and ornamental gravel. She imagined the sum of its parts deconstructed into haystacks sitting on the drive where the house had once sat: separate piles of gilt picture frames, blocks of parquet flooring, individual pats of butter from the restaurant, computer keyboards from the offices, lily pads from the lake, like some kind of giant build-your-own-stately-home kit that would take two hundred years to construct.

If she was able to take the whole house apart and put it back together, would Ralph be there again, sitting in his office, tucking a cigarette behind his ear to smoke as soon as he got out the door?

No he wouldn't. He was dead.

As Meredith rounded the corner behind the house, she braced herself for a phalanx of flashing lights, police vehicles, ambulances and CSI in paper suits – although of course George would've mentioned it had they actually arrived.

She dropped Dexter back with Ceri then went back downstairs, out across the courtyard to the stable block that housed the shop, with her cubbyhole of an office at the back. Swiping herself in, she checked that nothing was broken or moved.

All was normal – she had cleared up the broken china and shelf the previous day after the policeman left, and Ralph had fixed the shelf himself. She shut the door of her cubbyhole office and made herself a coffee with soya milk, which immediately curdled into cheesy clots.

As she stirred it, she thought back to what Pete had suggested the previous night. Could Ralph really have been strangled? His face had been purple, but the light in the ice house had been almost nonexistent. She had been so busy trying to restart his heart that she hadn't really been looking that closely at the exact hue of his skin. He'd have had marks on his neck if someone had throttled him – but, again, she hadn't been looking for them.

Her mobile buzzed on her desk, and when she saw who it was, her heart plummeted.

'Hi Paula,' she said, trying to keep the shake out of her voice as she answered. 'What's up?'

10

Meredith

Paula didn't sound overly worried – not then, as she was telling Meredith that Ralph hadn't come home the previous night. Meredith had a sudden urge to yell at her that she bloody well should be worried.

'Has he ever done it before?' she asked instead, fiddling with a loose thread on her top.

'No, never. And his phone's switched off.'

Meredith gave the thread a yank.

'But, you know, I'm guessing that he just ended up on some kind of bender and has been sleeping in a hedge all night. He'll probably limp home with a massive hangover and minus a shoe, any minute now. He might have left his phone at work. I just wondered if he'd crashed at your place last night. I know you had your monthly staff lunch, and he often has to get a cab home after that. I'm always asking him if the Earl knows how much of Minstead House's budgets go on Ralph's alcohol habit.' She laughed mirthlessly.

'I am a bit worried about his drinking,' Meredith said, feeling like the hypocrite she knew she was. 'He didn't stay at mine last night, but he *was* drinking in his office after lunch. He texted me about five-ish to ask if I wanted to come up and have a drink with him then, but I'm really busy at the moment, getting ready for the stocktake, so I didn't.'

She felt as if there was something obstructing her throat and swallowed hard.

'It's weird, Paula. His car's still here. I saw it this morning on my way in. If he hasn't come home, I think you should ring the hospitals. Maybe he couldn't get a cab and decided to walk into the village, and had some sort of accident on the way. Or perhaps he's collapsed some-where. You hear these stories. Ceri hasn't mentioned him leaving his phone in the office.'

'I'm worried about his drinking too,' Paula said in a small voice. 'It's got worse lately. You could be right. I've been thinking the same – but I was just waiting for him to come rolling in, in the early hours. I've been lying awake all night, planning the bollocking I was going to give him.'

'Are you seeing clients today?'

'No, I only had two booked in and I've cancelled them both.'

Paula was a psychotherapist, practising from a big studio in their garden. Meredith had often thought that was an unsafe thing to do, but Paula always brushed off her concerns with a blithe wave of the hand and pointed out that where Meredith lived was far riskier, being so isolated. 'Yeah, but I don't invite mentally unstable people to my house,' Meredith would counter.

'I've got to go upstairs for our heads of department meeting in a minute,' she said now. 'If he's not there, I'll check with Ceri to see if he's rung in sick. She didn't say he had this morning when I took Dexter out for his walk, though ... Keep me posted, won't you? And try not to worry...' To her horror, her voice cracked.

She covered it up with a cough and said a hasty goodbye to Paula. Then she lowered her head to the desk and banged it, gently and repeat-edly, on a catalogue of cashmere cushions and picnic blankets.

⊓⊔

Unsurprisingly, Ralph's seat was unoccupied at the start of the meeting. Ceri announced rather crossly that she hadn't heard from him.

The Earl frowned. 'What's his car doing here then? Parked the Rolls next to him this morning, thought the lazy bugger was in early for once!'

Meredith forced her mind not to flash back to yesterday and looked around the table at her colleagues. Both the Earl and his son, Sebastian, looked a bit the worse for wear, and she wondered if they had also continued drinking yesterday after the staff lunch. Could they have had anything to do with Ralph's disappearance?

Neither of them lived in the house any longer, although Sebastian had grown up here. When he'd gone off to uni, to study whatever young aristocrats study at Cambridge, the Earl and his wife had moved to a stunning eight-bedroomed Georgian vicarage in Minstead Village. 'Downsizing', they'd called it, which Pete and Meredith thought was hilarious.

Once Sebastian had left uni – after the first two terms – he'd bought a round-the-world ticket and set off travelling – probably with his own Sherpas – for a couple of years. On his return he'd promptly been employed by his dad as Minstead House's PR person. He was pleasant enough and well meaning, but absolutely rubbish at his job.

Meredith imagined the scandal that would ensue if yesterday's events were made public, and cringed. It would affect everybody, quite apart from the devastating impact it would have on Paula.

Please come back, Ralph, she exhorted mentally. If she tried hard, she was able to believe that he might just walk in now, clutching his head.

The Earl rotated a finger in his bristly ear and Sebastian gazed out of the window while Ceri poured cups of coffee from a large cafetière. The head of HR, Maureen – a willowy redhead nicknamed Mumblin' Mo because she spoke so low, so fast and in such a thick Scottish accent that nobody could understand her – was reading through the agenda with a look of barely concealed boredom.

The Earl called the meeting to order, and Ceri sat in Ralph's empty chair to take minutes, pen poised over a new page in her notebook and an expression of ferocious concentration on her lined face. Whatever her failings as an executive PA were, she was a whiz at shorthand and tended to write down absolutely everything, which meant that the minutes always ran to dozens of pages.

Halfway through a drone by Valerie, head of volunteers, about the recent volunteers' training day, Meredith's phone rang in her bag.

Everyone turned to glare as she fished it out, apologising, and went to kill the call. But then she saw that it was Paula again. She stood up and excused herself, mouthing, *I have to take this, sorry.* The Earl frowned at her – mobile phones turned on during meetings were one of his many *bête-noires* – but she barely noticed. Why would Paula ring again, half an hour after they last spoke, unless there was bad news?

What was she thinking? She *knew* there was bad news. It was Paula who didn't ... yet.

'Paula! Is he home?'

Paula was crying so much she couldn't speak.

'What's happened? Is he hurt?'

Meredith thought she was going to throw up. She walked to the top of the stairs and forced herself to stare out of the window at the sunlit treetops, trying to ground herself. The morning sun felt warm on her face through the glass.

So this was how lives unravelled.

'Nothing,' Paula said eventually, and Meredith managed to breathe again.

'Nothing?'

'No news. I've reported it to the police, and they're sending someone over. But I know something terrible's happened. He's never done this before; he just wouldn't. Even if he was mad at me for something, he'd let Jackson know he was OK – and he hasn't. Meredith...'

'Yes?'

'Will you come round later? I really don't want to be on my own.'

Meredith closed her eyes, sunlight laser-dappling her eyelids, a dozen fabricated excuses flitting through her mind. The thought of witnessing Paula's agony was intolerable.

'I'll see if I can get away a bit early. We're still in the meeting at the moment, and Hester has a dentist's appointment this afternoon, so I'll have to cover the till until she gets back. But I'll come after that, at about fourish, OK? Hang in there and let me know if there's any news.'

She went back into the meeting, not realising how much her stricken expression was giving away until Valerie stopped talking and everyone swivelled to face her.

'Meredith?' Ceri said with alarm. 'What's the matter?'

Meredith sat heavily back in her seat. 'Hopefully nothing ... but that was Paula. She's really worried because Ralph didn't come home last night. She's already told the police. It's so out of character for him.'

The Earl peered over his smeary half-moon glasses, worn on a chain round his neck. He had quite a soft spot for Paula, and Meredith and she used to giggle that if she, Paula, played her cards right, she could one day be the second Countess Winnet.

It didn't seem so amusing now.

'Good heavens. And his car's here. Do you think I should get the garden lads to do a search of the grounds? Did anybody see him leave last night?'

They all shook their heads. Meredith couldn't meet anybody's eye.

'He's walked into the village before, hasn't he? When he's...' Mo tailed off, not wanting to drop Ralph in it by saying 'been too pissed to drive', but they all knew what she meant.

'Has Paula rung round the hospitals?' the Earl asked Meredith.

'Yeah. Nothing. I said I'd go over and see her after work. I'll work through lunch and leave early, if that's OK?'

'Of course,' he said. 'Well, this is all most concerning. I do hope he hasn't come to any harm.'

Meredith thought of herself scattering Ralph's popped shirt buttons in her flowerbed like incriminating seeds. Seeds that, if they were to sprout roots, would only produce terrible seedlings of guilt and remorse.

'So do I,' she said fervently.

⊓⊔

The meeting dragged on for another half an hour or so, but it was clear nobody was really paying attention. Ceri's eyes kept going glassy and she had to stop doing her shorthand squiggles to press a tissue against her lower lids and sigh heavily, before half-heartedly resuming.

Eventually all thirteen items on the agenda had been raced through, and they were released back to their respective offices. The rest of the day passed without incident for Meredith, apart from a young woman with learning disabilities who tried to steal a packet of Minstead House fudge. She didn't even have the heart to tell the shoplifter off. The girl started to cry as soon as Meredith pointed out she'd spotted her dropping the fudge into the open top of her backpack, and gave her back the fudge.

Hester returned at around half past three, a hand pressed to her rapidly swelling cheek and her lip drooping slightly, and Meredith found herself wishing that Hester wasn't quite so stoic. She had no option now but to go to Paula's and face the music.

11

Meredith

Paula opened her front door, clinging onto it as if it was the only thing holding her up. Meredith had to prise her fingers off the frame and steer her by the elbow through to the kitchen.

The kitchen was a mess, the counters covered with a random selection of seemingly unconnected items: a heap of tarnished spoons in an untidy pile; flies buzzing around a huge pile of half-chopped tomatoes; a baking tray lined with silver foil next to some brown fluffy wool; a purple ukulele on one of the stools at the breakfast bar; some shrivelled-up leaves and a small pair of knitting needles.

It reminded Meredith again of her image of Minstead House in kit form. Perhaps this was the personification of what a mental breakdown looked like: foil, cutlery, tomatoes, knitting...

'Thanks for coming,' Paula managed eventually, pouring Meredith a huge glass of wine without asking. She looked terrible, grey as putty, dark circles under her eyes and a blotchy complexion. Meredith wanted to hug her but felt too guilty, so she merely nodded and held out her hand for the wine.

It was stiflingly hot in there, despite a fan listlessly rotating on the kitchen island.

'What's all this?' Meredith gestured towards the mess on the counter, then moved the ukulele so she could sit down.

Paula gave a strangled hysterical bark of laughter. 'I can't settle to anything,' she said. 'I keep starting things and not finishing them. I was going to make gazpacho. Then I thought I'd clean the spoons. Then I remembered I'd started knitting a fledgling for my niece. And I need to practise the ukulele.'

'Knitting a fledgling?'

Meredith wasn't really surprised, though. Paula's house was littered with the corpses of half-finished craft projects and the evidence of short-lived hobbies. Ralph had frequently complained about it at work.

Paula ran her hand through her usually sleek black straight hair, making it even more dishevelled. 'My sister's been rearing this baby bird. Put photos of it all over Facebook, but it died and she was so upset. So I thought I'd knit her one, you know, to sympathise.'

'Mmm,' Meredith said, tempted to add, '...as you do,' but it seemed insensitive under the circumstances. 'Tell you what, let me finish chopping the tomatoes. You sit down for a minute and talk to me.'

She gestured towards one of the stools at the breakfast bar and Paula obeyed, pouring herself an even bigger glass of wine first, half of which she gulped straight down.

'Have you eaten?'

Paula shook her head.

'Don't go crazy on the wine...'

Tears sprang into her eyes. 'Why? In case it looks bad that I'm pissed when the police show up to tell me my husband's dead?'

'Oh Paul, don't think the worst, please. It's not even twenty-four hours yet. Let me make this gazpacho and we'll have some. I haven't eaten either.'

Meredith had to stop chopping to rub her throat, to try and ease the constriction in it. You didn't shag your friends' husbands. How could she have done it?

'Can I ask you something?' Paula wasn't looking at her, but at her glass, running her thumb frantically up and down its stem.

Oh shit, please don't, Meredith thought. She had a flashback of Ralph's buttocks in the low mirror of the disabled loo, clenching and thrusting, her leg wrapped around his thigh. 'Of course.'

'Yesterday ... at work ... how drunk was Ralph? He rang me in the afternoon and he sounded pissed. Said you'd all been at the staff lunch, that it had gone on longer than intended, and he'd have to stay late to catch up. I teased him. I said, did he mean "catch up" or "sleep off the hangover under his desk"?'

Meredith cored a tomato, seeds spilling onto the chopping board in a gelatinous shiver. 'He's always quite pissed after the monthly lunch,' she replied carefully. 'I think he might have carried on drinking in his office.'

'How did he seem, at lunch?'

Meredith shrugged, turning away from Paula to start on a red pepper.

'Same as usual. He was on a different table so I didn't talk to him – he was sitting with the Earl and Sebastian and the other bigwigs.'

She remembered Ralph winking across at her, trapped between the Earl and Sebastian, all three of them knocking back the Chianti.

'I was sitting with Ceri and Mumblin' Mo. Ralph was still there when I left to go back to my office.'

Which was when Ralph had texted her to ask her to come and see him after work...

Where was his phone, she wondered?

'How can he just have disappeared?' wailed Paula.

'What did the police say?' Meredith pretended to be engrossed in scraping the brittle white seeds out of the pepper's heart.

'Not a lot. Someone came over, about an hour ago. She just took down all the details. They said they won't make it public for another day, though.'

'What else did she say?'

'Nothing very useful. Just "I'm sure he'll turn up" – that sort of thing. She wanted a photo of him and to know if he had any medical conditions, and so on.'

'And did he? Does he, I mean?' Meredith tried to keep the treacherous hope out of her voice, although she wasn't sure what exactly she was hoping *for*.

'Nothing serious. Oh Meredith, do you think he's left me? I know I moan about our lack of a sex life, but I do love him, you know.'

Meredith put down the knife and went over to Paula, putting her arms around her, trying to keep her juice-stained fingers away from Paula's crumpled, white linen shirt.

'He adores you too. He told me so just yesterday.'

About half an hour before he slipped his fingers inside my knickers. She cringed.

'Did he really?' Paula hugged her back. 'Where do you think he is, then? Surely he'd have rung if he could.'

Meredith extracted herself from the embrace. It felt too hypocritical. She hesitated. 'Like I said, he texted me, mid-afternoon sometime, asking me to pop into his office for a drink after work. That's what makes me think he kept going, that he was on a bit of bender.'

Paula was still for a moment. 'Does he do that often?' Her voice was very small. And then: 'Did you go? I can't remember if you said you did or not.'

Meredith looked straight at her. 'I don't know, and no I didn't. I didn't want to drink Scotch at five-thirty in the afternoon, especially not after I'd had two glasses of wine at lunch. I had to work late – getting ready for a stocktake next week.'

There were several truths in that sentence, but none of them went anywhere near diluting the one that was a barefaced lie.

'So we know that he was OK at – what time did he send the text?'

Meredith took her phone out of her bag and checked it, glad to be able to direct her gaze somewhere else. 'That was at ... four o'clockish.'

'Can I see? I should let that policewoman know.'

Handing it over, Meredith felt relieved that Ralph hadn't put anything suggestive in the text; it merely read: *Post-work snifter?*

She hadn't even intended to go, that was the irony, she thought.

'Let's just say, hypothetically, he kept drinking all afternoon, then felt too wasted to get home. He knew he couldn't drive, so he left the car there. Perhaps he lost his phone, felt ill, got a hotel room somewhere to sleep it off?'

'Why not just come home, then, if he felt ill?'

Paula slid off her stool and walked over to the jumble of items on the counter. She picked up several of the leaves and shuffled through them, holding one out. 'What's this one?'

Meredith shrugged. 'Not a clue. Ash? Oak? Sycamore? Not yew, I know that much.'

'That's my point.'

Sometimes talking to Paula was very tiring. 'Your point?'

'I don't know either. I'd have known when I was a kid. I knew them all then, everybody did. Now nobody knows. I thought I'd stick them in a scrapbook or something.'

'You can probably get an app that—' Meredith broke off. There was a sound from the front of the house, a faint crunching on the gravel, and she felt sick to see the way that Paula's entire appearance changed in a second; the years and cares fell away from her as she stuck her chin in the air, almost sniffing it like a pointer, already smiling with relief as they both held their breath and waited to hear the grind of a key in the door.

But there was no key. Just the rattle of the letterbox as someone stuffed a flyer through it and the faint swish of it sliding across the hall floor.

'He's dead,' said Paula flatly. 'I know he is.'

Meredith had no idea what to say to her.

12

Meredith

She left Paula's house in a daze. She'd had to put her to bed at 8.15 p.m. with a sleeping pill, Paula drunk and sobbing and clutching Meredith's arm with her bitten nails. Meredith didn't think she should leave her, but Jackson, Paula's taciturn twenty-year-old, home from uni for the summer, had come back from a fruitless search of Ralph's local haunts. He assured Meredith he would look after his mother.

Somewhat to her shame, Meredith couldn't get out of there fast enough, her guilt practically shoving her between the shoulders and through the front door. She was heading home, but as she drove through the village, past the immaculate, chocolate-box whitewashed cottages, the turning down to the marina loomed up ahead of her and suddenly she only wanted to be with Pete again.

She parked on the marina road and trudged down the metal steps to the water's edge. It was a perfect summer's evening, the river as calm as a millpond, the late sun creating a golden hue that suffused everything it touched. There were people out on the water, canoeing or punting, looking like they didn't have a care in the world, when Meredith felt as if she had a huge black cloud above her head.

'Evening Meredith! How's your week been? Want to come in for that trim I promised you?'

It was Pete's neighbour, Andrea, who was at the outdoor table on the rear deck of her wide-beam barge, a large drink in one hand and her phone in the other.

'That's bad for the baby,' Meredith said grumpily, gesturing towards her glass.

Andrea laughed. 'Is tonic only, silly! I am not so stupid. Come. You look like you need a drink too – one with gin.'

'Let me check if Pete's in – I need to talk to him. If he's not, I will. Thanks.'

'Bring him too,' Andrea said with a cheeky smile, and, despite herself, Meredith smiled too. Those two were crazy about each other, she was convinced of it, but neither would admit it.

'I'll try.'

Meredith was very fond of Andrea, who was unfailingly generous with her time and never, ever seemed to be miserable, despite getting knocked up on a one-night stand when she'd gone home to Hungary to visit her elderly parents earlier in the year.

Meredith climbed onto Pete's boat and tried the door, but it was padlocked. Peering in through the glass panel, it looked as if he hadn't been there all day – a cereal bowl and empty cafetière sat on the galley counter. She had a spare key to the padlock, but suddenly she was glad of Andrea's offer of company. She didn't want to be alone with the jumble of thoughts swarming around her snowglobe head like white noise.

She jumped off *Barton Bee* and strode up Andrea's gangplank to join her on the deck. Andrea was sitting at a slatted wooden table covered with a ferociously detailed puzzle on a roll-up jigsaw mat. Most of it was completed, with just one chunk of the middle left to do.

Meredith picked up the box lid and looked at the picture – a park scene with far too many identical-looking trees and white clouds, populated by people in sixties dress, boys fishing for minnows, girls in miniskirts and tank tops, skipping rope. She could see why Andrea had left that particular middle section till last – it was almost all pink cherry blossom. The remaining pieces in the bottom of the box were a muddle of pink and white.

Sun soaked into her tired bones, and she tipped her head back to feel its rays warm her cheeks, letting the box lid fall onto the deck.

'Lovely evening.'

'Yes. I get you a drink, then you tell me what's wrong.'

Meredith made a face. 'Don't ask. Really.'

Andrea came over and gave her a spontaneous hug. Then she picked up a strand of Meredith's hair. 'Let me cut. Is too long for you.'

Andrea had converted one of her tiny bedrooms into a fully equipped mini salon, complete with spotlit mirror, basin and one black chair for a customer. She was one of the most in-demand hairdressers in the area – as long as clients were nimble enough to get down the often-slippery steps to the waterside.

'Maybe later. Thanks, though.'

Andrea disappeared into the galley and Meredith sighed, feeling about ninety years old. She must only stay for one, she decided, otherwise she might end up telling Andrea what had gone on this week, and not just the bit about Ralph being missing. Meredith idly scrutinised the jigsaw, all the stylised caricatures of people going about their business, mostly on a pathway through the park. A glamorous-looking young mother sat smoking on a bench while holding the handle of one of those huge old prams, presumably rocking it.

She picked up a piece that looked like it might belong in the flower-bed next to the bench, but it didn't.

Meredith wished *she* could have a cigarette, but until last night she hadn't smoked for fifteen years, and she didn't want to start again now.

Andrea returned and handed her a tall, cold G&T, the condensation on the glass sparkling in the sun, a thick chunk of lime bobbing in the fizz. No drink had ever looked so appealing. Meredith took a long swallow.

'Thank you – oh God, that's so good. Just what I need.'

'The baby is missing,' Andrea said, seemingly apropos of nothing.

'What?' Meredith was alarmed, thinking Andrea meant her own baby.

'Look,' she said, pointing at the empty pram in the puzzle. 'And face is not in box, I have searched and searched.'

'Did you buy it in a charity shop? They often have missing pieces.'

Andrea shook her head. 'My dad give it to me for Christmas. We always give each other a new jigsaw.'

She was right, though; Meredith sifted through the few dozen pieces left in the box, but none had a baby's face on them. They were all cherry blossom.

'It must be on the floor somewhere.' Meredith leaned down and peered beneath the table. 'Could it have fallen through a crack in the decking?'

Andrea shrugged. 'Must have done. Is annoying.' She paused. 'And worrying.'

'Worrying?'

Her hand flew to her belly, and she rubbed it gently, looking embarrassed. 'I think is omen.'

Meredith had forgotten how superstitious she was. 'Oh Andrea! Of course it's not an omen. You mustn't think like that, you'll drive yourself crazy.'

She wondered if it would be insensitive or non-PC to suggest it might be Andrea's hormones. She'd never really known any pregnant women before and, obviously, hadn't ever been one herself. But was that the accepted wisdom, that your hormones went berserk? Or maybe that was after the birth ... She wasn't sure.

'How many weeks are you now?' she asked instead.

'Twenty-two,' Andrea replied, smiling properly. 'And he just kick me.'

She was such a beautiful woman, with delicate bone structure and high cheekbones. For the first time Meredith realised with a slight shock that she reminded her of Samantha. If her colouring hadn't been so different – dark, instead of a Celtic-looking freckly redhead – they'd have looked quite similar. It was the smile, the figure and the profile. She studied her, thinking about Samantha, wondering what ever happened to her. She hadn't seen her for more than thirty years. Strange how she didn't find Andrea sexually attractive, seeing as she'd found Samantha irresistible. But that was probably just because Samantha always looked at her as if she was the most beautiful woman in the world. She, Meredith, had been young and naïve, lapping it up. Meredith always wondered if she would ever have had any sort of gay relationship if she'd never met Samantha. She hadn't since.

'Want to feel?'

'He's letting you know he's fine,' Meredith said, reaching out her hand and tentatively touching Andrea's taut stomach through the layer of cotton jersey. 'Wow! That's amazing. I've never felt a baby kick before.'

For some reason it made her think of Ralph again, and she had to swallow hard. He'd been desperate for grandchildren, even though Jackson was only twenty. 'Give the poor boy a chance!' Paula and Meredith used to tease.

'So what is matter, Meredith?'

Meredith sat back in her chair and stared out over the water, watching a lone rower power past, and three ducks flying in a V formation towards the setting sun.

'I've just come from my friend Paula's house. Her husband, who's also my friend, and my work colleague, he's gone missing. Something's happened to him, it must have done. It's so out of character.'

Meredith felt an utter heel, being so disingenuous. She knew so much that might help find him, yet she was saying nothing to anybody.

'Oh no! How long is he missing for?'

'Just over a day so far. But there's no way he'd vanish without a word.'

'I am sorry, Meredith. That is very worrying.'

Meredith gave her a tight-lipped smile. 'Don't be nice to me. I might cry.'

'Let me give you haircut instead. Try to take your mind off it!'

'OK,' she said, thinking that it would take a lot more than a trim. 'Thanks Andrea – if you're sure. But you must let me pay you.'

Andrea flapped her hands. 'Certainly not! Come.'

Meredith brought her half-finished drink inside, following Andrea into her tiny little salon. Andrea settled her in the black leather chair and velcroed the plastic cape around her neck, before wetting her hair with water from a squirty bottle and combing it through. The gentle bite of the comb's teeth against Meredith's scalp was relaxing and she felt her shoulders drop just a little.

She had to stop worrying. Ralph would surely be found, or come home. He'd managed to get out of the ice house by himself – Meredith refused to believe anybody else could have been involved, in such a short time – so that meant he was still, contrary to all appearances, alive.

Andrea's salon had been squeezed into the prow, where the smaller of the two bedrooms had once been. It sported two portholes, one in front of Meredith's seat, overlooking the dockside, and one behind Andrea, who was beginning to snip at Meredith's split ends. This port-hole had a view across the river, and Meredith could see it, reflected in the big flat mirror, which also obscured the view directly in her eye line.

Something caught her eye, a reflected movement, and she jerked out of the chair, making Andrea gasp.

'Meredith! What is matter? I nearly stab you with scissors!'

Meredith leaped up, peering frantically out. 'There's someone on board! I saw a man's foot going past the porthole!'

'*What?*'

They both ran through the living room of the boat – salon, pro-nounced 'saloon', as Pete kept reminding Meredith – and up the three steps to the deck.

'You look this side, I'll go the other,' Meredith said, her heart pounding. The black cape was flapping out behind her and her hair was plastered to her head.

But there was nobody. Unless they'd immediately run back around to the port side, jumped back onto the dock and legged it to hide behind one of the upturned boats. Meredith decided she must have imagined it; they'd have had to be very speedy indeed to do that without being noticed.

Andrea was looking at her strangely. 'I am worried about you,' she said. 'It must have been a duck or something.'

'I'm sure I saw a foot, in a black trainer. Just a glimpse, and a shadow.'

'A shadowy foot with no leg?' Andrea asked in a faintly teasing voice.

'Well, obviously the leg had already gone past,' Meredith said, realis-ing how silly this sounded. 'On that little ledge thing round the side, what's it called?'

'The "cant", I think it is. Come on. Let me spray your hair again. Won't take long,' she said, and they went back inside.

'Just... lock up well tonight, won't you Andy?' she said, once she was seated back in the black chair. Their eyes met in the mirror and Meredith could tell Andrea thought she was being ludicrous. Their little dock community was so safe. Everyone looked out for everyone else; they had their own in-built neighbourhood watch. If some random stranger really had been tramping round the outside of Andrea's barge, Meredith was pretty sure that Pete or Trevor or Johnny would've been standing on the dock by now, demanding to know who he was and what he was doing there.

Meredith was the isolated one, since the Earl and his family had moved out of the house. At nights just her and Leonard on the whole fifteen-hundred-acre estate, and if someone *was* prowling round her cottage, Leonard would be at least five minutes' away, since her place wasn't even on his rounds.

It had never bothered her before, but now she felt spooked.

She wanted to tell Andrea about Ralph, how something weird was going on. She had no idea what, and maybe she was being totally self-obsessed and narcissistic by thinking it had anything to do with her. She couldn't help remembering the last time she felt like this, though, even though it was so long ago.

As if activated by her concern, the puckered purple scar over the hole on the back of her left hand started to burn and itch, and she had to press her right thumb down on it to keep the sensations at bay. Andrea, like most people, had always been too polite to ask what had happened, but Meredith saw the covert glances it received when she forgot to place her hand palm up, or cover it with her other hand. If anyone ever did ask, she had her story down pat: a knife, a late night, a drinking game that went horribly wrong...

But only Pete knew that this wasn't the truth.

13

Meredith

Six days of limbo passed. Nothing else strange happened; everything just carried on, as if Ralph had been beamed up by aliens. He was officially a missing person, and the staff at Minstead spoke about it in huddles, with hushed anxious whispers.

'I'm just going for lunch, OK?' Meredith told Doris, who was sitting precariously on the high stool behind the cash register, polishing stained-glass window decorations. Her bald skull shone disconcertingly under the shop's halogen spotlights, barely covered by a few remaining strands of candyfloss grey hair.

At eighty-three, Doris was by far the oldest and most doddery of the volunteers, but Meredith couldn't let her go. She'd been volunteering a day a week since her husband died thirty years before and, like Ceri, would probably lose the will to live herself if she no longer had the anchor of Minstead House tethering her to this mortal coil.

Meredith felt another pang of sorrow at the thought of Ceri, who was out of her mind with worry that Ralph was missing. Since last Friday, she'd been mostly sitting at her desk outside his office, twisting rosary beads between her fingers and staring vacantly at her telephone.

'Be careful on that stool. You know I worry about you up there,' Meredith said.

Doris looked over her glasses at her. 'I haven't fallen off it yet,' she said. 'See you in half an hour. Have you got a hat? It's sweltering out there.'

'Good point.' Meredith borrowed a branded baseball cap from the rack of merchandised apparel, and stuffed it in the bag with her foil-wrapped sandwich. 'Call me if you need me.'

Doris wasn't wrong. Opening the side door into the sunshine felt like walking into an oven, after the cool flagstone floors and air-conditioned shop. But the sun's soft fingers stroking her face felt good. She strolled away from the house, through the wrought-iron arbour arch and into the rose garden, which was in full, insanely colourful bloom, an explosion of scent and pastel shades.

There weren't many visitors about in the grounds – it was too hot, probably. They'd all be inside, their gazes sliding across boring oil paintings by minor eighteenth-century artists, and marquetry cabinets. It made Meredith smile that the words she heard most frequently when she walked through the public areas of the house were from children: 'I'm bored. Can we go now?'

At the end of the rose garden, she turned left into the vegetable patch, a regimented riot of tomatoes, marrows, netted strawberries and courgettes, then out through the gate marked *STAFF ONLY*, heading in the opposite direction from her cottage. This took her to her favourite part of the grounds, a once-ornamental pond with a low crumbling wall around it, closed off to the public while awaiting restoration. The pond was surrounded by a scramble of rhododendrons and bulrushes, and Meredith loved it because it was completely private, with a view to die for. The rest of the staff rarely bothered to walk this far from the house, so she almost always had it to herself.

She headed straight for 'her' bench, greedily taking in the view over the ha-ha, across the woods and to the Surrey Hills beyond, now shimmering in hazy layers under the cloudless cerulean sky. It soothed her without fail, particularly after a morning spent with the colourful busyness of all the shop's offerings in her eyeline. A blackbird chirped sweetly in the huge oak on the lawn a few feet away. For the first time since Ralph's body vanished a week ago, she felt the distant echo of a sense of peace. It wasn't back yet, but there was the hope that it might be.

Meredith pulled the borrowed baseball cap out of her bag and rammed it on her head to shade her eyes from the sun's dazzle, moving the label to one side so that it didn't dangle in her face. She unwrapped the cheese and pickle sandwich she'd made the night before and took a bite. As she chewed, she took the top off her juice and was about to take a swig, when something caught her eye.

The surface of the pond was usually still and bottle green, the only movement the stilted skedaddle of the water bugs. It had been many years since the curly-haired stone cherub in the centre had spat any water through his patinated trumpet. But something looked different today. There was something in the water, a lumpish mass breaking the surface, hidden in the rushes to the far side of the cherub.

Meredith wrapped her sandwich back up in its warm foil so that the wasps wouldn't get to it and went over to investigate. It was a huge, dark object. She stepped carefully round the pond on the chipped and uneven crazy paving.

At first she thought it was a duvet, or maybe some large coats that someone had, for some unfathomable reason, dumped in there. Her heart was in her throat as she climbed onto the low wall to try and get a better look, still refusing to allow herself the thought that it was anything other than a discarded sleeping bag or suchlike. But she still couldn't see properly because of the thickness of the unkempt reeds. She needed something to part them with; a stick or branch. There was no way she was getting into the pond herself – she didn't even know how deep it was. She jumped off the wall and searched around, but there were no sticks on the ground. Then she ran back into the kitchen garden and yanked a cane out of the raspberry bushes, the effort in the hot sunshine making her hands slippery with sweat and fear.

She approached the pond more slowly this time. Should she call security now, save her having to look herself?

No – that would be stupid, she thought. It still might turn out to be nothing. Small insects hummed and buzzed around her head, intensifying the white noise inside it. She got back onto the wall, already feeling unsteady. She focussed intently on the sight of a bee bouncing into a foxglove to help her keep her balance.

She reached forwards with the cane. Parted the rushes, touched the floating lump. Then prodded it, to try and push it out into more open water. It moved, turning slowly.

Later she thought that was the point she knew, deep down. Even though it just couldn't be ... Even though he was unrecognisable.

The body floated free, breaking the surface of the pond, pushing aside the waterlilies in a way that gave Meredith the grim, fleeting thought: *pushing up daisies.* It rolled slowly over onto its back, an actual dead bug in the water. She glanced at his bloated, greeny-grey face, the skin already beginning to slide off the skull. Then looked away, nausea rising fast.

It was impossible, surely? But from the faded sodden pattern of his shirt, the same shirt she'd ripped most of the buttons off, she knew it was Ralph.

14

1983

Meredith

I didn't go to Greenham Common because I wanted to make the world a better place. I only went to piss off my parents. That, and because I happened to own a teddy-bear suit.

It was my seventeenth birthday, but had that stopped Mum and Dad being really annoying? It had not. I'd been wondering if they were getting divorced or something: Dad was really quiet, and had been for a few weeks; and recently Mum seemed like one of those small plastic toys on a spring – the ones where you licked the suction base, pressed the top to stick down, waited a few seconds for the spit to dry and then watched it boing up and off the table. Mum was boinging up every five minutes, running her hands through her wiry hair, shouting at me for no apparent reason. Even though it was my birthday, after they'd given me and Pete our presents (driving lessons – brilliant – and some new guitar strings from my brother, ten pounds from my uncle and auntie), she asked me to run down to the newsagents to pick up a copy of the *Times Educational Supplement*.

'I can't, I haven't done my make-up yet,' I said, packing *The Anatomy of the Industrial Revolution* into my backpack. I couldn't see why she wanted the teachers' magazine right that minute, anyway. 'I'll bring one back this afternoon. I've only got fifteen minutes before I need to leave.'

'I need it now!' Mum's eyes were wild and bulging.

Dad sat on a bar stool at the counter, mute and miserable, like he wished he could be anywhere else.

'The new jobs will still be there later.'

'Meredith, please just do as you're told. It'll take you ten minutes!'

I looked at my watch. 'Why can't you ask Pete?'

'He's already left. Meredith. Please.'

I hitched up my backpack – the Industrial Revolution was heavy – and grabbed the only apple with fewer than two bruises from the fruit bowl. 'Sorry. I can't go in without my make-up on, and I'm not going to be late. I'll get a detention, and it's my birthday. I don't see why you can't go.'

To my shock, Mum burst into tears. She *never* cried. But – being selfish and seventeen – all I could think was, how could she cry on my birthday? Emotional blackmail!

Fuming, I ran up to my bedroom, grabbed my make-up bag then stomped out of the back door and down the garden path, without stopping to comfort her. I'd have to do my face at school, and if any of the boys saw me without mascara on, I'd be mortified.

'Happy fucking birthday, Meredith,' I said out loud.

I was, retrospectively, deeply embarrassed at how selfish I'd been as a teenager.

⊓

Caitlin was just pulling up the shutters outside Sarum Discs when I passed through the Old George Mall on my way to school, an unlit rollie stuck to her bottom lip. The little bells at the bottom of her crinkled Indian drawstring-waist skirt tinkled as she moved. 'Hi Meredith, beautiful day, isn't it!'

I grunted. Caitlin was one of life's relentlessly cheerful people; even more so in the past few weeks since she'd had a new boyfriend. It was 'Sam this, Sam that, Sam thinks ... Sam says...' all bloody day. It sometimes made it a bit hard to work with her on a Saturday, particularly if I was hungover. I usually just turned up the volume on the stereo to drown her out.

'Oh dear!' Her voice chimed like the tiny bells. 'What's the matter?'

'It's my birthday,' I said. 'And I hate my parents.'

She rushed over and gave me a tinkly hug, wafting patchouli as usual. 'Happy birthday! What a bummer you have to go to school. And don't worry, everyone hates their folks. Come in after and we'll have a special celebration, Alaric's got the new Bauhaus record in. I'll get a cake and ... Oh wait, what am I thinking? I can't. I took a half day. Guess where I'm going?'

My mood plummeted again at the immediate retraction of the offer – even though it wasn't like this was my only chance to mark the occasion; I was having a night out with friends at the weekend. 'Oh right. Don't know. Somewhere with lover boy, I imagine?'

A brief, agonised expression flitted across Caitlin's face, and I thought, *uh-oh, trouble at t'mill*?

'No – Sam's ... busy this weekend. We've had a bit of a fight, actually. Try again.'

I wanted to ask if she was going to dance naked in the moonlight at Stonehenge. Caitlin was what my mother called 'a loosely woven sort, probably knits her own yogurt'. Mum didn't like hippies.

'I'm going to Greenham!'

'Wow, no way. Really?' I probably sounded sarcastic, but was actually quite impressed. The women's peace camp had been on Greenham Common for more than two years, and apparently there were tens of thousands of women living there, camping around the airbase perimeter fence. Living! I'd often wondered how they supported themselves financially. Or bathed. Whenever it featured on the news, I was simultaneously curious and appalled at the sight of all the mud, filth and violence. A few months back they'd managed, just by sending out a chain letter, to get thirty thousand women linking hands around the fence. 'Embrace the Base', it was called, and the media attention had been huge.

Caitlin extracted a lighter from the pocket of her patchwork waistcoat. 'Yeah. This friend of mine's borrowed a camper van, and we're all going for a few days. I'm so psyched.' She dropped her voice. 'There's going to be a special protest tonight – well, two, apparently: a human chain all the way from Greenham to Burghfield – there's a big weapons factory there. We're not doing that, though. A load of us are going to dress up as teddy bears and break in while the human chain's happening. Honestly, Meredith, it's so amazing there at the moment. The vibe is incredible.'

I wasn't sure if I'd heard her correctly. 'Teddy bears?'

'Yeah. How brilliant is that? A sort of teddy bears' picnic, you know, to symbolise what those weapons could do to our children, and their children. And it'll be a statement, you know, contrasting with the macho militarisation of the base.'

'I've got a teddy-bear costume,' I said contemplatively, accepting a drag of the roll-up once she'd lit, inhaled and offered me it. 'You could've borrowed it, if I'd known. My granny made it for me for a school play when I was thirteen. Might be a bit small now, though...'

'No problem!' she chirped. 'I have one too. I sewed it myself last weekend. It's so cute, I want to wear it all the time!'

An idea formed in my mind, one that would really piss off my slightly right-wing parents. 'What time are you leaving?'

'After lunch,' she said vaguely. 'I wish you could come. It's gonna be epic. But Willow says they're squeezing me into the van as it is. I'm going to have to sit on someone's lap.'

So much for that, then. Nothing was going right today. Nothing.

'Oh well,' I said grumpily. 'Couldn't go anyway. Got a mock history exam at two. Just what you want on your birthday. Well, I better go, or I'll be late.'

I thought with a pang of guilt that in the time I'd spent stopping to chat to Caitlin, I could probably have run to the newsagent's and back for Mum.

⊓⊔

All that day I couldn't stop thinking about the protest, and the camper van full of militant teddy bears. As I daydreamed through each period, I realised I was desperate to go. In the free period before lunch, when I ought to have been doing revision on the role of Edmund Cartwright's power loom in the mass production of textiles, I went to the library, got a roadmap down from the shelf marked 'Maps of Britain' and worked out which trains I'd need to take to get me to Newbury, where RAF Greenham Common was. It was only an hour away, with one change at Westbury. Easy. And I had Uncle Mike's birthday money to buy the ticket with. Of course I didn't have any more details, like, what time this protest was, where the rendezvous point would be; because the whole camp surely couldn't be dressing in bear costumes – it must only be a breakaway faction. I had no idea of the size of it, but I knew it must be pretty big.

At lunchtime, as was our wont, my friends Julie and Charlotte and I set off down the path to the back of the school to sit in Julie's ancient two-tone 2-CV and drink Baileys (I only had one swig, since I did actually want to do well in the mock history exam). They'd bought me a piece of lardy cake on a paper plate from the baker's – my favourite – and stuck a candle in it, which Julie lit and I blew out. Then they sang 'Happy Birthday' lustily and tunelessly while Julie fluffed her perm in the rearview mirror. Charlotte lit a cigarette mid-refrain.

'Guess where I'm going later?' I announced indistinctly, my mouth full of dough and sugar, unintentionally echoing Caitlin's earlier words.

They thought I was insane when I told them. Julie, in the driver's seat, puckered her lips in horror. 'With all those ... old lesbians? Why?'

'I'm sure they aren't all lesbians. Lots of them have kids living there with them. And they definitely aren't all old. Caitlin's only twenty-six. Anyway, that's not important. What's important is...'

I paused. Why *were* they doing this? Did they really think it would make them take all the nuclear weapons away?

'Being *part* of something,' I said vaguely.

Julie and Charlotte looked at each other and rolled their eyes.

15

Present Day

Emad

Gemma and Emad bumped into one another on the steps of the police station; he was coming in, she was going out. He recognised her immediately, and was unable to believe his luck that their paths had crossed again, a good ten years after they'd last seen each other.

'Gemma McMeekin – Meeks!' He grabbed her sleeve then blushed puce and dropped it, thinking how presumptuous he was being. 'It's me, Emad. Emad Khan. Do you remember me?'

Gemma stared at him: a moment's confusion then delight all over her face, making it light up. She looked a bit tired, but fantastic, he thought. The extra decade had slimmed down her round cheeks and dissolved her puppy fat, and braces on her once appealingly goofy teeth were dragging them back in line. Emad remembered how he'd first fancied her in sixth form, precisely because, he guiltily thought, she *wasn't* one of the pretty and therefore unobtainable girls. She'd been the funniest, and the most outrageous, and she had gorgeous eyes – but she'd never been conventionally beautiful. And she'd always been kind to him, where most of the other girls had laughed at his shyness and how hirsute he was.

She was beautiful now, though, albeit still a bit plump and with traces of the old goofy teeth. All his long-forgotten feelings of lust for her came flooding back, reminding him of the times he used to lean against the wall outside the science lab, not having the nerve to go and speak to her, while she would clown around, giggling with her mates further along the same wall. She used to smile at him in class but otherwise mostly ignored him; apart from that one glorious time she'd played him 'Lose Yourself' on her iPod, sharing her earphones with him because she'd made some tenuous comment about Eminem and Emad being similar names.

'Emad Khan! Look at you all grown up. I didn't know you were one of us. Small world. Are you working here?' Gemma gave him a hug, beaming. Then she sniffed his shoulder, in a far more familiar way than she ever had when they were doing their A levels.

'New uniform, if I'm not mistaken? I remember that smell so well.'

He nodded, embarrassed and proud. 'Only passed out of basic training three weeks ago. Better late than never, eh? Turns out I wasn't cut out to be a photocopier salesman. Best decision I ever made ... Well, I hope it was anyway. Bit early to tell yet. You're a cop too? I don't believe it...'

'Detective, for the last five years,' Gemma said, clearly unable to hide the note of pride in her voice. 'DC. Maybe DS soon.'

'Wow,' he said with reverence. 'That's so cool. What are you working on at the moment?'

'Gang-related murder in Farnham,' she said. 'We got the guy two days ago. Right evil bastard, he is. Hope they throw away the key.'

Emad tried to look at her ring finger, but she had her left hand hooked around the strap of her handbag and he couldn't see it. She pressed a button on the Fitbit on her wrist.

'I've got to run. I'm due in court at ten. Great to see you, Emad! I'm sure we'll bump into each other again, now you're based here too. It'll be good to have an ally here.'

She clapped him affectionately on the shoulder and bounded down the steps, waving over her head at him without looking back.

Emad carried on into the station, his heart pounding with pleasure. He was already insanely proud to be a police officer. And now the job had just got a whole lot more appealing.

⊓⊔

They did not cross paths again for another week, even though Emad's eyes were out on stalks, looking for Gemma's curly blonde hair in every corridor. Perhaps she'd been tied up with her court case, he thought, and anyway he was kept busy out on calls and arrests, buddied up with more senior officers while he was still on probation. He asked around after her, just casually, saying how she was an old schoolfriend and he'd heard she worked here; but nobody else had heard of her – it was a big station.

Then, one Thursday morning he was making a tray of teas in the third-floor kitchenette when he felt soft hands cover his eyes. 'Guess who?' she said, and he smelled something floral and sensual in his nostrils.

'Hi!' He turned and grinned at her, then nodded at the eight mugs in front of him. 'You can tell I'm the newbie, eh?'

Gemma laughed. She looked even more gorgeous today, he thought, the dark shadows under her eyes a little less pronounced.

She wasn't wearing a wedding ring.

'We've all been there,' she said. 'Rite of passage...'

'I'm an expert already.' Emad busied himself pouring boiling water onto each teabag, and forced himself to keep his voice casual. 'What time is your shift finishing today? Want to grab a drink and have a catch-up? You know, one of those "do you remember so-and-so" conversations.'

She smiled, but briskly and – Emad worried – almost patronisingly. 'Another time, maybe. I'm knackered. But thanks. Don't you have a family to get back to?'

Could she be fishing for information? Or just being polite? Emad had no idea. 'No family,' he said, far too hastily. 'Single Pringle, that's me. What about you? You married? Kids?'

'Nope. One long-term relationship, ended a year ago when he cheated on me.'

Emad affected a look of outrage. 'What a moron! Sorry, though.'

'Yup.'

There was a slightly awkward silence. Emad stirred the teas one by one, fished out the teabags and left them in a steaming pile on the draining board, then pulled out a carton of milk from the little under-counter fridge.

'Better let you get on,' Gemma said.

'With my very important police work,' he added, sloshing milk into the teas.

'Very important,' she agreed, but her smile had fallen, and she looked bleak. In all their years at school together, he never remembered seeing that particular expression on her face. It must have been a bad break-up.

'Catch you later, Emad.'

16

Present Day
Emad

'Can I have a unit to deal please, immediate response, Minstead House, we have reports of an apparently lifeless male in the pond,' came the call over the radio.

Emad, in the passenger seat, picked up the handset. 'Control from GU22, show us assigned, ETA five minutes.'

'Do you know the place then?' PC Damian Jackman was driving, in a far more flashy way than Emad thought necessary.

'Been there as a kid. Know where it is, mile or so outside Minstead Village, right?'

As they drove up the long, tree-lined driveway to Minstead House, Emad only partly registered the verdant parkland with deer nosing around tree roots and the occasional bunny hopping away in fright; the first glimpse of the white bell tower appearing at the brow of the hill, and the car park full of visitors' cars, the sun glinting silver off their roofs.

Instead his thoughts were torn between anticipation about seeing his first real dead body and the memory of the expression on Gemma's face that morning when she'd told him about her cheating ex.

They rounded the corner, the turrets and pale, primrose-coloured stone of Minstead House looming up ahead of him. He had a deeper flash of memory: his mum bringing him here when he was a little boy. It had been a hot, sunny day much like this one, but inside the house had been dark and cooler – and, to his nine-year-old self, boring. Apart from the kitchens, which were fascinating. Plaster deer and pig carcasses, stuffed pheasants and geese hanging from hooks in the ceiling, wax fruit in bowls, fake loaves being pushed into a real furnace by a waxwork lady in a mobcap.

Damian parked at the front of the house, ignoring the curious looks of a bottleneck of tourists congregating at the main entrance, waiting to buy their tickets, and marched up to the desk. Emad had to force his attention back to the matter in hand.

A flustered and sturdy receptionist stood up as soon as she saw them come through the glass entrance doors. 'This way, Officers,' she said officiously after Damian had introduced them. She lifted up the counter with an arthritic-looking hand, the flesh of her ring finger puffing over and almost obscuring a wedding band. Her name badge read 'Angela Carruthers'.

'Wait a second,' Emad said, leaning over the counter so that the queuing tourists couldn't hear. 'Are you continuing to allow visitors inside?' He glanced at Damian, unsure if this was acceptable protocol or not. Damian's face looked impassive, suggesting that he didn't have a clue either. And he'd been a PC for a year.

Angela looked simultaneously appalled and self-important. 'Yes, until we're told otherwise,' she whispered. 'The ... ah ... body, has been discovered in an area of the grounds that's currently private. No member of the public has any sort of access to it, because the pond's been cordoned off, awaiting restoration. Security is guarding the site.'

Emad straightened his hat. 'I see. Well, you may shortly have to stop admitting visitors. It could all be a bit of a three-ring circus here soon, I'm afraid. Does the person who called us...' He took out his notebook to check the woman's name, feeling unprofessional that he hadn't remembered it, or checked before going in.

'Meredith Vincent,' said Angela. 'She's our shop manager. She was out there having her lunch next to Cherub Pond and she found ... it.'

'Does Ms Vincent know the identity of the body?'

'I don't know. She didn't say. She just called me to say you were on your way ... I thought there'd be more of you. Nothing like this has ever happened here before!'

Angela Carruthers looked out at the tourists, jostling impatiently outside the glass doors, trying to eavesdrop. 'The trouble is,' she said, stricken, 'if you wanted us to close, I'd need to run it past my boss, Ralph Allerton. And he's been missing for the last week.'

'You don't need to run it past anyone,' Emad said, more firmly than he felt. 'Shall we?'

Angela Carruthers now had an expression of mingled confusion and horror on her face, and wrung her hands with a dry scraping sound, clutching them to her ample bosom, a thought seeming to occur to her. 'I'm just really worried that ... that it's *Ralph* in the pond.'

Emad gave her a sympathetic smile. 'Please do just point me in the right direction, Mrs Carruthers, but stay at your desk. Someone will give you further instructions in due course, but for now you can carry on selling admission tickets. And when my colleague arrives, direct him to us, please.'

He hoped they were doing the right thing. If Dark Mavis – as he'd learned to call DS Mark Davis, who Emad had been delighted to discover happened to be Gemma's immediate superior – pitched up and immediately demanded the house be closed to the public, or even evacuated, they would look really stupid.

Angela took them out of another door to a lawned area studded with shady horse chestnut trees. An open-sided tourist bus – more like a large cart with rows of seats in it – waited to ferry tourists around the grounds, its driver slouched over the wheel. He looked to be in his mid-forties, yet he had startlingly bushy grey facial hair. He was staring into space, caressing his beard as if it was a beloved pet.

'It's about a five-minute walk through the cottage gardens,' she said, 'or you can ask Henry there to drive you.'

Emad thanked her and they approached Henry, who sat up guiltily at the sight of their uniforms. 'Could you run us over to the Cherub Pond as fast as you can, please?'

It was far too hot to walk; he was sweating cobs inside his hi-vis jacket and hat.

They rattled along yellow gravel paths, curious visitors looking up at them from their lawn picnics and strolls. The bus/cart shuddered to a halt next to a walled garden, and Henry turned around in his seat. 'Go through that archway,' he said, pointing away from the garden, 'across the open lawns, turn left at the far side, through the *No Entry* rope, left again by the greenhouses and you'll come to the pond.'

They thanked him and alighted, both wiping the sweat from their foreheads as they crossed the lawns and ducked under the rope, falling silent as they prepared themselves to see a dead body.

It was floating face up in the rushes. With dulled, bulging eyes and bloated, peeling skin, it was every bit as gruesome as Emad had feared it might be. A distraught woman came over to them, and Emad had to blink himself back into sharp focus. He realised his breath was coming in sharp, shallow puffs and he felt sick.

Hold it together, dickhead, he silently and furiously urged himself. But one glance at Damian told him his colleague felt the same – the man had turned like a traffic light from red to green.

The woman approaching was wearing a baseball cap with a large label hanging down over her left ear – which was the first image that came back to Emad whenever he mentally revisited the scene. It was odd, but infinitely preferable to that of the corpse. The woman was sobbing – nose running and eyes streaming from underneath her sunglasses. She was short and slim, of indeterminate age – she could have been anything from thirty-five to fifty.

'You must be Meredith Vincent? I'm PC Khan – call me Emad. Are you all right? I think you need to sit down for a minute. It's a terrible shock. I don't feel so hot myself, if I'm honest.'

Spotting the cracked, listing stone bench on the far side of the pond, weeds sprouting out from between the cracks, Emad took Meredith's arm and led her over to it. It didn't look appealing, but it was in the shade. The pair of them weaved through the unkempt grass and stumbled slightly over the crazy paving as Damian took a tentative step closer to the still, brackish water.

Emad realised how out of his depth he felt. Right then, despite his nerves about encountering the legendarily difficult Mavis, he'd have welcomed him there to tell him what to do. 'Isn't there someone you could call to be with you?' he asked gently.

Meredith just shook her head. 'Don't ... want ... anyone to see me like this,' she sobbed. 'Or anyone else seeing ... him.'

It was true what they said, he realised. Nothing really prepared you for your first victim of drowning. The shock of seeing the body like that was bad enough when it was a complete stranger; how much worse must it be if you knew the person?

'I believe you identified him when you rang us?' he prompted gently. 'Ralph Allerton? He's been missing since last Thursday, is that right? Are you absolutely sure it's him?'

Meredith gave another shuddering sob, managing a nod. 'He was my friend,' she whispered. 'I recognised his shirt; otherwise I wouldn't have known, not for sure. Seeing him like that ... it's just ... How did he get there? I don't understand it. He was fine...'

The poor woman was burbling with horror.

'When did you last see him?'

Meredith paused and stared hard at a dandelion that had forced its way through a crack, twisting the tissue round in her fingers. She wore several big chunks of rings, Emad noticed, with a different colourful stone set in each, making the knuckles of her right hand resemble traffic lights. They seemed at odds with her otherwise conservative appearance.

'Last Thursday afternoon. We'd had our monthly staff lunch. I went back to the shop before they'd all finished – it can drag on a bit sometimes and I don't like to leave the volunteers on their own for too long.'

'How was he?'

Meredith shrugged miserably. 'He seemed absolutely fine. Happy as Larry. Full of beans ... Just, he was quite drunk...' Her voice caught, and two more fat tears rolled over her cheeks and dropped into her lap. The label from her baseball cap was still dangling, but less obtrusively now – she must have turned it round a little.

Emad realised she must have just borrowed it from the shop to wear to lunch – not very professional, or hygienic, for the shop manager, but she obviously didn't expect to be seen by anybody.

'Well, we'll take a full statement in due course,' he said. 'But in the meantime I have to inform the duty inspector, see how he wants to proceed. Could you wait here a second while I make a call?'

Meredith nodded again, without looking up. Emad walked away, out of earshot and round the pond to the far side, where Ralph Allerton's body floated. He rang Mavis, who picked up immediately.

'DS Davis.'

'Yes, hi Sarge,' he said quietly. 'PC Emad Khan. I'm at Minstead House. There's a body in the pond, seems that it's a senior member of staff who went missing last week. Pond's in an area of the grounds not open to the public. I wasn't sure whether to tell them to stop admitting visitors to the house. Should we get the place evacuated?'

He heard Mark take a slurp of coffee. 'Hm. Nah. Not if it's definitely hidden from sight. Think it'd be too much of a palaver. So is it definitely him?'

'Seems like it. His name was Ralph Allerton. Found and ID'd by Minstead's gift-shop manager, Meredith Vincent. He's been in there a while. She saw him on the day he went AWOL; says he was pissed but in good spirits. Looks like he probably just fell in and drowned.'

'Sounds like that, yeah. I'll look up the MISPER report, hold on...'

Emad heard Mavis tap at his computer keyboard.

'Right. Yup. His missus says the same. He wasn't depressed or worried about anything – going missing was completely out of character. Liked a drink, etc, etc. Pretty obvious what's happened, as you say. I'll get everyone down there. Make sure you seal it off.'

'OK Sarge,' Emad said. 'Right you are. See you shortly.'

He returned to the stone bench, where Damian was already cordoning off the pond, unscrolling a roll of police tape and wrapping it around the leg of the bench, then tree trunks nearby.

Meredith was now fanning herself with the brim of the baseball cap. She'd stopped crying but was staring wildly at Emad.

'What happened to him? How did he *get* in there? It's just not ... possible.'

Emad grimaced sympathetically. 'I know, it seems so hard to believe he'd have just fallen in and not been able to get out again. The water must be so shallow. But I suppose if he was that drunk, he might have hit his head on the side or something ... we'll know when the post-mortem comes back.'

Meredith flinched and something caught Emad's eye. He tried not to stare, but couldn't help his eyes being drawn back to it: the big, puckered purply-black hole in the back of Meredith's hand, the one she was fanning herself with. She must have noticed him looking, because she hastily transferred the cap to her other hand and put the scarred one down on the bench slightly behind her, trying to hide it. Perhaps that was why she wore the rings on her other hand, he thought, to pull attention away from her left.

'You OK to sit there for a few minutes, till our scene-of-crime officers and the paramedics arrive? I'll take a statement once they do.'

She nodded, staring at her lap.

Emad started walking around the pond, checking the ground for anything unusual. The pond had stone edges, around which was a scrubby, balding lawn, some weed-choked flowerbeds, and the gravel path leading from the greenhouses. The soil was pretty dry after several weeks with little rain, but at the corner of path and lawn, Emad stopped and stared at a noticeable indentation.

'Damian,' he called. 'What do you think of this?' He pointed to the ground at his feet and Damian hurried across. 'It's a tyre track. Bike? Wheelbarrow?'

'Wheelbarrow – but so what? The gardeners presumably come through here all the time.'

'Yeah, but look how deep it is. That'd be a heavy barrow. Maybe...'

Damian snorted, then glanced over at Meredith. He dropped his voice. 'So, what? You think this guy was tipped into the pond from a *wheelbarrow*? Have you seen the size of him? I reckon he's as likely to have been dropped out of the hold of a plane.'

Emad scowled. 'Just a thought.' He'd been quite pleased at the thought of discovering some evidence, and now Damian had completely pooh-poohed it.

17

1983
Meredith

I spent my first two hours at Greenham wandering around in wellies, feeling alternately thrilled to be there and utterly humiliated, sweating in my bear suit, blisters forming, shiny and taut, on my toes after the long walk from the train station. But as time went on, and more and more smirks and sniggers were coming at me, any remaining thrill wore off. I'd made a terrible mistake in coming. Maybe Caitlin had been winding me up. I was going to kill her when I next saw her in the shop. While I overheard lots of talk about the human chain – apparently the turn-out had way exceeded expectations – there were no signs whatsoever of any other bears. Or what if Caitlin had got the wrong day?

By seven o'clock I wanted to cry. I hadn't had the nerve to stop and talk to any of the women huddled in groups around fires along the fence. There were not as many as I'd thought, but maybe most of them had gone out to do this human-chain thing. Many of the women I saw had grubby-looking, half-naked toddlers running around, brandishing sticks, so presumably it was all the mums who'd stayed in camp. I was getting funny looks too, which implied that none of them had heard about the teddy bears' picnic. I trailed miserably along the fence, which was bedecked with colourful banners and slogans, quilts embroidered with 'Ban the Bomb' and 'Protest and Survive'. The evening air was redolent with the scent of wood smoke, weed, lavender and patchouli. I could smell it, trapped in the fake-fur fibres of my bear suit.

What was I going to do if I didn't find them? Stupidly, I hadn't thought through the return part of the journey. I'd brought Pete's sleeping bag; it was strapped into the top part of his rucksack, which I'd nicked from his bedroom, so if the worst came to the worst I could sleep under a tree. Hopefully someone would take pity on me, though, and let me stay in their tent or something ... I shuddered with dread. I was way out of my depth.

'You all right, love?' came a voice from near the fence.

I looked up to see an elderly woman with long white hair, sitting on a camping chair, knitting something complicated-looking. A hand-painted placard saying 'I'M HERE BECAUSE I LOVE MY GRANDCHILDREN' rested against the fence next to her. I was so relieved to hear a friendly voice that tears leaped into my eyes.

'I'm fine,' I said, my lip trembling. 'It's just that it's so ... big here. I thought it would be easy to find the person I know, but that was stupid of me. Have you seen any other people dressed as bears? There's supposed to be some kind of teddy bears' picnic but I have no idea where and now I'm worried I'll never find them.'

She smiled, her eyes vanishing into a ruffle of crow's feet. 'Like them, do you mean?'

I turned and followed her gaze. Two women had just tramped past behind me, one dressed as Rupert the Bear, in a red jumper and yellow checked trousers with matching scarf, the other, a tall slim woman with long, wavy red hair tucked into the neck of a costume a bit like mine, only dark brown instead of my golden fake fur. Hers had a bear's face hood, pushed down so that it rested on her shoulders, the bear's upside-down eyes staring glassily skywards.

I thanked the knitting lady and dashed after them. 'Excuse me! Excuse me!'

They turned. The red-haired woman was strikingly beautiful – huge green eyes, high cheekbones and Pippi Longstocking freckles scattered over the bridge of her nose as if they'd been drawn on. 'Oh lookit! Another bear! And such a cute one,' she exclaimed, in a broad American accent not dissimilar to Daisy Duke's in *The Dukes of Hazzard*.

'I'm so relieved!' I gushed. 'I thought I'd got it wrong. I was told there'd be bears, but I've been here ages and haven't seen any...'

'"I was told there'd be bears"', quoted the American woman solemnly. 'I think I'll have that as the title of my autobiography, if you don't mind?' She stuck out her hand and smiled, her face lighting up. 'I'm Samantha. Pleased to meet you, little bear.'

I laughed too and shook it. 'Meredith. Very pleased to meet you.'

The other woman, who looked less interested, gave me a fleeting smile and a nod. 'I'm Sandrine.' Now that I could see her face, I thought she actually looked like Rupert the Bear, with a plump-cheeked face and beady eyes.

Samantha's approving eyes didn't leave mine. In anyone else I'd have found it disconcerting, but I felt myself relax in her gaze, opening up like a flower. I wondered if she was gay. I'd never met a lesbian up close before.

'So where is this picnic going to be?' I asked. 'Is it an actual picnic? I mean, I ate my sandwich on the train and I didn't bring a rug or a flask or anything.'

They both laughed then, Sandrine in a more mean way. 'Not a real picnic,' she said. 'It's symbolic.'

She said the word slowly and deliberately – as though I was a stupid person who had never heard it before.

'Right,' I said, staring her down. Somehow Samantha's warmth emboldened me.

'So where have you sprung from today?' Samantha asked, linking arms with me as we fell into step together. They seemed to know where they were going.

'I got the train up from Salisbury,' I said, thrilled by her familiarity.

Samantha stopped suddenly, gripping my arm harder. 'You're kidding – you're from Salisbury? Me too!'

'Ha,' I said. 'Yes.' I put on my thickest Wiltshire accent. 'Oi could tell az zoon as you opened yer mouth you woz one of uz.'

Samantha creased up, literally bending over at the waist and roaring. 'You are SO FUNNY!' she shrieked.

Sandrine looked pointedly at her wristwatch. 'Come on, girls, we're going in through the fence at Turquoise Gate at eight p.m. That's a ten-minute walk from here and it's already five to.'

I didn't care about her waspish tone. I was basking in the glory of Samantha's amusement. 'So where are you really from?' I asked, ignoring Sandrine.

'I'm from a town called Lawrence, in Kansas, but I truly have been living in Salisbury for the past couple of months. Staying with my sister's husband's sister. Such a small world, hey? And such a cool city.'

I nodded, delighted.

'What do you do?' she enquired. 'Something arty I'll bet.'

I beamed. 'No, I'm still at school actually. First year of A levels. What about you?'

'No way! You look a lot older. Me? I have a law degree from KU, but I decided to travel for a couple of years. Heard about Greenham' – she pronounced it Green Ham instead of Greenum, as everyone else did – 'and decided to come check it out. First came last year, and now I have a place to stay, in a yurt over at Turquoise Gate, so I spend quite a bit of time here. I love it!'

'That's so cool,' I said, mentally wincing that I'd copied her word; a word I never normally used.

Sandrine pointed ahead. 'Here we are. Just in time. They're cutting the holes.'

'Our people!' said Samantha, throwing her arms wide as we surveyed the crowd gathered close to the gate. Some had bear costumes like ours, some had made a token effort by wearing black and white and sporting panda masks. Bears of all different types and sizes were working in silence, huddled around the ones with wire cutters.

'I'd assumed they'd be chanting or singing,' I said, surprised at how quiet it was.

'Oh, we will be,' Samantha said. 'That comes later, once we're inside. Don't want to alert the pigs to what we're planning – we need the element of surprise.'

'What *are* we planning?' I asked nervously. This was getting serious.

A ripple of excitement went around as the first ladder was propped against the fence, thick blankets flung over the barbed wire, and a second ladder passed up and over by three overgrown teddy bears.

'Here we go,' whispered Samantha, and to my surprise she took my hand. 'Stick with me, OK?'

Sandrine rolled her eyes. 'Catch you later,' she said, vanishing into the crowd. 'Not in the mood for this today.'

'Oh that one, she's such a misery guts!' Samantha said, her eyes shining. 'This is the fun part – come on!'

I'd have preferred to go through rather than over the fence, but as we got closer, Samantha suddenly shoved me towards the foot of the ladder. She was ripping my backpack off my shoulders. 'Leave that here, you can come back for it. It'll be fine,' she said, and before I knew it, her hands were pushing my furry backside up the ladder. 'I'll be right behind you!'

Then I was at the top, straddling the barbed-wire fence. I could see for miles, wisps of smoke above the treetops to my left, rising from dozens of campfires and merging with the pinkening dusky clouds. To my right, the alien green mounds of the silos.

I froze, suddenly convinced I'd fall, but the encouraging faces of the women already inside were urging me over, their arms outstretched. Other women were pouring through the gap in the cut fence, racing towards the silos.

'Come on, honey, almost there,' said Samantha, halfway up the ladder behind me. There was a queue behind her. I couldn't hold them up. No going back now.

Taking a deep breath, I put my hands flat on the scratchy blankets, slid my right leg down to the top of the second ladder, and swung my left leg round to join it. I was over! I half climbed, half slid the rest of the way to the ground, my knees trembling with fear and exhilaration. I had never done anything illegal before. I had to banish the vision of my disappointed parents and my furious headmistress.

Seconds later, Samantha was next to me. 'We're IN!' She hissed, grabbing my hand again. 'Man, what a buzz!' Dragging me with her, she ran towards the silos, following the other bears, several of whom were already at the top of the grassy banks, dancing and hooting, chanting and singing.

It was the most exciting thing I'd ever been a part of, bar none. At first there were about twenty of us dancing up there, then thirty, forty, fifty, sixty ... beyond that I had no clue of numbers, just that I was part of this glorious sisterhood of impassioned faces, some shouting slogans with anger imprinted on their features, others, like me and Samantha, alight with a strange joy. I had to admit that nuclear weapons were the last thing on my mind then. I was caught up in the moment, and I never wanted to go home. I wanted to stay with Samantha and these women forever. At that moment she moved close to me, wrapped her arms around my neck and swung me with her. I could see her freckles up close, her wide black pupils in the bright-green irises. Nobody had ever had such an instant or strong effect on me.

We slowed, swayed together, my own arms shooting unbidden round her waist, eyes locked. Softly, gently, she reached forwards and kissed my lips, sending a stab of desire right down to my groin. Our lips began to part...

...But that was when it all turned nasty. Men in uniform – police, soldiers, military police – streamed through the gate, dozens and dozens of them, wielding truncheons, faces dark with fury and aggression, their yelling drowning out the ululations still going on all around us. We broke apart.

'Stick with me,' Samantha shouted as I turned to see a huge policeman charging straight for me. Women were being seized bodily and dragged away screaming. The huge cop bent at the waist, grabbed me around mine and in one swift move put me over his meaty shoulder and started running back towards the gate. How could I stick with her?

As he carried me, squirming as my breasts bumped against his back, I saw her through the melee, fighting with another, smaller guy.

'Stop resisting!' he was screaming at her, brandishing his truncheon above her head.

I mentally entreated her to stop resisting. The thought of her being injured made my pounding heart hurt.

As we got away from the main throng my own abductor seemed to relax a bit. He slowed to a jog and asked me where I got my bear outfit from. I didn't answer – I wasn't in the mood for small talk, bouncing upside-down over his back.

'Oi!' he said breathlessly, 'I asked you a question!'

I was scared now; scared, angry, aroused, confused. Had I really just kissed a girl on top of a silo? I'd never found a woman attractive before!

'My nan made it for me,' I panted. 'For a fancy-dress party.'

The copper's laugh made me livid, and I punched at his solid thigh until he told me, in a less nice voice, to cut it out. He even smacked my fake-fur arse at one point, quite hard, which made me scream, 'Police brutality!'

But that only made him laugh again.

18

1983
Meredith

Once we were through the gate, the cop put me down and grasped my sleeve instead, marching me towards a fleet of small, knackered-looking green-and-white coaches, where ragged queues of angry women were being herded, closely guarded by a phalanx of police. I looked wildly around for Samantha and felt a wave of relief as I saw her being dragged through the gates, seemingly unhurt, howling and swearing at her captor.

I was even more relieved when she was pushed into the same queue as me. 'Fucking pigs. How dare they!' she yelled.

'You were trespassing on Ministry of Defence property. I'm sure you're fully aware that that is an immediately arrestable offence,' said the policeman nearest us, his arms folded imperiously across his tunic.

Samantha spat in the grass at his feet. He merely raised his eyebrows. 'Nasty little dyke,' he commented, almost conversationally, and I had to pull Samantha's arm to stop her launching herself at him.

'Where are they taking us?' I asked, terrified now.

'Don't worry, honey, I'll be there. It's no big deal. They just take us to the nearest drunk tank and then let most of us go with a warning. Hell of a headache for them, though.'

We were almost at the head of the queue to get on one of the buses. Two bored-looking policemen were booking everyone in and doing perfunctory bag searches at a small card table near the coach door.

The woman ahead of us was clutching a worn shoebox, holding it to her chest as if it contained her worldly possessions.

'Hand it over, love,' said the younger of the two cops, who didn't look much older than me. He had a blancmange-pale face and looked like he was trying to act more bravely than he felt. 'We don't have all day.'

The woman with the shoebox, who had long, straggly pink hair and a baggy fabric bear costume, seemed reluctant. Her friend had already started laughing. 'Go on, Babs, give it to the little boy,' she said, and Babs made a show of slowly placing the shoebox on the table.

'Be careful with it!' she beseeched. 'It's very precious.'

The booking officer narrowed his eyes at her. As he took off the lid I was thinking, *Oh shit, what about Pete's rucksack? And his sleeping bag – he'll kill me!* I'd have to go back for them later.

A foul smell pervaded the air and the officers' disgusted exhalations brought my attention back to the shoebox.

'Search through that, then, sugar tits,' Babs said, the smirk in her voice clearly discernible. The box was full of smallish dark-red objects, meaty and metallic. I thought at first they were corpses of small skinned animals, then Samantha, looking over the woman's shoulder, started to laugh.

'Oh my god, that's genius,' she crowed, almost hysterical.

I looked closer. The shoebox was full of used tampons. Samantha clapped Babs on the back, and a ripple of mocking laughter went around the captive women. Personally, I thought it was as disgusting as the policemen did, and had to choke back a gag. The smell was unbelievable.

'Oh for God's sake, Babs,' said another officer, climbing out of the bus to see what the furore was. 'Not again!' He turned to the young policeman at the desk. 'She does this every time she's arrested. Thinks it's hilarious. Well what I'd say is hilarious is that she has to carry that rank fucking object round with her all day...'

'You ought to search it, officer,' said Babs's companion, putting on a faux-winsome voice. 'You'd be in terrible trouble if she was smuggling a knife on board, now wouldn't you?'

To my horror, the constable did actually don latex gloves and have a perfunctory poke around in the contents of the box, his other hand gripping his nose and mouth shut. Our entire queue, plus the queues waiting to get on the neighbouring coaches, hooted with derisive laughter, catcalling and roaring at him. The young copper had gone from white to puce with horror and embarrassment, and I almost ... almost ... felt sorry for him.

It was horrible on the coach. Freezing cold – I was starting to shiver now, from fear and the chill of recently dried sweat – and with stained velour seats and filthy Formica tables. Three military policemen got on board, one sliding behind the vast steering wheel and two hanging onto metal poles to keep an eye on us all as the engine shuddered into noisy life, the bus's big windows rattling so hard that I could feel my cheeks vibrating.

One of them, shouting to be heard above the engine noise and the heckling women, made a speech about how we were all arrested and being taken to Reading Police Station, where we would be held until further notice. I looked at Samantha apprehensively.

'Don't worry,' she repeated. 'It's going to be fine.' She held my hand and I gripped hers tightly, unspeakably relieved that she was there.

'How many times have you been arrested?' I asked, and she looked skywards, counting off on her fingers.

'Four,' she said. 'And never charged.'

That made me feel a little better.

'It's my birthday today,' I announced, as the coach rumbled through the main gates onto the Newbury Road.

'Oh WOW!' said Samantha, kissing my cheek effusively, like we'd known each other for years. 'Happy birthday, gorgeous girl! Eighteen?'

'Seventeen,' I said sheepishly, and she blanched slightly.

'Jeez. Listen,' she leaned into me and whispered in my ear, 'when you're booked in, for God's sake don't tell them you're underage.'

I was surprised. I'd been planning to milk it, in the hope they'd take pity on me as a child.

'Why not?'

'Because the whole thing will take ten times longer! I'm serious.

There was a sixteen-year old kid last time, and my God, the hassle. They had to get someone in to be an appropriate adult for her, and it took *hours*.'

'Oh. Right.' I mentally rehearsed my fake year of birth in case I was asked: 1965, not 1966. 1965, 1965, 1965...

Half an hour or so later, we arrived at Reading Police Station. I was dying for a pee, having not been since the train, but dreading what the arrangements would be. I'd seen *Porridge* on TV, the steel toilet in a corner ... I couldn't.

All sixteen of us were escorted into the station and herded up to the desk. The young arresting officer (whose face had returned to milky white again) announced to the custody sergeant: 'These ladies were caught at twenty-one nineteen on April the first, trespassing on MOD property, contrary to Section Five of the military defence law, and brought here to be detained...' I tuned out after that, still fretting about Pete's rucksack, my swelling bladder and my parents' reaction when I rang them to admit where I was. But then I heard him announce that we were all to submit to a full body search.

Shit! No. I felt my bowels turn liquid, and I clutched Samantha's furry sleeve. 'I can't do that!' I said, in a small panicky voice.

She hugged me. 'It's fine, really. It's over real fast.'

I was so glad she was there, but it didn't make me feel a whole lot better.

We shuffled forwards to be booked in, and when it was my turn, I stared into the custody sergeant's weary bloodshot eyes as he cautioned me: 'You're entitled to a solicitor free of charge, and you're entitled to have someone informed of your arrest. Do you want us to inform someone?'

As advised by Samantha, I shook my head, but I couldn't prevent tears of longing rolling down my face at the thought of Mum and Dad coming to my rescue. It would be worth all the inevitable shouting, the disappointment, the grounding, just to be home tucked up in my own bed – after a long sit on the toilet, in my own bathroom...

But she'd told me not to let the police tell them, and I trusted her.

I signed my acknowledgement of the caution – which, Samantha said, meant I'd be released sooner – then joined another queue of women waiting to be searched by two WPCs. We were being taken one by one into a room. The door was shut, I noticed, which was a relief – at least there'd be privacy, I thought. The women emerging again wore a variety of expressions from weariness to grumpiness. Nobody seemed traumatised though. My turn came, and I was ushered into the room, which was empty except for a desk with an overhead projector and two bored-looking female officers. My stomach was churning.

'Oh look, another teddy bear,' said the taller of the two – a woman with a ferocious, blonde Vera Duckworth perm. 'Slip that off for me, love.'

I unzipped the front of my bear costume and let the furry shoulders drop to the floor so I was standing quivering in my bra and pants. It was cold in here, and I felt goosebumps sweep across the bare skin of my chest and stomach.

'Good girl. Just pull your pants forwards; let's have a quick check.'

It was the most humiliating moment of my life. Even worse than when I got my period as I walked into town wearing white jeans.

I hooked my thumbs into my flowery M&S knickers and pulled them away from my abdomen, staring hard at the ceiling tiles and trying very hard not to cry. But it was a) painless, b) over in a second, and c) neither of the women donned rubber gloves and stuck their fingers inside me as I'd feared they might, so that was a win. They were the first people ever to see my pubic hair.

I told Samantha that later, in a blurt of confession, and she laughed, which made my heart leap.

'Funny old world,' she said affectionately, in a mock-British accent.

19
Present Day
Meredith

Meredith heard them clatter down the metal steps from the carpark to the wharf – a man and a woman, unmistakably detectives; dressed like middle management, walking with authority. The man was broad-shouldered and morose, his jacket sleeves too short for the length of his arms. The woman was younger and friendlier-looking, with a mass of curly blonde hair and slightly protuberant front teeth.

'I'd like to live on a boat,' the woman was saying. 'So cosy. Wood-burning stove, sunrises on the water...'

'Icy decks in winter,' her colleague retorted. 'Rats running up the ropes. Can't think of anything worse.'

So he was as cheery as he looked, then. Meredith ducked out of sight behind a porthole, wondering if she had time to get dressed. The PC who'd come to Minstead when she'd rung 999 had said someone would come and interview her, but not who or what time.

It was Saturday morning – late enough for the sun to have burned all the summer mist off the water, but still, she'd have thought, too early to go round to interview people.

'Which one's her brother's?' the man said, consulting his phone. 'It's called *Barton Bee*.' Even though Meredith could no longer see him, she could hear the sneer in his words, as if he thought they were particularly ridiculous.

'Not sure. We can always ring her if we can't find it.' The woman dropped her voice, but Meredith still heard. 'Hopefully she'll be in less of a state than she was the other day. Emad said she was in bits. Is she staying here with her brother, then?'

'Dunno.'

There was a pause, and then a confident rap on one of the boat's portholes. Reluctantly, Meredith tied her short dressing gown tighter round her waist and went to let them in.

They were both flashing badges at her.

'Meredith Vincent? DS Mark Davis and DC Gemma McMeekin,' said the man. 'May we come in?'

'Of course. Sorry, I didn't sleep last night, and now I've only been awake long enough to make coffee ... I didn't know what time you were coming. My brother's gone to his workshop already, he's got a big commission to finish. But I suppose you don't need to speak to him, do you?'

Shut. Up, she mentally commanded, realising how hideously rambly and defensive she must sound.

She stood aside to admit them as they hunkered down and squeezed through the low door, which was particularly difficult for the guy, who must have been about 6'5". He almost had to fold himself in half to get in. Her left hand was on the door frame, and the woman, Gemma, clocked her scar as she came past her into the barge.

Meredith saw Gemma's eyes widen and hastily pulled her arm behind her back, furious with herself for blushing.

'Please, sit down,' she said, gesturing towards Pete's faded, saggy old corner sofa next to the wood stove.

They all sat, Meredith at one end, DS Davis's long legs a trip hazard as first he stretched them out across the kelim rug, then crossed them, then decided again and went for a manspreading stance instead. She didn't warm to the man at all.

'I'll just get a few details down, if I may,' Gemma said, taking a notebook and pen out of her shoulder bag. Now that she was closer, Meredith saw that she had braces on her teeth, which made her voice sound a little thicker than it probably was normally. She couldn't have had them on for long, because her teeth were still quite prominent. She had a plump, guileless face which, with the braces, made her look much younger than she probably was.

Davis gave a sudden exclamation. Gemma and Meredith both looked up to see what he was looking at. His eyes were bulging out of his head with a sort of delighted awe as he seemed to drink Meredith in.

'No *way*! I don't believe it. It's you, isn't it! You're Merry Heather! Fuck m— Um, sorry. I mean, wow, that's amazing. I am a *huge* fan.'

Meredith felt the blood drain from her face. No. Surely not … Nobody, but nobody had recognised her in years! How could this guy, who didn't even look old enough to have been buying records when the band were famous…?

For so long it was what she had been dreading more than anything; far more so since Iain's phone call last year. She sat on her hands to stop them shaking. *It's OK*, she told herself. *If anyone's going to recognise you, it's good that it's a policeman. Safe. Nothing bad will happen.*

Gemma stood up, concerned. 'Are you OK? You've gone a funny grey colour. Let me get you some water.' She turned to Davis. 'Merry Heather?'

'Merry Heather!' he crowed, slightly less effusively now that he'd witnessed Meredith's shock. 'Lead singer of Cohen, one of the best bands on the planet!' The excitement in his tone ramped up again. 'My big brother had all your records, and I really got into you through him. I don't think I'd have made the connection though, if I hadn't spotted *that*.' He pointed at a mug on the coffee table, with the logo COHEN emblazoned on it. 'You look very different.'

Yes, that was certainly her intention, Meredith thought, scowling at the offending mug. Pete had had it for so long, she'd forgotten it was there.

'God, I adored you when I was a teenager.' He was practically gushing now, and Meredith had the urge to punch him in the throat.

'It was a very long time ago,' she said eventually, in a voice that she hoped did not invite further discussion. 'I don't talk about it. It's all in the past now.'

Gemma had found a glass on the draining board and filled it. She brought it over and handed it to Meredith who took an obedient sip, but Gemma hadn't let the tap run first and the water tasted warm and brackish.

Meredith still couldn't figure out, even with the *aide-memoire* of the mug, how Davis could have made the connection. In the band's heyday she had resembled a female Robert Smith from The Cure, with wild backcombed black hair, not the mousy short bob that she had now worn for several years.

Davis stood up, wandering around Pete's boat in a proprietorial sort of way that Meredith found doubly infuriating. He peered at book titles on the shelves and even, when he thought she wasn't looking, flicked through a large stack of vinyl next to a turntable. He still looked like all his birthdays had come at once.

'So what did you need to ask me?' she enquired pointedly, setting the glass back on the coffee table with a too-loud clatter, glaring at Davis until he came and sat down again. For a horrible moment she thought he was going to ask for her autograph.

'I know our colleague, PC Khan, took some details from you on Thursday at the scene. We thought we'd come and see how you're feeling today?' Gemma said. 'Could you talk us through it again, what happened? In case we missed anything important.'

Meredith opened her mouth to speak, but had a shocking mental image of Ralph's mouth, gaping, full of green slimy water, and felt as if she was being choked by it. 'I still just can't believe it,' was all she managed. 'I just can't...'

'It must have been a terrible shock to find him like that.'

Meredith wrapped the dressing gown tighter around her body. She could see Davis trying not to stare at her legs. Under normal circumstances, she was sure he'd never fancy someone like her – older than him, lines around her eyes, no make-up. She bet his usual type was a WAG in vertiginous stilettos, she thought bitterly, trying to rid herself of the memory of Ralph's bloated body.

'Do you go down to that pond a lot when you're at work?'

She nodded slowly. 'I quite often eat my sandwiches there in summer. There are no tourists. A bench with a view that gets the sun. The shop's so hectic at this time of year that I crave a bit of solitude, you know? To not speak to anybody for half an hour.'

'How long have you worked at Minstead House?'

Meredith thought about it, counting off the years on her fingers. Her brain felt like soup. Or like slimy pond water. She'd got the job two years after *it* happened.

Two swans sailed majestically past the porthole, the movement making Gemma jump.

'Over twenty years ... twenty-one now.'

'Wow. Long time to be in the same job.'

Meredith wondered if the woman meant it to sound that patronising. It *was* a long time, though. Twenty-one years ago was 1997.

They must have been wondering how – or why – she'd gone from being at the top of the music business to being a gift-shop manager. She was well aware it was an odd choice of post-fame career.

'Do you enjoy your job?' Davis asked, a slightly high break in his voice betraying that he wasn't over his rush of starstruckness.

'I adore it,' she said, her eyes suddenly brimming with tears. 'It's everything to me. Nothing like this has ever happened there before; it's just so horrible.' She sniffed hard. 'I'm sorry. I almost never cry. But I don't seem to have stopped since ... since ... it happened. I can't believe he's gone.'

To her own ears, the words sounded shallow and insincere. She hoped they didn't to the two officers.

Gemma put a sympathetic hand on her leg, but Meredith twitched it off. Davis glared at his colleague.

'Can you tell us about your relationship with Ralph Allerton?'

Meredith panicked for a moment, thinking, *Shit, how do they know*? Then she realised he just meant a work relationship. Her heart pounded in her ribcage, and she felt sweat break out on her forehead. *Stay calm*. From the way they were both regarding her, it was clear that they had both noticed her reaction.

'He was my boss,' she said flatly. 'Sorry, I thought you meant were we in a relationship! And obviously, no we weren't – he's married to my best friend Paula. *Was* married to … She's beside herself.'

'I'm sure,' Gemma said. 'So which came first, Paula becoming your friend, or Ralph becoming your boss?'

'The latter. He invited me round to dinner a couple of months after he started – about ten years ago? Paula and I hit it off straight away, and we've been friends ever since. I've been on holidays with them. They … they both made me laugh. I'll miss that…'

'I see,' Davis said. He seemed to have pulled himself together a bit. 'Can you talk us through the last few days before Ralph went missing? I mean, when did you last see him?'

Meredith stared straight ahead, at a kitsch knitted deer's head trophy on the wall of the boat. One of Pete's ex-girlfriends had made it for him. Rhiannon, that was her name. Meredith had liked her. She was earthy and fun and always making stuff: earrings and candles and body lotion. But Rhiannon went the same way as all the others – dumped.

'The last time I spoke to him was in his office a week last Thursday. We'd had our monthly staff lunch, although I wasn't on the same table as him; he was sitting in between the Earl and Sebastian – that's the Earl's son. They were all drinking quite a lot – they always do. I went to his office later that day to discuss a new line of gardening equipment I'm buying in, and to ask if he'd spare some of the gardeners to do a photoshoot showing them using it, but he was pretty legless by that time. I couldn't get much sense out of him to be honest. I've talked to Paula about my concerns over his drinking. He shouldn't have been drunk at work. She's worried too.'

'Does everyone go to the monthly lunch?' Davis asked, as Gemma scribbled frantically.

Meredith shook her head. 'Only the senior staff, and people like Ceri, Ralph's PA, who've been there for donkey's years. There's dozens of staff; we couldn't all meet at the same time. We only do that at the summer party. Ralph established it – the monthly lunch – a few years ago, with the Earl's blessing. Pretty sure it was so that they could all legitimately get pissed at lunchtime once a month.'

'What's Ralph got to do with the house's gardeners?'

'He's – he *was* – head of estates, so that means he was line manager to the head gardener, Eric Nicholson, who all the other gardeners report to. It's the same with me in the shop: the head of HR makes all the hirings, but all my volunteers report to me.'

'Thanks. So what time did you leave Ralph's office last Thursday?' Gemma's pen was poised over her notebook.

'About five-thirty, I think? I had a whisky or two with him, tried to make him drink some water – and I wanted to be sure he didn't try to drive home. I'd have taken his car keys, but he wouldn't let me have them. He did promise not to drive though, so when I saw his car the next morning I assumed ... I assumed he'd got a cab home. I didn't leave the house myself till about nine-fifteen. My twin and I were planning to go for a drink, so I decided to stay late to catch up on some invoicing. So I was in my own office till he – Pete – arrived. He was late, as usual. He was meant to come and meet me at eight-thirty. By then we decided we couldn't be bothered to drive to the pub, so we just went back to my cottage.'

'And neither of you saw Ralph again before you left?'

'No. Only Leonard, the security guard. Everyone else had gone home. I thought they had, anyway.'

'How do you think Ralph could've been found in the pond a week later, Meredith?' Gemma asked. 'Do you have any idea?'

Meredith stared down at her unscarred hand. She was still sitting on the other one. 'I'd imagine he just fell in; he was definitely drunk enough. But I don't understand what he was doing down there in the first place. There was no reason for him to be in that part of the grounds. Unless he wanted some fresh air or something ... But he was never one for walks...' She tailed off.

'We've spoken to Mrs Allerton – Paula – and she's sure her husband didn't have any enemies. Although last week's events might suggest otherwise. Do you know of anybody? Any sort of situation he might have tried to hide from her? An affair? Debts of some description?'

Meredith felt like she couldn't breathe.

'No,' she said eventually, realising she was chewing her bottom lip. 'Everyone liked Ralph. The only thing that he might have hidden from Paula, or downplayed, was his alcoholism. He was a functioning alcoholic, I guess. I feel bad that I didn't talk to her about it before, because he admitted that he didn't drink much at home. Only at work. Although it can't have been anything to do with that, surely?' She paused. 'When do you think it happened?'

'The pathologist will hopefully be able to give us a better indication of time of death. The post-mortem was conducted yesterday.'

'Right,' said Meredith, trying not to think of all the post-mortems she'd read about in crime novels; seeing in her mind's eye the grim vision of the top of Ralph's sawn-off skull, his organs bagged up to be weighed and put back, the tag on his toe...

'We saw on the system that you'd recently had a suspected break-in at the shop. Our colleagues did take a look at the CCTV, but as you know, the main shop camera had been deactivated, and nothing suspicious showed up on any of the other nearby cameras, so that all seems to be a bit of a dead end. You don't think there's any sort of connection, do you?'

Apart from me, thought Meredith, her mind now swimming with images of dead rats, beheaded flowers, the splash of green paint...

Davis cleared his throat. 'Do you mind me asking, Merr— ... Meredith: what happened to your hand? That's a nasty scar.'

Fucking hell. Meredith stuffed the offending hand further underneath a cushion, feeling two spots of colour flaring suddenly on her cheeks. How dare he ask her?

'Yes, I do mind, as it happens. I don't like to talk about it.'

Davis shifted from buttock to buttock, and Gemma's eyes slid away, her expression unreadable.

20

Meredith

Paula turned up unannounced at Pete's barge that afternoon. Meredith had been sitting in the sun on the roof, trying to read a battered paperback she'd selected from Pete's bookshelf. It was Raymond Carver's short stories; apart from the fact they were genius, she thought short stories might accommodate her current severely limited attention span, but she was still struggling to concentrate.

When she saw Paula swaying at the top of the steps to the pontoon, she leaped up. Paula looked as if she was about to topple head first down them. Meredith jumped off the boat, barefoot, and ran over to meet her.

'I'm sorry,' she said as Meredith came up the steps, wincing as small stones pressed into her bare soles. Paula had put on make-up, but there was lipstick on her teeth and black blobs of eyeliner clogged the corners of her eyes, which were so red and puffy she looked as if she'd had an allergic reaction. 'I had to get out. I remembered you said you were staying here this weekend. I hope you don't mind. Will Pete? I can't stand it at home. Ralph's things are everywhere, and he's not there. I feel like I don't ever want to go back. I'm going to have to sell the house, aren't I? I mean, how can I stay there now? Jackson doesn't even live there anymore...'

Meredith took Paula by the hand, which felt dry and crepey in hers, and led her into the barge. 'It's fine. Of course Pete won't mind. He's at the workshop today anyway. Where's Jackson now? He should be with you.'

'He's at his girlfriend's in Guildford. He was so upset, I told him to go and spend some time with her. He can't cope with me like this. And why should he? He's twenty years old and he's just lost his dad. But he'll be back later, he said.'

Poor Jackson, thought Meredith as she steered Paula over to the sofa. The cushions still had two indentations from where the two cops had sat; DS Davis's deeper than the one left by the woman with braces. Meredith couldn't remember her name. She'd been so much nicer than DS Davis.

As she put the kettle on for Paula, Meredith thought about how creepy it was that Davis had fawned over her so much. It had been so awkward and inappropriate. He'd gone from a sneery sort of disdain to puppyish adoration that didn't at all suit his sallow, stubbly face. If he hadn't been a police officer and hadn't spotted Pete's bloody Cohen mug, she'd have lied and said she wasn't Merry Heather at all. She was so far away now from that person, it was risible.

She wanted to forget that Merry Heather had ever existed.

'Don't you have any wine?' Paula asked, appearing next to her and making her jump. 'I've had so much tea my tonsils are floating. Everyone keeps offering me fucking tea, like it's going to make everything all better. I don't want tea. I want alcohol.'

'OK. If you're sure.'

Meredith had a sudden flashback to Ralph's purpled tongue and lips, and unscrewed a bottle of white from the fridge instead of the already-opened Merlot on the galley counter.

'Did you drive here?'

Paula's lip trembled like a little girl's. 'No. Can't drive. The police impounded the car for evidence. God knows why. So I walked. I needed some air.'

Meredith poured her a glass, having a Pavlovian reaction to the greedy glugging sound. Sod the tea. She took down a second glass and filled that too. 'Let's go and sit on the roof.'

They took their wine, and the bottle, and climbed up on the roof of the barge, where Pete kept two folding garden chairs. It was a beautiful day, not as hot as the previous week, thanks to the bright white clouds scudding intermittently across the sun and diluting its bite for a few minutes, before it pushed them aside again to make the river sparkle. The towpath opposite was busy with families out cycling or walking.

Meredith picked the open Chandler paperback off one of the chairs and gestured for Paula to sit down.

'Look at them,' Paula said in a choked voice, watching a little girl scooting along the towpath opposite, two thin pigtails flying straight out behind her, a fluffy sort of dog cavorting next to her, barking its head off, and the girl's parents walking behind, hand in hand, in matching sunglasses, laughing. The dog's barks carrying across the river made a metallic scraping sort of sound. 'Not a fucking care in the world.'

'You don't know that,' Meredith said, as sympathetically as she could. 'They're probably going through all sorts of shit too.'

'*Her* husband hasn't just turned up dead in a pond,' Paula said, and began to cry.

Meredith didn't know what to do. She felt suddenly overcome by a huge wave of exhaustion. Probably guilt-induced, because she didn't want to have to cope with Paula and her emotions. She knew she owed it to her, sure, but at that moment she felt an overwhelming urge to unburden herself. She could almost visualise the look on Paula's face as she, Meredith, told her that she and Ralph had shagged in the bog at work just minutes before his death, and that someone must have taken his body and dumped it in the pond. Surely anything would be better than this torturous limbo.

Of course, she said nothing, apart from clucking and cooing – things that had never come naturally to her. She topped up Paula's wine, which was already getting warm.

Meredith saw Andrea emerge from her barge with a very large lady who'd just had a perm, or a set and blow-dry, or whatever she'd done that had given the lady the resultant helmet of tight curls. Andrea was escorting the matronly woman over the narrow wire-sided gangplank.

'Goodbye Mrs Macaulay,' chirped Andrea, waving the lady off. 'See you in three weeks.'

She turned and climbed back aboard, catching sight of them on the roof.

'Hello up there Meredith! Lovely day to catch some rays!' But then she saw Paula sobbing, and grimaced. 'Oh ... Everything is OK?'

Meredith made a face back at her. 'All fine! You remember my friend Paula?'

'Yes.' Andrea gazed at Paula with sympathy. 'Your husband he is still missing?'

This prompted a fresh outbreak of sobs.

'I'll fill you in later, Andy,' Meredith said, and Andrea nodded sombrely, disappearing back inside.

Meredith took a long swig of the wine and handed Paula a tissue she found in her skirt pocket. 'I had the police here again this morning,' she said. 'What do you think of that DS Davis? I don't like him.'

Paula shrugged. 'Didn't really notice,' she said, her voice thick with tears.

'The other one was much nicer – the girl with the braces. How old do you think she is?' She was trying to keep Paula talking, take her mind off things.

She was rubbish at this, she thought, but then, what did you say to someone whose husband had just been murdered, and you were withholding what was probably crucial evidence?

'Don't know. She looks young. Late twenties maybe.' Paula gave a long, hard sniff and wiped her finger underneath her eyes. 'Too young. Everyone's too young. But do you know what, Meredith? I don't know how I'm ever going to carry on. I can't even kill myself because of bloody Jackson. I'm trapped here, in this body, in this life, and I don't want to be here without Ralph. I spent thirty years with that man, for all his faults, and I spent twenty with Jackson and now he's at uni, he probably won't ever live with me again. I've got nobody and I'm nothing without them.'

Meredith rushed over and put her arms around her. 'Oh please don't say that! You have your friends. You have me. Jackson will always need you, even if he's not at home.'

Paula remained sitting bolt upright, not relaxing into the embrace, and Meredith felt awkward and devastated for her. This, she thought, was why she didn't hug people, apart from Pete. And Ralph ... And look where that had got them...

'I don't have you,' Paula said. 'You're my friend, but you're not going to be there in the middle of the night when I wake up and can't get back to sleep, or when I'm sick and need someone to rub my back. Or to cuddle when I'm sad, or go on holiday with, or...'

'I can do the last two,' Meredith said miserably, not pointing out that Paula *was* sad and she *was* currently trying to cuddle her. 'But I know what you mean. I don't have anyone for those things either, if it's any sort of consolation. Living on your own is fine once you get used to it. Really. It's all in the mindset.'

Meredith saw Paula's face and hastily backtracked. 'Not that I'm saying grin and bear it, or be positive, or any of that shit. You need to give yourself time to mourn Ralph, but it will get better. It will...'

Paula gave her a perfunctory hug back, then pushed her away to drink more wine. Leaning forwards in her chair she stared at Meredith through her bloodshot and swollen eyes, her mouth in a tight, angry line. Meredith wondered if, subliminally, she knew that it was her she was quite right to be angry with.

'Have you ever lost anybody you really, really loved, Meredith?'

Meredith gave it some serious thought. She'd loved her parents, especially her dad. She thought she'd loved the various partners she'd had over the years, although she'd barely given any of them a second thought once they'd broken up. 'No,' she said slowly. 'Pete's the only one who would break my heart.'

Then: a sudden memory of freckles like sunshine and red hair that smelled of wheat and lavender, a smile as wide as a country mile and a sexy midwestern accent...

'Actually. There was someone once, when I was young. I was really in love with ... her.'

It was the first time she had ever admitted to anybody other than Pete that she'd been in a gay relationship.

'Her?' Paula's face relaxed a little, and Meredith thought, *Well, at least that's taken her mind off Ralph for a second or two.*

'Yeah. I was only about seventeen when we met – in fact, it was my seventeenth birthday. I met her the day I went to a Greenham Common protest and got arrested. We went out for a couple of years after that, but nobody really knew, apart from Pete, and he only found out near the end that we were anything more than friends. I moved to a squat in London to live with her.'

Paula's eyes were like saucers. 'Really? I didn't know you were bisexual.'

Meredith shrugged. 'I don't know that I am – it was a lifetime ago. If she hadn't come on to me in the first place it would never have occurred to me to want a relationship with her. She was just … very hard to say no to, and I was young and impressionable.'

'What happened?'

She hesitated. Samantha had been locked in a small, dusty box in the recesses of her memory for decades now. 'Nothing that dramatic … I haven't thought about her in years.'

Paula nodded. 'That was one of the things I loved about Ralph.' Her eyes brimmed again. 'He drank too much but apart from that he was so … *dependable*. He'd never have let me down or cheated on me. I always knew where I was with him. And now he's not there, it feels like I'm losing my mind. I even thought there was someone in the bloody house yesterday, creeping around! I heard something, and the back door was open … I thought I was about to be murdered. Crazy, eh? If Ralph was still alive, he'd have gone to check and then given me a cuddle and told me I was safe with him.'

Tears dropped down her cheeks unchecked. Meredith thought again of the break-in in the shop, the beheaded flowers, her own sense of unease. Should she tell Paula to be careful? Maybe there *had* been someone in her house. But she couldn't bear to risk upsetting her even more.

'And there was definitely nobody there?' she asked cautiously.

'Of course not. Can I have some more wine?'

21

Meredith

Pete returned half an hour later, smelling of mastic and sawdust, looking tired. His expression didn't betray anything, but Meredith could tell from the slight droop of his lips that he wasn't best pleased to have to deal with a grief-stricken Paula on his barge – although of course he was far too kind to let her see that.

He joined them on the roof, glancing at the empty wine bottle and their flushed cheeks.

'Nice day for it,' he commented after he'd said hello, giving Paula a warm hug then sitting down and tipping his face to the sun. Meredith noticed he hadn't offered Paula any verbal condolences, but she knew him well enough to understand that the awkwardness of it all would probably have brought him out in hives. And it would only have set Paula off again, so on balance it was just as well.

'Yeah. Did you get your cabinet finished?'

He nodded. 'Yup. Just got to let the glue dry and then varnish it tomorrow. Deliver on Monday. I'm knackered. It's looking good, though. Check it out.' He took his phone from his back pocket and brought up a photo, turning the screen so they could see it. It was an intricate mahogany Chinoise-influenced cupboard with inlaid mother-of-pearl cranes and flowers.

'Wow, Pete, that's amazing. Really beautiful,' said Meredith. 'Isn't it, Paula?'

Paula didn't say anything. She was just twirling the stem of her empty wineglass round and round, perhaps as a hint that she wanted yet another drink.

Meredith didn't want her to carry on drinking. It would only make her more maudlin.

'Do you fancy a walk down the towpath, Paula? I could do with stretching my legs and clearing my head. I'm not used to drinking in the daytime.'

Liar! she shouted at herself. It was at almost the same time of day that she'd been knocking back Jack Daniels with Paula's dead husband during the last couple of hours of his life.

'Not really,' Paula said in a small voice.

Meredith shot Pete a glance. She could tell that he was reluctantly wondering if he had to invite her to stay for dinner. She felt guiltily relieved that she was at Pete's rather than in her own cottage, because if she'd been home there'd have been no excuse not to extend the offer.

'What time did you say Jackson's coming back?' she asked, as gently as she could.

Paula shrugged. 'He's going to cook dinner. Not that I could eat anything.'

'Oh that's so nice, he's cooking!' exclaimed the twins in tandem, and Meredith hoped Paula didn't pick up that their enthusiasm was as much for their own sakes as hers.

Grief did strange things to people. Which of them knew how they'd react in that situation; become maudlin and morose, quiet and withdrawn, inconsolably tearful – or all of the above? When their dad died, Mum had been like Paula was being right now – tetchy and unbearable, and Meredith remembered it felt to Pete and her as seventeen-year-olds that their mother just wanted to make everyone else suffer the way she was.

That was partly what had driven Meredith away. That, and Samantha of course. The fact that Pete had forgiven her for abandoning him to deal with Mum was yet another testament to his kind heart. Even if it had taken him a few years...

Would Paula ever forgive her, though, for what she'd done to her? Of course she wouldn't, if she ever found out, and who could blame her?

Meredith looked over at Paula. She'd put the wineglass down on the roof and was biting her nails, working at them with her teeth, trying to pull off bits of cuticle, a vacant expression in her bloodshot eyes.

'What time are you having dinner?' Meredith asked, tentatively.

'Are you trying to get rid of me?' Paula bit back.

'No! Of course not, Paul. Honestly, you can stay as long as you want. Can't she, Pete?'

Pete nodded, looking faintly terrified.

Then Paula burst into tears again. 'I'm so sorry,' she sobbed. 'I just … I can't … it's all … have you got any more wine?'

'There's some red,' said Pete, bolting down into the barge and disappearing for a disproportionately long time, although Meredith had been about to try suggesting a cup of tea again. She felt personally responsible for the loss of the woman Paula had been – the brilliant, creative, scatty, well-groomed person who couldn't be further from this broken human slumped in the picnic chair in front of her, whose life had been blown apart forever.

Meredith had to keep remembering that it wasn't her fault. Ralph's death wasn't her fault.

Pete's tousled head reappeared, bent to avoid bumping it on the low barge doorway as he came back up the steps holding a half-full bottle of red.

'I'll buy you some more to replace what we've drunk,' Meredith said, noticing he hadn't brought out a glass for himself.

'Too right you will,' he said, with a faint smile.

'Not joining us?'

He shook his head. 'Too much invoicing to do,' he said. 'If I start drinking now that'll be the rest of the day blown out.' He topped up their glasses and retreated.

'He should've brought us clean ones,' Meredith grumbled mildly, although she was feeling more annoyed about having to drink more wine to keep Paula company. White wine and sunshine always gave her a headache, and she could feel one burgeoning behind her ears and across her temples. Adding Merlot to the mix was guaranteed to make it set in for the day. Still, she thought, it was the least she could do.

On the quayside, Pete's neighbour Trevor was splitting logs to replenish the communal woodpile, and Meredith idly watched his biceps flex as he swung the axe. Trevor was a nice man. In a civil partnership with Johnny, both of them were from Zimbabwe originally; a lovely couple. Sometimes Meredith envied Pete and Andrea. All the residents of the river boats had formed themselves into a proper, tight little community. They were always having impromptu get-togethers and leaving each other little gifts on deck – homemade lemon curd, bottles of fizz, pot plants. She herself had no neighbours and rarely received any visitors, unless someone she knew decided to have a day out at Minstead House and popped into the shop to say hello.

Then she reminded herself that solitude and isolation had been her own choice. It would drive her crazy having people just dropping by at all hours.

'Post-mortem was yesterday,' Paula said tersely, and Meredith felt a tiny jolt of fearful adrenaline, even though she already knew this.

She forced her thoughts to the possible results, praying that it wouldn't show that Ralph had recently had sexual intercourse ... Surely it wouldn't, she thought. Not if he'd been in the water for days. 'Yeah, I heard, but they haven't had the report in yet.'

Paula fixed her gaze on her and for a moment Meredith thought, *She knows*. But then she just said, 'Maybe it'll show that he had some sort of terminal illness, and drowned himself rather than facing it.'

'Maybe. Although,' Meredith added with reluctance, 'he seemed fine that day. He was on great form.'

'I'll find out on Monday, I suppose,' Paula said thickly, looking at her phone. 'Fun, fun, fun. Not. Oh. I've had a text from Jackson, checking where I am. I'd better go.'

'I'll walk you home.' Meredith got to her feet.

'No need, it's only through the village.' Paula stood up too, swaying slightly, knocking over her empty wine glass. Meredith managed to catch it before it rolled off the boat into the water.

'No, really. I need some fresh air.'

Pete was sitting at his galley table with reading glasses on the end of his nose and a sheaf of paperwork in front of him. He looked up as they climbed unsteadily down off the roof. Meredith stuck her head through the doorway to tell him where they were going.

'Staying here tonight?'

'Do you mind?'

'Of course not.'

'As long as I won't be putting the kibosh on any potential action you might have been contemplating.'

He rolled his eyes. 'As if. Although I thought I'd invite Andrea over to supper.'

'Well in that case I'd better—'

'No. I want you there,' he said firmly. 'Please. I don't want her to think I'm going to try it on with her.'

Meredith sighed. 'Pete. Dude. What's the matter with you? She's lovely, and you fancy each other.'

'She's my neighbour, Mez, and she's pregnant. It's far too complicated, and I wouldn't want to lead her on by letting anything happen.'

It was Meredith's turn to roll her eyes, although she did understand. It would be terrible if they slept together and then Pete got cold feet – as he was prone to. Andrea was far too vulnerable to be messed around.

'Well, maybe the time isn't right now,' she conceded dully. 'Right. See you in a bit. Text me if you want me to pick anything up in the shop on the way back.'

'More wine!' he called after them.

⊓⌐

Paula trudged through the village next to Meredith, several people stopping to hug her, tears in their eyes as they gushed condolences, which Paula accepted as gracefully as she could manage. Meredith could tell that she wanted to tell them all to sod off.

Paula and Ralph had been a popular couple in the village, and Ralph's death had been broadcast on the local news the previous night: 'Death at Minstead,' the newsreader had intoned, over a backdrop of

Minstead House looking particularly glorious. At least they hadn't shown the actual pond.

'Now it's *really* like sodding *Midsomer Murders* here,' Paula said savagely after she'd been accosted for the third time. They had often laughed about how Midsomer-ish the village was, with its chocolate-box cottages and petty, complicated village politics. Now they even had a mysterious death to boot.

Meredith couldn't muster a smile.

They reached Paula's house, a stocky-looking whitewashed 1920s villa on the far edge of the village, wisteria climbing around a front door that was usually flanked by two big stone lions, which Ralph had loved and Paula hated. But as soon as the door came into view, they knew something was wrong.

Meredith did a double take. The right-hand lion was still there, standing proud, but the left-hand one had been smashed; its head was severed from its body and was lying next to it, staring up at the sky.

She put her hand on Paula's arm. 'Paul ... look at that.'

She waited for Paula to confess that she herself had done it in a fit of grief – although how she'd have had the strength to, without pushing the whole statue over, Meredith couldn't imagine. But as she watched Paula's eyes widen with shock and incomprehension, she knew that this was the first Paula had seen of it too.

'It was probably Jackson,' Paula said uncertainly. 'He's been so upset. He never liked those lions either.'

Meredith wasn't so sure. She had a very bad feeling in the pit of her belly, and, as Paula opened the front door and dumped her bag in the hallway, she realised she was holding her breath, waiting for Jackson to appear and confirm or deny it.

'Jack?' called Paula. 'I'm home. What's happened to the lion?'

Jackson appeared at the top of the stairs – a gangly tousled youth, eyes pink-rimmed. He was usually handsome, in an unformed sort of way, but today he looked like a pale facsimile of himself.

He shrugged. 'It was like that when I got home. I thought you'd done it. I know you hated them...'

'It wasn't me,' Paula said, kicking off her shoes and sitting down wearily on the bottom stair, leaning her head against the wall with an expression of utter defeat.

Meredith's heart sank. 'I don't want to worry you,' she said, 'but I think you need to let the police know.'

22

Pete

Once Meredith and Paula had left, Pete located his phone – it was on top of the unlit stove – and texted Andrea to see if she'd come over for fish pie and wine later. He made sure to stress that Meredith would be there too, to assuage his nerves at extending the invitation in the first place. He considered Andrea, with her silky black hair and endless legs, to be way out of his league, and the thought that she might assume she was being invited over to be seduced made him grimace with discomfort, despite the fact that there was nothing he'd have liked to do more. If she was interested in him romantically, surely she would have given some sort of signal by now? She was unfailingly smiley and sparkly around him, and quite touchy-feely after a couple of drinks – not that she was drinking, now that she was pregnant. But then, she was like that around everyone else too.

It seemed odd, if not wrong, to be having what was essentially a dinner party when Meredith could be mixed up in something that may at any moment be deemed to be a murder investigation; but what were they supposed to do, if not 'keep calm and carry on'? He knew it was important to Meredith to do just that, otherwise she'd just sit around and obsess, and become increasingly scared and paranoid. And if the police were to investigate her further, it was essential that it looked as if she was just in her usual routine, untroubled by conscience.

Plus, to have Andrea over would be good for them both. They wouldn't be able to discuss Ralph if she was here, and she unfailingly made them feel happier – she was just that sort of person.

Meredith was always telling him to go for it with Andrea – to be more confident, that he was gorgeous, a catch for any woman, he'd just been unlucky with previous relationships; but he never believed her. She was biased, anyway. Whenever he looked in the mirror all *he* saw was a gangly, weedy middle-aged bloke losing his hair. And the clothes he favoured – retro tank tops, baggy cords, collarless shirts, brogues – looked fine on Shoreditch hipsters, but, he suspected, on him just made him look like a 1950s throwback or someone who could only afford to shop in charity shops. All he was missing, he'd thought grumpily that morning as he was shaving, was a pipe and a comb-over – the latter wasn't far off being doable.

He was just putting some music on – Hubert Parry's *Songs of Farewell*, his favourite choral work; Meredith always gave him shit about it, so when she got back he'd change it to Tom Waits, or Joni or something more likely to meet with her approval – when his phone buzzed in his hand.

It was a reply from Andrea, saying she'd love to come and she'd bring wine and pudding. He cranked up the volume of Parry's 'My Soul There Is a Country' so loudly that the sound bounced off the barge's low ceilings and he realised that, for the first time since Meredith had rung him in panic the other day, hope was fluttering in his chest.

He really didn't mind that Andrea was pregnant – in fact, it made her more appealing, although he wouldn't admit that to anyone. He'd love to have children, so why not? It would be like having a ready-made family. Meredith would make a fantastic auntie. Of course, it was too late for her to have kids of her own now.

Poor Mez, he thought, melting butter in a pan to make a white sauce. Meredith always pushed people away when they got too close. She complained about being single, yet usually dumped whichever bloke she'd been raving about just weeks earlier. He suspected it was really because she couldn't handle someone in her life full-time after so many years alone. Not to mention her decades-entrenched trust issues. And now this...

He wasn't particularly surprised that she'd shagged Ralph. Starved of sexual attention and affection, needing the validation of knowing she was still attractive, whisky-vulnerable, her guard down from already knowing and trusting him as a friend ... It was easily done.

As he stirred flour into the butter, he wondered again what the hell had gone on in that ice house. Could Mez have been mistaken in her conviction that Ralph had really been dead? It almost felt as if Ralph was playing some mean-spirited trick on her. But Pete had met Ralph, and he was the last person Pete could imagine doing that.

He was peeling potatoes when Meredith returned, empty-handed and sniffing the air.

'Stinks of fish in here.'

He gestured to the peelings and bubbling pans on the stove. 'Fish pie! Where's the wine?'

'Shit, sorry Pete, I forgot. I'll go now. I can't concentrate on anything. My head's still all over the place.'

'Don't worry. Get two bottles, then. How was Paula, when you left her?'

'Turn this crap down and I'll tell you.' She cocked an ear at the speaker. The choir had just sung '*I know my life's a pain and but a span*' and she laughed mirthlessly. '"I know my life's a pain"? They're not kidding. What a dirge! I hope you're not going to play this later.'

Usually Pete would have teased her about being a philistine, but he sensed that she was close to tears and so did as she asked.

'OK,' he said mildly.

Meredith sat down heavily on the sofa. 'She's in a terrible state, Pete,' she said. 'Luckily Jackson had arrived, so he'll look after her. I just don't even know what to say to her. And ... something weird happened. You know their stone lions? Someone smashed one today. Jackson said it was like that when he arrived home, so it must have happened this afternoon while she was here.'

Pete turned off the gas under the simmering fish and turned to face her. 'Could've been an accident – a delivery man knocked it over, or something?'

'It wasn't knocked over. It looked like it had been deliberately smashed, just the top half. And, Pete, when she was here earlier she mentioned she thought there was someone in the house last night, when she was on her own.'

They stared at each other. Pete saw Meredith's face and knew she was thinking of another time, another big empty house with her in it; just her, and the stranger creeping up the stairs...

He came to put an arm around her. 'Has she reported it?'

'She promised she would. Oh God. What if...?'

Pete held her more tightly. 'Let the police sort it. We don't know, it's almost certainly all just coincidence.'

He hoped his use of the word 'all' didn't betray his fears that it encompassed that creeping stranger, and now a dead rat, a shop break-in, a body dumped in a pond. He didn't want to freak her out any more than she already was.

'It's all shit, that's for sure. Let's just try and have a chilled evening tonight and forget about it for a bit, at least till we know the worst. Andrea's coming, so we'll have to act normal; we won't be able to dwell on it.'

Meredith leaned against him for a moment, then took a deep breath and stood up again. 'Mm. OK. Normal, right. I'll go and get more wine. But I'm going to ring that Gemma Whatsername on the way – the cop – and tell her about Paula's lion, because I'm not sure that Paula will.' She left the barge, pulling her mobile out of her pocket.

Pete watched her stomp away towards the steps, wishing he could make everything right for her.

⊓⊔

Five hours later, they were full of fish pie and apple crumble, and the twins were drunk. Somehow, even though Andrea was on the sparkling water, they seemed to have got through the two bottles Meredith bought earlier, plus the one that Andrea had brought as a gift. Meredith kept wailing that she mustn't drink any more as she was going for a run in the morning, then topping up her and Pete's glasses. Her leaden misery of earlier had changed into an alcoholic sort of mania that, Pete knew, was her way of coping. He wondered if Andrea could tell that Meredith was far from her usual self.

Pete was struggling to take his eyes off his glamorous neighbour. She was wearing some sort of shimmery short dress that emphasised her neat, round bump, full breasts and long bare legs. With her long hair cascading down her back, he thought she looked like a sixties icon; a more beautiful Cher, perhaps. Despite being sober, Andrea had become so giggly that she couldn't fail to cheer them both up. Pete had put on a playlist of mostly Meredith-approved music – The Cure, Gil Scott-Heron, Tower of Power – but a couple of choral pieces had slipped through, and Meredith had pounced on something.

'Did I just hear them singing about a *pelican?*' she'd said. 'What the actual fuck are we listening to now?'

'What is a pelican?' Andrea asked.

She was on the sofa next to Pete, shoes off, her legs curled up under her, twiddling a strand of hair, her bare arm tantalisingly close to his. Meredith was sitting in the armchair next to the unlit stove, elbow on its arm, her wineglass at a perilous angle.

'You know, that sea bird with the massive double chin for storing fish in,' Meredith said, sketching a pelican's bill in the air in front of her own neck.

'Ah, that,' said Andrea, nodding. 'Yes, is same in Hungarian. Pelikan.'

Pete googled the lyrics to the song they'd been listening to. Finzi, 'Lo, the Full and Final Sacrifice'. 'Yup. It's "O soft self-wounding Pelican! Whose breast weeps Balm for wounded man".'

'What the hell is a self-wounding pelican?' demanded Meredith.

'Is like self-harming penguin perhaps?' Andrea said.

'Or a self-service parrot?' Pete suggested, and they laughed, although Meredith's hoot sounded contrived, like someone had pinched her hard and told her to laugh.

Andrea glanced first at her then, with raised eyebrow, at him. He shook his head briefly and smiled, touched by her concern.

He had to declare himself to her. Not now, not when Meredith was in the middle of this crisis, but soon. It was time, surely. Andrea was so beautiful, and if he left it any longer someone else would be braver than him. He'd always been too afraid of the rebuttal, or of it ruining their friendship – but he'd caught her glancing at him, her pupils flaring when he spoke, the way her smile stretched right up to the corners of her eyes when she listened to him. She was touching his arm now, just brushing her fingers against his skin; and she was sober, so it couldn't be the wine talking. He would. He'd invite her over again, soon, dinner for two this time. He imagined how soft her lips would feel, how gently they would have to make love with the baby between them…

As if she read his mind, she turned and looked at him again, uncurling her legs and sliding her bare feet into her trainers, crushing the backs down rather than putting them on properly. She grasped his arm to help steady herself as she stood up in the ungainly way that pregnant women did – although in her case, she still managed to look graceful – and Pete stood too, to help her.

'Well, my sides are aching and my belly is full of pie and baby,' she said. 'But I must go to bed now, to dream of self-wounding pelicans. Thank you for a wonderful evening. Next time you must come to me.' She was looking Pete straight in the eye, and he caught Meredith's triumphant smirk as she gave Andrea a quick hug goodbye, then excused herself to go to the loo, leaving the two of them alone.

'I'd love to,' he said, and before he let himself think too closely about it, he leaned down and kissed her gently on the lips. They felt exactly as soft as he'd thought they would.

⊓⊔

'Well?' demanded Meredith when she returned, staggering slightly, as if the barge was cutting through choppy sea instead of on the millpond-flat river.

Pete changed the subject. If he confessed his intentions to her, he'd never hear the end of it. 'Are you really going for a run in the morning?'

'Yup,' she said, grabbing a pack of Nurofen from the kitchen counter and popping three out. 'If I take these now, that should nip the worst of the hangover in the bud. I brought my trainers and jogging gear ... cos it'll be more of a jog than a run for sure. I'm hoping it will clear my head, in all ways. Come with me?'

'No bloody way,' he said. 'I'm having a lie-in tomorrow. You're a better woman than I am.'

Meredith gathered up the dirty plates and scraped the leftovers into the food bin. 'So, did you ask her out? Even you must have noticed the way she was looking at you!'

Pete looked briefly self-conscious. 'I think I did notice, yeah. I didn't ask her out...' He saw Meredith's mouth open to protest and rushed on, '*But* she invited me over. Soon. So I will then.'

Meredith nodded, a tiny flash of pleasure crossing her face as she piled all the dishes next to the sink, and then she sank back into gloom. 'Leave these, I'll do them in the morning. I'm going to turn in. I need to try and sleep off all that wine you made me drink.' She came over and hugged him. 'Thanks for dinner, bro. Really helped take my mind off ... things.'

Sadness scudded anew across her features, then she snapped herself back. 'And excellent news about Andrea. So nice that something positive is happening in the middle of all this ... shit.'

23

Pete

Pete slept soundly for the first five hours of that night, serenaded as always by the cheep and chatter of the sedge warbler that nested in the tree nearest the barge. He always slept so much better when Meredith was on board, it occurred to him as he dropped off. Perhaps it was because he could be sure she was safe.

Later, he wasn't sure if it was the splash that had woken him, but he recalled that something had, because he'd opened his eyes and tried to figure out why he was suddenly no longer asleep. He told the police it must have been around 5.00 a.m., because the faintest peachy light had been coming through the thin curtains. All was silent, though. No splashing, not even the tiny, thin flip of a fish's fin, or a duck's feet paddling over the surface as it lifted off.

He'd gone back to sleep, closing his eyes against the encroaching tannin headache, until, at about 7.30 a.m., he was vaguely aware of hearing Meredith get up – she never was any good at sleeping in: the pump and flush of the chemical toilet, the click of the kettle and the bubble of the boil, mugs clashing as she reached one down for her tea. He remembered hoping that she wasn't going to bring him one because he was nowhere near done with slumber – but then heard nothing.

Until the scream came, piercing his dream. He'd never heard Meredith scream before, but even before he'd sprung out of bed, he knew it was her. He was outside on the pontoon in his boxers before he was even properly aware of being awake, rushing towards his sister, who had collapsed to her knees in the cool morning air, issuing an unearthly banshee sound, incongruous in her Lycra and trainers.

'Mez! What's the matter!' He realised he was almost shaking her to try and get her to stop, so he wrapped one arm tight around her body and with the other, pressed her face into his neck as if his skin could gag her into silence. She struggled against his bare torso, trying to free herself, but at least she stopped screaming. Pushing his chest to loosen his grip, she stared into his face with wild bloodshot eyes, her cheeks chalky white.

'*What?*'

She pointed towards the river with a shaking finger, in the direction of Andrea's barge. For a moment he wondered stupidly if it was on fire, but there was no smoke or smell of burning. It looked fine, exactly as it had done the night before, its navy livery smarter than *Barton Bee*'s shabby dark green ... He shook his head with incomprehension but Meredith still couldn't speak.

The neighbours were popping alarmed heads out of their hatches, and Trevor and Johnny were pounding towards them, both in slippers, Trevor in a towelling robe and Johnny still in his pyjamas. They stopped in front of Pete and Meredith, who had now folded down to the ground like a malfunctioning garden chair, then they too followed the direction of her still-pointing finger. Pete stood up slowly and began to advance towards the edge of the pontoon, Trevor behind him, Johnny crouching down to take over comforting Meredith, who had begun to babble and sob.

Pete wanted to put his fingers in his ears. He had never heard Meredith like that, not even last week with the trauma of Ralph's disappearance. Shit, he thought, what could be worse for her than *that?*

Then he peered over the edge of the pontoon, in the gap between his boat and Andrea's, and he saw what Meredith had seen. Long strands of black hair rippling out like seaweed across the water's dark surface, a body bobbing up against the wall, face down, clad in a spotty pyjama top. He recognised it – he saw it every morning when she came out for her morning herbal tea on her deck table, frowning at whatever jigsaw she currently had on the go; the little triumphant noise she made when she managed to slot in another piece. It was a sound she didn't even realise she was uttering but which always made him grin to himself.

He'd never hear it again. She'd never cook him that supper; he'd never have the opportunity to tell her how beautiful she was, and how much he would love both her and the baby.

The baby.

His face contorted with grief and he too fell to his knees.

'Fucking hell!' Trevor shouted in panic next to him. 'We have to get her out!' He started stripping off his robe as if to dive in, but Pete reached out and gripped his ankle. 'No point. She's clearly gone.'

'We can't just leave her in there!'

'Who is it?' moaned Johnny. 'It's not Andy, is it? Please tell me it's not her. Not her!'

Pete nodded slowly without turning. *Andy,* he thought. *Andrea. I love you.* Then he began to cry.

24

Pete

'What's wrong with us?'

They had returned to Meredith's cottage after the police had taken their statements. Meredith parked her Morris Traveller in the car park, and both of them gazed momentarily at the space that had held Ralph's car before the police had towed it away.

'What do you mean?' she asked flatly as they trudged down the steps to the cottage gate.

Pete rubbed a hand across his face, as if he was trying to wipe away the memory of Andrea's body in the water.

'Did a gypsy put a curse on us as babies, or something? I mean, what the fuck is going on? It doesn't make sense. It's as if everybody we get close to is being bumped off.'

As Meredith jiggled the key in the lock, he turned away to look over her cottage garden, a riot of hollyhocks and tea roses that blurred into a floral cloud. He blinked hard and took a deep breath.

'"Everybody we get close to" is a bit of a stretch,' Meredith said, her voice sounding as strained as he felt. 'And you've got *me*. I know it's not the same as a wife or anything, but at least we have each other ... I don't think I would ever trust anybody else.'

Poor Meredith, he thought. Her trauma had been stitched so well into the fabric of their lives that he just didn't see it any longer, like the invisible mending that their mother used to do on his school trousers; like the hole in Meredith's hand that he no longer noticed, because after a while it had become too painful to see. His head was a mess.

'Andrea and I kissed last night when you were in the loo,' he said, heading straight for the living room and flopping down on the sofa, as he always did. He put his face in his hands. 'It was so bloody lovely. And I told you she invited me over, right...? I was so excited. I thought at last something was going to happen; that it was time, that I'd been right to wait and not rush it. And now she's fucking *dead*. How can she be dead?' His voice cracked. 'And her baby. Can't stop thinking about that little baby too, it's just so...'

Meredith knelt at his feet and wrapped her arms tightly around his neck. 'I know,' she said. She was crying too; he could feel her hot tears on the skin below his ear. 'I'm so sorry. It's not fair, it's just not fair. She was such a lovely person, and could have been so right for you...'

They wept together, rocking, taking comfort from their closeness, as if their grief was halved by sharing it.

Eventually Meredith sniffed and sat back on her heels, scrubbing her eyes. 'I still haven't told the police that I slept with Ralph.'

Pete blew his nose with the cotton hanky he kept in his pocket for when he had hay fever. 'Shit, Mez. You can't now. Especially not after Andrea. They're going to think you've got something to do with it!'

'That's crazy, why would they? Ralph and Andrea were both my friends. Why the hell would I ever *drown* them? I suppose it depends what the post-mortems show. At the very least they'd have me for obstructing the course of justice, or withholding evidence, or something.'

'That Davis guy would probably forgive you anything. I doubt you can do any wrong as far as he's concerned.'

'He might be a fan but he's a cop first, Pete. I mean, seriously – you think if I'd killed them he'd, like, just let me off with a warning because he had all Cohen's albums?'

Pete stood up slowly, like an old man, a hand in the small of his back. 'I'm not thinking straight. I just keep seeing her...'

'Me too,' Meredith said, idly tracing the edges of her scar with a forefinger. Pete had long ago observed it was a thing she often did when she felt unhappy, as if she was reading her pain like Braille. Meredith drawing attention to it herself was pretty much the only time he ever noticed it these days. 'How are you going to go back to the barge after this? I don't know how I am.'

Pete sighed heavily. 'I don't know either.' He walked towards the kitchen and opened the fridge door. 'I'm not hungry, but we haven't eaten all day. What have you got in?'

'Eggs. Might be a bit of bacon left. I really don't want anything though, apart from wine, and I don't even have any of that.'

'Is that all? You need to go shopping.'

Meredith leaned on the kitchen door frame and scowled at him. 'Well, sorry, Pete, but I've had other things on my mind.'

He turned, egg box in hand. 'Are you wondering...?'

'What?' They held each other's gaze. Meredith put her damaged hand defensively behind her back.

'That,' Pete said, glancing towards her concealed hand. 'You are, aren't you? And you were after Ralph, too. I tried to ask you then but you cut me off. But we can't not talk about it now. You're wondering if he—'

'Don't.'

'You have to tell—'

'No! There's no way. It was a lifetime ago!'

'But you said that twat at the record company found you last year.'

Meredith's face had turned a sickly yellowish colour, and Pete felt compassion flood through him like an adrenaline rush. He put the eggs down on the counter, went across and hooked his arm casually around her neck. 'Tell them what happened, Mez. It's important. It's probably nothing to do with it at all, but...'

'Yeah. OK. I'll tell Gemma about it. And about me and Ralph.'

'Promise?'

'Um ... I'll try.'

25

Gemma

Gemma could still faintly smell the bitterness of burnt orange on her
fingers the next morning as she keyed in the request for information
on Meredith Vincent from the General Registry. The last thing she'd
seen before leaving for work was a row of empty sterilised jars, still
waiting to be filled. They were like some sort of metaphor for her life –
the marmalade she spent much of her free weekend making had never
set and had to be flushed down the toilet. Why did work always seem
easier than the rest of her life? It was a relief to be back at her desk –
less so when Mavis strode in, however, his trousers slightly too tight
around the crotch, his clean-shaven face like a cross-looking Action
Man.

'Morning, Mark,' she said. 'Nice weekend?'

'PM results are in on both vics,' he replied, staring at a polysty-
rene ceiling tile over her desk as if it was about to reveal some sort of
profound secret. 'Tell the team there's a briefing for ten a.m., please.
Lincoln's coming in as SIO. This is an MIT investigation now.'

'What, so they were dead before going in the water? Both of them?
No!'

'I'll tell you in the meeting.'

He marched past her desk and on to the coffee machine. Gemma's
thoughts whirled – a maelstrom, with Meredith Vincent in the eye of
the storm. What were the chances of two people close to the woman –
both in terms of geography and their relationships – being murdered
then dumped in water within a week of each other? This surely made
Meredith a prime suspect; yet she had no motive, no beef with either

victim and both were her good friends. She hadn't had any sort of breakdown or psychiatric problems, to their knowledge.

Could someone be trying to get at *Meredith*? The thought seemed preposterous. A respectable, fifty-something gift-shop manager didn't have those sorts of enemies.

A world-famous household name pop star, however, could easily have crossed someone at some point in her career – and they still didn't know what had caused Meredith's sudden withdrawal from the public eye. She'd been wondering if it was something to do with the hole in her hand that Meredith wouldn't discuss. Gemma made a mental note to look into this further. And Meredith herself seemed worried, albeit more about Paula Allerton than herself. She'd rung Gemma a couple of days before to report that a statue outside the Allertons' house had been vandalised, and that Paula had told her she thought someone had been creeping around there the night before.

An hour later the conference room was packed – Gemma had sent out a blanket email. Emad sidled in at the last moment with another newish PC – Damian someone – and took a seat at the back. When she flashed him a brief grin, she noticed the sheepish, pleased expression that crossed his face. He was such a sweetheart.

Mavis and DI Lincoln stood at the front, next to a board on which were pinned photographs of Andrea Horvath and Ralph Allerton, pre- and post-mortem.

'Right. Morning everyone,' Detective Superintendent Lincoln began. He was a tall, handsome, chisel-jawed man with wavy blond hair and just the right amount of darker stubble, but he had an unfortunate voice and a weird way of coughing, where he flung back his head and coughed into the back of his hand with short staccato barks. This looked very melodramatic, like a speeded-up swooning Victorian heroine. He did it so often it had to be a sort of tic, and this, plus the nasal voice, instantly cancelled out much of the sex appeal of his appearance. Gemma could tell, though, that Mavis still felt threatened in his proximity.

'I'm now the SIO on this, so, for those who don't know the details,

I'll fill you in. Thursday, fourteenth of June, PCs Khan and Jackman here were called to Minstead House, where the shop manager, Meredith Vincent, had been on her lunch break by the pond and had found Ralph Allerton's body in the pond. He'd been reported as a misper the previous Thursday after not returning from work. Two days later, Ms Vincent was also at the scene of discovery of a second body: Andrea Horvath, a Hungarian national who'd lived in the UK for ten years. She worked as a hairdresser off her boat at the Wey Wharf, next to Meredith Vincent's twin brother's boat. Meredith had been staying with her twin, Pete, the night before and found Andrea's body in the water when she left for a run in the morning. We've now had PM results in on both vics, which has ruled out accidental deaths, definitely on Allerton, who'd been strangled, and probably on Andrea Horvath, who suffered a blow to the head before she went into the river. It's possible that she banged her head and fell in, but unlikely – the severity of the blow and shape of the wound indicates something like a baseball bat. Seems a bit of a coincidence that Ms Vincent finds two bodies in the same week, wouldn't you agree?'

Nods from around the room.

'So obviously she's the primary focus of our investigations. Her brother's the alibi for both occasions, and there are no motives for either death – vics were her friends – and she seems genuinely distraught. But we need to look at both twins, check out their relationships with the deceased.'

Gemma put up her hand.

'Yes? You're DC McMeekin, correct?'

Lincoln did the weird coughing thing, so Gemma nodded and waited till he'd finished barking. 'Sir, I'm wondering if someone is after Meredith herself, trying to hurt her. I think there's something she's not telling us, maybe from years ago. You know she was the lead singer in the band Cohen? They were big in the eighties and nineties.'

This information elicited a ripple of excited murmurs from around the room, particularly from the personnel who were in the forty-plus age bracket.

'Davis did mention this, yes,' Lincoln said, scratching his ear. 'But I'm not sure that—'

Gemma interrupted him. 'She was really freaked out when Mark – DS Davis recognised her.' Flustered that she'd spoken over him, she rushed on: 'And she's got this massive scar – well, hole thing, really – on the back of her hand that she's very cagey about. She just says she doesn't like to talk about it and clams up. I Googled Cohen, and it turns out she quit the band really suddenly in' – she consulted her notes – 'ninety-five. When they were at the height of their success. She seems scared, and paranoid. I was wondering...'

Mavis was shooting daggers at her, presumably thinking that it should have been him who imparted this information. She gritted her teeth, hoping that the blush she could feel sweeping across her face wasn't too obvious to everybody else. She willed her voice to stay firm as she continued:

'...I was wondering if I could go and be her FLO for a few days? Partly because she's in a state; she lives in this isolated cottage in the grounds of Minstead House, and I'm worried, if someone's trying to target her, she could be next. But also so I can really get to know her better. Like, why is she working in a gift shop and renting a tiny cottage? She must have made a fortune during her time with the band. She might tell me whatever it is she doesn't want us to know...?'

Lincoln coughed again, and Mavis pressed his lips together in a tight line of disapproval. Gemma stared at her hands, willing them to agree so that she didn't look like a complete twat in front of everybody. It had been a spur-of-the-moment idea, to get herself involved in the investigation, but it wasn't normal to assign Family Liaison Officers to anyone outside of family members of the victims.

'Are you an experienced FLO?' Lincoln scrutinised her, his head on one side.

'Yes, boss. I've had more than twenty placements over the past five years. I've already met Meredith. I'm sure I could establish a good rapport with her. I know it's not standard procedure to stay over, but under the circumstances I think it would be a good idea...?'

She didn't dare to look around to see the scowl she knew would be on Mavis's face at this. Meredith hadn't warmed to him at that first interview, and he'd acted as if it was a personal affront ever since. And now she was suggesting that she broke official FLO protocols.

'She's got her brother. Why doesn't he go and stay with her?' said Mavis. 'And surely she's working during the day. What are you going to do, hang around her shop all day?'

Gemma stood her ground. 'She told me she's taking a few days off – compassionate leave. Her brother's working – got some big commission to finish apparently, so he'll be holed up in his workshop in Minstead Village. Just think how much intel I could get out of her if she's at home alone for a few days. She trusts me, I know she does. She said before she'd only talk to me.'

'Maybe,' said Lincoln. 'But first can you look at all the CCTV available from the day Ralph Allerton vanished? Let's see if that throws anything up.'

Gemma had to avert her eyes in order not to throw Mavis a smug look. 'Already done, boss. He's not seen on camera coming down from his office that afternoon, but the cameras are only on the main staircase and external doors. He must have used the back staircase, the one the servants would have used, but Meredith Vincent said that wasn't unusual – staff often use that one when the house is closed to the public. Cameras also picked up Meredith's brother arriving on his bike at around eight-forty p.m., which tallies with her statement.'

'What about interviews with all the staff working that day? Did anybody see Allerton leave?'

'We haven't done any other interviews yet. Of course we'd have done them straight away,' Mavis said defensively, 'if we'd known it was going to be a crime scene.'

If you'd *realised it was a crime scene, you twat,* thought Gemma, somewhat unfairly. There had been no reason at first to suspect that Allerton's death was anything other than an accident.

'So now that we know it is,' said Lincoln, not even trying to keep the sarcasm out of his voice, 'I suggest you get back over there and do a search around the pond. Please tell me the pond was cordoned off in the golden hour?'

Mavis nodded, chastened. 'Of course, boss. PC Khan here closed down the scene when he got there.'

Emad had opened his mouth to agree, nodding furiously, but Lincoln spoke first.

'Well, that's something at least. Get a team down there to do a thorough search of the area surrounding the pond again. If he was dumped, there should be footprints, tyre tracks, something. He was a big guy; he can't have been that easy to transport. Mark, you go back and speak to the wife, tell her about these new developments.'

At the mention of tyre tracks, Gemma caught Emad glaring in an uncharacteristically confrontational way at Damian, who was studiously avoiding his eye. 'There were wheelbarrow tracks,' Emad blurted. 'Deep ones, leading to the pond.'

'Why the hell didn't you put them in your report, then?' Lincoln's brows furrowed with irritation as he stabbed with a thick finger at the printout of Emad and Damian's report about the scene.

Poor Emad, thought Gemma. His expression had reverted to its default one of humility, and it took her straight back to their schooldays, how cowed he looked when the teacher asked him a question he couldn't answer.

'It's an area that the house's gardeners go through a lot – the pond lies between the greenhouses and the vegetable gardens. But surely Allerton wouldn't have fitted into a wheelbarrow?' she said.

'He could have done,' Lincoln said grimly. 'If he was already dead, and the person or people wheeling him were strong enough to lift him into it.'

'Right,' said Gemma. 'We'll talk to all the gardeners, see who was around that night. Emad, can you make a start on that?'

Emad nodded, opened his mouth to speak, then hesitated. Gemma smiled encouragingly at him, and Lincoln spotted it. 'Was there something else, Emad?'

'It might be nothing, sir,' he said reluctantly, his voice barely audible over the judder of the elderly aircon unit, 'but I was thinking: you mentioned that Meredith's twin arrived at eight-fortyish on the night Allerton went missing. She said that she and Pete were going out for a drink but then decided against it. I was just wondering why he would have cycled all the way up to Minstead House? I mean, why didn't she just meet him in the pub, if they'd intended to go out? The nearest pub's The Ship in Minstead Village. No reason for him to go up to the house first. And she said he was "picking her up" for a drink, but he arrived on his bike. I don't think he even has a car, does he?'

Gemma was about to agree, but Mavis jumped in: 'I'm sure that's no big deal, Emad. They probably hadn't decided whether to go out or stay in, that's all, so they'd agreed he'd come up to her and then they'd see how they felt.'

Chastened, Emad looked down, not meeting anybody's eyes. Gemma made a mental note to congratulate him later for thinking of it. It *was* a good point. Why *wouldn't* Pete have just gone to meet Meredith at the pub? The Ship was only up the road from Pete's boat. It didn't make sense. She would pay Meredith another visit and ask her.

26

1983
Meredith

When I remembered back, that birthday at Greenham marked the first major turning point of my life. It had been a day of firsts, both good and bad: first demo, first kiss, first arrest, first body search.

First time I learned what I'd been too self-obsessed to realise; that I was about to lose my dad.

I couldn't take it in. In fact, to begin with, I thought it was some kind of sick joke; perhaps a punishment for me absconding to Greenham and getting arrested on my birthday, leaving just a note.

Samantha and I, and all the other women, had been released with a caution at 2.00 a.m. I'd rung home from a payphone outside the police station, reversing the charges. Dad had answered, wearily, and hadn't said a word while I apologised down the phone, suddenly mortified at my reckless behaviour. I saw myself from high above, a small, dirty bear in wellies, tear-stained and sobbing in a phone box.

Samantha waited outside, wandering a little way down the road when she heard my sobs. I was glad that she was still there, and more glad that she was being discreet. It was all so embarrassing, but a combination of delayed shock, tiredness and Dad's familiar voice combined to set me off, and I cried so much that Dad had to keep telling me to take deep breaths as I 'sorried' until I almost puked. When I told him I'd been arrested and released with a caution for public-order offences, at first he assumed I had been arrested in Salisbury after a raucous birthday celebration with my friends.

'Reading? Why did they bring you to *Reading*?' I heard the alarm in his voice.

'Because that's the nearest police station to Greenham Common,' I hiccupped.

'*Greenham Common*?'

Mum, who'd obviously woken up and joined Dad at the phone at the bottom of the stairs, squawked in horror. I pictured her ear jostling for receiver space next to his.

'Yes. I told you that's where I was!'

'No you didn't!' Mum shrieked. 'What the hell were you doing *there*?'

'I left you a note. In Pete's room.'

'Pete went straight out after dinner. We thought we heard you both come back about midnight, but it must just have been him.'

Oh shit. None of them had seen the note. They hadn't even been aware I'd gone. This made me feel both better and worse.

'So you thought I'd just ignored the birthday dinner?'

'Yes,' Dad said mildly down the phone. 'For reasons we couldn't quite fathom.'

I heard Mum snort at his restraint, and it made me cry harder. I'd have preferred her outraged censure to Dad's understated disappointment.

'Daddy,' I said, even though I'd stopped calling him 'Daddy' when I was thirteen, 'please could you come and pick me up?'

ГU

Bless him, he did come. He said he'd pick me up from Reading Police Station at four o'clock. Samantha and I drank stewed brown tea in an all-night cafe in town, talking nonstop, and then wandered back to wait outside the station at the appointed time. He arrived at bang on 4.00 a.m., pulling up in our bottle-green Ford Escort. I'd never been so pleased to see him. We dropped Samantha off at the camp – I'd been hoping she'd want to come back to Salisbury with me, but she said all her stuff was in her tent – and then embarked on the empty road home.

'She seems like quite a character,' Dad said, after Samantha had slammed the rear passenger door and chirped her goodbyes, telling me she'd see me soon, thankfully not trying to kiss me in front of him.

'She is.' I pulled off my wellies and put my sweaty feet up on the dashboard. They smelled, but Dad didn't remark on it. 'I only just met her, yesterday. She lives in Salisbury too; that's how we got talking. She really looked after me, it was so kind of her. I – I left Pete's rucksack there. She's going to bring it back.'

Dad was silent for a while, an unlit pipe clamped between his lips as he drove carefully along the deserted dual carriageway.

'I could ask you what you were thinking, and why you did it,' he said. 'Your mum was in tears earlier when she realised you'd gone out before your birthday dinner. She spent a long time cooking that for you, you know. Pete was there, but it wasn't the same without you.'

My own tears immediately returned to my eyes. Mum and I had a fractious relationship, but I hated the thought that I had made her cry. I hadn't thought she'd be that bothered.

'I seem to be upsetting her a lot recently,' I said, wiping the back of my hand under my nose. 'I understand about the dinner, and I'm sorry. I'll tell her I am. But why did she have a fit yesterday morning, about me not wanting to pick up that stupid magazine from the newsagent's? And why's she always yelling at me?'

Dad sighed. 'That wasn't about you. Not yesterday. She was upset about something else.'

'What?' I tried not to sound belligerent, but did anyway.

There was a long pause. Dad's eyes were fixed on the dark road.

'Dad, what is it? You're not getting divorced, are you?'

'It's nothing like that, love.' He sounded so sad.

'Please, just tell me.'

'Well, Mum wanted you to go out because we had to phone the hospital at eight-fifteen for some test results.'

'On...?'

'On me. I haven't been feeling very well lately. You've probably noticed that I'm very tired at the moment and a bit yellow-looking? And I've had this awful backache?'

Apart from witnessing him clutching his back and groaning occasionally, I'd been oblivious, but I nodded.

'I had a few tests at the Infirmary a couple of weeks ago. I can't … I'm sorry, but…'

His voice suddenly sounded as if someone had their hand clamped around his throat while he was trying to be sick. My heart clenched with fear.

'No,' I whispered.

Dad changed down a gear to take a corner and the Escort shuddered.

'Darling girl. I'm so sorry. When we rang up yesterday, they told us to come in. So we did. And the consultant told us. I'm afraid it's … it's cancer. Pancreatic cancer.'

I burst into tears again. I wanted to jump into his arms but he was driving, so I hugged myself instead, wrapping my arms tightly around my body till my hands were clutching my own shoulder blades.

'But … but, they can operate, right? Can you have a … a transplant? A pancreas transplant?'

Dad smiled faintly. 'I can't.'

'Why *not*?'

'It wouldn't work. It's already spread to my liver and kidneys and spine.'

'No, no. No!' I railed, rocking. This couldn't be happening. 'What else can they do?'

Over the engine noise, I heard the gulp as he swallowed hard.

'Nothing, unfortunately. The trouble with this type of … of, *cancer*' – he extruded the word with difficulty – 'is that you don't get any noticeable symptoms of it for a very long time. They think I've had it for months, maybe even years. And once it spreads, it's impossible to treat. It's really too late to do anything.'

'Oh, Daddy.' I plucked uselessly at the sleeve of his tweed jacket, almost howling, regretting every snappy word and stroppy flounce I'd ever said and performed. Every possible thing I'd ever done to cause him sorrow.

'The dinner. My birthday dinner…' I'd blown out what was probably the last birthday dinner Pete and I would ever have with him. 'I wouldn't have gone off to Greenham if I'd known. I swear I wouldn't.'

'Of course, darling girl. Of course.'

I cried the rest of the way home, pulling up my knees and sobbing into them until the fur was matted and humid with my tears.

Once Dad had finally killed the engine and coasted into our driveway, we both climbed stiffly out of the car, and I saw for the first time how thin and weary he looked, how hunched and pained. I ran into his arms, the tears still coming thick and fast, and we stood hugging each other outside the house in the pre-dawn chill, me still in wellies and the stupid bear costume.

'Come on,' he whispered eventually. 'Get yourself to bed for a few hours. And, Meredith?'

'Yes?'

'Please ... look after Mum for me. When I'm gone.'

'I will, Dad, I promise.'

27

1983

Meredith

For the first time, I was disappointed not to smell Caitlin's patchouli scent and hear the little bells jingling on her Indian skirt when I arrived at nine o'clock the Saturday after my birthday.

It had been a horrible week at home, now that the news was out about Dad. Mum was no longer trying to hide her emotions and would grab any of us who passed within arm's reach in long, tight hugs that took every ounce of my self-restraint not to break out of. I'd never been a very huggy person – unless the bestower was Samantha, as I'd recently discovered.

Pete wouldn't talk about it at all, and was in a massive mood with me for leaving his rucksack and sleeping bag at Greenham, even though I kept saying he'd get it back, and if he didn't, I'd buy him new ones. Dad looked worse every day. Now that I knew, I couldn't believe I hadn't noticed before. It was as if he was shrinking before our eyes. I couldn't take it in.

School was increasingly tedious, and I couldn't concentrate on my A levels because my head was so full of panic: panic about Dad's condition; panic about never seeing Samantha again – I hadn't heard a word from her; panic about failing my exams...

So it was a relief to get to work on Saturday, and I'd been dying to compare notes with Caitlin about the teddy bears' picnic.

The shop door was unlocked when I arrived, but the shutters were still down. Alaric, Sarum Discs' owner, was behind the shop counter making himself a cup of tea from the kettle in the alcove. He didn't offer to make me one. In fact, he had a face like a slapped arse – probably because he loathed getting up before eleven, especially on a Saturday.

'Where's Caitlin?'

He scratched his black stubble and scowled. 'In prison.'

'*What*?'

'She only went and got herself arrested at Greenham Common last weekend.'

I ripped off my jacket, joined him behind the counter and hung it on the back of the battered swivel chair next to the till. 'Oh my God! Actually, I got arrested there last weekend too.' I couldn't keep the pride out of my voice. 'But how come she's in prison? I got released with a warning. She doesn't have any previous, does she?'

I said 'previous' oh-so-casually, the vocabulary of being arrested tripping off my tongue as if it was a regular occurrence.

Alaric didn't seem impressed, though. 'Well, actually, she's not in prison as such, not at the moment, but she's been charged and she's out on bail. She's had to go and stay with her folks in Cornwall pending a trial, which might not be for a few months.'

Pressing the 'open' button on the till, I enjoyed as always the satisfyingly heavy *ker-chunk* sound as the drawer shot out, even while my mind was reeling from the news of Caitlin's tribulations. I began emptying the float into the tray compartments from the plastic bags full of coin denominations that Alaric had dumped next to it.

This was one of my favourite jobs at work, reminding me of the toy till I had when I was about nine, and how much I'd loved compartmentalising coppers even back then. As I did it, I felt a huge surge of guilty relief at briefly escaping the stifling, sad atmosphere at home. The knowledge of Dad's imminent demise was so crushing that I found myself repeatedly trying to ignore it altogether; pretend it wasn't happening – which was a lot easier to manage when I was busy elsewhere.

'Don't do that yet,' Alaric said irritably. 'Shutters aren't even up!'

I rolled my eyes, making sure he couldn't see me. I hated opening the shutters, they were so heavy and had a tendency to come sliding back down with a huge screech and thud if you didn't click them into place fast enough at the top. 'OK. But why's Caitlin been sent to trial? Surely not just for trespassing?'

Alaric took a milk bottle from his satchel and popped the foil top, pouring it into his tea. 'She didn't go into too many details on the phone, but she's been charged with GBH. Apparently she poked a copper in the face with a stick while avoiding arrest. He's been blinded in one eye. I reckon she's looking at doing time – a couple of years at least.'

'Shit.' I was horrified.

As I went outside and grappled with the heavy shutters, my mind reeled. I felt sorry for Caitlin. I could see how easy it might be, in the heat and fear of dozens of angry uniformed men charging at us, shouting and swearing, to lash out in self-defence. If I'd had a stick in my hands before I was bodily carried off the silo, who was to say I wouldn't have done the same? Caitlin was tiny, about seven stone; no wonder she'd felt that she needed to defend herself.

I imagined the devastation on my folks' faces if they'd had to actually bail me out, then sit in the public gallery watching me be tried in a court of law. It was bad enough having just been arrested! I felt a cold sweat of horror at my recklessness, and relief at having been let off without charge, especially in the light of the discovery of Dad's terminal diagnosis.

Caitlin and I hadn't been best mates or anything, but she didn't deserve that. And even if she never knew it, I owed her a debt of eternal gratitude for putting the idea in my head in the first place, and therefore giving me the chance to meet Samantha.

I shoved the shutters into place with the long pole and went back into the now much-lighter shop, propping the pole back in the corner. 'I didn't even see her when I was there. Mind you, the place is huge,' I said, noticing how dusty the till was. I found a grimy duster behind the counter and set to. 'I don't blame her for lashing out at them. The police literally carried us all off – it was pretty terrifying. She must have just been really unlucky that she injured one of them.'

Dusting done, I flicked the kettle back on to reboil and pointedly threw a teabag into one of the other tannin-stained mugs; an ancient chipped Southampton FC one emblazoned with the words 'When the Saints Come Marching In'.

'Do you have her folks' phone number?' I asked. 'I'll give her a ring to say I'm sorry she got nicked.'

Alaric shook his head. He'd sat down on the swivel chair with his tea and lit a cigarette, flicking through the pages of last week's *Melody Maker* and scratching his black arm hair. He was the hairiest man I'd ever seen.

'When's the trial? Is she going to come back? What about her boyfriend? Will you have to get another full-time person?'

'Blimey, Meredith, enough with the questions. I told her I'd keep a job open for her, but she was a bit rude about it. I let it go because she's obviously under a lot of stress, but she basically implied that I could stick it.'

I suppressed a smile. Caitlin couldn't stand Alaric – said he ogled her tits and made suggestive comments to her.

'I think she's broken up with that bloke of hers too. She made some self-pitying comment about how she's lost everything, including the love of her life...'

He sighed dramatically, as if Caitlin's misfortunes were nothing more than an irritation to him – which they doubtless were. Alaric had never been big on empathy.

'Gonna put an ad in the *Journal* today, and I'll do a sign for the window too. Now, could you unwrap those Heaven 17 albums and top up the bin? We sold out last week.'

He slurped his tea and turned away from me, while I cut open the box of records and wondered if Samantha needed a job. It would be so cool to have her working here too. I wished I didn't have to do my A levels. I wouldn't have minded a full-time job here myself, aside from the obvious downside of having to work with Werewolf Al.

Then I thought: *Did* I have to do my A levels? Who said? Everyone just expected it, that was all. Because I was bright, they expected I'd go to university and get a good degree, then ... then what? I had no idea what I wanted to do. Until now, the future had always just stretched ahead of me in a fluffy cloud of vague non-specific achievement. But what my day at Greenham Common had shown me all too clearly was that there were people – women – out there making decisions based on their principles, not on some woolly sense of entitlement. Women to whom the expression 'changing the world' was not an aphorism but an actual goal. Women like Samantha.

My thoughts were never far from Samantha, mostly in the form of fretting, and almost certainly as a displacement activity – something to stop me dwelling on Dad's illness. She had warned me she would be staying at Greenham for a bit and would therefore be incommunicado, but I worried constantly that I would never see her again. She had my phone number; she could easily have gone out to a phone box and rung me if she'd wanted to. I'd seen a little queue of women at the one on the road just outside the camp.

I couldn't bear the thought of never seeing her again. I relived our kisses over and over again, feeling the same guilty thrill as her soft lips pressed against mine and her tongue slipped inside my mouth. I couldn't tell anybody about her, particularly not Charlotte and Julie, after their disgusted comments about lesbians being at Greenham. It seemed like such an embarrassing cliché, to have gone there once for a few hours and come away as a newly gay woman. They'd probably either take the piss out of me for it, or go weird on me and start assuming I fancied *them* or something. To my knowledge there were no lesbians at all in my school – amongst the pupils, anyway. We all knew that the PE teachers were 'lezzers': a word that I would never allow to cross my lips again.

Thinking of lips brought me right back to Samantha. I stared out of the shop window at the passers-by, mostly determined-looking housewives with empty wheely shopping bags, heading to the marketplace for the best selection of fruit and veg. Bet none of them had ever felt another woman's breast. They didn't know what they were missing.

'Oi, Earth to Meredith,' said Alaric crossly. 'If you've got nothing better to do, go and sweep the dust bunnies out from under the display racks while we're still quiet.'

I scowled but obeyed. With men like Alaric about, who *wouldn't* want to date a woman instead?

28

1983
Meredith

One day before the end of term I was walking into town after school with Julie and Charlotte. We'd just sat our first mock A level – English lit – and had decided to treat ourselves to tea and a jam doughnut at Reeves the Baker. We were ambling along the gravel riverside path that was the more scenic route into the centre of town, our waistbands rolled over so many times that our grey skirts resembled wide fabric belts, and our ties in knots bigger than our fists.

I had tuned out of the conversation they were having about whether Steve Francis and Neil Hart fancied them – mostly because I could have told them the answer was almost certainly 'no', at least, not half as much as they fancied themselves. My head was full of Keats, *The Fall of Hyperion,* particularly a line that ran, 'one minute before death, my iced foot touch'd the lowest stair...'

That line stuck with me. I'd laughed about it with the girls – 'my iced foot', like an iced bun or a foot in a bath of ice cubes. But secretly it haunted me, the cold descent to your fate, the knowledge that you'd reached the end of your life, the bottom of the staircase, no going back, not ever...

Dad's iced foot had touched the lowest stair three weeks ago. It was as if, from the moment he told me he was dying, back in April, he had to get down to the business of actually doing it. Almost overnight his eyes turned yellow and the knobs of bones sprouted everywhere on him, like a grim budding magnolia but in reverse.

It was unbearable to watch, so I'd closed my eyes and turned the other way.

Selfish.

During the funeral I had yearned for Samantha. She was my future, but I hadn't heard from her since April. I didn't think I'd ever see her again, and to my shame, this upset me almost as much as losing Dad.

I hadn't thought about Mum at all.

The girls were talking fast, gesticulating wildly, as if all the words they hadn't been allowed to speak during the three-hour exam were now spurting out of them in a saved-up torrent. I probably couldn't have got a word in edgeways even if I'd wanted to. They usually made me laugh with their intense diatribes on boys, but today I felt too spent to engage. Or perhaps I felt that I'd grown apart from them, since Greenham and Samantha and Dad's death. I really didn't care whether Neil Hart got the highlights in his hair done at a salon or just used Sun-In like the rest of us.

I drew a short way away and was idly watching the hypnotic dark-green swirl of the river weed under the surface as I walked, trying to spot the minnows and occasional freckled trout darting through it.

Someone was cycling towards us, and I instinctively moved closer to the riverbank to allow the cyclist to pass between us. She was almost upon us when the sun suddenly glinted on her hair, like a celestial arrow pointing her out to me. I gasped so hard and stopped so suddenly that Julie ceased mid-sentence in her impassioned rant about how much it hurt to get highlights, especially from her hairdresser, who seemed to take pleasure in snapping on the thick rubber sieve-hat, then dragging the hair strands through with the metal crochet-hook.

It was Samantha.

'I swear she's trying to stab me with that thing ... What's the *matter*, Meredith?'

I ignored the question. Samantha screeched to a halt beside me, the edge of the wicker basket on her handlebars touching my right breast, her eyes greedily latching onto mine and holding me in her amber gaze. She looked astonishingly beautiful, red hair streaming, like a Valkyrie on two wheels; an angel of death who would rip me away from my old life forever. I felt a slow smile spread across my face and wanted to run into her arms, yelling with joy. But then I saw Julie and Charlotte gawping first at her, then at me, then at each other, and I felt gauche in my rolled-up skirt, jumper tied round my waist, ankle socks and – the shame – I even had a naff flowery hairband in my hair, the one I'd had since I was eleven years old. I wanted to rip it off and throw it in the river. I couldn't have looked more like the schoolgirl I was unless my hair had actually been in pigtails and I'd had ink splotches all over my fingers.

'Hiya,' I said, grinning at Samantha, questions tumbling over themselves behind the dam of my mouth. I immediately firmly closed it to prevent myself either kissing her or giving her the Spanish Inquisition.

'Hey, you,' she drawled, grinning back and pushing her hair out of her face. 'Long time, no see. I have your brother's rucksack and sleeping bag back at my place. Got time for a coffee?'

I glanced across at my friends, who both raised their eyebrows at me. 'Sure,' I said. 'Great, about Pete's things. He's been moaning about them for weeks. Samantha, these are my mates Charlotte and Julie. Charlotte and Julie, this is Samantha; we met at Greenham a couple of months ago.'

'Ohhhh,' they chorused, their faces alight with prurient interest. I immediately flushed scarlet, agonising that they could see how turned on I was just to be in Samantha's presence. I had to glance down at my nipples to make sure they weren't betraying me through my thin bra and white shirt. Samantha clocked me looking and I could have sworn she read my mind. Her lips twitched with amusement, and my blush developed a blush of its own.

'Jump on. You can ride shotgun,' Samantha said, wheeling her bicycle around on the path in a brisk 180-degree turn and patting the spring-loaded metal rack on the back of it.

I slung my schoolbag over my shoulder, climbed on and held myself steady by grasping the edges of the rack behind me in the way I'd seen teenage boys do, although I'd have preferred to wrap my arms around her waist. She pushed off and began to pedal hard back the way she'd just come.

'I'll see you tomorrow,' I called over my shoulder to the girls, sticking my legs out to the sides to get them off the ground. As Samantha managed to get up a bit of speed, I could feel their eyes burning into the back of my head. There would be questions, I could tell, although I didn't think they would suspect that there was anything sexual between us ... would they?

Oh, who cares, I thought, as Samantha's wheels crunched over the sandy gravel.

'Follow the yellow brick road,' I called.

'Well, I am from Kansas,' she called back, laughing, and I felt pure happiness – for the first time since Dad's death.

'So,' she said, once we got into town, the girls mere specks in the distance behind us when I'd glanced back. 'Where shall we go?'

I directed her to another tea shop, one as far away from my friends' usual haunt, Reeves, as I could think of, with lots of upstairs nooks and dark little corners. We ordered a pot of tea and toasted teacakes and found the most distant table, in a top room that only held two, the other one unoccupied. Once the elderly, cross waitress had struggled up with our tray and dumped it accusingly in front of us, Samantha poured the tea. Then she stopped, mid-pour, leaned forwards and kissed me before I had a chance to ask her where she'd been, what she'd been doing, why she hadn't been in touch, whose camper van she had been sleeping in, whose pillow had her head been on for the past two months...

'My dad died,' I said instead, when we came up for air. I waited for the gasps of sympathy, but all she said was, 'Move to London with me' – more of a command than a question. 'My mate Marsh has got an awesome squat in Willesden we can live in. I've been sorting it all out these last few weeks. Sorry about your daddy, he seemed real nice.'

'OK,' I replied, all the questions fleeing, forgetting that I had four more mock exam papers to sit; forgetting my promise to Dad to look after Mum, forgetting that Pete would be left to cope on his own. 'When do we leave?'

So this was what being in love felt like. No wonder people raved about it.

29

Present Day
Meredith

The woman detective, Gemma, texted Meredith that afternoon asking if she could come over and see her at Minstead.

Now what? thought Meredith, but she texted obediently back to say yes, of course, and to remind Gemma that she was at home in the cottage, having taken a few days compassionate leave. She couldn't face being in the shop, knowing that Ralph wasn't upstairs in his office, or around for coffee, or to have a laugh with in staff meetings.

She had been in the front garden, ostensibly weeding, but also trying to make sure that none of Ralph's shirt buttons were visible after she'd thrown them into the flowerbed in panic the previous week. The weather had changed, banks of dark grey clouds rolling across the hills, heavy with threatened rain, casting a pall over the grounds. Her mood felt as dark as the sky and wasn't helped by Paula, who rang her as she was wrestling with the root of a stubborn bramble.

'Why did you ring the police to tell them about the lion?' Paula demanded as soon as Meredith answered. 'I told you I'd let them know! Now they're all suspicious, like I'm hiding something!'

Meredith wiped her free hand across her sweaty forehead. She wasn't sure what to say – she didn't want to freak her out any more than she already was. 'Oh Paula,' she began carefully. She'd been going to say something like, *we have to tell the police everything, no matter how inconsequential it seems*, but then realised how massively hypocritical that would be.

A robin hopped along the crazy-paving path, stopping with its head on one side to regard her. They stared at each other for a long while. Meredith couldn't shake the sensation that it was judging her.

'Look,' she continued to Paula, and the robin. 'I'm sorry if you thought I was interfering, but I'm worried. It's not just the lion. You said the door was left open. I really don't want to freak you out, and I'm not saying there's any connection to any of it, but with ... what happened to Ralph and Andrea, unless the post-mortems show that they both died accidentally, I just think we can't be too careful.'

She tailed off, rubbing a burgeoning blister on her thumb made by the spade's handle. She had decided not to burden Paula with all the other weird stuff that had been going on with her. And neither Paula nor Ralph ever knew the truth about who she used to be, nor how she really got the scar on her hand.

'DS Davis is coming over to see me today,' Paula said. 'It might be with the results of the post-mortem. I asked him, but he wouldn't tell me on the phone. Which means it's not good news.'

It was as if she was refusing to accept Meredith's fears that someone might be targeting them.

'That Gemma woman, the detective, is coming over to see me as well,' said Meredith.

'Why would she do that?' Paula sounded almost outraged. 'Why would they need to tell *you*?'

Meredith immediately wished she hadn't mentioned it. 'Because I knew both Ralph and Andrea, I suppose.'

'I'm going to go to Norfolk to stay with my sister for a bit,' Paula said. 'Jackson's going away with his girlfriend for a couple of weeks, some last-minute package holiday. We can't have a funeral till the police release Ralph's body anyway. DS Davis said it was OK as long as he knows where we are. I've cancelled all my clients indefinitely.'

The rain began to fall, fat drops on the parched earth. Meredith retreated inside the cottage, leaving piles of weeds on the path and the robin's reproachful stare. She felt inordinately relieved at the news that Paula was taking herself out of harm's way, and that she was doing it without Meredith having to spell out her fears. Even before all this, she and Ralph had expressed concerns about Paula's potential vulner-ability, seeing mentally unstable clients in the detached summerhouse that was her consulting room.

It was raining heavily when Gemma arrived, soaked just from the short walk down the steps from the car park. Meredith heard the click of the gate and watched her come up the path, stepping over the uprooted weeds, her normally pleasant face set in a grimace of something that was either discomfort at the rain, or knowledge of the news she had to deliver.

'Come in, come in,' Meredith said, opening the door and forcing a smile. 'I'll get you a towel.'

'Thanks. I didn't think to bring an umbrella.'

After a bit of fussing around with tea and towels, Gemma finally delivered the news Meredith had been dreading.

'Meredith, I'm so sorry, but the post-mortems showed that both Ralph and Andrea were murdered. Ralph was strangled, and Andrea was hit on the head before she fell into the water. It could be the work of two separate killers, but we really don't think that's likely.'

Meredith stared down at the jagged hole in the back of her hand.

Black boots, thumping across a van floor.

Black boots, kicking her in the face.

The flash of a blade, plunging down towards her.

Her own screams, amplified by the van's metal sides...

They sat in silence for a few moments, then Gemma leaned forwards and said, her voice barely audible over the noise of the rain drumming at the window, 'I think there's something you haven't told us about all this. Am I right?'

Meredith was going to tell her. She opened her mouth to speak, but the words just wouldn't come. She couldn't say it. If she said it; if she said, *I think it's me he's after*, then it made it real. And as for, *I had sex with Ralph right before he died*; shame mingled with the terror and stilled her tongue.

In the end, all she said was, 'You don't think *I* did it, do you?'

Gemma met her eyes. 'Personally, no I don't. But I think you have something to do with it, whether you're aware of it or not.'

Another long pause.

'Meredith, I know what happened to you; the abduction. I found the details on our system. I'm sorry – that must have been unspeakably traumatic. I know they never found the perpetrator. Which is what makes me concerned that these murders of your friends are new warnings to you. I know it seems unlikely, since so much time has passed – but we can't rule it out. Perhaps your attacker has been out of the country, or has only just tracked you down...'

Meredith felt the room tip and sway. She sank back against the sofa cushions and waited for the nausea to pass.

'Surely this has occurred to you as well?'

They knew. It was real; she couldn't keep denying it any longer. All she could do was nod, her eyes closed.

'Please help me,' she said.

Gemma came and sat beside her, and even though the girl was half her age, Meredith had an urge to collapse into her arms.

'I will. I promise,' Gemma said. 'But you have to help us too. I'm reopening your case. We're going to look again at all the evidence you gave last time, see if we can make any sort of connection. And...' She hesitated.

'What?' Meredith braced herself, but Gemma's next words, when they came, were a relief.

'...I've asked my boss if I could base myself here with you for a few days, in my role as Family Liaison Officer. We wouldn't normally stay overnight, but given how remote you are out here, I think it's a good idea. Partly for your own safety, and partly so we can have a proper chance to talk. Just you and me. Anything you can tell me, about Ralph or Andrea as well as about you, could help catch this guy, Meredith.'

Meredith could tell that Gemma was expecting her to refuse immediately, and under any other circumstances, the idea of someone other than Pete staying in her cottage was anathema, but all she could do was nod again.

'OK.'

30

1984
Meredith

Eighteen years old was far too young to be living in a crumbling derelict apartment block in Willesden Green, sleeping on a stained mattress like a tramp, condensation running down the walls and no heating apart from a brazier we all huddled round in the bare upstairs bedroom we'd made into our living room, since the ground floor rooms were too unspeakable, even for us.

Later, I came to realise that there was a subconscious element of penance about the squalidness of my surroundings. I told myself I was free; free of exams, school uniform, the oppressive clutch of Mum's misery, Dad's empty armchair in the corner. But the truth was that I'd merely tried to run away from my own grief. I'd thought that by putting miles between me and my family's vast loss, it would diminish its perspective. But in hindsight all it did was add a bucket of guilt to the already potent cocktail of suppressed negativity and unexpressed sorrow. I'd abandoned Pete and Mum when they needed me most – even though Samantha, on the rare occasions I tried to articulate this, merely shrugged and said, 'Baby, what use would you be to them, feeling this fucked up? You'll be much more useful once you get your head straight.' I pretended to believe her.

I missed Pete, and Dad of course, and I hated that Pete was so angry with me for leaving him with Mum, but it was done. I had failed Dad. They were better off without me.

⊓⊔

Apart from my guilt, the other blot on my hippie landscape was Samantha's excessive free spiritedness. She hated being in one place for more than a few days at a time and spent increasingly lengthy periods of time at Greenham, which made me itchy with insecurity. Mostly because she never invited me to go with her – although I was secretly quite glad about this, being terrified of getting arrested again; the last thing I wanted was more police officers peering into my knickers. And Samantha was so effervescent with love and affection whenever she came back that I refused to read anything into it more than her desire to rid the world of nuclear weapons. I was utterly besotted. I'd even thought about how we could have children together and which of my fellow squatters we'd ask to be sperm donor – Marsh was the answer; he was gorgeous.

Despite the privations, I loved living in the squat. I adored the bunch of guys I lived with: mild-mannered twenty-something Goth eco-warriors to a dreadlocked man: Spike, Matty, Marsh and Webbo. Every night the five of us – six, when Samantha was there to share my mattress – sat around the brazier and smoked weed until I wove a hazy web inside my head, rolled up in my sleeping bag and drifted off into a comfortable night's sleep. Often we would sing – Matty was a really good guitar player and Webbo brought out bongos. Those were the best nights. We wrote music together – mostly rage-filled protest songs, but they were pretty good. The boys treated me like a kid sister and were unfailingly protective, and in return I cooked and kept the squat as clean as I could while they were out busking and working odd jobs for pittances that were then pooled.

Feminism? What feminism? I later thought.

One day after I'd lived there about six months, Marsh shouted up the stairs from the kitchen – we had to come in and out through the forced back door – 'Come and see what the *fuck* we've got!'

I raced downstairs as fast as was possible, while avoiding the broken stair treads, hoping it was something really nice to eat. I'd have killed for roast chicken, and Marsh was the only other non-vegetarian, although we both pretended to the others that we were. I was so sick of veggie curry made with chickpeas and tinned plum tomatoes – or, as they were for some reason referred to in the squat, 'wombat's afterbirth'.

But it wasn't a chicken, or a few packets of sausages he'd foraged from the bins at the back of Safeway. It was an amp, a couple of microphone stands and a bass guitar, all sitting on the filthy, peeling lino of the kitchen floor.

Marsh grabbed me round the waist and hugged me effusively, stinking of frib juice – as I'd learned to call patchouli oil – and weed. 'It's for *us*! Man, we're starting a *band*!'

He always spoke like that, putting heavy emphasis on certain words as if he had to conserve his energy for the rest of them. I laughed, mentally picturing our motley, unwashed crew in a line-up next to sequinned and styled favourites like ABC and Duran Duran. 'A band?'

'Yeah *man*! The landlord at The Five Bells wanted to get rid of it all cos he's getting a better rig. He said I could take it off his hands if I repainted the bogs for him.'

'Wow.' I examined the battered amplifier and the random cables and boxes, not having a clue how any of it worked. 'But how will Matty's guitar be heard over the top of this lot?'

Marsh smirked at my ignorance, scratching his long wispy beard to hide it. 'His guitar's got a pick-up. We just plug this' – he held up a long cable – 'into *this* and we're in business. I'll play bass, and for now we'll have to do with bongos till we can get a drum kit, but, you know, it's gonna be epic!'

'Who's going to be the lead singer?' I foresaw fireworks – Marsh and Matty were both pretty competitive.

'You are!'

I laughed, thinking he was joking. 'No, really. I'll do backing vocals.' Then I saw the intense expression on his face. 'What? You're not serious.'

'Totally serious! Why not? You're way more interesting to look at than the rest of us, and you've got a *great* voice! We've got, like, ten songs now, plus covers? That's more than enough for a set.'

I leaned back against the sticky kitchen counter. 'Wow,' I repeated, a slow smile spreading across my face. For the first time I was glad that Samantha was away. I wouldn't have stood a chance if she'd been in the running. She looked like a red-headed Kate Bush, and her voice was just as good as mine. 'Cool.'

I wouldn't have had *this* if I'd stayed in Salisbury.

31

1984
Meredith

Two months later, on an impulse during one of my weekly calls home from the phone box on the corner of the street, I invited Pete to come and watch the band's first-ever live gig. I was so excited about it, and I suddenly really wanted to see a friendly face in the audience – assuming there would even be an audience. We were playing in the function room of The Five Bells. Every time I'd been in that pub previously, the only clientele had been elderly gentlemen in raincoats hunched on bar stools, grimly sipping pints and ignoring each other.

'Up to London?' Pete repeated, as if London was a four-day camel ride away.

'Yes, up to London. Don't, if you don't want to!'

'Well, I could, I suppose. It'll be half term. Can I stay on your sofa?'

I looked out of the phone box window and could see the pathetic excuse for a sofa that even we squatters had rejected as being too disgusting. It was languishing on its back in the front garden, looking drunk, stuffing spilling from its stained cushions. Fortunately, it was highly unlikely that any of the neighbours would complain – apparently the entire street, a once-handsome crescent of redbrick terraced apartment buildings, was a squat. Europe's largest squat, we found out some years later when it was raided by the police and it was on the local news.

I hadn't confessed to Mum and Pete that I was squatting. They thought I was in a flatshare funded by my job in the local leisure centre. I did have a job there as a receptionist, but only one day a week.

'Um ... yeah, you can crash at our place, sure. Bring the sleeping bag.'

I thought it would be better to let him see my current living arrangements when he arrived, rather than whip him up into a frenzy of stress about it beforehand. Pete could be a right old woman at times. But I was reasonably confident that once he'd seen how nice the boys were and how homely we'd made the place, he wouldn't freak out as much as if I told him outright I was living in a squat.

He didn't know about me and Samantha yet either. I decided I'd cross that bridge when I came to it too; and that would depend entirely on whether she deigned to put in an appearance at the gig. She'd better, I thought. She'd been away at Greenham for the past three weeks, but she knew it was our first – I'd made her write the date down in her notebook last time I saw her.

It would be a lot for Pete to take in, but I didn't like lying to him and I felt bad that we were already so distant from one another.

'So will you come?'

'I'd like to, but I'm not sure I'll be able to afford the train. And how do I get to your place from Waterloo?'

I tutted. 'It's not hard. Just get the tube. We're a one-minute walk away from Willesden Green station. You could always hitch up if you can't afford the train.'

'*Hitchhike?*' Pete sounded appalled, and I rolled my eyes.

'God, Pete, grow a pair! It's how we all get around.'

Samantha did, anyhow. She never went to Greenham by any other means, unless someone gave her a lift.

'Mez, you mustn't! It's so dangerous. Mum would have an eppy.'

'Oh, put a sock in it, Pete, it's fine. Look, I've got to go, I don't have any more ten pences. Just aim to be there between one and three on Friday. We have to go and set up and soundcheck about four.'

I just had time to give him the address, directions from the tube and the name of the pub in case he was late, then the beeps went, and the line was dead. I wasn't convinced he'd really come, but I hoped he would. I missed him.

And I wanted him to see me fronting the band. After my initial nerves, I *loved* being the lead singer. I became someone else in front of that microphone. I'm sure a psychiatrist would have had a field day with it, but it was as if all my grief and rage at Dad's death channelled itself into my voice and out through the speakers.

'Woah,' Marsh had said, the first time I screamed out one of the more militant protest numbers we'd written, staring at me as if seeing me for the first time. 'You're *terrifying*.'

I beamed. I felt like *I* was seeing me for the first time too.

There was no mirror large enough in the squat to practise my snarl into, but I did it in the mirrors at work instead. As a member of staff I got free swimming passes too, and I went three times a week to swim and, more importantly, shower afterwards, the song lyrics churning through my head in constant earworms as I ploughed up and down the lane. I took all my dirty knickers into the shower with me once a week and washed them with the same shampoo I used on my hair.

I did that on the morning of the gig – I wanted at least to have clean hair and pants for my debut. We'd practised so hard for it and, even though I said so myself, we weren't half bad. Webbo had borrowed a mate's drum kit, and the pub already had a backline so we had everything we needed. As I dried my hair with the wall dryer in the women's changing room, my nostrils were filled with the scent of chlorine and my brain with the random to-do list of what needed completing before showtime: write set lists; take Pete for a pint to calm him down after he'd seen the squat; shoplift some gaffer tape as we were nearly out; put make-up on; inspect the sheet on my mattress to make sure it wasn't too revolting, since Pete and I would have to top and tail; fill my oil lamps up so we'd have some light when we got home; buy – or nick – shoelaces for my DMs as the old ones kept breaking...

I didn't approve of stealing anything, by the way, and always wrote the purloined items down in the back of my diary. As soon as I had any money, I bought the same thing somewhere else and replaced it on the shelf of the original shop I'd nicked it from.

I'd wanted to make a banner bearing our name, to put behind Webbo's drum kit, but I wouldn't have time for this gig and I didn't have a spare sheet or any black paint. We'd called ourselves Cohen, which was the name of the people who used to live in the flat before we took it over. Their post still arrived in surprising quantities and we burned it all in the brazier. It never looked like anything interesting.

I turned the corner into our terrace, these thoughts still chasing themselves through my mind, and was about twenty feet along the pavement before I noticed the tall figure of the woman ahead, shoulders bowed by the heavy rucksack on her back, red hair obscured by the roll of her sleeping bag...

'Samantha!' I shouted joyfully, pounding towards her as she turned and opened her arms wide, beaming at me.

I threw myself at her. 'You came back!'

'Of course, honey – as if I'd miss your first show!'

Then she kissed me, long and hard, and I didn't even care that a passing dog walker sucked his teeth at us. It was only when we finally came up for air that I had the thought, *Oh shit, now I'm going to have to tell Pete.*

32

1984
Meredith

As debut gigs went, the first twenty minutes were pretty much par for the course. Five people in the audience, all of them connected in some way with the band. A few others stuck their heads around the door of the small function room to see what the racket was, recoiled at the wall of sound and retreated.

Samantha had promised to drum up a gang of mates who so far hadn't materialised, and there'd been no sign of Pete before we left to set up, so I assumed he chickened out and wasn't coming. I told myself I didn't care, that it didn't matter because I had Samantha there, standing right near the front with a pint glass clutched in her long, slim fingers, beaming at me, her auburn hair loose, cascading over her shoulders, and her eyes rarely leaving mine. Even just looking at her turned me on. And in that respect I was glad that Pete was a no-show, because it meant I'd be sharing my mattress with Samantha tonight instead of him.

During our third number, the door opened wider, light spilled in from the saloon bar and a group of eight Goths – five women and three guys – burst in, shuffle-dancing as soon as they were through the door, immediately bringing the room to a dark sort of life. One of them, a short slim woman in combats with a mass of black curls, was far more animated than the others. She leaped on Samantha and hugged her around the neck effusively, her lit roll-up – or was it a joint? – dangling from her fingers.

Back off, bitch, I thought, turning up my snarl and raising my voice to a banshee howl as we launched into a cover of The Cure's 'Subway

Song', which only made the black-haired woman jump around to the beat more wildly. I wondered who she was. She and Samantha were obviously old friends, but Samantha hadn't mentioned anyone specific coming, just 'some of my buddies from when I lived in Wandsworth'.

She had all sorts of buddies in different places – buddies I knew nothing about. I wasn't even really clear who she'd been living with in Salisbury when I first met her – she never mentioned them anymore and was irritatingly vague whenever I asked her. Something about someone's sister-in-law, I recalled.

After five songs we stopped for a beer and fag break. I was hyped and jittery, and it was strange to be outside in the June dusk of the pub's garden, my ears ringing in the summery silence, the birds' evensong replacing our angry anticapitalist paeans. Matty brought me a pint of lager, and its fizz was soothing on my scratchy throat.

'It's going wicked!' he enthused. 'Samantha's mates are loving it, they just told me. They love our songs! That guy with the white dreads, he says his brother-in-law's in the music business, and if we make a demo he'll give it to him.'

I laughed. 'Matty, are you mental? There's no way we'd get a record deal singing this sort of stuff! We're hardly New Romantic, are we? We live in a squat!'

Matty snorted dismissively. 'New Romantics? That crap's so nineteen eighty-one. And there's tons of bands out there doing what we're doing. Look at Siouxsie and the Banshees. The Cure. There's this new band, The Cult, everyone's raving about. And we're better than all of them. Definitely more fucking authentic. I bet Robert Smith never went on a protest march in his life, and he's probably never even set foot in a squat.'

Samantha appeared in the garden then, looking flushed and high. 'Honey, this is awesome! I'm dead proud of you.' She slid her arms round my waist and hugged me, and I blushed with pride. She did look proud. Usually she had a kind of almost maternally fond expression on her face when we were getting off with each other, but this was different. There was actual respect in her eyes.

'Where's your brother? I thought he was coming? I'm dying to meet him.'

'So did I,' I said, rolling my eyes. 'He's being a flake. I think he's pissed at me for leaving him on his own with our m-mum.' I stuttered slightly over the word 'mum', having been about to say 'mom' then realising that was a step too far, linguistically, on top of the words 'flake' and 'pissed'. Neither of which, in that context, I'd ever used before I met Samantha. It was the first time I noticed how much I parroted her.

The boys joined us too, and we drank pints of snakebite, courtesy of the management and in lieu of actual payment, while Samantha went around the whole pub garden exhorting the punters to 'come check them out, they're awesome'. I watched her gesticulate towards us, pushing her wavy hair impatiently back from her freckled face, and at that moment felt completely content with my odd life and the unexpected direction it had taken the second I met her. She was wearing a 1940s nipped-waist navy-blue dress with white polka dots and the ubiquitous DMs, and she looked amazing, particularly in contrast with all the sartorial Goth gloom surrounding her.

Her gang of friends who'd bundled in during the first set was still in the function room, leaning against the walls, smoking and chatting when we returned for the second round. I noticed her black-haired pal eyeing me up in a not entirely friendly way as I climbed back up onto the little stage and adjusted my mike on the stand. Halfway through the first song I turned my back on the audience – swelled now to around twenty – windmilling my arms and stomping my DMs in time with the drums in the instrumental break. When I turned back, Samantha and the black-haired girl had left the room. I didn't think anything of it at the time, particularly not when the door opened and a familiar tousled head peered around it. Pete!

I broke into a wide beam that made everyone turn to see who I was looking at, and sang with renewed joy, shrieking out the lyrics of our song 'Flare', about what the world would look like after the next huge set of solar flares: '*Scorched earth, no TV, no need for microwaves, all your food already fried...*'

Pete beamed back at me from the doorway, spreading his hands wide and shyly inclining his head as I moved my hips, pointing at him with both forefingers. He edged inside, slid off the straps of his rucksack – the same one Samantha had rescued from Greenham for me – and leaned against the wall, sipping at a half. A half! What a wuss, I thought affectionately, suddenly beyond happy that he was there to witness this fantastic evening.

Fuelled by alcohol and spliff, our small audience's inhibitions gradually dispersed like the threads of blue smoke caught in the lights, and one by one they all began to dance. I'd never imagined what a buzz it would be to write and sing songs that people were *dancing* to! Fantastic, I thought from the stage, raising my pint glass high in triumph.

After our last song, plus a repeat of one from the first half as an encore, I jumped off the stage and leaped into Pete's arms, as the DJ put on some James Brown to indicate that we were done. Pete blushed crimson to the tips of his ears, but he whirled me around self-consciously and allowed me to ruffle his hair and bestow smacking kisses repeatedly on his cheeks.

'My bro!' I called to the watching audience, who were taking breathers from the dancing to crowd around me and the other band members. 'My twin, believe it or not! All the way from Salisbury. Come on, Pete, let's get to the bar. Leave your rucksack at the back of the stage, it'll be fine.'

Pete did as he was told, nodding at Webbo, who was beginning to dismantle his borrowed drum kit. I took drinks orders from the guys and, linking arms with Pete, headed towards the bar. 'I can't wait for you to meet Samantha,' I enthused. 'You'll love her, she's just so cool.'

How was Pete going to react when he learned I'd become a lesbian? As far as I knew, he was still a virgin. There was something very square about him as a teenager.

As I handed him a pint – ignoring his protests – I regarded him with fondness, his tufty hair, ruddy cheeks and farm-boy jeans. You could tell a mile off he wasn't from London.

'Let's go shopping tomorrow,' I said. 'I'll take you to Flip and we should get you some decent gear. They do awesome checked shirts and stuff; vintage, you know?'

'*Awesome* checked shirts?' he mimicked. 'Why have you gone all American? Watching too much *Cagney and Lacey* are you?'

'Samantha's from Kansas. I spend a lot of time with her. It's obviously rubbed off on me. Where is she, anyway?'

I looked around the bar, and then out in the garden, but there was no sign of her. While Pete went off to the loo I asked the barman if he'd seen her. 'Pretty girl with long curly red hair. Blue-and-white spotty dress, American?'

'Oh her,' he said, his hand inside a tea towel rotating in a tankard. He was a mean-looking skinhead. 'Yeah, hard to miss *her*. She took off about twenty minutes ago – said something had come up. You Meredith? She told me to tell you she'd see you back at the squat later, and *well done*.' He said the last two words with a sneer, as if it pained him to pass on the message.

'Oh. Thanks,' I said, hauling myself up onto a bar stool and picking at a beer mat, until he reached forwards and removed it from my fidgeting fingers. Pete came back and joined me at the bar.

'Samantha's pissed off somewhere,' I said. 'You'll meet her back at the sq— er ... house, though.'

Thankfully, someone had put a very loud Deep Purple track on the jukebox, so Pete didn't seem to have heard my near slip. I was worried if I told him in advance, he wouldn't come and stay.

'So your mate Samantha is your flatmate too?'

'Sort of,' I agreed, suddenly not able to meet his eyes. 'It's us, and the boys in the band. They look after us. Not that we can't look after ourselves,' I added.

Matty and Marsh struggled through the doors from the function room, carrying a big speaker each from the PA. 'Oi, just because you're the singer don't mean you don't have to help us load out!' Marsh called, his skinny legs bowing with the weight.

'Coming,' I said, taking a long swig of my drink.

33

1984
Meredith

I felt pretty annoyed with Samantha for bailing on me before the gig was even over, but I tried to swallow it down. After all, she had hitched all the way back from Greenham specially to support me; she'd mustered up a gang of friends to come and watch – without whom we'd have had almost no audience at all; she'd danced and looked proud and given me loads of thumbs-ups. I reminded myself that she was a free spirit. She never liked being in one place for long. She'd left a message for me with the barman. I'd see her back at the squat...

But where had she been for the past three hours? There was a worm of unease squiggling around in the pit of my belly when I realised that her friend, the girl with black curly hair, was also nowhere to be seen. The rest of their mates were still in the pub garden, smoking and laughing, but she definitely wasn't with them.

I was so keen for Samantha to meet Pete; I'd talked incessantly about him to her, and she claimed to be fascinated that I was a twin. Keen – but simultaneously nervous about admitting the truth of our relationship. Pete did have a 'live and let live' policy – he wasn't a prude – but he was quite old-fashioned, and innocent. And perhaps he might not be quite so tolerant when the 'deviance' – as my mother would call it – was so close to home.

For the first time ever, I felt a tiny bit glad that my dad wasn't around anymore. I realised my lip was curling, even just thinking about his reaction. He'd have been completely appalled that I was gay.

It helped with the pain of his loss. Small mercies, and all that shit.

We got all the equipment loaded into the van that Matty had borrowed from his work, and declared the evening a success, celebrating our first live gig with a couple more pints of snakebite and black. Pete was almost as drunk as me, I realised, loosening up as the night went on, losing his country-bumpkin shyness and joining in the banter with the boys at the bar. By the time the skinhead barman called last orders, we'd all had so much snakebite that none of us seemed to be in possession of knees anymore, sagging and staggering and bellowing our songs as we pushed our way out of the pub and wobbled towards the squat. Matty was too drunk to drive, so he said he would pick up the van in the morning.

Samantha wasn't home when we got in, but my first main concern was monitoring Pete's reaction to my new abode. He didn't baulk at the rubbish-tip front garden, with the sofa lying on its back like an old drunk, all its rusty springs on display, or at the boarded-up downstairs windows, but he did a double-take as we got inside and Matty switched on the hurricane lamp in the hallway, which illuminated the damp, peeling walls and bare floorboards.

'Are you redecorating?' he asked dubiously as I steered him towards the stairs, pointing out the broken treads and the missing banisters. He stepped gingerly up them as Webbo guffawed behind us.

'Yeah, darling, this place will look *divine* by the time the interior designers have finished next week! New carpets are arriving tomorrow, and the chandeliers are being flown in from Paris, and—'

'Oh shut up, Webbo!' I said, seeing Pete's shoulder blades jam hard together as he stiffened his back in embarrassment, chin jutting forwards; a well-worn gesture. I half expected him to click his heels together and salute at the same time whenever he did it. It harked back to his time in his early teens in the Salisbury Sea Cadets (I never understood why Salisbury had Sea Cadets being, as it was, firmly inland). Pete had hated every minute of it, so the back-stiffening was, I thought, some kind of Pavlovian reaction; parade equalling mortification.

'Why's there no electricity then?' he asked.

'You never been in a squat before, mate?' Marsh enquired cheerfully.

Pete stopped in the upstairs hallway, so suddenly that I bumped into the back of him. He turned and stared at me. 'What, you mean you don't pay *rent*? You're living here illegally? Oh my god, Mez! What's the matter with you? Mum'll have a conniption fit!'

I rolled my eyes and dragged him into my bedroom, which was illuminated by the sodium-orange glow of the street lamp outside the window. 'Sit,' I commanded, pointing to the bare mattress. 'Mum doesn't need to know it's a squat. It's fine. Stop being such an old woman about it.'

Pete flopped back on my mattress, spreading his arms wide, as I lit the two oil lamps on the floor. 'She's already going nuts about you moving out and bailing on your A levels, you know.'

Guilt bolted through me, an emotional pile-driver boring down through the beery haze as I set the match to the second wick quickly, before it burned my fingers. 'I might still do them and go to uni. It's no big deal!'

Pete wasn't satisfied. 'What if you get evicted? Then what?'

I shrugged. 'I'll come home, I suppose. Or I'll go somewhere else, with Samantha.'

'The famous Samantha. When am I going to meet her?'

At that exact moment, I heard the front door close, and soft footsteps on the stairs, pauses where the feet stepped over the broken ones. I knew the sound of her tread, like I knew the sound of the beat of her heart and the number of freckles on her nose. 'Now, by the sound of it.'

I couldn't help glancing at my watch. Almost midnight. She'd been AWOL for more than three hours.

Samantha burst into the room, a crumpled cigarette tucked behind her ear and her hair a wild mess at the back of her head, as if she'd been asleep for hours. Or, as Dad used to say, 'dragged through a hedge backwards'.

'Honey! Well done *you*,' she drawled, rushing over to me and hugging me in the effusive way she always did, the way that ensured no other hug would ever compare.

'Was it OK?' I asked, ever anxious for her approval. The hug may have been big, but the words sounded patronising to my insecure ears.

She kissed me full on the lips. 'It was fine, for a first gig.'

This was not the high praise I'd hoped for, and my face must have fallen.

'Mez, that's bollocks. It was brilliant!' Pete sat up and glared at Samantha, the flickering flame of the oil lamps casting weird shadows across his face.

He obviously wasn't going to take it well, then. Part of me was impressed that he'd worked it out so quickly. We hadn't snogged in front of him, so how did he know Samantha wasn't just a friend? While intuitive in many practical ways, when it came to emotions and love, he could be remarkably slow on the uptake.

'You must be Pete! I've heard *so* much about you. I'm Samantha. Delighted to meet you.' She stuck out her hand and subjected him to her highest-watt, most cornfed smile.

To my dismay and horror, Pete completely dissed her. He stared at her for a moment, as if she was some sort of alien, got up from the mattress and acting as if she wasn't even there, turned to me. 'Where's the loo? I'm dying for a slash. If you even have a bog in this dump – or do you just piss out of a window?'

He stomped out of the room before I'd had time to answer, and for a moment Samantha and I just stared at each other.

'Wow,' she said contemptuously. 'You didn't tell me he was a homophobic prick.'

'He's not!' I replied hotly. 'He must have just ... worked it out, and it's a shock for him because I'm his sister. He'll come round.'

Samantha pouted and put a hand on her hip. 'What, so I have to suck up to him till he forgives me for turning his precious twin into a nasty dyke like me? He can go screw himself!'

I'd never heard her talk like that before. She was occasionally terse when she had PMT, but this was a new and very unwelcome tone.

'Samantha, what's the matter?' I asked. 'Where have you been all evening, babe? We missed you after our set.'

Samantha plucked the cigarette from behind her ear, stuck it between her lips, squatted down on her haunches and picked up the matchbox from the floor. Her spotty dress had some kind of net under-skirt that bunched out around her. I wondered where she'd got it from – I'd never seen them before; neither the dress nor the petticoat. Not for the first time, I realised how little I knew about her. How did she have the cash for new clothes?

I waited, but she didn't speak, just sucked on her cigarette.

'Nice dress, by the way. That new?'

Still no answer. Then, 'What's it to you?'

I was flabbergasted. 'Pardon?'

'*Pardon?*' she mimicked, and I felt tears of confusion spring into my eyes. It had been the best night of my life, and now she and Pete were ruining it.

'Don't you sodding talk to my sister like that.' Pete was back – there must have been someone in the bathroom. He stood in the doorway glowering at us both. Samantha got to her feet in one lithe moment, squaring up to him.

'Pete! What the fuck?'

He approached her and with a forefinger jabbed her in the chest, above her right breast. She growled – an actual low growl of rage.

Then he turned to me. 'You're sleeping with her, aren't you?'

'We're in love,' I said defensively, and Pete snorted.

I put my hand on his arm but he shook it off. The three of us were standing in a small circle around the oil lamp, angry elves around a magic toadstool. A poisonous toadstool, I thought, drunkenly.

I took a deep breath. 'Pete, I realise this is a bit of a shock. Perhaps I should've told you first, but I wanted you to meet Samantha...' My voice wobbled. 'Please don't judge her – us – until you know her better. I'm so happy, Pete, honestly. I've never been happier.'

Pete looked me in the face. Suddenly, and for the first time, he seemed so much older than me. There was sadness as well as anger in his eyes.

'Yeah, you really look it right now.'

Samantha lunged for him then, eyes narrowed, cigarette still in the corner of her mouth. I had to put my arms round her waist from behind and drag her away from him, kicking and screaming so loudly that Webbo and Marsh appeared in the doorway, their eyes bloodshot and their movements sluggish.

'What's going on?'

Samantha wrestled her way out of my grip, grabbed her still-full rucksack and pushed past the boys. 'I'm gonna leave you *children* to it,' she said coldly. 'Seeya, Meredith. It's been real, but I've got more important things to do with my life.'

I was reeling. Surely she couldn't mean what it sounded like she meant?

'Samantha! Stay. Please!' I moved towards her, but Pete held my forearm, then hugged me so tightly that I couldn't extricate myself before I heard the bang of the front door.

Samantha was gone.

几

Webbo and Marsh sloped away, leaving Pete to deal with me. He tried to comfort me, but I was too drunk and distraught, and I lashed out at him.

'This is your fault! You wound her up and now she's gone!'

'Mez, if that's how easily wound-up she gets, you don't want to hang around with her.'

I made furious speech marks with my fingers. 'I don't "hang around" with her. We were – are – in a relationship! Why is that so hard for you to accept? We've been together for over a year!'

I refused to allow myself to consider that Samantha had been AWOL for at least three-quarters of this time.

Pete slumped back on my mattress, looking utterly shell-shocked. It was a surprise, for both of us – we almost never argued. But at that moment I wanted to punish him, make him feel the same pain I was feeling. He scrubbed the back of his hand across his eyes but I couldn't tell if he was crying. Even in my fury, I hoped not. I'd never seen him cry, not since we were little kids. He hadn't even cried at Dad's funeral.

'I didn't want to tell you this, Mez, but I saw her earlier. She was in the pub garden when I arrived, kissing that girl with the black hair, when you were on stage. I didn't think that much of it, apart from the fact I've never seen girls snogging before so, you know, I noticed. That's why I was frosty with her when she showed up here.'

'I don't believe you,' I sobbed, although of course I did. Deep down I'd known all along, as soon as I saw Samantha look at that girl. I just couldn't bear to admit it.

'Oh, come on. You think I'd make up something like that? Of course I wouldn't!'

'You just can't cope with me being gay.'

'THIS IS NOT ABOUT ME!' he yelled, suddenly as furious as I was. 'Why can't you just stop blaming me? In fact, why can't you think about someone other than yourself for a change? You just walk out, leave me to cope with Mum, who's in a right state by the way, not that you give a shit. You haven't even asked how she is!'

'I talk to her!' I shouted back. 'I ring her once a week!'

'Whoop-de-doo,' said Pete. 'You ring her for five minutes once a week from a phone box and think you've done your duty; but every single day of the week I have to deal with her crying her eyes out. She misses Dad like crazy, and now she has to worry about you too, living on your own, dropping out of school, moving in with people she's never met and knows nothing about. Now I can see why you haven't told her anything about them, because they're a bunch of druggy, benefit-scrounging losers, aren't they?'

He did at least drop his voice when he said that, but I was in too much of a frenzy to do the same.

'How dare you talk about my friends like that! You know what, why don't you just fuck off back to Salisbury? Go running back to Mum and tell her what a mess I'm making of my life. I'm sure you'll take great pleasure in it. I wish you'd never come!'

'Oh, and here comes the self-pity. That's predictable. OK, well, fine.

I'll go. And don't worry, I won't tell Mum anything that will stress her out even more than she already is. You just carry on, pleasing yourself and letting everyone else pick up the pieces. You always do.'

He hauled himself off the mattress and picked up his backpack and sleeping bag and for the second time that night, someone I loved walked out of my life.

'Oh, and by the way,' was his parting shot. 'You aren't even gay. You're just *weak*.'

ப

It would be eleven years before I next saw him, and I never saw Samantha again. I never had another gay relationship, either. So as much as I resented him saying what he said, I guess he was right.

34

Present Day

Gemma

Gemma drove up to the main gates of the estate for the second time that day and switched off the car engine. It was a perfect English summer's evening, everything an even more vibrant green than usual after the earlier thunderstorm, sheep grazing placidly in the field outside the estate, all the previous humidity replaced by a cool, brisk breeze.

She had been home to pack an overnight bag, then back to the station to finish writing up her daily report, and to inform Mavis and Lincoln that she was relocating to Minstead for a few days.

It was 6.00 p.m. precisely, the time she'd asked Meredith to get the security guard to let her in. She craned her neck to look through the tall wrought-iron gates to the house, thinking back to Mavis's earlier words: 'Let's hope you can get some significant intel off of her, or there'd be no need for you to be there. I mean, it's pretty secure, isn't it? Security twenty-four/seven, a locked gate, fence around the perimeter...'

'I'm going in as her FLO, not her bodyguard,' Gemma had said, trying not to shudder at the words 'off of'. She had once, during a dull stake-out, compiled a mental top ten of irritating things Mavis said, and 'off of' was definitely in the top three. 'She's just lost two people close to her.'

'Why don't you just go in tomorrow? You'll only have a few hours with her tonight.'

'I wish I could. But she doesn't want to be on her own, and her brother's busy tonight. She specifically asked if I could come now, and she doesn't strike me as the needy type.'

'How did she seem, in herself, when you were talking to her? Doesn't sound like she's coping.'

'No, I don't think she is. She sounded scared. She admitted that she thinks the same person who killed both of them only did it to get at her, after what happened to her in the nineties. It's just a case of trying to figure out if she's got reason to believe it, or if she's just being paranoid. Lots of people who've been in the public eye – people who've never been through anything like what she went through – are paranoid too.'

'Or lying,' Mavis said, darkly. 'We can't rule that out yet, either. But, assuming she didn't do it, *somebody* killed Ralph Allerton and Andrea Horvath. It's pretty unlikely that it was two separate random murderers.'

'I know,' Gemma said, taking the keys of a pool car off a peg and signing them out. 'Leave it to me. I'll report in to the guv later.'

'Give me a bell too, let me know. And ... look after yourself, Gemma,' said Mavis, much to her astonishment.

⊓⊔

An elderly uniformed man on a golf buggy finally drove up on the other side of the gates, heaved himself off it, came towards her, and fumbled with the large padlock.

'Hello. DC Gemma McMeekin,' she said after he'd hauled open the gates, holding her hand out through the window. 'Thanks for coming to meet me.'

The guard shook it. His hand was fat, with a calloused palm, and he smiled at her with a mouthful of teeth so yellow and crooked that it made her happy she had braces.

'George. Good of you to be 'ere to keep an eye on our Meredith. I'd do it meself, like, but I've got to do me rounds. Can't be everywhere at once, can I? But, I tell you, this is a bloody terrible business. The thought of it. Nothing like that's never happened 'ere in all thirty years I bin 'ere. Shall I show you to the cottage?'

Gemma explained that she'd already been there once today, so George locked the gates again and drove off with a sombre nod, his buggy making a loud whining noise. It reminded Gemma of her mum's sewing machine, when you tried to press the treadle but the needle was jammed in the material and wouldn't move.

There was a team of gardeners turning over the soil in an empty border on the far side of a lawn, white marble statues flanking them like the weeping angels in an old episode of *Doctor Who,* but Gemma's attention was mostly on the stunning view, layers of violet hills in the distance. No wonder Lady Whatshername had wanted to build her home here.

She parked in the staff car park and retraced her steps down to the cottage. A flowerbed by the downstairs window was bursting with hollyhocks in various pastel shades. Gemma hadn't noticed it earlier in the pouring rain.

'Hi again. Nice not to arrive drenched this time,' Gemma said, dumping her bag on a chair and inspecting Meredith's face. She looked a bit more composed than she had earlier, but her already-pale skin still bore the greenish tint of stress and shock.

'Come on through, I'll put the kettle on. I'm just making dinner – stew. It's almost ready. You're not a vegetarian, are you?'

'Great,' said Gemma. 'And no. I'll eat anything.' She gazed at two framed prints on the wall – cats wearing glasses superimposed against a background of dictionary entries. Like many of the objects and much of the decor in the cottage and, Gemma reflected, on Pete's boat, they could easily look naff in a different context, but here they actually weren't at all. That purple velvet chaise-longue had seen better days, and the Chinese rug looked faded and threadbare.

'It's a gorgeous cottage. I wish I lived somewhere like this.' Gemma followed her into the kitchen, admiring the potted orchids on every surface and ledge. It was instantly about ten degrees hotter in there, a warm fug of cooking meat that made Gemma's stomach rumble. 'My flat's in a block of identical ones, built twenty years ago. It's like they were intended to have no character whatsoever. But it was all I could afford.'

Meredith made a noncommittal noise and clicked open the latch on the door next to the sink, revealing a small utility room, where she opened a drawer and removed a clean dishcloth.

A cat had been lying curled up on a pile of clean laundry on top of a dryer, but when it saw Meredith, it jumped up and ran into the kitchen, leaving a circle of black fur on the top white towel.

'That's actually not even my cat,' Meredith said, crossly. 'He comes in through the cat flap and waits till he can get onto a bed. He's called Gavin. He's actually the house cat, but he seems to prefer it here.'

Gemma laughed. 'Gavin! Excellent name.'

Meredith dried two mugs and threw in tea bags. 'Ralph named him.' Her voice sounded strangled. 'Just got to mash these spuds then we're done. Would you like a glass of wine as well as the tea?'

'No thanks, I'm fine,' said Gemma, although she'd have loved one. She was feeling strangely unsettled. She'd had numerous previous FLO postings, but never one to a solo woman, and never overnight. She couldn't shake the faint feeling that rather than being assigned to Meredith, she, Gemma, was more like a foster child – or an exchange student – than the one who was meant to be taking charge of the situation; it was as if she needed Meredith, rather than the other way around. Although of course, she did need Meredith. The investigation needed Meredith.

Meredith needed to be kept safe.

35

1992
Meredith

That April evening was one of the highlights of my life ... until it was ruined. It was certainly the pinnacle of the band's trajectory. It was what we had all fantasised about since our days in the squat, nine years previously. *Secretly* fantasised about. None of us ever articulated it, beyond a vague 'we want to get the message out' and an earnest agreement that, should we ever hit the big time, we would use the money to help the needy. But we'd come such a long way since the days of really having a message, of ranting about consumerism and elitism and cronyism. Perhaps if we had been more honest we would have admitted the truth: *Yeah, and obviously it would be great to be millionaires too.*

Our progress had been slow and steady, but what Cohen had worked and argued and sacrificed for finally paid off. All those circuits of the country in the knackered, old red van; the student unions and pubs and crappy festivals; the flexi-discs and home-printed T-shirts, building up our rabidly loyal fanbase, Goth by Goth.

That momentous evening saw the launch of our album, our third, but the first of a new deal with a major label, and said label had pushed the boat right out. They'd given us a five-million-pound advance for it, so they had to make sure they did all they could to recoup it – and the marketing and promotional spend started with the launch.

It sounded a lot, five million, we all agreed, almost sheepishly. And it was, of course. We rationalised it by pointing out that those were the days of stupid advances. Bowie and U2 got close to forty million for deals in the late eighties and early nineties.

The launch was held in a swanky recording studio venue in Chiswick, the live room decorated with huge floor-to-ceiling black-and-white photographs of each of us. People milled around – other popstars, looking haughty and vaguely peed off that they weren't the centre of attention. Journalists, TV celebrities and record-company staff from bigwigs to postroom boys had all just started arriving. The plan was to do an exclusive full playback of the new album, once enough free champagne had been circulated, followed by us performing an acoustic version of the first single, 'Old Boys' Club'.

Marsh was grumbling about the champagne and 'fuckin' ridiculous canapés' that a dozen besuited waiters were offering on silver trays. 'It's not right,' he kept saying.

'Oh, chill out, Marsh,' Webbo said, swigging back a full glass of fizz. 'We've been over this a thousand times. The more well-known we are, the more of a platform we have to effect change.'

I took a glass of orange juice from a passing waiter's tray. I didn't like champagne, and didn't want to drink anything alcoholic before we performed to such a starry and select crowd. Even though it was just one acoustic number, I wanted to give the best performance I'd ever given.

'Or,' I said, 'we could've done a press release saying that we were offered this big swanky launch with ten grand's worth of booze and cocktail sausages, but we turned it down and gave the dosh to homeless people. That'd get us publicity, right?'

'Might do,' said Marsh, lighting up his rollie and using an empty glass as an ashtray, 'but it's a bit *late* now.'

'Shame,' said Spike. 'It's a top idea. Wish we'd have thought of it earlier.'

The boys, once more, all looked slightly sheepish. I knew that our huge advance didn't sit well with many of our fans either, who'd been very vociferous about it – sending letters written in green ink to the *NME* about how we'd sold out, and so on. But as Iain McKinnon, our new marketing manager, explained, the size of the advance had a direct correlation with how much the company would promote us, so in terms of giving our music the best possible chance to reach a big audience, it was the one thing that could ensure our worldwide success.

'Give the money away if you don't want it, hey?' he'd said, his smooth forehead furrowed with confusion at the idea that anybody would be that insane.

In the end we all agreed to make sizeable donations to charity, and I actually did it. I wasn't a hundred percent sure that the boys had got around to it yet, but that was for their consciences to worry about. None of my business. Marsh bought his parents a new three-piece suite, so perhaps that was his idea of 'giving back'.

They were here tonight – a nice middle-aged couple, her in pearls and twinset, him in slacks and a tie, standing awkwardly against the wall, drinking juice and looking nervous whenever a waiter appeared with canapés. 'You should talk to your mum and dad,' I chided, poking Marsh in the side.

He rolled his eyes. 'Man, it's so embarrassing they're even here. I didn't think they'd really come when I invited them. They hardly ever leave Northamptonshire.'

'You're lucky to have them,' I said wistfully.

I was the only member of the band who didn't have anyone there to support me. Webbo and Spike were both with their girlfriends, and at least Marsh *had* a mum and dad to be there, even if he was mortified by them. Despite the fact she'd turned out to be a two-timing bitch, I had a flash of wishing Samantha could be there to see us. But Marsh had heard on the grapevine that she'd gone back to the States and was now working at a Californian university as a lecturer in English literature.

Mum had passed away two years ago from a sudden stroke. I'd been on tour in Japan at the time, Cohen's first international tour, supporting Radiohead, and I hadn't even been able to come home for the funeral. I tried to explain to Pete on the phone, but he'd just shouted at me – the same old stuff: how selfish I was, how I never thought of anyone but myself, until I slammed down the phone.

I hadn't spoken to him since. The band were my only family now.

Once everyone had downed a few drinks, Ray Newton-Berry, the company MD, gave an effusively OTT speech about Cohen and our 'incredible' first album for the label, how honoured they were to be releasing it, how he was sure it was going to be a worldwide smash, how delighted they all were to be working with us ... blah, blah, blah. Marsh was staring at his shoes, Matty and Webbo were smirking delightedly at each other and Spike was examining the end of a dreadlock between his fingers, twirling it like a little girl fiddling with a ringlet. All the while, a photographer discreetly snapped away at us, standing under our huge monochrome portraits on the walls. We weren't asked if we would like to speak – which was fine by me – then the album was duly played out at top volume through the studio's sound system. I had to admit it sounded pretty amazing, and I could tell from everyone else's expressions that they thought the same, as they whooped and hollered with genuine enthusiasm between every track. When it was over, Ray got back up and announced, to yet more ecstatic applause, that we would perform 'Old Boys' Club'.

Marsh heaved up the string bass hc was playing on this pared-down version, and Webbo sat down with the bongos rammed between his knees. Spike and Matty slung their guitars round their necks, and I took my place at the microphone, taking a few belly breaths as the boys began the intro.

Some songs just flowed out of me on a river of emotion, and that was one of them. It wasn't a sad song, but it resonated deeply; a tale of privilege versus hardship and poverty; a postcode lottery in which plenty was given to the few but denied to the many. You could have heard a pin drop in the room as I howled out the chorus. Even the too-cool-for-school celebs and supermodels were transfixed. When we finished, there was a second's silence, then a roar of approval, far more genuine than the applause at the start.

I felt a moment of pure happiness – followed instantly by a stab of grief so deep I wanted to double over.

I wanted Pete to be there, clapping. I wanted Mum to be wiping away a tear of pride, just like Mrs Marsh over there. I wanted Dad to be nodding slowly and appreciatively. I wanted someone to give me a huge hug, in the way that Spike's girlfriend was embracing him.

So it was with a mixture of delight and a dragging sense of loss in my belly that I left the venue a couple of hours later, walking with the boys through the studio doors and along a short pathway to the pavement, where the uniformed drivers of several executive cars waited to whisk us home.

That was when it happened, as we were all milling around, ignoring the paparazzi gathered outside the gates.

Later, I remembered it was a balmy evening – the sort of June night England does so well, when the air was warm yet still fresh and redolent with the scent of petrol, fast food and cut grass.

I'd just been chatting to Webbo, discussing when we'd next meet and what a great night it had been, when a huge and sudden howl of rage made us both swing around, jerking our heads with shock. The security guard at the studio doors started to bolt down the path, but he wasn't quick enough: a bulky person in a clown mask leaped out, literally from the bushes he'd been hiding in a few feet away, we realised later, and threw something. At me.

I saw a flash of lime green and put my arm up over my eyes, just in time as it transpired, before I was completely drenched with paint flung from a five-litre can. The assailant's aim was deadly accurate; there was barely a square inch of me that he hadn't coated. Thankfully I had managed to protect my eyes, but it was in my open mouth, my nostrils and ears, deafening and humiliating me. Bright green, stinking, dripping off me, splattering everyone in a seven-foot radius.

Later, I remembered the gasp that went up, followed immediately by shouts and uproar, and the click-click-click of the camera shutters as the delighted paparazzi got the scoop of a lifetime. I remembered the balmy London night smell was eradicated in a second, replaced by the oily pungent stink of gloss paint – it was gloss; the bastard wanted it to be almost impossible to get off. The venue staff had to call an ambulance and take me away to make sure it hadn't poisoned my blood. You couldn't just wash off gloss paint, as I discovered – the hard way.

The A&E nurses were amazing. They stripped me off and sponge-bathed me with white spirit, which was cold and stung like buggery, three of them wiping me down as fast as possible to minimise the exposure to both the paint and the astringently toxic white spirit. I was too shocked to cry, but all I was thinking about was Pete.

I yearned for my twin then, with a longing stronger than I'd felt in all the years since we'd fallen out. I'd have rung him then and there and begged him to come and see me, thrown myself on his mercy, apologised till the green on my face turned to blue, but I was too busy vomiting into a cardboard kidney bowl.

The paint was so difficult to get out of my hair that I told them to just shave it off. All of it. I didn't want it.

I'd have got them to shave my skin off too, if they could.

Everything was ruined.

From the peak straight into the trough.

⊓⊔

Spike and Webbo came to the hospital with me that night – Marsh had to take his folks to their hotel and Matty had apparently crashed out somewhere, too stoned to be any use. After my hosing-down, we gave statements to the police in a small, private visitors' room. They had to keep the windows wide open, because even after a long, hot shower to wash off all the white spirit, my skin still stank of it to the point that the fumes were making everyone else feel slightly dizzy too.

It was in every pore. I felt as if the spirit and the paint were coating my internal organs too, as if I'd been glossed inside and out. My scalp was the only place that felt clean, and I kept obsessively rubbing my newly bald head. I was dressed in paper knickers, braless in hospital scrubs and borrowed flip-flops, my launch-party black dress now in an incinerator somewhere. I felt like a convict.

'They've caught him, right?' Spike demanded when the two policemen turned up.

But it turned out they hadn't. And they never did. My assailant had dropped the paint can and legged it before anyone, even the security guard, had managed to catch him. He'd been wearing gloves, so there were no retrievable fingerprints, and no description other than a vague 'six feet tall with broad shoulders' – no idea of ethnicity or age or anything. The recording studio was in a residential area, so he could've disappeared into any front garden to hide, or into a waiting getaway car. It wasn't a murder or even serious GBH, and the cops clearly weren't going to deploy the resources to try and find him.

Everyone assumed it was an aggrieved fan protesting at our perceived sell-out. Although, even then, I thought differently. The attacker hadn't shouted anything. Those sorts of protests weren't usually solo; they were carried out by small groups not afraid to let their grievances be known. The point of protest was that there *was* a point.

As it turned out, I wasn't wrong. The paint incident was just the start of a whole campaign of harassment that, on numerous occasions, made me wish I had never joined the band in the first place. Anonymous vitriolic letters, vandalism of the tour bus, violent threats to my safety – always mine, never the boys – until we had to have 24/7 security whenever we went anywhere; the cost of extra security at our gigs almost made it financially unviable for us to play in the UK.

The worst thing was the fear. The cold finger of dread on my spine, which had me constantly looking over my shoulder, unable ever to fully enjoy the buzz of playing stadiums and appearing on *Top of the Pops,* always thinking the masked assailant was out there, waiting to pounce, next time maybe with a knife or a gun.

I hated him for this. He ruined what ought to have been the most incredible time of my life.

The threats stopped as abruptly as they'd started – a year or so after the green-paint incident, but my fear and sense of foreboding never went away.

With good reason, as it turned out.

36

Present Day

Gemma

Gemma sat on the faded velvet sofa in Meredith's front room, propped herself up with cushions and opened her laptop.

'Can I have your wifi code, please, Meredith?' she called. If she was honest, it was kind of nice to be neither at home nor in the strip-lit office, which was always redolent of poor aftershave choices and testosterone. This room smelled of lavender and summer.

'Here you go,' Meredith said, returning with a small sticker on which were printed the relevant details.

Gemma thanked her, typed them in, then Googled *Merry Heather + Cohen*. While she had already found Meredith in the system, she knew little about her career as a popstar, nor about her fellow band members.

There was a Wikipedia entry about the band, which Gemma read through – a long list of chart singles and albums, the various changes of line-up after Meredith left suddenly in 1995, links to articles endlessly discussing the reasons why she might have quit so abruptly, statements from a spokesperson from her record company saying that she had left the country indefinitely for 'personal reasons'. There were also a lot of photos and reports of an incident in which Meredith had had paint thrown over her; Gemma made a mental note to speak to her about it. Nobody seemed to have made a connection between this and the abduction, three years later. She clicked back to the Google search results, and something caught her eye – a link from a site called TMZ, which Gemma knew was a celebrity gossip site: 'The Mystery of Merry Heather – Solved at Last?'

Her breath caught in her throat. How had nobody spotted this? Clicking on the article, she saw an old photo of Meredith, much younger and thinner, and in full stage make-up, accepting a BRIT Award, with an inset video still of a smarmy-looking man. The banner underneath read: 'Breaking News – Record Company Exec Iain McKinnon Speaks Out.' She clicked on the video.

'I can't say much,' said this Iain bloke self-importantly, looking like he was dying to say everything. 'Just that I have exclusive information that Merry Heather has been back in the UK for some time, living a very different life in rural Surrey, and currently considering a summer reunion with Cohen. Obviously this is most exciting, but I'm not at liberty to disclose the details until contracts have been finalised. It would be Cohen's first performance in twenty years, and their first with the original line-up in over twenty-five. I'm sure Merry is dying to get back in the spotlight again! Working in a gift shop in a stately home is very far from what she does best.'

A brief shadow crossed his face as if he knew he'd said too much, and the interviewer, off-camera, pounced, demanding, 'She works in a *shop*? In a stately home? Merry Heather? Which stately home? Has she said why she left the band so suddenly all those years ago?'

Iain McKinnon smirked guiltily and gave a dismissive wave of his hand. 'As I'm sure you appreciate, I can't divulge that information. Merry's privacy is very important to us.'

The video ended abruptly, and Gemma sat back on her pillows, bewildered. A reunion? That couldn't be right, surely. The thought of Meredith on stage again was almost laughable. The woman couldn't even bear to mention the band, let alone want to rejoin it.

She peered at the date on the article – last August, almost a year ago. If someone had really wanted to discover Meredith's whereabouts and go about making her life a misery, it wouldn't be that difficult. How many stately homes – with gift shops – were there in Surrey? Quite a few, but not so many that it would be difficult to figure out which one she ran. A handful of phonecalls would probably do it; or a lot of visits to country piles.

Gemma hadn't realised there had been a big mystery around why Meredith dropped out of the band all those years ago. But why would she? She'd been five years old in 1995. She barely even remembered Kurt Cobain.

Her thoughts returned to the scar on Meredith's hand, the hooded expression in her eyes whenever anybody asked her any questions about the past. Gemma had just sort of assumed that the woman had got fed up with being in the public eye, as she herself would very quickly. Gemma couldn't imagine anything worse than being hassled wherever she went, photographers lurking in corners to leap out at her, long-lensed, capturing her least flattering angles. She imagined being in the *Daily Mail*'s Sidebar of Shame, pictured all sweaty leaving the gym, or caught having a row with her ex, Rich, shouting puce-faced in a park at him, under the caption: 'Gemma McMeekin in Screaming Argument with Boyfriend!'

She shuddered, closed the laptop and wandered through to the kitchen in socked feet, delicious smells of lamb and rosemary wafting through to her from the Aga. Meredith was laying a tiny table with knives and forks. A jam jar of fresh bright-blue cornflowers had been placed in the middle and an uncorked bottle of red sat on the counter with two empty glasses next to it.

Meredith looked up and caught Gemma looking longingly at it. 'Hi. I know you said you didn't want to drink as you're on duty, but it's there if you want to. I'm going to have one. At *least* one.'

'It smells delicious.'

'It's just a lamb stew. You do eat meat, don't you?' Meredith said it in a way that implied *tough shit if you don't.*

'Yeah.' Gemma had already told her this, just a few minutes ago.

'Good. I'll dish up then. Have a seat.'

Gemma sat down, mentally rehearsing the questions she wanted to ask. 'Um, Meredith, I didn't know you were planning a reunion with your band?' Perhaps a bit abrupt to kick off with, she thought, but she wanted to see what reaction it got.

Meredith had just turned to stir the stew with a ladle, ready to spoon it onto plates, but she froze; her back to Gemma, so Gemma couldn't see the expression on her face.

'I'm fucking well not. Not in a million years. What makes you think that?'

Gemma felt alarmed at the vehemence of her tone. That was a reaction all right.

'I saw something on line. A video interview with some record company guy – Iain McSomething – who claims you are. Or were, last year.'

Meredith dropped the ladle back into the pan, stew splattering with a sizzle over the Aga's hotplates. When she turned round, her face was green with shock. '*What*? Show me.'

'I'll get my laptop. Hold on.'

Gemma galloped back into the front room and grabbed the laptop. When she re-entered the kitchen ten seconds later, Meredith had filled a glass of red to the brim and was sitting, legs splayed, on one of the kitchen chairs, swigging at it. Her eyes were pink and she was blinking furiously. 'I'm not crying,' she said. 'I'm *livid*. How fucking dare he?'

Gemma navigated back to the TMZ clip. 'I think he let it slip,' she said as they watched in silence. 'Look at his face when he says it. I'm sure he didn't mean to.'

'He hired a private detective to find me,' Meredith said in a strained voice.

'You knew?'

'I knew he wanted me to do these stupid gigs, because he found my phone number and rang me up last year. I told him where to stick his offer, obviously. But I can't believe he then let it go out on the internet as if it was actually a done deal! He's the most arrogant dickhead I've ever met. He was, twenty-five years ago, and he still is. I just can't believe it. Can I sue him? Let me see that again.'

They watched the clip a second time, Meredith's face a mask as she stared intently at it. Gemma kept glancing at her. She was glad she was here with the woman. Meredith increasingly seemed like someone who really did need protecting.

'I guess it's lucky that other media outlets didn't pick up on it,' Gemma said gently. 'It could have been worse. But ... if someone has been looking for you for years and they've seen this, it might have given them the clue they've needed to track you down.' The unspoken words 'and start killing your friends' seemed to hang between them like a miasma.

'Do you remember anybody ringing the shop to ask if Merry Heather worked there, or anything like that? Anything out of the ordinary at all? Any of your staff mentioning that someone was asking questions or hanging around?'

Meredith shook her head. On the Aga the stew had begun to bubble ferociously. She stood up slowly, picked up the oven gloves and lifted the pot off the burner. 'Don't want it to stick,' she said. 'Do you mind if we eat a bit later? I've lost my appetite.'

'That's fine,' said Gemma, 'but please think hard. We can't ignore this. I'll need to let M— ... Mark, I mean DI Davis, know.'

She stammered over his name, almost calling him Mavis.

'I can't remember anything like that happening, no. But if it was someone who found me based on this – why didn't they kill *me*? Why kill Ralph and Andrea? Or...' she swallowed, '...Pete, God forbid, if they're after people close to me? And why now?'

The two women gazed at one another. Gemma wanted to reassure her, but found she couldn't. 'We don't know that Pete isn't in danger,' she said, absolutely dying to pour herself a glass of the wine. Red stained her braces though, she reminded herself, but it didn't stop the craving. 'Or you. We have to work out who's done this and stop them, before it escalates any further. There's something else I've been meaning to ask you: the night Ralph went missing, Pete came to "pick you up" to go for a drink. But he doesn't have a car, does he?'

'He's got a van, for his furniture deliveries,' said Meredith slowly. 'But yes, that night he was on his bike.'

'So why did you say he was picking you up? Why not just meet him at the pub in the village, near his workshop?'

There was a long silence. Finally, Meredith raised her eyes to Gemma's. 'There's something I have to tell you,' Meredith blurted, leaning back against the kitchen counter. 'I didn't before, because ... well, you'll see why ... but...'

'What?' Gemma was concerned that Meredith was going to pass out. Beads of sweat had popped onto her brow. 'Sit down, Meredith. I'm worried about you. What is it?'

Meredith paused then spoke in a gabble, as if the faster she said the words, the less impact they'd have.

'I had sex with Ralph on the evening he went missing. We were both pissed. I regretted it straight away and went home, but when I got back here I realised I'd lost my key – it had fallen out of my pocket. I went back for it and he was dead on the floor. I must have been the last person to see him alive ... apart from whoever killed him.'

'*What?*'

'I did CPR on him for ages, but nothing. I panicked. I thought he'd had a heart attack. I knew it was too late to call an ambulance so I rang Pete instead, because I was in a state. He came over – on his bike because the van was in the garage. I took him to where it happened, and we were going to ring the police then, but when I got there, the body was gone. Someone took it, and they must have dumped it in the pond that night. Then I found him the following week. I'm sorry, I'm so sorry. I know I should've said something before, but Paula ... Paula's my friend. I just couldn't risk her thinking I had anything to do with it, because I didn't, at least not intentionally. I think the same person killed Andrea. And whoever it was might have found out where I live and work because of that twat Iain McKinnon, and now everything's ruined and I'm scared and I don't know what to do...'

Gemma just gaped at her for a moment. When she'd hoped that going in as a FLO would encourage Meredith to open up about stuff she might have been hiding, she never in a million years expected *this*.

This changed everything.

'Meredith ... I'm sorry ... I'm going to have to arrest you for withholding vital evidence. It's unlikely you'll be charged, but ... You do understand, don't you?'

Meredith nodded, eyes downcast. She seemed almost relieved.

37

1995
Meredith

I'd always had a terror of being broken into at night; it stemmed from my childhood, after Mum, Dad, Pete and I once came home to a burgled house after a holiday. It was when Pete and I were about thirteen. The glass in the back door had been smashed and the lock forced, and all our stuff was strewn about the place. All Mum's jewellery had been taken, and our television. Worst of all, the burglar had taken a huge runny shit on the carpet in Pete's bedroom. The police told us at the time that this was not uncommon. The stress of breaking in made the intruder's bowels loose, and opening them on the floor was their little calling card. I was secretly relieved that it hadn't happened in *my* bedroom – I'd never have been able to sleep in there again. I think that was partly why I liked living in the squat – security may not have been tight, but I was never there on my own.

After the green-paint incident and all the other threatening things that happened, that little lump of fear started growing out of control. I imagined it like a ball of elastic bands inside me, more and more individual fears being stretched over it until it felt as if it was pushing all my internal organs out of the way to accommodate it, squashing the breath out of me, compressing my heart so it could only manage wing-flutters instead of proper beats.

I'd honestly have stayed in the squat if I could, even after we signed our record contract, but the police and property developers launched a dawn raid one day soon after our second album came out. Using police helicopters and riot gear and dogs, they evicted everyone. Fortunately

we were all away on the road at the time, so we had our meagre possessions with us. It was our neighbours who bore the brunt of it. The raid
made the papers: 'Europe's Largest Squat Evicted: Famous Residents
Include Band Cohen'.

The boys and I rented a flat together for a year or so after that, but
as we amassed more royalties and had more success, one by one they
drifted off to buy their own houses with their girlfriends and wives.
Then, after we got our big advance, I felt I might as well do the same.
Put down some roots, finally. I couldn't count on the band being
around forever.

Things changed.

So, a year or so after Cohen had its first million-selling single, I
bought a big Georgian house in a smart London street of identical
houses. Naturally, security was high on my list of priorities, and ironi-
cally, I had an appointment with a bespoke security firm to come and
fit cameras and a panic button in my bedroom. I'd booked them for a
date that turned out to be exactly a week after *it* happened. The police
did later pursue that line of enquiry, because how obvious would that
have been? Raid the house, knowing that it had no alarm. But every
member of the security company had a solid alibi.

And I knew who it was, anyway. It had to have been him – the personification of my nightmares; my paint-throwing tormentor. I was
sure of it. I'd been waiting for him, in the sweat-soaked green-painted
nightmares I'd been having ever since the album launch.

⊓⊔

I'd only been living in the house a month or so, coming and going via
the narrow, claustrophobic, weed-choked alley that ran behind it so
that nobody recognised me and realised they had a million-selling pop
star living in their street. I'd only met my immediate neighbours, both
elderly couples who didn't, as far as I was aware, have a clue who I was.

All I had at the time in the way of personal protection was a lock on
the bedroom door and a rubber wedge to jam underneath it – token

gestures that I'd naïvely thought would give me enough time at least to ring the police, should the worst happen.

It had been an unremarkable evening and I'd been feeling chilled – until Iain phoned, anyway. I remembered wandering the hallways of my magnolia-painted house, holding up swatches of every grey in existence – dove, soft, dark, pewter – wondering what combination of them to paint the walls in. I could've employed the services of an interior designer, but I didn't want to take the risk that word would get out. I was loving my solitude and seclusion. My own place. I'd come a long way since the squat.

Everything had been going so well. Cohen was at number three in the UK charts, having just slipped down from number one, where we'd been for the preceding month or so. Unless I went out with a wig and dark glasses on, I was pestered for autographs wherever I went, mostly by students and hippies. So my home was my haven; I was sure I'd managed to keep my new address hidden from the world. Even at the record label, nobody knew it – apart from the accountant who sent out my royalty statements, and, at my behest, she posted them with a fake management company name on the envelope so that nobody knew they were going to me. The band didn't have a manager – we'd never needed one. We were a collective, not a product.

Another, less credible, reason I didn't want anybody, specifically the press, to know where I lived was that Cohen's ethos was firmly anti-capitalist. I dreaded to think about the field day they'd have had when they discovered I'd recently purchased a sizeable Georgian 'mansion'. I'd struggled with the decision, but ultimately decided that I would leave it to charity in my will, if I never managed to have any children. I was still embarrassed by it, though; until that point, my terror of word getting out about the house was probably on a par with my terror at the thought of an intruder getting into it.

Despite the capitalist guilt, I loved my new home. At that point I felt much safer mid-terrace than I would have done in an isolated house in a remote village somewhere; and, once I had moved in, it went a long way to providing me with the security I lacked in any other area of my life.

Strange that I later ended up living in a cottage in the grounds of a huge country estate that was almost empty at nights; but by then I was in full recluse mode and craved the isolation. Even at the time of the break-in I was already on my way to becoming reclusive. Mum was dead and I hadn't seen Pete for more than ten years – since we had the row over Samantha, who I also never saw again after that horrible night. I had nobody except the band. But I was fine. Happy, mostly. Loving my success. I didn't even miss Pete and Samantha anymore. I didn't need anybody.

On the night of the break-in, I cooked myself a chickpea curry, watched something mindless on TV and drank one more glass of red than I ought to have, considering I'd been intending to have an alcohol-free day. My phone rang just before the ten o'clock news, and I glared at it. Who was calling me at this time of night?

When I saw that it was 'The Pointless I', I contemplated ignoring it, but I knew that he'd just keep ringing until I picked up. It infuriated me that he knew I was unlikely to be out partying.

'It's a bit late, Iain; could it wait till the morning?'

'Hello Merry, how you doing, darling?' Just from those words I could tell he was drunk.

I rolled my eyes. 'In fact, let me call you back, I'm about to—'

'Let me stop you there. Tomorrow's no good. It's tonight I'm interested in. And what I'm interested in is you and me getting together – a little nightcap, see where the mood takes us, and—'

It was my turn to cut him off. 'Iain. I'm sorry, you're a…' I couldn't bring myself to say 'great guy', '…really good marketing manager,' I finished instead. 'But I'm about to go to bed. I have no intention of any sort of nightcap with you. And I don't know why you're asking. The answer hasn't changed since the last time you propositioned me. Or the time before.'

It was becoming boring, actually, and I was sure that he only tried it because he couldn't bear the thought of any woman *not* wanting to sleep with him. I was pretty certain he didn't even fancy me. He was a good-looking man but he left me cold, with his bulgy pecs in too-tight T-shirts, overpowering aftershave and thickly oiled black hair.

'Well, there's something *pacif ... spec ... spas*,' he stumbled over the word, but I couldn't muster even a wry smile.

'Specific.'

'Yah, that. I'm round the corner from you and—'

'*You know where I live?*'

'For sure, Merry, how else do you think we know where to send your royalty statements?'

'Fuck's sake, it's supposed to be confidential!'

The thought of Iain flirting with the record company's accountant to coax it out of her made goosebumps of disgust skitter down my spine.

I imagined him out there now, swaying on a bar stool in the pub on the corner of my square, possibly even staring at my house through the mullioned bar windows.

'Like I said, Iain, I'm getting ready for bed now; there's no way I'm going out.'

'Well, don't let me stop you.' I heard the lasciviousness in his voice. Bloody men. I should've stayed gay; women were just so much *nicer*.

But then I remembered Samantha's behaviour, and thought, well, not all women.

It was as if Iain read my mind, because what he said next made me want to storm round to the pub – assuming that was where he was – and punch his Afrikaaner lights out.

'I just thought you should be aware that I'm doing you a massive favour here. You see, I've learned something about you that you're not going to want anybody else to know, and unless we're ... careful, they will find out. They will be very interested. And believe me, it would not be good for the band's image.'

I tried to sound bored, but panicked butterflies were beginning to flap inside me. 'What are you talking about, Iain?'

'I've had a letter.'

'Right. A letter from who?'

'A letter from someone who used to know you very well. Samantha Applebaum.'

At the sound of Samantha's name, the butterflies almost carved their way out of my solar plexus, their wings tiny knives. 'What did she want? Did she write to *you*?'

'Not personally, but lucky for you, it landed on my desk unopened. It was a To Whom It May Concern. Pretty snarky letter, in my opinion. She's not happy with you, is she? But more to the point ... I didn't know you were a lesbian, Merry, you sly old dog!'

'I'm bisexual,' I said, too hastily. 'Not that it's anybody's business.'

'Ah, but it is. Some would argue that it's everybody's business. And you know what all your fans would think? They'd think that you'd lied to them, by omission; that you're a fake...'

'I'm not a fake!' I realised I was almost shouting, and had to force myself to calm down. 'Why did she write?'

Iain exhaled, a great smug gleeful breath. 'She wants money. She said that unless we pay her ten grand, she's going to the papers with the story of your relationship, and how she was the reason that you're even in the band in the first place, how she was the obvious choice for lead singer but you pushed her out of the running for the job. She even provides a handy PO Box number for us to send the cheque to.'

'Evil bitch. She never even said she wanted to be in the band! She was always away. And anyway, I was just a kid...' I stopped abruptly. I didn't want to give him the satisfaction of knowing how much this was panicking me. And puzzling me, too. Surely a now-respectable university professor had better things to do?

At the back of my mind, I'd always had a fearful thought that she might have had something to do with the paint incident – paid someone to do it, perhaps. Or, knowing Samantha, egged them on.

I was terrified at the thought that Iain or anyone else might know about my past – my relationship with Samantha, and my shameful abandonment of Mum when she'd needed me most.

The weird threatening letters in green ink addressed to me care of the fan club had been scary enough, and even without the paint incident we – I – had endured more stalkerish behaviour than our peers seemed to get.

The letter from Samantha was very different.

In a way, though, I wasn't surprised we'd heard from her. Her silence all these years was what had been more surprising – she'd always been a terrible star-fucker, basking in the reflected glory of anybody even remotely famous.

'So is Big World going to pay her off?' I realised I was holding my breath.

'Well that depends. On you,' said Iain, and my heart sank. Surely he couldn't mean what I feared he did? 'We could come to a little private arrangement, you and I,' he went on, and I thought, shit, he does.

I looked at my bare toes and had to swallow hard not to vomit over them.

'So you are actually blackmailing me into having sex with you. That's classy.'

'Oh, Merry! Don't look at it like that. Let's just call it a situation where you can scratch my back, and I'll scratch yours.'

'I'll consider it. Don't even think of coming over tonight though,' I said, and hung up, shaking, before he could say anything else.

After that I pottered about, trying to calm down, cleaning up the kitchen, making a cup of tea to drink in bed. I retired upstairs, taking deep breaths in an attempt to quell the tension and fury in my solar plexus. I took a sleeping pill and eventually managed to fall asleep, mindlessly watching some terrible film with the bedroom television on a timer, as I often did when we weren't touring, gigging or promoting anything.

A noise from downstairs woke me at 2.55 a.m. – a suppressed but distinct cough. I remember jerking awake, the digital clock on my bedside table imprinting the neon-green time on my bleary, drugged retinas. Foxes often came into my garden, crashing around in the shrubbery and having screaming sex sessions, both of which activities sounded scarily human. But after that cough there was no crashing or shrieking, just an ominous silence ... and then, my heart swooping into my throat ... a creak on the stairs.

I must have imagined it. Surely I had! I swallowed hard, and my heart changed its mind and decided to try and hammer its way out of my chest instead. I switched on the bedside lamp and leaped out from under the duvet, darted across the room and carefully turned the key in the lock. And that was when I saw the door handle move, slowly and silently.

38

Present Day
Gemma

'Excuse me. I have to make a call – I'll go outside.'

Gemma left Meredith sitting in the kitchen, looking as stunned as if someone had just told her this shocking news, instead of the other way around.

She let herself out of the back door and walked a little way from the house, her heart pounding. Shit, she thought. This changed everything. She felt simultaneously furious with and sympathetic towards Meredith, for not saying anything sooner.

But then, if you shagged your mate's husband, you really wouldn't want to admit it, would you?

'Boss, sorry to call you out of hours but there's been a big development,' she said when Lincoln picked up the phone. She could hear loud music in the background, something grungy that she would never have expected Lincoln to enjoy; the Smashing Pumpkins or Nirvana or something from the nineties. He'd turned it down to a background hum before she could identify it. It could even have been Cohen.

'I'm at Meredith Vincent's cottage. She says Ralph Allerton died in an abandoned ice house in the grounds of Minstead House and that someone dumped his body in the pond later.'

She heard a splutter. Lincoln had presumably taken a swig of whatever he was drinking at the wrong moment.

'*What?*'

'Meredith Vincent just confessed to finding his body and not saying anything.'

'Why the hell not?'

'Because they got pissed at the office staff lunch the day his wife reported him missing, and had a sneaky shag after work. Meredith said he was fine when she left him in the ice house, but she realised she'd dropped her keys, and when she went back for them, he was lying on the floor, dead. She did mouth-to-mouth but he was definitely gone.'

Gemma heard Lincoln whistle with incredulity. 'Good grief. This is astonishing. Do you believe her?'

'I think so, boss. Obviously we need to bring her in, but she was clearly very fond of the man.'

'Do you think it was some sort of sex game that went wrong?'

'I don't think it was anything to do with the sex,' Gemma said. 'Though I suppose we can't rule it out. If she did strangle him while they were shagging, she'd have to be stronger than she looks.'

'And if she was all that fond of him, why did she just leave his body in there?' Lincoln mused.

'She wasn't going to, she said.' Gemma glanced over her shoulder back at the house, hoping Meredith couldn't hear her. It was so deathly quiet in these hills, sound must carry for miles. She walked a little further away, into a large walled vegetable garden – huge beds of netted strawberry plants, their delicate foliage in stark contrast with the obscenely broad leaves of the pinkening rhubarb stems in the neighbouring beds. The smell of warm fruit was intoxicating.

Gemma gave a start when she saw a figure crouching over one of the far beds. Then she realised the person was in the green uniform of Minstead House's gardening team, and they were pulling weeds out from around what looked like carrots. She couldn't tell if it was a man or woman, but they showed no signs of having noticed or overheard her, so she paced in the opposite direction.

'She rang her brother in a panic. He told her to stay put till he got there, and then they'd go back; pretend to discover Allerton "by chance" and call the police. But when they went back to the ice house, he was gone.'

'Right,' Lincoln said. 'I'll meet you at the station in an hour. We'll interview her. Let's get all the CCTV from inside the house that day, as well as any in the grounds near the ice house. I'll get someone stationed over there twenty-four/seven; it's a new crime scene. I don't want any gap in the evidence chain, now we've finally got one. Oh, and Gemma?'

'Sir?'

'Nice work, getting her to tell you that.'

Gemma returned to the cottage, her cheeks flushed the same pink as the rhubarb at DI Lincoln's praise.

Meredith was still sitting in the same position in the kitchen, her arms hanging uselessly by her sides, looking more like an old woman than she ever had before. The stew still bubbled gently on the Aga's hotplate, the soft plopping sounds somehow comforting.

She touched Meredith's shoulder gently.

'OK Meredith, we're going to have to go to the station – but I think you should eat something first. You've made this lovely stew, and all that'll be on offer down there will be some dodgy sandwiches.'

'I'm not hungry now,' Meredith said, in a dull monotone.

'I'm sure. I'm not really either – but let's try. Just a small amount. You sit there, I'll sort it.'

Gemma took two glasses down from a shelf and ran the tap to fill them with cold water, thinking how glad she was that she hadn't succumbed to the sneaky glass of Rioja she'd been tempted by just half an hour ago. Imagine Lincoln smelling it on her breath! She glanced at Meredith's wineglass – it didn't look like she'd downed any more since Gemma had been on the phone to Lincoln. That was good. It would be far from ideal if Meredith was under the influence when interviewed.

'Do I need a lawyer?' Meredith's voice was tiny and thin.

'You're not under arrest so, no, not unless you want one. We just need to get a proper record of what happened, on tape. OK?'

'OK.'

There were oven gloves on a hook near the Aga, so Gemma slotted one hand into each end, lifting the heavy iron pot off the stove and placing it on a mat on the table. Steam rushed out in a thick cloud when she took off the lid, and the smell of the succulent meat made her mouth water. She ladled a couple of spoonfuls into two bowls and handed one to Meredith, who merely gazed at it as if she didn't know what she was meant to do with it.

As Gemma hung the gloves back up, something else glove-related occurred to her:

'Can I ask you a slightly personal question, Meredith?'

Meredith shrugged, not meeting her eyes.

'Your scar ... I know Mark asked you about it before, but it's obvious that you're self-conscious about it. How come you don't wear gloves? Wouldn't that be easier for you than people staring at it all the time?'

As if to demonstrate, Meredith slid her damaged hand under her buttock on the chair; an instinctive movement.

'I used to,' she said, quietly. 'When I first got the job here. It's hard to hide it when you work in a shop. But one glove makes you look like a weirdo – I kept getting comments about Michael Jackson, or people just outright sniggered. Two gloves isn't much better – not to mention just being totally impractical. You can't use a phone, wash your hands, type – none of the things I need to do a lot of the time...'

She paused, pulled out her hand and studied the scar, turning her hand this way and that as the steam from the bowls gradually died down.

'I thought I'd get used to it, but I never have. I did plan to have reconstructive surgery – you know, a skin graft – but once I took the job here, I never got round to it, I suppose. I just learned to block out the sight of it; and I do, most of the time.'

Gemma took a seat at the table with her, digging a fork into the stew and blowing on it before putting it in her mouth. It tasted as delicious as it had smelled.

'I know what happened; how you got it,' she said carefully. It felt the right time, having broached the subject already.

Meredith's head jerked up. 'How?'

'I did a search for your name on the General Registry – sorry, our database – and saw the report about the attack on you. I'm so sorry, Meredith; it sounds like a horrific experience. A terrible thing to happen to you.'

Meredith sat completely still, glassy-eyed, and Gemma felt it would be insensitive to take another mouthful of the stew. She gently picked up Meredith's fork and placed it into her hand. 'Please, try and eat if you can.'

'I don't want anyone to know,' Meredith blurted eventually. 'It would be in the papers. I couldn't bear it all being raked up again, when I did everything to avoid people knowing last time.'

39

1995
Meredith

Someone was actually trying to get into my bedroom; a real-life horror movie. I'd locked the door, but as the intruder pushed I didn't trust the lock to hold. I wedged the rubber door stop in the gap under the door, screaming as loudly as I could.

That was when it all kicked off. The intruder shoved and rattled the door, hard this time. I rammed my foot up against the doorstop to prevent it slipping, but the person on the other side was now banging on the door panels. Why, why hadn't I put in an alarm the day I moved in? A panic button? A sturdy bolt as well as the lock and key? My telephone was on the bedside table on the far side of the bed. I had a choice – either lunge for it now and call 999, or keep my bodyweight against the door in case the lock gave way.

My elderly neighbours were all deaf, and although the houses were terraced, they were so solidly built that no noise leached through the walls. I screamed more loudly though, just in case someone heard through the window. But my bedroom was at the back of the house, not over the street.

I was wearing flowery cotton pyjamas. I remembered looking down at them and having the inane thought: I couldn't be murdered wearing flowery cotton pyjamas, I just couldn't.

The intruder kicked the door with all his force, splintering the bottom panel. With a jerk of shock I saw a huge black boot briefly appear through the hole, then withdraw. Then, worse, a black-gloved hand shot through and grabbed me in an iron-pincerlike grip around my calf, crushing the cotton flowers. When I tried to disengage it, his other hand reached through the hole too, and then he had my arm.

'Unlock this fucking door right now and stop screaming,' he hissed, 'otherwise you're a dead woman.'

I struggled but I felt like a car in a scrapyard being lifted in metal jaws, about to be crushed. He had pulled my arm through the hole, up to my shoulder, and was now twisting it backwards, threatening to dislocate it.

'Open. The. Door.'

'What do you want?' I gasped in agony, as a stream of warm urine gushed down my inner thigh and puddled on the wooden floor. 'Please stop.'

'Do as I say, bitch,' he ordered, 'or I'll snap your arm in two.'

'I can't reach the key unless you let me go,' I screamed, and he released his grip enough to allow me to twist around, but kept tight hold on my wrist.

What should I do? I had no choice. I had to open it. If I didn't, he'd destroy the door completely and break my arm. There was nowhere to run apart from into the bathroom, which didn't have any lock on the door. My phone was out of reach. Perhaps if I just gave him my jewellery and the stack of notes I kept hidden at the back of my knicker drawer, he'd go away.

Or should I just jump through the window and take my chances? No, too risky; I'd land on the flagstoned patio and probably break my neck.

I grabbed hold of the rubber doorstop and unlocked and opened the ruined door, feeling like I'd just sealed my own fate. He let go of me, just for a moment, and I pulled my arm back through the hole, pain shooting up into my neck and through my shoulder. I turned to run, planning to barricade myself inside my ensuite bathroom with the doorstop; the door of that was more solid than the original pine-panelled bedroom one. But I didn't take more than two paces before he was on me, shoving me face-down on the bed and twisting my arm up behind my back – the arm he'd already hurt. My screams were muffled by the duvet.

I'd caught a glimpse of a well-built, featureless figure: he was wearing a balaclava – not a standard-issue, ghoul-rapists black one, but bizarrely, one in dark autumnal stripes of russet, brown and green. Like someone's nan had knitted it. A nightmare personified, nonetheless.

'This will be so much easier if you fucking cooperate.' His voice was a weird combination of gruff and simultaneously high, for a man; at odds with his muscled frame.

'I will,' I mumbled, above the sound of the shriek of pain from my shoulder. The foxes had nothing on me. 'Take whatever you want. I'll tell you where it is.'

'Just you.' Then I heard the rip of gaffer tape being detached and he rolled me over, securing my arms together at the front and taping them together at the wrists. Next my head was pulled forwards off the mattress so he could wrap the tape round and round, covering my mouth. In his haste and my fight, at first he managed to cover my nose too, and I had to vigorously shake my head, trying to make him see that I'd actually die before he could do whatever the hell he wanted me to cooperate with. He must have seen me starting to turn blue, and pulled it down, away from my nostrils, kneeling astride me as he did so. He was wearing a massive, bulky waterproof black coat thing; I remember it rustled whenever he moved. He smelled of sweat and engine oil and just a whiff of patchouli.

When he knelt over me I assumed that was it: he was going to rape me.

But he didn't.

No grinding or grabbing. Instead he yanked me up by the elbow and frogmarched me to the wrecked door. 'Let's go,' he said.

As he dragged me down the stairs, fighting as much as I could, given my bound arms – why could nobody *hear*? – I had a fleeting thought, clear and sharp in the panic soup of my brain, of Keats' 'iced foot on the bottom stair'. It was from that poem I did for A level English, the one that reminded me of Dad's death. I hadn't thought of it for decades, but as I saw my own bare feet stumbling and sliding, I knew it was because I was facing my own point of no return; my very own descent into oblivion.

He bundled me, resisting all the way, out of the jemmied-open kitchen door, down the garden and out to the dark street via the alleyway. I struggled, but his meaty arms were firm around my waist, the wet-wool stink of his breath in my face. There was a Luton van backed up at the end of the alley. He pulled open the rear shutter just enough to get me inside, lifting me off my feet and stuffing me through the gap and into its black maw, then climbing in after me and slamming the door back down. Surely my neighbours would hear that? It was such a loud, metallic crashing sound, like someone hitting saucepans with metal serving spoons.

Even now, the sound of the shutter door at the rear of a van, any van, going up or down makes me weak with terror. I have to sit down and jam my head between my knees to stop myself fainting, no matter where I am. On the kerb, or the middle of the car park, if there's nowhere else. In my mind it has become conflated with another, long-ago sound; the metal shutters across the windows of the record shop in Salisbury. I've always thought that was a shame. I'd liked that job, working with little hippie Caitlin and grumpy Alaric. Now the memory of it is ruined, in a jumble of other bad stuff, like Dad dying, what happened with Samantha, falling out with Pete. That grinding, shuddering sound would forever confuse and shut me down.

As I lay panting with shock, the floor cold and smooth beneath my right hip and shoulder, I felt my ankle being yanked, then encircled in cold metal – handcuffs, with a chain welded to one half. The other end of the chain was attached to a metal ring, and I had a mental flash of a defeated, bow-backed donkey chained to a fence. Why was the floor so smooth and slippery beneath me? It wasn't like the rough floor of a normal van.

It took me a moment to realise I was lying on thick plastic sheeting. Oh Jesus, oh God, I knew what that was for; it was so my guts wouldn't stain his van.

He heaved himself in, the engine juddering into life with the turn of the ignition key. The radio came on at the same time – some sort of hideous techno – quiet at first, then he turned it up, presumably once we were out of my street. It seemed to represent my panic. I tried to force myself to breathe deeply, to listen to the music and subsume myself into it, use it like mental blotting paper to soak up the terror.

He drove for some time – twenty minutes, half an hour? I couldn't tell, and couldn't see my watch. I was freezing cold in my PJs, with a soaked crotch and piss-stained legs. I could smell my own urine, further soured with fear, and my shivers had turned into shudders that convulsed me as I lay on the slippery van floor in a foetal position, convinced I had just minutes to live.

If I survived, I vowed to make up with Pete. Fresh tears rose in my eyes at a brief mental flash of throwing myself into his embrace. The scent of urine was replaced, just for a second, by a memory of the smell of home: woodsmoke and Dad's pipe – which, in my fevered, senti-mental imagination still lingered all these years after he'd gone; Pete's teenage aftershave; Mum's gentle lavender. *Oh God, please,* I prayed. *Please let me see Pete again.* It seemed so trivial now, and me so stub-born. I'd treated him badly, him and Mum. No wonder they'd been angry with me for just walking out on my family, leaving Pete to pick up the pieces, too arrogant to think it mattered, too traumatised by Dad's death to think about anyone else's feelings.

Family was *all* that mattered. And now I'd never get the chance to tell him that.

Eventually the van came to an abrupt stop, somewhere so silent that my ears rang with it after the techno and engine noise. Door opening again. Heavy footsteps. Shutter up.

'I have to do this, *Merry,*' he said as he hauled himself in and put a hurricane lamp in the corner, his weird, high voice indistinct behind the hot, damp wool of the stripy balaclava. The emphasis on my stage name sounded mocking, full of intent.

He pulled the shutter back down again, sealing us in this window-less Tardis of torture. When he turned around I saw he was holding a knife so long and sharp-looking that I almost fainted.

'Why?' I tried to say through my tape gag and the encroaching blackness, but it just came out as a moan. I had backed myself into the corner, my knees hugged to my chest, the metal ring pressing into the small of my back, instinctively and pointlessly trying to make myself as small as possible. I didn't want to die here, not in this cold metal box, with the lamp casting menacing shadows in the van's interior and making the knife's blade flash. He was actually waving it around, as if he'd seen too many martial arts movies, like the crazy person he must be. But he couldn't be that crazy, surely; were full-on mad people capable of buying or hiring vans, working out how to get into my house, how to get me out without anybody seeing, all the logistics that must have been involved? He knew my name, so it must have been premeditated.

Much later, I wondered if the waving around of the knife was some kind of prevarication. He didn't seem to hate me, particularly; at least not until he dragged me out of the corner of the van by my wrists as far as the chain would reach, and repeatedly kicked me in the kidneys and spine until I felt like my body was a sack filled with shards of vertebrae and feared I'd never walk again. I couldn't believe my back wasn't broken.

'You had it coming, you bitch,' he said almost casually, his voice mean, although not angry. Then he stopped, took one step towards me, raised the knife up high, and held it with both hands, like a sacrificial sword. I put my own bound hands in front of my face to protect me, looking desperately from side to side to see where I could escape to – somewhere to roll out of his reach – but there was nowhere to go, and my back was too sore to move anyway. For a moment I thought this was it, it was all over. I closed my eyes, not even realising that it was me making the high-pitched squealing sound that was all I could manage inside the gag.

Then, out of nowhere, a banging, and a quavery but firm voice from outside of the van: 'Everything all right in there? What's going on? I'm going to go and telephone the police!'

My attacker brought the knife down towards me, full force. The voice must have thrown him, though, because the knife missed whatever target he'd been aiming at – eye, throat, heart? Instead he caught my hand, the knife striking and breaking the bone leading to my middle finger, then slipping between that bone and the next, my ring fingerbone.

I rolled back, the knife still stuck in me, blood spurting everywhere and splashing my face as I kicked out at him with my free leg now that he was disarmed, determined that he wasn't going to get another go. The knife was mine now – in me, through me, of me – and the shock was so great that it kept the pain at bay, just for a few seconds.

I'm sure he'd have had another go, had there not been someone outside. It would have been easy for him to overpower me and pull out the knife, but he must have panicked, or decided to cut his losses and make a run for it, shoving up the shutter just far enough to throw himself out and vanish into the dark stillness of the night.

I'd never believed in God, but the appearance of that Good Samaritan, right at that moment, made me change my mind.

40

Present Day
Gemma

'Interview by DS Mark Davis and DC Gemma McMeekin with Meredith Vincent, commenced at nineteen forty on Monday, June the eighteenth, 2018. Right, Meredith, thanks for coming in. We already have your statements from the scenes about the discovery of the bodies of both Ralph Allerton and Andrea Horvath, but now that we have the results of the post-mortems back, and in the light of the new information you gave DC McMeekin earlier, we need to have another chat. Let's start with Andrea. Talk us through the night before you found her, if you can?'

As Mavis spoke, Gemma scrutinised Meredith's small figure, hunched in the chair opposite. It was almost impossible to imagine her ever screaming into a microphone on a stage, rapt fans – like Mavis, or at least his older brother – moshing in the front rows of the audience in front of her, commanding their attention, soaking it up, the trademark thick, black eye make-up and wild spiky black hair making her instantly recognisable. 'Riot Grrls', they were known as, apparently, back in those days. Gemma was young enough to be confused about the distinctions between them and punks – as far as she could tell, there was no difference. Perhaps it was an era thing.

Today Meredith Vincent couldn't have looked anything less like a pop star. She sat staring at the table, her face bare and her thin mousy hair held back from her face with a plain band. She wore the running gear she'd been wearing earlier to do the gardening; not the expensive patterned stuff that cost a fortune from Sweaty Betty, but some faded grey Lycra leggings and a zip-up hoody that had bleach spots down the front of it. There were black circles beneath her eyes, and her skin had a parchment-like pallor to it, which had intensified when Gemma mentioned the autopsies. Her cheekbones were still high, and her eyes large and vivid – echoes of her past beauty, but it was clear to Gemma that the woman had made a conscious effort to minimise her assets, not enhance them.

'This is a nightmare,' she whispered, picking at the skin around her fingernails.

Mavis attempted to arrange his features into a sympathetic expression. 'I appreciate it's very difficult. Just talk us through what you know. It doesn't matter if you're repeating stuff you said before.'

Meredith swallowed. 'She – Andrea – came over on Saturday night. Pete invited her and cooked dinner for the three of us. We were all good friends. Well, I think we were all hoping that Pete and her would get together, they have – had – such a spark. Me and Pete were hoping that, anyway, although he'd only just admitted it. He's really slow at picking up on when women like him. I told him on Saturday he needed to make a move, and something did happen between them: a goodnight kiss when I was in the loo...' She caught the glance that Mark shot Gemma. 'It was reciprocated! Pete was floating on air after it. He said she'd invited him round to hers next, to return the favour. He thought it was finally the start of something.'

'Finally?' Gemma asked. 'How long had they known each other?'

'A while,' said Meredith. 'Since Pete moved to the marina about a year ago. Andrea was there already – I think she bought her barge shortly after she got divorced in Hungary and moved to the UK. She was neighbourly to him when they moved in. They all are, on their pontoon; they're like a little commune – or community anyway. They became friends quite quickly, and then I got to know her too, because I'm there a lot.'

'And nothing had ever happened between them before?' Mavis sounded incredulous, and Gemma thought how crass he was. As if he was implying that Andrea had been so attractive, it was impossible that Pete would have been able to resist. She could see from Meredith's expression that she felt the same as her.

'No. Pete's shy, and I think Andy was reluctant to upset the status quo and possibly ruin their friendship. If you ask me, it's because she was pregnant and saw that Pete still liked her in spite of that. She realised she could trust him...'

'Who was the father of Andrea's baby?' Mark asked, clasping his hands together as if he was about to pray. Gemma, not for the first time, regarded his beautifully white, strong nails and wondered at them. Did the man go to a nail bar? She'd never seen a bloke with such perfect nails. Her own were bitten and ridged.

'Nobody knows,' Meredith said. 'We all wondered. Apparently it was a result of a one-night stand she had in Hungary when she went back to visit her parents last year ... Oh! Her parents...'

'Her parents have been informed,' Gemma said. 'They're planning to come over soon and sort out her possessions, try and organise selling the barge and so on.'

Meredith's face was stricken. 'They did know she was pregnant, didn't they?'

'No. They didn't know. It came as a shock – another shock – to them.' Gemma spoke quietly, and she and Meredith exhaled simultaneously, a breath of pure empathy, one woman to another.

'How awful.' There were tears in Meredith's eyes. She couldn't possibly have had anything to do with it, Gemma thought, not unless she was a consummate actress.

'Did you hear anything on Saturday night, after Andrea left?' Mavis said, in an unnecessarily loud voice. 'And did you see her leave? What time was it?'

Meredith sighed. 'I did tell you this on Sunday. No, I didn't hear a thing. Pete thought something had woken him, maybe a splash, but I sleep really heavily and I'd had a few glasses of wine. I didn't wake up till seven. I didn't see her leave that night. She said goodbye to me before I went to the loo – I was in there a while because I wanted to give them some time alone without making it look obvious. I was hoping they'd kiss ... and they did. First and last time.' Her voice shook.

'And what time was that?'

She heaved another great sigh. 'I'm not sure exactly. It wasn't really late. She wasn't drinking, of course, being pregnant, and said she was tired. I think it was about half past ten.'

'What time did you and Pete turn in that night? And why did you stay there instead of going home?' Mavis wasn't even looking at her as he asked this, so Gemma sought out Meredith's eyes and held them, in a gesture of solidarity.

'I often sleep on the boat. Pete's got a spare berth he calls my bedroom.'

'What did you do during the day on Saturday? Did you see Andrea at all before she came over?'

Mavis was scribbling notes in his illegible spidery scrawl. He had terrible handwriting and held his pen in a hunched-over way, as if shielding what he was writing from prying eyes.

'I'd stayed there on Friday night too. Got up about nine – Pete had already gone, he left for his workshop about half eight. I was awake from sevenish – I always am – but I was kind of messing round on my phone, and dozing for a couple of hours because it was Saturday. Then I made some bread, cleaned the place up a bit for Pete, had a shower.'

'Did you see Andrea in the daytime, before she came over in the evening?' Gemma asked. 'We're not clear on her movements that day.'

Meredith shook her head, then nodded, remembering. 'Yeah, just briefly. I went and sat on the roof for a while, reading in the sun, then Paula – you know, Ralph's wife ... widow ... came over in the afternoon. She was in a state and just wanted to drink wine and cry. She wanted me to get drunk with her, but I didn't want to. I can't drink in the daytime; it gives me a headache. I had a glass, though, to keep her company. That's when I saw Andy ... Andrea. She was accompanying one of her clients off the boat, then she came over and asked after Ralph, if he'd been found. She saw that Paula was upset, and I told her I'd fill her in later. She went back to her boat and I walked Paula home.'

'And how did Andrea seem?'

'Absolutely fine, then and in the evening.' Meredith paused and looked up, her eyes huge and grey. 'Please tell me – can you be sure that she didn't just fall in and hit her head on the way?'

Gemma held her gaze. 'From the nature and position of the blow to the back of her head, the pathologist's opinion is that it's highly likely someone inflicted that injury on Andrea prior to her falling into the water.'

Meredith's good hand stole contemplatively up to the back of her own head as if in sympathy. 'It's so horrible.' Then she froze. 'Oh God,' she whispered, 'I've just remembered something I forgot to tell you last time. It might be nothing ... but...'

'Anything you can tell us could be helpful.'

Gemma saw a very faint stain of pink rise on Meredith's cheeks. Guilt, at more stuff she hadn't told them about?

'The other day – last week? – Andrea trimmed my hair for me, in her salon on the boat. It was after Ralph went missing, but I didn't think anything of it, not really. I thought I'd imagined it...'

Gemma shot a glance at Mavis, but he was staring intently at Meredith.

'Go on,' he said, in an uncharacteristically gentle voice.

'It's just that I could have sworn I saw someone passing the port-hole – a flash of a leg, like someone was walking round the edge of the boat.'

Mavis somehow managed to combine a neutral expression with one of scepticism. Gemma wondered if he knew he was doing it. 'What time of day was this?'

'That's the thing – it was only about four in the afternoon, broad daylight, and I really doubt that her murderer would be strolling round the edge of the boat for anyone to see. They'd have some nerve, if they were. I just thought I should mention it.'

Gemma mentally agreed with her at the unlikeliness. 'I don't know anything about boats, but would there be any other reason for someone to do that? Could it have been one of the neighbours?'

'I suppose so,' Meredith said, tracing a line on the tabletop with the side of her thumbnail. 'They do sometimes jump from boat to boat.

There was no-one out there when we went and looked. But it gave me a fright. Also...'

'Yes?'

'This does sound stupid, but when I went over there, Andrea had been doing a jigsaw on a table out on deck; she used to do them all the time. This one was almost done, everything except some cherry blossom on a tree – but there was one bit missing. We talked about it – Andrea was freaked out because the missing bit was a baby, in a pram. I remember she said she thought it was an omen...'

Gemma willed Mavis not to let his expression show what he doubtless thought of *that*. He thought that anything involving superstition or religion – the two were interchangeable as far as he was concerned – was for morons and sheep.

'I know it sounds mad; it's so easy to lose a jigsaw piece,' Meredith ploughed on. 'Like I said, it could be nothing. But then seeing that foot outside, it felt so creepy, after the stuff that had been going on even before all this.'

'We'll check to see if there's any CCTV on the wharf,' Mavis said, making a note. 'And of course we're talking to all the residents. We'll ask if anyone saw anything that day.'

'There's no CCTV,' said Meredith. 'The council won't put it in, so Pete's been organising everyone to chip in for it themselves, because there's been some petty vandalism. It's due to be installed next month.' She hesitated. 'Could you tell me ... What about Ralph? Do you have any idea how he ended up in that pond yet?'

Gemma cleared her throat. 'Nothing's shown up on CCTV. But at least now we know where he died. Forensics are working on the ice house and surrounding area.'

Meredith looked as though she had suddenly aged ten years.

'DC McMeekin has explained what you told her earlier. Why on earth did you not let us know all this in your first statement?' Mavis asked, in a tone of detached curiosity, as if he was Meredith's therapist, Gemma thought, feeling faintly irritated. 'For the benefit of the tape,' he added, 'this is the information that Ms Vincent was the last person to see Ralph Allerton alive. They had sexual intercourse in the ice house, she left, but forgot her keys, and when she returned for them, he was lying dead on the floor. Is that correct?'

Meredith cleared her throat. Tears sprang into her eyes. 'Not quite,' she said. 'We, er, had sex in the disabled loo in the house. We went for a walk afterwards and he showed me the ice house. We kissed in there; he wanted to do it again, but I was already feeling guilty, so I went home.'

'And how long had you and Ralph been having an affair?' Mavis asked.

'We hadn't!' Meredith replied hotly. 'Honestly. We've been friends for years, but I swear on my life that was the first and only time anything ever happened between us. It was just a moment of madness, when I was feeling vulnerable and he was pissed.'

Gulping, she wiped away the two tears that had fallen at the same time, one from each eye, perfectly synchronised and straight down her pallid cheeks.

'I was in shock. I couldn't tell you because Paula's my friend and I felt so guilty. And I was worried you'd think *I* did it.' She looked up. 'And I *didn't* do it. I would never hurt either of them, Ralph or Andrea. I loved them. I think that's why they're dead. They were both killed because someone wants to get at *me*.'

41

1995
Meredith

My guardian angel's name, I later found out, was Mr Martindale. I would be forever grateful that he'd been brave enough to shout, rather than just going off to call the police and not saying anything, because I'd have been dead if he'd done the latter. The strike of the knife had already severed several major veins in my hand; if I hadn't got out then, I'd have bled to death.

Mr Martindale had heard the thuds and my muffled moans from the interior of the van as he took his corgi out for its middle-of-the-night constitutional. They were both elderly and insomniac. A war hero, even aged eighty-four he wasn't afraid of confrontation, of speaking out when something was wrong. And it was clear that something was very wrong.

I would never forget the sound of Mr. Martindale's voice, the firm, 'Hello? Anyone still in there?' to which I heaved and groaned and made whatever noise I could through my gaffer-tape gag, even though stars were exploding in my vision and black was creeping across my brain as I struggled to stay conscious. The pain in my body where the man had kicked me was nothing compared to the volcanic new agony of the knife piercing through my bones and sinews.

Mr Martindale shoved the shutter higher and shone his torch inside the van. I remembered his gasp at the slick crimson puddle illuminated in the beam, and the gentlemanly but heartfelt imprecation that he uttered when he saw me, gagged and chained by the ankle to a metal ring bolted into the side of the van, the knife still sticking through my hand. The bastard had plunged it in with such force that the tip was showing through my palm. I had neither strength nor stomach to try to pull it out, or to think about the reality that if my hand hadn't been in the way, the knife would instead be residing in my jugular, or my eye, or my heart...

I was too far gone to think about anything by then. Fading fast, I watched two Mr Martindales heave themselves stiffly up over the lip of the van, valiantly ignore the crimson puddle, and rush towards me in duplicate, before slipping in my blood and ricocheting off the van's other side like a grim sort of comedy double-act. Double-vision act...

'Oh my dear girl,' they were both saying, tears of shock and panic in their voices. 'What is your name? Don't go to sleep! There's a phone-box on the corner, I'll call for help then come straight back, I promise...'

I didn't want him to leave, even though he was going for help. I was so terrified that the man was going to come back and kill us both. But I must have passed out then, because I didn't know anything else until I woke up in St Thomas' Hospital.

ПɈ

Several days later, Mr Martindale asked permission to visit me, and I agreed. He was the only visitor I'd had the whole five days I was an inpatient. I missed Pete more than I had at any point over the decade we'd been estranged. But I just couldn't bring myself to ring him; not yet. I was too afraid he'd reject me.

Mr Martindale turned up with an African violet in a little pot and a box of chocolates, those horrible sickly seashell ones I couldn't stand. His kind eyes and compassionate tones were the things that made me lose it and break down, and I sobbed in his arms for the whole duration of his visit. He didn't even seem to mind that I left snail-trails of mucus all over his Fair Isle tank top. It smelled of potpourri and tobacco – exactly as my dad would have smelled if he'd still been alive. When I had that thought, I howled so much that the policewoman who sat outside my door came in, thinking that Mr Martindale had done something awful. She saw him patting me tentatively on my hospital gown-clad back with his veined and shaky hand, and withdrew again tactfully.

Reece Martindale was my undoing and simultaneously my future strength, the only one who kept me going. The awareness that I owed my life to someone was an overwhelming and inexplicable sensation. All I knew was that every time the horror revisited me, followed by the terror that my intruder would one day find me again, I saw Mr Martindale's face swim into my mind, and his steady, rheumy eyes calmed me. I really did think he was an angel. What, after all, were the chances of him happening across me in the van, in that remote part of Clapham Common – for that was where it turned out the man had taken me – at 4.00 a.m.?

Mr Martindale died a few months later. Heart attack. I never did find out what happened to his corgi. I still think about that dog occasionally. I should have offered to take it in. It was a nice dog, like he was a nice man.

When I was well enough, I moved out of London, to a tiny thatched holiday cottage in Minstead, for no other reason than it was a small village where nobody knew me. I didn't leave the house for weeks.

Several months later I sold my London place, for tens of thousands less than the market value. I lied to the band, telling them I'd had enough of fame and had emigrated to New Zealand to start a new life.

Iain McKinnon was the only one who knew about the attack – the police had arrested and interviewed him about his threats that night. He had a solid alibi though – a woman in the pub he'd picked up and taken home that night after I refused his offer. He was released, after being sworn to secrecy. It behoved him to keep quiet about it, because he and I both knew he'd get the sack if it came out he'd tried to blackmail me.

The police never managed to track down my abductor, despite many hours of interviews, trying to ascertain who might hate me enough to orchestrate such an attack. They liaised with their Kansas City counterparts, who went to interview an apparently very indignant Professor Samantha Applebaum in her office at the University of Kansas. She hotly and vociferously denied ever writing a letter demanding hush money from Big World Records in exchange for keeping her secrets about me safe, and had no idea who else even knew about our relationship, apart from Pete and the boys in the band.

'Preposterous!' was, reportedly, her reaction, and the police believed her. The letter had a UK postmark on it, and Samantha had been teaching in Kansas at the time it was sent. 'After all,' she pointed out, 'if I wanted to make money in a sordid way, I'd have sold my story to the British tabloids instead, wouldn't I? I have a good job and, more importantly, a good reputation. I would never risk that.'

Part of me hoped that this might prompt her to try and get in contact with me, perhaps apologise for her desertion – but only a small part. I was in too much of a state to care about that anymore.

The detectives went over and over every detail of the attack, but in the end all they could conclude was that my assailant was a mentally ill person with an imaginary grudge – a spurned fan, perhaps. Possibly Green-Paint Guy, but there was nothing to link them, apart from a similar build. None of us had a clue who might have written that letter, if it wasn't Samantha. I half suspected Iain himself. Perhaps he had somehow managed to uncover Samantha's name and the details of our love affair – perhaps one of the band had let it slip in conversation, but I very much doubted it. They weren't the sort for idle gossip, and they didn't like 'The Pointless I' much either.

I had trauma counselling, and we managed to keep it out of the papers. It wasn't that difficult in the end, because of the police's failure to catch the perpetrator. They made appeals, of course, for witnesses to the 'serious kidnap and torture of an unnamed female victim', but nobody apart from my rescuer had seen anything; not the man's van, not his arrival or departure from my house, nor his escape over Clapham Common. CCTV picked up the van in a couple of places en route, and detectives were able to confirm that it had been stolen from a scrapyard in Falmouth three days earlier, but that was about as far as they got. CID left the case open and, off the record, admitted to me that it had probably been a 'random nutter'.

Finally, a few months after I moved to Minstead, I plucked up the courage to do something I wished I'd done years before: I got hold of Pete's phone number. I rang our old next-door neighbour in Salisbury, who confirmed that Pete had moved to London and that she had a number for him.

Another week later, I dialled it, my heart pounding in my chest, the fresh scar on my hand throbbing.

'Hello?'

I started crying at the sound of his voice. 'Pete, it's me ... I'm so, so sorry, for everything. I've been a selfish bitch. Please forgive me?'

'Of course,' was all he said, a tremor in his own voice. 'I've missed you so much, Mez.'

42

Present Day
Gemma

Mavis put on his reading glasses with a frown and an air of reluctance that implied he resented having to wear them. As if either of us cared, thought Gemma, suppressing an eye roll. He cleared his throat.

'I've been looking again at the details of your previous attack, back in 1995. Obviously it was a very long time ago, but we can't rule out the possibility that whoever's behind it has been out of the country, or in jail for another crime, in the intervening years. I see from the transcripts that you had a conversation on the night of the attack with somebody from your record company, an Iain McKinnon, who tried to blackmail you into having sex with him, in exchange for keeping some personal information to himself; and that a third party, a woman named Samantha Applebaum, had tried to extort money out of the record company, threatening to go to the papers with the same information: i.e., that you'd had a sexual relationship with her.'

Meredith turned to Gemma. 'Iain's the guy we were talking about earlier. Sleazebag who did that interview for TMZ and let slip where I worked. He's a nightmare. But I'm sure it's not him. He had an alibi for the night of my attack – that night, after I turned him down, he apparently went home with some girl he picked up in the pub.'

'But if your attacker has been trying to track you down for years, that interview could have given him the clues they needed,' Gemma said.

'Yeah, maybe,' said Meredith miserably.

'And both McKinnon and the woman denied the blackmail

attempts,' Mavis said. 'Who else knew about your relationship with Samantha Appelbaum at that time?'

Meredith thought back. 'Not many people. I was so young. At first I was embarrassed to tell anyone – I told my best friends from school that I was moving to London, but not who with. The boys in the band were the only ones who knew, unless someone was stalking me and found out that way. We – I – did have a stalker, but that was a lot later. You know about the green-paint thing, but there were loads of other things too: hate mail and death threats and so on.'

'Did you not go to the police then?' Mavis sounded incredulous.

Meredith glared at him. 'Yeah. They didn't get anywhere, not even after the paint incident.'

'And you're sure it couldn't have been a friend of one of the other band members – someone hanging round with you back in the day, who you pissed off somehow?'

Meredith thought back. 'We were living in a squat for a few years when we started out. I guess there were people coming and going, but I honestly don't think I ever upset anyone to that extent. Samantha was the only one who ended up having an issue with me, but she wouldn't have gone to all that trouble, especially not once she was back in the States. She could be a right diva, but she would never kill anyone, or have wanted me to suffer like that, I'm absolutely sure. I can't believe that any of it was anything to do with her.'

43

Pete

Even though the commission had to be shipped to the client by the end of the week and he still had several inches of mother-of-pearl blossom and branches to inlay and lacquer, Pete found himself locking up the workshop at two in the afternoon and wandering back to the barge. He was completely unable to concentrate after Meredith had rung him to tell him the results of the post-mortems, and that she'd come clean to the police about her and Ralph. He wondered how she was getting on at the station. They'd want to speak to him at some point too, he supposed. Would he be in trouble as well? He found that he didn't really care, not as long as he and Meredith were safe. The police would protect them ... wouldn't they?

He stopped at the shop to buy a six-pack of beers from the local microbrewery, and the bottles chattered glassily in their cardboard compartments, banging against his leg as he walked home through the village, taking the shortcut through the back lanes to the marina. There had been heavy rainfall the night before and the lanes smelled of summer, of blooming roses and turned earth, dandelion and fresh spears of grass, a scent that usually made the sap of his spirits rise with joy – but today he took no pleasure from it. This feeling of being constantly close to tears was a new and unfamiliar one. He reached the steps and looked down at Andrea's boat, still cordoned off with police tape. The sight made him want to howl.

He descended the steps and climbed heavily aboard *Barton Bee*, which rocked to accommodate his weight. The river was swollen and angry after the rain, streaming under him, its watery scowl personifying his mood.

He put the beers down on the deck to fiddle with the new and very stiff padlock and hasp he'd attached to the door a few days ago. The previous rusty little hasp had been half hanging off and any intruder wishing to come aboard could have dispensed with it in one sharp twist. Since the post-mortem results, he didn't want to be next. There were two shiny new bolts affixed to the inside, too.

He had more bolts still in their packaging, intended for Meredith's front and back doors. He was far more worried about her than himself – although at least that cop was with her for a few days. That knowledge did help. It looked very much like someone was trying to get at Meredith – or maybe even frame her for the two murders. Who, and why now? His thoughts drifted back to the attack on her all those years ago. It was a subject he tried to avoid in the already-overcrowded chambers of his mind. There was no space for it; no benefit to imagining the horrors she had endured in that Luton van.

However, he had no choice. The guy had never been caught.

The stiff padlock refused to allow the key to turn, and Pete kicked at the door in frustration and rage. 'Open, you bastard,' he growled at it.

Still, at least its solid stiffness meant he'd be safe. If he couldn't get in, nobody else could already be in there, lying in wait for him.

He wiggled the key until the lock clicked open, thinking again that he would insist Meredith came to stay for the foreseeable. That policewoman couldn't be there for long, surely – didn't she have a home of her own to go to? And besides, it was *his* job to protect his sister, not some teenage cop. He had no idea of Gemma's age; late twenties, presumably, but with the braces she looked about thirteen. The pair of them would be no match for a determined assailant.

Assassin.

Pete decided to go back to 'assailant'. It was a less terrifying word.

He took the bag of beers and the padlock inside, bolting the door shut behind him, and had uncapped the first bottle on the edge of the kitchen counter before he'd even kicked off his trainers and dropped his backpack to the floor.

It tasted like nectar, its cold hoppy fizz immediately calming his nerves. He chugged the first and immediately started on the second. Flopping onto the sofa and putting his socked feet on the coffee table, he pressed Meredith's name in his phone's favourite contacts list – which, he noticed, only contained her number and Andrea's; he pushed down the stab of pain that this observation induced.

'Hi, Mez, are you OK?' he said as soon as she answered.

'Hi, Pete. Yup. Back from the police station. They're not pressing charges, thank God. I just got a telling-off. I decided to go into work for a few hours. Gemma's still with me.'

'Anybody ... unusual in the shop?'

'Nope. I was dreading paparazzi and shit, but nothing out of the ordinary. What about you? Are you at the workshop?'

He took another gulp of the beer. 'Nah. Couldn't concentrate. Locked up and came home. I'm going to drink a six-pack, watch shit TV and get an early night. How long is Gemma going to be with you?'

'A day or two more, she thinks. Then her boss will make her go back.'

'I think you should come and stay with me after that.'

He heard her sigh. 'Pete, thanks, but I don't want to. I'm safe in the cottage, I'm sure. I mean, I've got my own twenty-four/seven security; how many people have that in their house?'

Pete snorted. 'What, that ancient tubby guy we met – the one who wheezes when he walks? I'm not sure that he counts as a crack security team. If someone came to your door, and he – what's his name?'

'There's two main ones. That was Leonard, on nights. George is the daytime one.'

'Leonard, then. He could be miles away in the house if something happened in your cottage! I've bought you a couple more bolts, I'll come and put them on tomorrow.'

'Oh Pete. Thanks. But please stop worrying; there's really no point. When Gemma goes, I'll come and stay for a few days if it makes you feel better, but I can't live on your boat. It's far too small, and we'd drive each other crazy. Anyway listen, I have to go, a coach party's just come in.'

Pete heard an increased humming in the background, the chatter of voices in an unfamiliar language. 'OK, sis. Love you. I'll call you later.'

'OK. Love you too.'

⊓⊔

By 9.00 p.m. there were six empty beer bottles lined up neatly on the rug next to the coffee table. Pete couldn't be bothered to move them into the recycling box, but even in his inebriated state, didn't like the sight of them scattered haphazardly. He'd only got up to pee and make himself a toasted sandwich. He was now lying back on the sofa, contemplating the bottle of Glenfiddich on a shelf in the galley.

When he closed his eyes he saw the empty spaces where the shiny mother-of-pearl trees were meant to go on the unfinished chest. They were nagging at him – but not enough to make him want to sober up and get back to work. The trees could wait. Drinking and doing nothing couldn't.

Darkness seemed to have fallen fast on the river, unless he'd nodded off for a while. He must have done, because his heart was hammering, and he recalled a dream in which he'd seen Meredith darting between creamy-white branches, vanishing into the velvety blackness, leaving just a pearlescent glimmer behind her.

But next time he opened his eyes, all his possessions could only be seen in silhouette, crowding him silently. He pulled out his phone and checked the time – just after 10.00 p.m. He thought about calling Meredith again, but then felt overcome with sleepiness and texted her instead:

Going to bed now. Knackered and full of beer. Talk in the morning. Love ya.

Leaving the bottles where they were, he did at least get up and check that both bolts were firmly shot across before filling a pint glass with water and staggering into bed, via a final visit to the loo to clean his teeth and have a last pee. He was asleep within minutes of tearing off his clothes and flopping down on the mattress.

ᒪᑎ

A knocking sound awoke him some hours later; like knuckles on glass, persistent and loud. It was still pitch-dark, but something felt wrong; something more than just his dry mouth and slight biliousness. Who the hell was rapping on his window? The boat was rocking, far more than the gentle bobbing it made when moored. He sat up, ignoring the dizziness, and pulled back the curtain covering the porthole in his berth. Usually, his view would have been of the marina's stone walls, faintly orange-tinted from the light thrown by the street lamp in the car park above.

But there was no light visible. Shapes of trees loomed in mono-chrome, and as Pete's hearing sharpened into wakefulness, he heard the slap of water against *Barton Bee*'s sides. The moon came out from behind a cloud and suddenly light refracted off the water; not the enclosed sides of the marina, but open water.

He was drifting, mid-river. Shit!

At first he couldn't think how this could be. There was a strong offshore wind blowing an ebb tide that night, but that couldn't have disturbed the lines, unless they'd been tampered with. The lines had been secure when he'd boarded that afternoon – he always checked them, bow and stern, ever since some teenagers had untied him a couple of years ago. Fortunately he'd spotted them then, snickering and riding away on their bikes, another dare completed, and he'd started the engine, swearing loudly as he steered *Barton Bee* back to her mooring.

The bedside clock's red digital letters showed it was 3.30 a.m. Unlikely to be kids, then. But what had that knocking sound been?

Pete pulled on the shorts and T-shirt he'd only discarded a few hours before and stuck his feet into flip-flops, before racing the length of the boat back towards the engine room, to see if he could tell how far he'd drifted and if the ropes had been cut or untied. He was so familiar with the riverbank scenery that if it was anywhere less than a few miles, he'd probably be able to tell where he was from the shapes of the trees and the curve of the moonlit path. He shot back the two bolts on the door to the deck, focussing only on grabbing the tiller and getting his bearings.

A blast of cool, night, river-weed-scented air blew into his face as he pushed open the door, the moonlight showing him the unwelcome sight that he really was drifting mid-river, carried fast on the ebb tide, apparently several miles from the marina.

Swearing volubly, he was just clambering out when a hand clamped something over his nose and mouth, something that smelled weirdly like a vodka cocktail, only synthetic and super sickly, as if shovelfuls of sweetener had been added to the alcohol.

Out of the blue, into the black.

He didn't see it coming at all, nor whose hand it was. His knees buckled and he stumbled backwards, down the two steps into the saloon. The smash of his skull as it bounced off the barge's worn parquet floor was the last thing he remembered.

44

Meredith

The morning after her police interview Meredith awoke, confused and sweaty, from a horrible dream about Samantha.

In the nightmare, Samantha had been rising like one of the zombies in the 'Thriller' video, only instead of from a grave, it was from the top of one of the silos at Greenham. There were other women around her, and they were all chasing Meredith off the stage she'd been performing on with the band, the entire stadium audience coming for her in the lurching gait of the undead in horror movies, arms stretched straight ahead. Samantha was leading them, her eyes bright red and her mouth twisted in a smile of pure evil. Meredith remembered thinking, *Oh shit, they know it's me, they know who I am*, because every zombie audience member was wearing a Minstead House T-shirt. Even as she was fleeing, she thought, *I must re-order those, we'll definitely have run out...*

'Fuck,' she muttered, sitting up and reaching for her mobile. There were no messages or missed calls, which was weird. Pete usually texted her first thing, just a 'good morning' GIF or a cute photo of a cat, or his misty morning view of the river. She went to her favourites folder and pressed his number – he and 'Work' were the only numbers in there.

'Hi, Pete, it's me, ringing to properly fill you in on my police interview. Just woke up. Hope you're not too hungover after your beerfest last night...'

Meredith stopped mid-message, her voice cutting out as if someone had unplugged her. She realised she didn't even have the energy to speak.

'Just call me?' she begged instead, hanging up. At least she didn't have to work today, and she was safe. Gemma was here. They could just stay holed up in the cottage all day, hopefully.

She went for a pee, opened the curtains, drank the glass of slightly stale water on her bedside table, put on her dressing gown and climbed back into bed, where, propped up on her pillows, she gazed for a long time out of her bedroom window at the fresh green morning outside. She wanted the sound of the birds tweeting in the branches and the sight of puffy clouds scudding across the sharp blue sky to wipe the mustardy-putrid nightmare rot from her head, but after ten minutes they still hadn't. And Pete hadn't called her back.

A worm of concern began to wriggle in her chest. Why hadn't Pete picked up, or returned her call? He was never far from his phone and, since Ralph's disappearance, he'd been extra-vigilant about getting back to her immediately if she called or texted. It wasn't like him not to respond at all.

She checked the time on her phone. 08.46. He usually left the barge around now to get to the studio, so she supposed he might have been cycling over there when she was recording the voicemail.

She hadn't had a lot of sleep before the nightmare; she'd lain staring at the dark ceiling with her eyes wide open, clutching the duvet up under her chin like a child, her thoughts racing, wishing she'd asked Gemma to drop her over at Pete's after the interview rather than back here. She could have stayed and helped him drink the beers.

Meredith called him again, but once more the call went straight to voicemail. She tried the landline number of the studio, but that just rang out. She wished she had Johnny or Trevor's numbers, but she didn't. Just Andrea's, she thought, a lump rising to her throat.

On a whim, she rang Andrea's number and heard her familiar, accented voice: 'Hello! I am so sorry I am not able to come to the phone, but please—'

Meredith killed the call, a tear spilling down her face. Why had she done that? It hadn't made her feel remotely less crap – in fact, the opposite. She sniffed hard and swung her legs out of the bed, slowly, like an old lady.

She dressed and went downstairs, where she found Gemma sitting at the Formica kitchen table in a pink towelling dressing gown and slippers, working at her laptop, a cup of tea by her right hand. Her face, bare of make-up, was shiny and rosy. The woman looked about sixteen.

'Morning Meredith,' she said. 'Kettle's just boiled. Sorry, I was about to get dressed.'

'I can't get hold of Pete,' Meredith said, not bothering with the small talk. 'He isn't picking up, or ringing me back.'

She opened the fridge door out of habit and stood for a long time looking inside. There was a bit of yogurt left, a heel of bread, enough milk for tea ... but in the end she merely closed the door again. 'I'm really worried.'

Gemma stood up. 'Let's get over there, then. Give me five minutes to get dressed.'

⊓⊔

As they got into Gemma's Ford Focus, Meredith averted her eyes away from the space that had held Ralph's car. She wondered how Paula was getting on at her sister's. She should ring her ... once she knew that Pete was safe, of course. There was little room in her head for anything else at the moment.

Gemma drove them slowly out onto the access road that ran behind the house and fed into the public car park and to the main exit. Hardly anyone was around this early, and they didn't even pass another car on the short drive into Minstead Village.

Parking up at the top of the steps leading to the pontoon, Gemma was just pulling the handbrake up when a gentle rap on the passenger window made Meredith jump. It was Trevor, Pete's neighbour. She wound down the window and managed a smile, which he didn't reciprocate – in fact his expression was a mixture of puzzlement and worry.

'Hi Meredith ... hopefully you can solve the mystery.'

'Hi Trevor. What mystery?'

'Where your twin's taken himself off to.'

The breath stopped in her throat, and she had to cough to get it started again. 'What do you mean?'

Trevor moved to one side and made a gesture with his arm towards the river. 'He's moved the boat. Didn't tell any of us he was going, though, and he must have gone in the middle of the night. Is everything OK?' He scratched his head contemplatively. 'I mean, obviously everything is not OK...'

They both stared at Andrea's barge, still taped off and now, next to it, the empty mooring where *Barton Bee* had been.

'Oh my God,' Meredith said, opening the car door so fast she caught Trevor's elbow on the edge of the door. 'Sorry,' she said automatically, running over to the edge of the pontoon to look again at the space. 'Fucking hell. Gemma! I knew something was wrong. I've been trying to ring him but it just goes to voicemail. He wouldn't go anywhere – I mean, not without telling me. Shit, Trevor, something's happened to him, I know it has. When did you last see his boat?'

Trevor gripped her shoulders gently, kindly, trying to get her to make eye contact. Gemma rushed over too, her brow creased with concern.

'Shhh,' Trevor soothed, as if she was a teething toddler. 'Don't panic, sweetie. Stay calm. It could be nothing. Someone could've undone his moorings. You know kids were doing that last summer, the little bastards...'

'But why isn't he answering his phone?' Meredith wailed, hyperventilating, clutching Trevor. It seemed only minutes since the last time she was losing the plot, Andrea's body bobbing against the pontoon, her hair in black ribbons swirling around her head ... Meredith tried to shake off the horrific mental image of Pete's bloated corpse in the same place.

'I'll call it in,' Gemma said, pulling out her phone and stepping a short distance away.

Footsteps rang out on the iron stairs, and Johnny's head appeared. 'What's going on? Where's Pete?'

Meredith was shaking so much that she thought her legs were about to give way. 'Not Pete. Oh God, not Pete. Help, please, we have to find him...' she beseeched.

Trevor folded her into a claustrophobic and unwelcome hug, which she fought her way out of.

'Come on board with us,' Johnny said, exchanging worried looks with his partner. 'In fact, stay here today, in case there's any news. We'll look after you.'

They walked her slowly down the stairs, flanking her as if they were prison guards taking her to the gallows, Meredith thought, a flash of her zombie nightmare coming back to her. She had to grasp the handrail tightly on both sides, worried that her knees were about to buckle.

They'd just managed to persuade Meredith to sit down in the galley, and Trevor had put the kettle on, when Gemma climbed on board, her face grave. Meredith jumped straight back up.

'Is he dead? Please don't tell me he's dead.' She was almost howling out the words.

Gemma came over to her and put a hand on her arm. 'We have no reports of that,' she said gently. 'But his boat was reported this morning, found drifting about ten miles downstream. Nobody on board. We'll launch an investigation immediately.'

45

Pete

When Pete juddered back into consciousness, he couldn't at first work out where he was or what was going on. It felt like he was in a spin-dryer in the dark, until he realised that was just because his head was swimming so badly. Then he had a weird flying, falling sensation, as if he was plummeting off a dream cliff – no hands, no idea how far below him the water was or how hard he'd hit it, just a freakish sensation of free-falling through his own pain.

And he was in pain. Bad pain. His whole skull throbbed, his eyeballs pressing painfully against their sockets, huge and swollen, like his teeth, ears, nose. Everything ached, worse than the most severe hangover he'd ever had. He tried to lift his hands to stop himself belly flopping into the water; but there was no water. And he could not move his arms from where they were lifted behind him. He tugged, feeling the pull in the sockets of his shoulders. Nothing.

Gradually, he became aware that he was in a dark place, moving, but in a strange, immobile position. Kneeling, arms pinned by his sides, forehead resting on a thin metal edge as if he was about to be executed.

Was he about to be executed?

He tried to call out but he couldn't open his mouth – couldn't part his lips at all. Tape across his face. He lifted his head with difficulty, but the pain was too great and bile rose in his throat.

No, man. Fuck no. You can't be sick, he thought in panic. If he was sick he could choke and die.

He brought his head gently back down to feel the metal edge again, but at that moment the moving floor beneath him jumped, hard, and the metal edge smacked against his brow, making his head hurt even more.

A bump, he thought. *That was like a bump, in a road. I'm in a van, being taken somewhere.*

Meredith had been taken somewhere in a van, all those years ago.

He tried to push away the thought of her poor ruined hand, the constant reminder of the torture she'd endured that night, forcing himself instead to stay calm, work out what was happening.

He wasn't on the van floor. He realised he was in some kind of open container, which in turn was in the van. The container was small, just large enough to accommodate his kneeling form, and cold against his bare knees and shins. Metal, he thought, puzzled. It feels like metal. He slumped over to his left and then, with difficulty, to his right, to see where the sides were. It seemed wider at the front than the back. Could he be in a *wheelbarrow*? The sides were about that height. He tried to unfold his legs and climb out, but then became aware that his hands and ankles were bound together too.

This must be how Meredith had felt, he thought, and had to swallow back down the vomit in his throat. The thought of her feeling half as terrified as he did now made tears of horror spring thickly into his eyes. How had he never properly understood before? He'd been a terrible brother. They hadn't even been talking at that stage. She'd gone through all that – all *this* – on her own.

Stop it, Pete. Focus.

His kidnapper must have used the wheelbarrow to transport him from the barge into the van. Perhaps he put a plank across to wheel it ashore. Couldn't have been easy. Pete was skinny, but six feet tall. He must have been forced into the kneeling position first, taped together like a Christmas turkey, then lifted into the wheelbarrow. Jesus. There must be at least two of them; surely that would be too hard on your own? He strained his ears to hear if there was any conversation going on in the van's cabin, but he heard nothing apart from his own panting breaths and the van's engine. He couldn't tell what sort of vehicle it was. He didn't think the engine was throaty enough to be a lorry, and although he couldn't see anything, the space felt bigger than a micro van.

He needed to get out of this wheelbarrow.

He rocked himself from side to side, as vigorously as he could, trying to ignore the howling pain in his head. If it was a twin-wheeled one, he was screwed, but if it was a traditional one-wheeler, he might just be able to tip himself...

Crash. He'd done it! He lay gasping on his side on the van floor, his heart hammering as he waited for the van's driver to slam on the brakes and come round to see what the noise was. But nothing. The vehicle continued to bounce along. They hadn't noticed.

But what good had it done him? He was still immobilised.

The van seemed to be going uphill. Pete could hear the strain of the engine, and feel the tilt of gravity as it made him slide backwards a little way. They'd been driving for at least twenty minutes, he guessed – but it could've been much longer, depending on how long he was unconscious for. Twenty minutes or so since he came round.

With the long fingernails of his right hand, the ones he'd cultivated to be able to play the guitar without a plectrum, he scratched away at the tape around his ankles. But it felt like that thick black electrical tape, and it wasn't giving an inch. Straining against it did no good at all, of course, but he found himself repeatedly doing so anyway, making his wrists cramp and throb in tandem with his head.

It was hopeless. He'd just have to take his chances when the van finally stopped.

His heart thudded with fear. Meredith had once – just once – told him about what happened when the van she was in had stopped.

As if prompted by his terror, the van's gears changed down with a crunch, and Pete felt it slow to a halt.

This was it.

⊓⊔

Van door opening. Heavy footsteps, no voices. The click of a lighter. A pause. Pete couldn't hear the inhalation, but imagined his kidnapper sucking on a cigarette, leaning contemplatively against the van side just inches away from him, perhaps keeping it alight to burn him with...

Then a few more footsteps, the crunch of the door opening. The glare of a torch in his eyes, and the sweet scent of country night air. A familiar, comforting smell: sheep and grass and sleepy, droopy-headed flowers after dark.

'Rolled out, you bastard, did ya?'

A strange growly voice; Pete honestly couldn't tell if it was high or low.

At least there only seemed to be one person out there. He could take him on. Kick him, hard, even though his feet were bare; his flip-flops having vanished at some point. Maybe kicking wouldn't be so effective. He decided to think of him as Rolli, as the word 'rolled' had snagged in his head. Better to give him a name; made him feel less monstrous. Rolli was small, cute and cuddly. He, Pete, could take a Rolli.

He'd just have to bide his time.

'Rolli' hauled himself into the van, making it creak and rock. Silhouetted against the black night, he was barrel-shaped, solid. Wearing a balaclava. Not remotely small, cuddly or cute.

Pete's heart sank. It was the same guy who'd taken Meredith, it had to be. Van, tape, balaclava. When would the knife be brandished? Pete could already see it glinting in the moonlight; imagine its flash through the air and the slice – or stab. Perhaps he'd be branded in the same place that Meredith was; they could have twin injuries. There was something faintly reassuring about that, even while the skin on his hands twitched with fearful anticipation at how much it would hurt to be impaled by a knife. But what could this guy *want*? What could they have ever done to deserve this?

He watched Rolli's shape pull the wheelbarrow out and place it with a bang on the ground beneath the ledge of the van. Rolli heaved himself back inside the vehicle and now it was Pete he was coming for.

He got behind him and, grunting with effort, shoved him towards the edge, as if Pete was a rock. Pete felt his shins scrape and protest on the van's metal floor. Then he was unceremoniously rolled off the edge, back into the barrow. He landed painfully, face upwards, which spared his poor head from more trauma, but meant his tied feet and arms took the impact. He feared he'd broken something in one of his arms – he couldn't even tell which – so intense was the pain.

Rolli loomed forwards over him, into his eyeline, and Pete's heart almost seized up in his chest. He was panting with fear. His assailant wore a woolly beanie hat pulled low over his forehead, and a scarf tied tightly around the lower half of his face, so that only his eyes were on display. Not the balaclava Pete had at first assumed it was. If he survived this, he thought, he'd recognise those eyes again anywhere. Even in the dark, he could see how pale they were, washed-out looking, with light, stubby lashes.

But instead of the knife Pete expected, when Rolli's hands shot forwards they were holding a long, thin piece of fabric, like a strip ripped from a curtain. Was he going to be throttled? His windpipe shrank and recoiled in his throat. But instead, Rolli tied the fabric around his eyes, wrapping it around Pete's head twice and securing it at the front, squeezing the bridge of Pete's nose.

Then he felt himself being wheeled off, which jarred his arm further. On his back in a haze of agony and confusion, Pete had the weird sensation of being a baby again, wheeled along in a pram in the dark, but instead of his loving mother's face peering in at him with clucks and smiles, there was just blackness where her face should be. Silence, apart from the squeak of the barrow's wheel and the man's breathing, still laboured from the effort of moving him.

He remembered again the missing piece of Andrea's jigsaw, the one that she had obsessed about. The face of the baby in the pram. She and Meredith had discussed it that night on his boat.

He was that missing baby. Andrea had been right to obsess about it, and he hadn't listened. If he had, perhaps they could've saved her.

He wanted Andrea.

He wanted his mother.

The silence became like a blanket of fear pressing down on him. They must be in deep countryside. Why was he being moved? And to where?

They proceeded at a slow, bumpy pace for what seemed like miles, up and down inclines, mostly over grass but once or twice across what must have been gravel paths. There was a level of unreality that Pete was vaguely aware of – he was in a *wheelbarrow*, for fuck's sake. His legs were hanging over the handles and his neck bent uncomfortably backwards, perilously close to the wheel when the barrow was tipped up and pushed.

What a way to die.

He thought of all the things he'd never done: been a husband, a dad. Never even owned a dog. If he got out of this, he'd bite the bullet and do online dating. He would enter his furniture into design competitions like Meredith was always telling him to. Maybe he could persuade her to go travelling with him. Backpacking around South-East Asia. Was that weird, to want to go travelling with your sister?

It didn't really matter, whether it was or not.

The barrow slid down a small slope, and his head banged painfully against a hard surface at the bottom. A door creaked open. Pete thought of deserted beaches at sunset, cold beers, fine, pale sand between his toes.

The temperature and humidity changed. He was inside, somewhere damp and cool. A sudden inversion and he was tipped out onto a chilly stone floor, like a pile of horseshit being dumped into the corner of a stable.

It felt a bit like a stable, in fact, although it didn't smell of horses. Pete struggled to roll over and right himself, his head and arm still hurting more than anything he'd ever injured before; even more so when Rolli grabbed him by the elbow of his bad arm, getting him into a sitting position.

The cloth was ripped off his eyes but it wasn't any lighter. For a moment Pete wondered if the blow to his head had knocked out his sight, but then a dim blue light appeared – a phone screen – followed by the bright white glare of the phone's torch function, shining right into his face.

'Home sweet home,' Rolli said in his strange, high-low voice, putting the phone down. Torchlight shimmered like a laser beam across a rough tiled floor and Pete could see walls, which might once have been whitewashed, and lighter areas that looked like boarded-up windows. He was in some sort of big shed, maybe. But there was a bench seat running around the walls, about a foot from the ground. Pegs attached, higher up. An old changing room? Was he in an abandoned school or something? It wasn't big enough to be a public baths.

Rolli approached him again, this time holding a length of rope, which he looped through something behind him and then attached it to whatever had restrained his wrists.

Oh God, Pete thought. *Please don't leave me here with my arms tied this tightly behind me. I'll die.* The pain was unbelievable, pulsing in waves up his arms and into his neck and head.

'Right. We'll be back tomorrow...'

Back? *We?*

Those words were chilling enough, redolent with threat, but what Rolli said next was what made Pete howl through his gag, struggling futilely against all his restraints, not even caring that it made everything hurt even more.

He'd failed. Failed Andrea, failed Ralph, failed himself...

'...with your sister. And that's when the fun starts. Sweet dreams, Pete.'

The phone was picked up. The door opened and closed again, the barrow wheel squeaking as it was wheeled away. The man was gone.

Sobbing and choking, Pete slumped forwards to try and relieve the pressure on his arms. Most of all, he'd failed Meredith.

46

Graeme

Graeme sits waiting in the van, parked in the small car park outside the dental surgery, heart banging painfully against his ribcage, thick hands shaking as they grip the steering wheel. His nails are filthy from the dirt he rubbed on the van's number plates this morning.

No matter how many times he's done it, it never feels any less stressful, even though everything has gone smoothly this time – so far anyway. But it's not a fear of danger he feels; it's a fear of messing up, of risking Catherine's displeasure.

Catherine used to say she loved his hands, how strong they were. Now they'll be together as a couple, will she say it again?

Graeme looks down at them, thinking back on some of the actions his hands have performed, the power they have wielded, the lives they've changed.

He doesn't often get this philosophical, but this is a big day, with so much at stake.

A very big day. In fact, it feels as if this moment is the pinnacle of his life. All the planning, all the worrying, his secret fear that something will go wrong and he'll be back inside too, or that he'll fuck it up like last time – that stupid man out walking his stupid dog. It took Catherine years to forgive him for that. But now he has another chance. They both do. There can be no mistakes this time.

⊓

In the event, he didn't need to be so stressed about it. It couldn't have been easier. All those months and years of prep, and now here Catherine is, in the back of an old red Honda that is just pulling into the car park. Graeme doesn't recognise the female driver – must be a new nurse – but the one sitting chatting to her on the back seat is Penny, a small plump sister that Graeme knows Catherine gets on well with. Will that make it harder to hurt her?

Silly question, Graeme thinks. Nothing makes it harder for Catherine to hurt anyone.

Catherine and Penny get out of the car, Catherine holding her jaw as if in great pain, but cracking some kind of a joke, because Penny's laughing in a scandalised way. She leans down and speaks to the driver, tapping her wrist, presumably saying she'll call her when they're done. Graeme catches the words, '...and small fries please.'

Tut, tut, thinks Graeme with a slow smile, they both ought to be coming in with Catherine. But it bodes very well that they aren't. The driver waves and drives out of the car park, crunching the gears as she exits.

Catherine looks in his direction, and Graeme raises his eyebrows, but Catherine gives an infinitesimally tiny shake of her head when Penny isn't looking. They've agreed that Graeme will only get out of the van if needed. Less chance of being spotted on CCTV.

Catherine and Penny begin to stroll across the car park. The only other pedestrians in sight are an old lady tottering out of the surgery entrance with a Zimmer frame and her carer, or daughter, opening the door for her.

Catherine's almost level with the space that Graeme has parked in. Graeme, in the driver's seat, pretends to be scrolling through his phone with one hand, but he keeps his eye firmly on them, and his other hand, out of sight, grips the heavy motorcycle chain that is his current weapon of choice. *Go on babes*, he urges silently. *We're so close. Get on with it, or I will.*

Violence ignites in his belly, raw and hungry like the craving of a recently reformed smoker when someone lights up next to them. For a moment he forgets who he's meant to be saving the rage for, and he wants to jump out of the van and stave in Penny's skull, imagining her dull-brown curls all matted, the blood pooling out around her...

Just as the two women are level with the van's bonnet, Catherine crouches down. 'Stone in my shoe,' Graeme hears her say.

Graeme forces the ball of anger down, loosens his grip on the chain, starts the van engine and leans across to open the passenger door. This is the sign.

Penny is waiting, still chatting away, while Catherine pokes around inside her shoe. Then, instead of straightening up in the normal way, she pushes herself away from the ground with the energy of a swimmer doing a racing dive off the side of a pool, her clenched fist swinging forcefully upwards and straight into the underside of Penny's jaw, a flawless uppercut.

The blow sends the woman flying backwards in an almost cartoonish fashion. She lands flat on her back, a stunned expression on her face as her skull smacks the tarmac hard, blood spraying out of her mouth. Is that a tooth, flying off in the opposite direction?

Catherine has jumped into the van and Graeme has driven out of the car park before she's even had time to get her seatbelt on.

Graeme drives steadily, nothing flashy, nothing to draw attention to them. Even if there is CCTV in the car park, there is nothing to identify the van. His hands have stopped shaking. A huge beam spreads across his face, even though they aren't high and dry just yet.

'We did it!'

'I did it, you mean.'

'Yeah, babes, I know.'

Conciliatory as always, Graeme does know. But he also knows that it has been all these months and years of preparation on his part that has got them to this stage. Making sure Catherine took her meds, back when she was still in Rampton; urging her not to blow her top whenever someone wound her up. Both of them knowing how crucial her good behaviour was.

Catherine has behaved herself for the last three years. It's a record.

But then, when Catherine really, really wants something, she'll do anything to get it. Graeme likes to think that Catherine's good behaviour was due to his influence – and perhaps too the fact that he persuaded the board to let him be Catherine's advocate. All the dozens of Care Plan Approach meetings he's attended on her behalf, feeling like a proper responsible citizen.

The joy they both felt when it was deemed that Catherine's condition was finally stable enough for her to be moved from high-security Rampton into this medium-security place in Surrey ... The plan was working, he thought. For the first time in his life, Graeme had a purpose, a mission. Not to mention all the other planning he had to do, to set everything up for Catherine. Convincing the CPA board to consider transferring her hadn't been easy, but they'd done it. Graeme had insisted it was because he'd got a new job, as a gardener, and he wouldn't be able to continue driving up to Northampton to visit Catherine. They wanted to be closer to each other; that was fair enough, wasn't it? They were a couple.

And the board bought it, not having a clue why Graeme had got a gardening job at that particular venue.

Graeme remembers with glee the day three years ago when he discovered that the Pop Bitch – PB – lived in Minstead and worked up at the house. He was boarding a bus in Kingston after a visit to his parole officer, and he saw PB walking to the next bus stop. Nobody else would ever recognise her; she looked completely different these days. But Graeme would have known her anywhere, even with the very short blonde hairstyle. Catherine had made him study so many photos of her that the woman's features were indelibly imprinted on his mind. Graeme immediately jumped off his bus and followed PB onto hers, sitting so close behind her that he could see the short, fine hairs sticking to the back of PB's collar – she'd obviously just had it cut. Why was she travelling by bus? Surely someone like her had a car? Maybe it was in for a repair or something.

Graeme sniffed the air in front of him, trying to see if PB was wearing the same perfume as she had when he'd met her last. He could still remember how she'd smelled; before the scent of her piss and fear and blood overpowered everything else.

That bus ride took at least thirty-five minutes, out into the arse-end of nowhere in the Surrey Hills, a place Graeme didn't even know existed. PB – and Graeme – finally alighted somewhere called Minstead House – a massive yellow place, where Graeme stalked her to that stupid shop full of overpriced pottery and other shit that posh people and ignorant tourists threw their money at.

He couldn't wait to tell Catherine that he had, completely by chance, found Pop Bitch, and that she worked in a *shop*. It was the biggest stroke of luck he'd ever had.

They gave themselves two years to work out phase two of the plan. Two years to start to put right what had gone so wrong last time.

And now here they are.

In the van, Catherine clips in her seatbelt. 'How did it go last night?' she asks.

'Like clockwork. Everything in place.' Graeme can't help the note of pride in his voice. He thinks of the man's eyes meeting his, his pain and fury and bewilderment. In that moment he almost felt sorry for him, for he was as much of a pawn as Graeme himself was.

'Good. Knew I could rely on you.'

Graeme smiles, all thoughts of pity forgotten.

'Let's get over there now.'

'Now?' Graeme has assumed Catherine would want to have a quiet night in first. See the flat, unpack, maybe even go to bed. The thought of Catherine's warm, pale body in his arms again makes him feel woozy with delight.

'You've got him. What if someone finds him? We need to get her there too, before they notice I'm missing.'

Graeme sighs. He knows Catherine is right. Obviously, when it's discovered that Catherine has escaped, Graeme will be the first one they'll call. But they thought of this too. Graeme has given a false address in Surrey, and has already ditched the SIM card of the mobile that is on Catherine's records as her next-of-kin contact number. The van will be well hidden.

'This time tomorrow...' Catherine says gleefully.

Graeme looks across at his beloved and feels a brief metallic twinge in his teeth, another little thrill of joy, to see her smiling so widely as she gazes out of the window at trees and fences speeding past.

'I know!' Graeme says. 'We'll wake up together. Our new lives start here. I can't wait for you to see the flat. I tidied up special.'

Catherine gives a dismissive wave. 'Yeah, yeah, that'll be great. But I'm not thinking about that.'

Crestfallen, Graeme indicates left onto a dual carriageway. 'Oh. What was you thinking then?'

Catherine turns in the passenger seat to face him, clasping her knee with excitement, rocking slightly, Graeme notices, in time with the fuzzy-felt cartoon air-freshener dangling from the rearview mirror.

'This time tomorrow, I'll finally be quits with Pop Bitch. She'll have suffered as bad as I did, all these years. A life ruined for a life ruined. Only fair, isn't it? And all this will have been worth it!'

Graeme wonders why his heart sinks. After all, he knows that this is at the heart of it all; has always been. But why can't Catherine just be happy that they are finally together?

47

Emad

Later that day, Emad messaged Gemma to say he wanted to run something by her, so they agreed to meet for a quick drink at 7.30 p.m., in the pub round the corner from the station. The Prince of Wales was not usually frequented by cops because it was generally deemed too upmarket, with its ostentatious flower arrangements, coir matting floors and uniformed bar staff, but, as Gemma said, eyeing the tweedy clientele, 'We can go posh just for one. At least we can hear ourselves think in here. Meredith's been spending the day with Pete's neighbours at the marina. I'm picking her up about nine and we'll go back to her place together.'

Emad wished it wasn't just the one. He wished they were going out for a romantic dinner, followed by a cosy nightcap, followed by going back to Gemma's flat and a night of passion. It was the second time they'd had a drink after work, just the two of them, and each time they met they got a little more relaxed and jokey with each other. He tried not to wonder if her heart skipped a beat whenever she saw him. He suspected not. And she looked particularly stressed today.

'So, what's so urgent?' she asked, when they were settled at a table with a pint of IPA for him and a Diet Coke for her.

Emad was bursting to tell her. 'I just got back from a call-out to Ashworth – you know, the mental institution near the A3?'

'Oh yeah? Natives revolting, are they?'

Emad took a gulp of his pint, swallowing a hiccup and putting a hand over his mouth, embarrassed. Gemma laughed, but not meanly.

'Not exactly, but someone escaped this morning.'

'It's low security, that place, isn't it? Can't they pretty much come and go as they please anyway?'

'Medium security. And they definitely *can't*. Anyway, this one did, and she's not the sort of woman we want on the outside, not if she's not taking her meds.'

'Well, surely she can't be that dangerous if she's in Ashworth?'

'The governor told me that she'd calmed down massively in the past couple of years; that's why she was moved over there from Rampton. Long-term inmate – first went in when she was in her twenties. History of extreme violence, manipulation, coercion, you name it. Has tried to kill other staff and inmates on several occasions over the years, but not recently. Several suicide attempts – the most recent five years ago when she made a swallow dive head first off her bunk onto the concrete floor. Smashed her nose in and gave herself severe concussion.'

'Ouch. How old is she now?'

'Mid-fifties.'

'No spring chicken, then.'

'No, but she managed to knock out a nurse with no difficulty – the woman's in hospital. The nurse had taken her for a dentist's appointment, and the prisoner did a runner in the car park. She had a getaway driver.'

Gemma didn't seem overly interested, so Emad thought it was time to play his trump card: 'Thing is, Gemma, there's a connection to Meredith Vincent.'

'What? How?' Gemma had a slight habit, Emad had noticed, of not concentrating on what he was saying, looking over his shoulder or, occasionally, fiddling with her phone – but he had her full attention now.

'I went to look at the woman's room in Ashworth, and when I got in there, one wall had bits of Blu Tack all over it. When I asked what she'd had up there, the nurse who took me in said – and you won't believe it – "Oh she was obsessed with some band from the eighties ... Funny, she must have taken all the pictures with her".'

Gemma's glass stopped en route to her mouth. Her jaw dropped. 'You're not going to tell me it was Meredith's band? Cohen?'

'Yup. Took the nurse a few minutes to remember, but when she did, she was sure. And she said that it was a bit weird, because Catherine had a few CDs on a shelf as well – but none of Cohen's. The nurse said it was a bit of a joke because Catherine had loads of pics of the band, particularly the lead singer, and yet she couldn't stand their music. They said they used to think it was funny – not that they'd ever have dared say that to her face.'

'Oh my God. Have you called it in yet? Catherine ... Her name's Catherine? Catherine what?' Gemma had whipped out her phone and was already dialling.

Then she stopped. 'Wait. You said Catherine's been in institutions for decades? It couldn't be her, then. When did she escape?'

'This morning. Catherine Brown. And, no, I haven't told Mavis yet. I wanted to run it past you first.'

'So if Pete Vincent's been kidnapped, it couldn't have been her, because it happened last night. Was she locked up in 1995 when Meredith was abducted?'

Emad shook his head, then turned it into a nod. 'That's the thing. She was in Rampton for years, all of the nineties. Couldn't have been her; not unless she's got someone on the outside working for her. That's why I didn't want to bother Mavis and Lincoln with it – in case they thought I was wasting their time.'

He was still having flashbacks to the humiliation he'd felt at the station, both when his wheelbarrow suggestion had been pooh-poohed in the meeting, and the look of withering contempt Mavis shot him when he'd queried why Pete had cycled up to Minstead when the twins were meant to be going for a drink.

Gemma put the phone to her ear. 'Damn, it's gone to answerphone,' she said to Emad. Then, into the phone: 'Hi – Meredith, it's me, Gemma. Quick question: have you ever known anybody in a mental institution; a woman called Catherine? Call me back and I'll explain. I'm coming to get you from Trevor and Johnny's a bit earlier – I'm in Guildford at the moment so I guess I'll be about an hour. I don't want to alarm you or them, but please don't open the door to anyone except me, OK? It might be nothing, but just to be on the safe side...'

Emad downed the rest of his pint as Gemma stood up, her Coke abandoned. 'Should I have told Mavis?'

'Could you do it now? Sorry to cut our drink short. Did you already know about her twin brother going missing?'

Emad was momentarily hurt that Gemma didn't even remember he'd been present at the morning meeting. 'Yeah, I was at the briefing. I was just about to ask about that. No news today, I assume? She's either having a run of right bad luck, or someone really is after her.'

'I know.' Gemma opened her mouth as if to say something else, then thought better of it. She stood up and gathered her things.

'I'll come with you,' Emad said.

'No – it's fine, you're not on duty. Just please call Mavis and tell him and Lincoln what you found out about Catherine Brown. I want to get over to Meredith's pronto, she sent me away earlier, and I thought she'd be OK with those two guys at the marina, but she could be in danger.'

'Well, OK. But...' Emad paused. They were colleagues, and friends, but he didn't want to sound patronising.

'What?' Gemma made a face at him.

'Just be careful. Will you call me when you get there?'

'Sure,' she said. 'Oh, by the way, you know in that meeting the other day, when you picked up on why Pete had cycled up to Minstead House when they were meant to be going to the pub in the village, the night Ralph Allerton went missing?'

'Yes,' said Emad cautiously.

'When I asked Meredith about it, she got all flustered and couldn't answer. It's what prompted her to 'fess up about shagging Ralph then ringing Pete for help. Nice work, my friend. That was a massive help.'

Emad sank his chin into the collar of his jacket, to hide the big smile on his face.

48

Meredith

Trevor and Johnny had been lovely, but having tolerated them fussing over her for most of a day, Meredith realised she just wanted to be at home. Their cloying concern and empty exhortations of optimism – 'he'll be FINE, I promise' – were making her feel very stabby and irritable. How could they make groundless promises like that?

In the end, she begged Trevor to drive her back to the cottage, saying she was exhausted and needed to try and have a nap, in her own bed. And reminding him that not only would Gemma be back with her later that night, there was also a police presence on the estate already, guarding the ice house, now that it was officially a crime scene, so she'd be perfectly safe.

He acquiesced, albeit reluctantly, making her promise to keep the doors locked and her phone on her at all times.

Once home, Meredith couldn't settle to anything. She wandered from room to room. It felt all wrong to be in her house; she should be out there searching for Pete – but where? How? The world outside her four walls felt vast and threatening.

Do something. Do something practical, she thought, remembering how her mum used to say that, if you were in a state, or feeling miserable, just 'clean out a cupboard'. Do something mundane and dull to take your mind off it.

How the fuck was cleaning out a cupboard going to help find Pete?

Her hands were shaking and her thoughts whirling round in circles. Gemma would be staying again tonight. Meredith realised she wanted her to come back. Gemma was taking it seriously. Gemma knew, like she did, that Pete was in serious danger.

Perhaps she should call her now; ask her to come. She should let her know that she was back at the cottage anyway; Gemma thought she was at Johnny and Trevor's.

But her phone was in her bag by the front door, and Meredith was so distracted, her thoughts flitting around like butterflies, that she didn't bother to get it. As she cast her eyes around the kitchen, trying to think of something to occupy her, she spotted the faulty secateurs on the windowsill. She'd brought them home from the gardening section of the shop the other day, to try and fix them. The manufacturers had erroneously bolted the blades of this pair to the canvas fabric of the case, so it looked as if the only way to remove the secateurs was by using pliers to dismantle them completely. If she could get them out of the case, she could probably put them in the bargain bucket and sell them half price.

Meredith found a pair of pliers in a drawer and took the secateurs out into the cottage's tiny back garden, forgetting not only to text Gemma but also her promise to Trevor to keep the doors locked. Sitting on the step to fiddle with the task at hand in the still evening air, silent bar the distant drumming of a woodpecker, she couldn't say it took her mind off anything, but at least it gave her something to do. In the pocket of the case she found a separate sharp little gardening tool, which she slid into the bib pocket of her dungarees so as not to lose it.

The bolt on the secateurs was stiff and it took all her strength to turn it, Pete's face in her mind the whole time, until she had a terror that he was being tortured like this: clamped, turned, pincered, stabbed ... The two blades of the secateurs were lying separated and she thought how menacing they looked, like the claws of a monster – but the bolt was still stubbornly attached to the case. Meredith sighed and gave up, bolting them plus the case back together. She'd stick them in the bargain bucket anyway and hope nobody spotted the major flaw.

She went to check her phone for any news, and was just crouching in the entrance hall, fishing it out of her handbag, when there was a heavy knock at the front door right next to her, making her jump. It would be Gemma, she thought, or even – hope flashed, a silver-minnow twist in her chest – Pete? No, that would be too much to hope for. It must be Gemma, or Leonard. Nobody else would come to the cottage at this time. She glanced at the phone in her hand and noticed that there were notifications from Gemma on the screen: a missed call and a voicemail.

'Did you just ring me?' she was starting to say as she opened the door, but it wasn't Gemma. A short, heavy woman loomed in the narrow porch, like a troll under a bridge. Her hair was thin and lank and her skin pasty, with black circles beneath her eyes, as if she hadn't seen daylight for years. Disconcertingly, her nose seemed to be plastered across her face, like a boxer's. A roll-up burned perilously close to her fingers, which made Meredith – somewhat irrationally – wonder if she was a friend of Pete's. The woman looked at her expectantly, unsmiling, so Meredith didn't smile either. Belatedly, she remembered her promise to keep the doors locked.

'Can I help you?' she asked cautiously. Then: 'Is this about Pete?'

The woman stared for a moment longer, with a glassy attentiveness. 'More about you, really.' Her voice was low and nasal.

For a moment Meredith's heart leaped with hope. 'Have you seen him? Where is he? Is he safe?'

The woman leaned against the door frame, her massive shoulder seeming to envelope it. 'First things first. You don't recognise me, do you? And why would you? Last time you saw me, I was seven stone. *You* don't look so different though. A fair bit more weight yourself, but then that's middle age for you, isn't it? The dreaded spread.'

Why was she making small talk? 'Just tell me what you know about Pete. Are you an old college friend of his?'

The woman laughed, a deep rattling sound coming from her chest. 'I don't think he'd consider himself my friend at the moment, no.'

Even then, Meredith didn't get it. 'Please. I'm sorry I don't recognise you. Unless you've got something to tell me about Pete – my brother, he's missing, you see – you'll have to forgive me, this is a very stressful time for me.'

'I'll come in,' the woman announced, flicking her roll-up into the flowerbed and pushing past Meredith into the house, crushing her back into the coat rack so that she almost fell against the wall. The entrance hall was too small for them both.

Meredith felt bewildered, invaded, the beginnings of fear, even though this was clearly not an attacker. Just some fat, annoying old woman. She followed her into her living room – a room where almost nobody aside from Pete, Ralph, Paula and Andrea had ever been – and found the woman lowering herself with difficulty onto the worn velvet sofa, her large arse sending up a little cloud of dust on impact.

'Do I know you?' Meredith demanded. She didn't feel like being polite any longer. 'Like I said, this is really not a good time for me. Please just tell me what you want.'

'Cuppa tea would be nice.'

The woman leaned her elbows on her legs and rested her chins in her hand. She was dressed in a shapeless tube skirt, a cross-body ethnic sort of bag with little mirrors embroidered on it, a long, cheap-looking sweatshirt and sandals that cut into the flesh of her puffy feet, which swelled over the straps.

'I must say I'm disappointed you don't remember me, Meredith,' she said. Her toenails were thick and yellowed.

'I know it's been a long time, but I suppose it figures that I was just completely ... *disposable* to you. Someone you could use and abuse and then forget about.'

Meredith had been fiddling with a magazine on the table, but this made her head jerk up in alarm. Who the hell was this? Someone from a rival band to Cohen's? Someone she'd known in the squat, or at the record company? For a minute she wondered if this was Iain's doing.

'I don't know what you're talking about. Please get to the point, otherwise you're going to have to leave, now.'

The woman smiled meanly, displaying small brown teeth. 'Sarum Discs, 1983?'

Meredith stared at her, the penny still not dropping. 'The record shop in Salisbury? Yeah, I worked there for a while. For Alaric. Did you know him?'

'Meredith, I worked there too. All week, and you came in on Saturdays.'

Meredith frowned. The only person she remembered working there too was little hippie Caitlin. She studied the woman's doughy face more carefully. This woman surely had nothing to do with her brother and the murders. '*Caitlin?*'

She laughed. 'Well done. Throw that girl a biscuit – we got there in the end. Except I'm not Caitlin anymore. I prefer Catherine these days. Cait. However you want to spell it. Catherine sounds classier, don't you think? My old bitch of a mum was an Irish tinker. Oh, sorry, you can't call them that anymore can you. Traveller. Whatever. She turned her back on me when I first got put away. Twenty-six, I was! Imagine your mum turning her back on you just because you weren't right in the head! And whose fault was that in the first place, I ask you? Bloody right: hers! She smokes skunk all through her pregnancy and then blames *me* for having a screw loose? Unbelievable. So naturally I didn't want to be called the name she gave me, not after that.'

Meredith was still finding it difficult to reconcile the Caitlin she remembered with the bloated, red-faced, ruined-looking woman in front of her. She remembered admiring Caitlin's neat little nose, back then, but this Caitlin's nose was an aberration – squashed and flattened and almost bulbous. And yet ... perhaps the resemblance was there. The dimple in the chin, the way her lip curled slightly when she spoke. It *could* be her, Meredith thought. Just about.

The woman placed her hands on her thighs and heaved herself heavily to her feet. 'There we have it.' She had a trace of a West Country accent.

'I don't understand why you're here, or how you found me,' Meredith said warily. She wanted to add, *And I don't give a shit about your relationship with your mother*, but thought she'd better not.

This woman had the weirdest air of loose cannon Meredith had ever seen, as if at any moment she would grow three-inch fangs and launch herself at her throat. She'd never witnessed anything like it. She tried to remember if she had ever had an inkling back when they worked together, but was pretty sure she hadn't. The only thing linking young Caitlin with this one was the roll-up that had been a constant between her fingers back then too.

Caitlin/Catherine narrowed her eyes at her, a mean grin squinching them up further still. 'Ah now, this is where it gets interesting,' she said. 'Make me a cuppa first, would you? I'd better come with you to supervise, I suppose.' Her tone was grumbling, as if she'd been badly inconvenienced.

'Supervise me?' Meredith said, half bemused, half furious. 'In my own house?'

The woman just nodded, heaving herself back up again and gesturing Meredith to accompany her to the kitchen, where she flicked on the kettle and proprietorially unhooked two mugs from the mug tree on the counter. 'I'll let you take it from here,' she said.

Meredith glared at her. It felt like a weird dream.

'You left the back door open. That's not wise – anybody could come in. Let me fix that for you,' Caitlin/Catherine said, waddling over to it, locking the door and pocketing the key. Meredith was about to shout at her when she turned, and the expression of sheer malevolence on her face made Meredith pause: 'I have something of yours,' Caitlin said. 'Or should I say *someone*? I have someone of yours.'

The breath stopped in Meredith's throat. '*Pete.* You've got Pete. Why? Is he OK? What happened? Where is he?'

She couldn't stop herself grabbing at Caitlin's arm. Caitlin looked down at her hand with utter disdain, peeling her fingers away.

That was the moment Meredith lost it. All the stress and tension of Pete's disappearance crammed itself into her head until she felt as if it was about to explode. She got so close to the other woman's face that she could see all her disgusting blackheads and open pores and smell her rancid breath.

She screamed at her, any sense of reality slipping away, as if she was in a film or a weird nightmare. 'Stop playing with me, you mad bitch. Where is he? Tell me right now or I'm calling the police and you'll get carted back off to whatever loony asylum you've been mouldering in for the last thirty fucking years.'

Caitlin pushed strong hands into Meredith's chest, palms landing hard on her breasts – whether accidentally or purposefully Meredith didn't know; all she could see was the rage in her eyes as Caitlin shoved her away, hard, then shook her head.

'Oh, dear, dear, dear, Meredith, that won't do at all. You don't speak to me like that. Ever. Not if you want to see your brother alive again. Do you understand? I wouldn't have thought you could afford to risk losing someone else, after Ralph and Andrea. I mean, apart from Ralph's pathetic little wifey, you don't actually seem to *have* anybody else. Bit weird, isn't it, to get to fifty-two years of age and have so few friends? I was almost running out of people to choose! But Pete's obviously the prize.'

Meredith realised she was hyperventilating, fear rising off her in waves.

'Why? Why would you do this to me? To Paula, and Pete? I haven't even set eyes on you for decades!'

Caitlin barked out a laugh. 'And that, Meredith, is your answer. You haven't seen me in FUCKING DECADES because YOU fucking got me locked up in 1983 and I haven't been out since. Not till NOW! How do you THINK that makes me feel about you, you cheating slut?'

Even through the terror, Meredith felt an outraged sense of injustice. What the hell was this madwoman talking about?

'How could that possibly have been my fault?'

Caitlin rolled her eyes and shook her head, as if Meredith was a particularly stupid child.

'Because you just take whatever you want, even when it doesn't belong to you, without giving a shit about anybody else's feelings, don't you?'

It was Meredith's turn to shake her head. 'I'm sorry, I don't know...'

She felt in her back pocket for her phone, to see if there was some discreet way she could call 999, or Gemma, yell at her to get back here with help, then barricade herself in the bathroom. But what if Caitlin then went straight off and killed Pete?

What if she'd *already* killed Pete?

'Greenham Common,' Caitlin spat. 'I saw you.'

Meredith frowned. She didn't recall seeing *her*. 'I remember you telling me about it, that you were going, in a camper van with a load of others. That was why I went, because I had a teddy-bear costume. We all got arrested. Next thing I heard was that you'd been charged with assault. But what did that have to do with me?'

In her head she was whispering, *Hold on Pete, I'll get you out. I'll get you back. Just hold on a bit longer. Please don't be dead.*

'God, you really haven't a clue, have you?'

Caitlin advanced towards her, suddenly snaking out an arm and grabbing Meredith's throat in her fingers. It felt like an iron pincer. Meredith couldn't breathe.

With her free hand, Caitlin delved behind Meredith, into the back pocket of her dungarees, and whipped out the phone, stuffing it deep about her own person – Meredith couldn't see where, because so many white spots were dancing jigs in front of her eyes.

Caitlin frisked her one-handed, hard and efficient, slapping rather than patting her down: hips, crotch, front and back pockets. She slapped harder and harder, until the slaps turned to punches; kidney, belly, side, breast…

She spoke fast and low, the words seeming to run together: 'You stole the love of my life. You ruined my life, you left me with nothing. You took Sam. You just fucking *took* her. It's *your* fault they locked me up. Seeing you with her, seeing you kissing each other in your stupid fucking teddy-bear costumes, it's your fault I went mental. You're lucky it wasn't you. If I'd been close enough it'd have been *your* fucking eye I poked out.'

Sam.

Samantha.

Caitlin was still on her hitting spree. Finding nothing else in

Meredith's pockets, she punched her hard in the eye, and Meredith would have fallen backwards if Caitlin's hand hadn't still been around her throat. Through the agonising crimson haze, she had a flash of memory: being in the shop with Caitlin wittering on and on about Sam, how wonderful Sam was, how much she loved Sam.

She'd thought Sam was a boy. They all had. Caitlin never said she was gay. She hadn't wanted us to know Sam was a girl!

Fucking Samantha. That bitch had been nothing but trouble in her life. If it wasn't for her, Meredith thought frantically, she'd never have dropped out of school, broken her promise to look after Mum, abandoned Pete ... and for what? To have this maniac stalk and kill everyone she loved?

Caitlin dropped her hand, and Meredith fell to the floor, gagging and clutching her throat, holding her palm tight over her eye because it felt as if it was about to pop out.

Caitlin crouched down next to her, her knees cracking like dry twigs. 'But hey, you were worth waiting for. *This* has been worth waiting for. And the fun's only just starting. All we need to do now is one more tiny bit of waiting. We'll just wait till it starts getting dark. Anything good on the telly?'

When Meredith opened the one eye that still would, there was a gun pointing right at the end of her nose, and beyond it, Caitlin's sickly smile.

Get back here, Gemma. I need you. Don't leave me with this crazy person.

The only possible consolation was that if Crazy Caitlin was here with her, Meredith, then at least she couldn't be anywhere torturing Pete...

Caitlin sat down on the sofa first, jerking the gun to indicate Meredith should join her. Meredith sat cautiously, terrified, but at the same time with a slow, dawning understanding. All the years of threats, memories of the slow swoosh of green paint, abusive letters, mean-spirited snipes and intimidation. The person responsible for all of this, for her near-death experience in the van that night, for her ruined hand.

For Ralph's death, and Andrea's. That person was sitting right next to her on a sofa. If it wasn't for Pete's life being under threat, Meredith would have launched herself at her then and there.

In a tiny way, it was almost – almost – a relief, to put a face to the tormentor, to know that there was a reason; and there was someone to be held accountable for it.

But as she had that thought, another simultaneous one occurred: so it *was* her own fault that Ralph and Andrea had been killed.

She couldn't let it happen to Pete as well. She wouldn't let it.

49

Meredith

They sat on the sofa together in silence for more than two interminable hours, as dusk then gradual darkness pressed against the small square panes of the cottage windows. Where the hell was Gemma?

Caitlin had the gun in one hand in her lap and the TV remote in the other, her eyes glued to the screen. At one point she even slipped off her unattractive sandals and put her bare feet up on the coffee table, a warped facsimile of domesticity. When Meredith caught the first whiff of cheesy odour she felt bile rise in her throat and had to swallow hard not to gag.

Instead, she forced herself to concentrate; alternating between glancing at the gun and keeping her attention outside the cottage – Leonard sometimes popped in on his night rounds, for a chinwag and a cup of tea. She didn't love the unannounced visits, since Leonard had a habit of wittering mindlessly on until Meredith had to feign a yawn and tell him she needed to get to bed, but she tolerated him doing this as she could tell the man was lonely. And he only dropped in occasionally – anything past the orchard and vegetable gardens wasn't, strictly speaking, in his patrol remit.

She'd have given anything to hear his footsteps on the gravel now though – but would that just precipitate something worse? Caitlin didn't seem like she would be reluctant to use that gun. *I can't be responsible for another death,* Meredith thought.

She needed to pee, but guessed that Caitlin would insist on coming into the bathroom with her. That was too humiliating to contemplate. She'd just have to hold it.

Finally, as Big Ben bonged on screen to signify the ten o'clock news,

Caitlin put down the remote and fished a mobile out of her skirt pocket, tapping out a text with her free thumb. The phone was on silent but a reply must have come almost immediately, as she nodded with satisfaction and hauled herself off the sofa, pushing the gun into Meredith's side and sliding her feet back into her shoes.

Shit, Meredith thought. *She's got an accomplice.* It would be two against one, assuming that Pete was in some way incapacitated.

Oh God, perhaps it was the man from the Luton van ... Meredith's bowels contorted in a twist of terror.

'Righty ho, time to go. Hey, that rhymes!' Caitlin cackled. 'Let's go visit your precious twinny. I'm sure he's missing you. And guess what? He's only five minutes' walk away!'

Meredith stared up at her. 'Pete's here, on the estate?' she croaked. 'You know we have security. CCTV cameras everywhere. Night security guards.'

Her thoughts immediately turned to the ice house, Ralph's body in the pond. There had been a round-the-clock police cordon put on the ice house now it was a crime scene. Caitlin had some nerve, coming back here.

Unless she had disposed of the police guards ... And even if she hadn't, how could she, Meredith, raise the alarm? The ice house was a ten-minute walk away.

'Is he in the ice house?' Meredith tried to keep the fear out of her voice, but the feel of the gun barrel pressing into her liver was as petrifying as that night in the van; as if the gun's mouth was literally tapping into her terror; it was somehow more visceral like this than seeing it trained on her face.

Caitlin just smiled, an infuriating little smirk that pushed her cheeks into two puffy cushions and made her eyes almost vanish. 'I know all about how good your "security" is, Meredith.'

She gave a manic thumbs-up, like someone about to watch a favourite TV show, something she'd looked forward to all week. It was impossible to imagine Samantha in a relationship with this insane woman, thought Meredith.

But then Caitlin had been young and gorgeous once too. Perhaps Samantha was just as bloated, her strawberry-red hair now dulled and grey, her teeth as misshapen and stained as Caitlin's. For a furious moment, Meredith wished Samantha *was* there, standing in front of her right now. She'd grab Caitlin's gun and kill her without hesitation, for all the pain she'd blithely inflicted for so many years.

But first she had to rescue Pete.

The fear returned, and Meredith realised it was fear for Pete, not for herself. That helped, in a small way: took it outside of herself, gave it a name and a purpose.

'Hey,' Caitlin said as they left the house, pushing Meredith ahead of her and closing the door behind them. 'I love your dungarees, where did you get them?'

What the fuck? The woman was off her head. Meredith didn't answer, shoving her hands into the deep pockets of the dungarees as they walked along the gravel path in the shadow of the huge old wall of the vegetable garden. The moon was bright, illuminating their way, and the gentle hoot of an owl felt very slightly reassuring.

'Charity shop,' Meredith muttered at last.

'Ew,' said Caitlin. 'How you can wear other people's cast-offs I just don't know. Disgusting. You might find anything in the pockets.'

Meredith almost stopped in her tracks. A huge jolt of fresh adrenaline swept up and down her body. The pockets! Could it still be in there? Very, very slowly, as Caitlin walked behind her, she crept the fingers of her right hand up towards her belly button and a few inches higher, to feel through the denim at the bottom of the dungarees' bib pocket.

It was still there! Caitlin hadn't thought to check that pocket when she'd been frisking/slapping her – perhaps she hadn't realised there was even a pocket up there.

She had a weapon! Albeit a very small one, but it was better than nothing; a tiny claw of a gardening knife, folded in on itself like a curved penknife. It had been in the side pocket of the case of the faulty secateurs. She'd forgotten all about it until Caitlin had unwittingly reminded her.

With her right elbow pressed close to her side, since Caitlin was slightly to the left and behind her, Meredith sneaked her fingers into the pocket and fished out the knife. It was small enough to fit in the palm of her hand. She dropped it into the more accessible side pocket of the dungarees, then slid her hand in after it, clutching it tightly until its plastic shaft was as warm as her feverish skin.

Caitlin hadn't noticed.

Meredith's heart pounded so hard that she could feel its throb in her throat, like a drum beat on the cool summer night air. If she could flip open the knife fast enough, and undetected, there was hope.

They walked for five minutes or so, downhill, towards the fringes of the Minstead Estate, through the orchard and out the other side to where the rough parkland began. They were heading, Meredith realised, towards the tennis court and the old swimming pool. On one of the first Lady Minstead's whims, the pool had been built quite far from the house – apparently she wanted the daily walk through the grounds to get to it, and didn't want it to be visible from the house. The Minstead House Trust had latterly decided that, since it was of no interest to the general public, it wasn't worth maintaining, and it had been abandoned once the house had been opened to the public two decades before. Meredith often thought what a shame that was; she'd have loved a lunchtime swim during her workday.

Nobody had played on the tennis court for years either. It stood, net-less, weeds sprouting from fissures in the tarmac, the white lines blurred and obscured by time and bird crap. Meredith and Caitlin walked across it now, the light from Caitlin's phone screen bobbing ahead of them. Meredith could see another faint flickering light coming from the window of the pool house. Her heart leaped in anticipation then cramped with pain. Was *this* where Pete had been all this time, so close by, practically hidden in plain sight? Why hadn't the police searched the grounds? Why hadn't *she*?

Caitlin heaved open the heavy pool house door, one of those old lead-paned glass ones. It gave an exaggerated haunted-house creak. 'We're here,' she called out, quietly, presumably to the person who'd sent her that text earlier.

A candle flame wavered in a jam jar on the side of the empty swimming pool, the only pinprick of light in the cold musty air of the place. Meredith felt a deep chill – the temperature seemed to have dropped by ten degrees from the summer night air of the grounds outside. At first she couldn't make out anything apart from the tiny flickering light – Caitlin had switched off the torch function on her phone.

Where was her own phone, Meredith wondered? Was it still in Caitlin's pocket or had the woman left it behind?

The pool house seemed so still. Caitlin must have thought so too because she called again, a faint tone of irritation in her voice: 'Graeme!'

Graeme? Who was Graeme?

50

Meredith

'Here,' came a strange, high-low, echoey voice in reply, seemingly from the depths of the empty pool.

That voice, speaking just one word, triggered something in Meredith, some long-suppressed memory. A black-gloved hand snaking through the hole kicked in her bedroom door and grabbing her ankle. Being driven away in the black interior of a Luton van, death reaching for her with cold fingers under its metal door. The shouting, the flash of the knife plunging into the back of her hand ... the terror.

It was him.

Meredith made a sound, an involuntary gasp, and felt her knees buckle. Warm urine released from her full bladder and streamed down her legs, filling the chill air with a sweet, straw-like smell, the exact same reaction she'd had when this person had broken into her bedroom. Just for a moment the relief of pressure in her belly, and the warmth on her cold skin, were welcome.

'Oh God,' she whispered, on her knees. 'Help us.' He'd rescued her before. Now they needed another Mr Martindale...

'Ugh,' said Caitlin in disgust, her voice suddenly loud in the darkness. 'She's pissed herself. Gross. Where are you?'

'Checking on the brother. He's down here, in a right state. Not sure how we're gonna get him out.'

Meredith's head shot up. 'What have you done to him? Pete! Pete? Can you hear me?'

'Shut up, bitch,' snapped Caitlin. 'One more word, one movement, and I'll shoot you both right now.'

She flicked the torch function back again and shone it into the empty pool. Pain pierced Meredith's heart as she saw Pete caught in the yellow beam, curled up naked on the blue-tiled floor, not moving. That ... *person* knelt over him.

It was the first time Meredith had seen the man's face, and with yet another shock she realised it was a face she recognised. She gasped again, but didn't dare speak, not with the glint of the gun barrel pointing in her direction.

The person – Graeme – worked here, at Minstead. One of the gardeners. Meredith felt a furious pulse throb in her neck. She'd seen him many times, crouching in a flowerbed, pruning, digging, weeding, never meeting Meredith's eye or returning her 'morning' when she passed him on the way to work, or was out walking Ceri's dog. Meredith had always assumed the man had learning difficulties, or was extremely shy, or just terminally antisocial. He'd even come into the shop once.

Oh God, she thought. *No wonder he knew my movements, and Pete's.* He could've been watching them for months. Probably had been. It was him who decapitated the flowers in the front garden, who knocked all the stuff off the shelves, probably left the dead rat in the fireplace.

It was starting to make sense. This Graeme was Caitlin's bitch. *Caitlin* was the one who ordered the attack on her all those years ago. Maybe Graeme had been inside too, in the intervening years, when things had gone quiet. Now they were both out – and Graeme clearly had been for some time.

Meredith was desperate to get to Pete, to climb into the pool and hug him, but it was as if Caitlin read her mind – or maybe she had unknowingly made a move forwards – because Caitlin snapped again: 'I told you, don't move. We're going in a minute.'

Going? Going where?

'I'm not going to kill you here,' Caitlin added. 'Thought we'd take a little walk first. So while we get him out, you can get your kit off too. Chop, chop.'

Meredith stared at her, stunned. 'What?'

'Kit off, cloth ears. I want you both naked.'

'Why?'

Caitlin chuckled meanly. 'Why not? You're an exhibitionist, aren't you? Prancing round for all those years like a cunt on stages, singing your stupid little songs ... You both came into the world at the same time starkers, so you should both leave the same way.'

The woman wasn't even making sense. This could not be happening, Meredith thought. It was just impossible.

If she stripped, she'd lose the knife. She couldn't lose the knife; it was all she had. Also – Pete didn't look like he could go anywhere, let alone climb a ladder.

Graeme seemed to agree. 'Cath ... you'll have to help me get him out. Maybe we should do it here. Put him out of his misery.'

Caitlin tutted irritably. 'Not doing it here; they'd be found too soon. Too much evidence. We'll stick to the plan. He's probably just faking anyway. You.' She turned to Meredith. 'Strip off.'

She tucked the gun into the waistband of her skirt and hauled herself, puffing with exertion, over the edge of the pool, down a rusty iron ladder at what was once the shallow end. Meredith palmed the knife once more then, still clutching it, unhooked the clasps on the bib of her dungarees, and let them slip off to the floor. The darkness was a help – neither Caitlin nor Graeme should be able to see that she was holding anything.

The air was cool, particularly on her piss-wet thighs, but there was too much adrenaline flowing round her body to allow her to feel cold. She stripped off her T-shirt and bra, and hooked off her knickers, so intent on concealing the knife that she didn't even feel shame at her nakedness. She had to do it fast, before Caitlin got close again.

In the pool, Caitlin laughed. 'Look at that: what a show-off. Didn't I say she was an exhibitionist? Nice tits too, what I can see of them. Shame it's so dark in here.'

As Caitlin and Graeme took hold of Pete and hauled him to his feet, his head hanging like a crucified man's, Meredith surreptitiously wedged the knife into her armpit. She'd briefly considered concealing it inside her vagina, but that would have been harder to do unnoticed, and harder to deploy fast if an opportunity to use it arose ... As long as Caitlin didn't make her walk with her arms in the air, this was probably the only option.

Pete moaned as the pair shoved him towards the ladder: a long, guttural sound that made Meredith's skin crawl with sympathy and shared pain. What the fuck had Graeme done to him? It was too dark to see if he had any obvious injuries or was bleeding. But as they reached the steps again, he was able to grasp its rails. They shoved him up, each with a meaty hand on one of his buttocks, but he seemed too far gone to care.

Finally he reached the top of the ladder and flopped over on the tiles at her feet, twisting and gasping like a landed fish. Meredith couldn't stop herself rushing towards him.

'Stop,' barked Caitlin, the gun again trained on her. Then she slowly swung it round to Pete. 'You touch him and I'll shoot you both right here.'

'Pete,' Meredith said, unable to prevent a strangled sob escaping. 'I'm so sorry.'

He couldn't speak, but their eyes met in a silent glint of love and desperation. *I love you*, Meredith mouthed, and he nodded, once, although it was too dark for him to have seen. He must have just known.

'Up,' Caitlin commanded. Graeme had joined her and was staring at the twins with an expression of gleeful fascination on his face.

Pete staggered to his feet, swaying, and it was only the tool wedged in her armpit that held Meredith back from helping him up.

'Off we go, then,' said Caitlin cheerfully, pushing them out into the warm night.

We're not the first to be in this position, thought Meredith numbly. *We're not unique.* She thought of killing fields and concentration camps; massacres; people being frogmarched towards open graves they'd been forced to dig themselves first. *It's just death. Comes to us all at some point.* What did she have to live for anyway, if Pete was going to die too? Nothing. It was better this way.

Just a month earlier she'd had a twin she adored and three close friends, which was actually more than enough for her, these days. Only one of them was still alive – but once all this shit came out, there was no way Paula would ever still be her friend.

All that hate and revenge, for one kiss on a silo, dressed as a teddy bear, almost thirty-five years ago. Meredith wished again she'd never laid eyes on that toxic Kansan, blithely lying her way through a hedonistic life, knowing that her red hair and green eyes would dazzle any doubts away. She probably never even had any desire for nuclear disarmament – all Greenham was to her was an endless supply of open legs and sleeping bags for her to lick her way into. Then Meredith wished that Caitlin had been honest enough to admit that her precious Sam was a girl.

And that Caitlin wasn't a lunatic.

But then, she thought, *there's no point in all that, is there?* What's done is done, as her mother used to say. And now she was done, too. If wishes were horses ... something else her mother would quote. Meredith never understood what it meant.

It was a tiny bit of comfort knowing she would die in the grounds of the estate, with the person she loved most in the world. At least the last thing she'd see and hear was the sway of dark branches, the reassuring little noises she heard through the open window of her bedroom every night, tiny claws digging, black snouts snuffling.

The grass felt soft and cool under her bare feet. Death opened her arms and smiled a dark, welcoming smile, and for a moment Meredith felt a transcendent calm as she and Pete began to stumble barefoot towards their destiny.

51

Gemma

By the time Gemma drove around the side of Minstead House to the staff gate, she was feeling flustered and anxious. It was now an hour later than she said she'd pick Meredith up, and the woman wasn't answering her phone, nor had she replied to her texts. Nor was she where she was supposed to have been.

Gemma had gone to collect Meredith from Trevor and Johnny's barge as agreed, only to find it locked up and empty, no sign of life inside when she peered through the portholes. She'd had to go round all the other boats, knocking and calling, to see if anybody knew where they were. Nobody did, so she then drove around the three nearest pubs in the village, eventually finding the couple having a pint in the garden of the third. They were sitting in silence, looking glum, both wearing shades although the last soft rays of the evening sun had slid across to the other side of the garden. Trevor was twirling the tips of his moustache in an absent-minded way, and Johnny was flicking through his phone.

Gemma walked across to them, her heels sinking into the soft grass, exhaling with relief that she'd found them – while simultaneously swallowing irritation that she'd had to chase around the village to do it.

'Hi – is Meredith here? I've just been to pick her up from the wharf, but she didn't tell me you were all going to the pub.'

'Oh, she went home this afternoon. She promised she'd let you know...' Johnny said, looking up from his phone. 'She didn't want to stay. Said it was fine, as you were coming later.' He paused. 'Have you not seen her all day?'

'No!' Gemma said, more loudly than she'd intended. Worry had made her feel scratchy. 'For God's sake, why did she do that? Why did you let her?'

The two men raised their eyebrows at one another. 'We're not her keepers,' Trevor said huffily. 'She can do what she wants, and she asked me to drive her home, so I did. How were we meant to know she wouldn't do as she was told?'

'We were just trying to help,' Johnny added, in a more conciliatory voice. 'Poor woman's in a right state. Is there any news about Pete?'

Gemma took a deep breath. 'Yes, of course. It was very kind of you. No, I'm afraid there's still no sign as to his whereabouts.'

She thought about vengeful, psychopathic Catherine Brown, Pete's disappearance and Meredith's vulnerability, and felt sick. In her mind's eye she had a brief mental flash of Meredith's little cottage, seen from above, a mere pinprick on the map of the Minstead Estate.

'I need to go,' she said abruptly. 'Thanks guys. Enjoy your pint.'

⊓⊔

Gemma keyed the code Meredith had given her into the keypad to open the side gate, reading the digits off the palm of her hand where she'd written them in biro. She could barely see them as dusk tipped into dark; black splodges of sheep moving in the field behind her, the soft rip of their teeth tearing at the grass the only sound she could hear.

Dark, and eerily quiet. Not for the first time, she wondered how Meredith could bear to live in such a secluded place. But it was one of many contradictions in the woman's personality. She seemed so lonely and isolated, and yet chose to live out here on her own. She shunned people, yet worked in a customer-facing role – and did a great job with it. Gemma had sat in the shop with her the day before, and despite all the trauma Meredith had recently suffered, she was unfailingly polite, good-natured and helpful to each and every visitor who trailed in and out of the door in search of Minstead House toffee and tea towels. It was as if she was able to shut out the unwelcome emotions completely. Perhaps, Gemma thought, that was a throwback from her days in the public eye, where constant media scrutiny had taught her extreme self-possession.

The gate slid open and Gemma drove slowly in. She parked in the staff car park, which was empty apart from Meredith's quirky little vintage car and two others, presumably night security. So she was likely still on the premises. That was good – wasn't it? As Gemma approached the steps at the far end of the car park, down to Meredith's cottage, she could see a light or two burning in the windows. Feeling prematurely relieved that everything looked normal, she walked up to the cottage, noting that the gate had swung open.

She banged the door knocker, loudly, the sound reverberating around the silent grounds. Nobody came, so she banged again, then moved across and peered through the living-room window. The curtains were drawn, but she was able to see a sliver of the room through a gap. It didn't look as if anyone was there.

Gemma checked the time on her phone – 10.20 p.m. It was possible that Meredith was in the bath, or had gone to bed, but surely she wouldn't sleep through the sound of hammering on the door? She'd be down, to check it wasn't Pete coming back – or to see if someone was bringing news of him. She rang Meredith's mobile again and held her ear to the letterbox to see if she could hear its ringtone coming from inside the house. Still nothing.

She wasn't there. This was now seriously worrying.

Gemma took out her phone, realising she'd left her radio in the car: 'Mav— … Mark? It's me again, Gemma. Sorry to ring you so late, but I'm worried. I'm at Minstead but can't get hold of Meredith Vincent. Has Emad rung you and told you what he found out about that escaped prisoner? The thing is, Meredith's car's here but there's no sign of her at home.'

'Yep, Emad filled me in,' he said, when Gemma had finished. 'Let's get a trace on Meredith's mobile. Leave it with me – I'll get an oral authorisation from the Sup. It'll only show the nearest tower, obviously, but at least we should be able to tell if she's still on site. I'll get straight back to you when I hear. What are you going to do now?'

Good question, Gemma thought. 'Wait in the car for a bit, I guess.'

'Not sure you should be there on your own, Meeks,' he said, which was the closest thing he'd ever said to her that expressed concern and affection. She'd certainly never heard him call her by her nickname. Was he worried, or just mellowing?

'Do you think I should come back?'

'Hang fire for a few minutes, let's see if she's on the premises. If she is, I'll send some backup over. Wait – isn't there still someone up there on duty at the ice house? I'll call you right back.'

Gemma trudged back up the steps to the car park, feeling in a strange sort of limbo. She was just opening her car door when her phone rang again. It was Emad.

'Hi, Gemma,' he said diffidently. 'How's it going?'

'She wasn't on the boat. Pete's neighbours dropped her back home earlier – but she's not here. I'm really worried now.'

Emad cleared his throat, a sudden harsh sound in Gemma's ear, at such odds with his gentle voice that it made her recoil. 'Um. Actually – I'm outside the staff gate. Do you know the code? Thought you could do with some company.'

Gemma laughed, half relieved and half annoyed. 'You're off duty!'

'Yeah. Nothing better to do. I called in and asked them to create a CAD for me up at Minstead, in case you needed backup, so I'll take the flak if it turns out to be nothing.'

She gave him the gate code, realising that she did feel happier that she wasn't there on her own and that there was a CAD in place – Computer Aided Dispatch. She would have done it herself if necessary, but this covered them both, and frankly, didn't make her the one who'd gone a bit OTT.

Her phone beeped. Mavis again, texting her:

Tried to call but line busy. Just seen Emad's CAD. Cordon at ice house now lifted – forensics complete – glad he's there instead. I'll let you know if I get a trace on MV's phone. Keep me posted pls. Mark.

Two minutes later she heard Emad putter down the gravel path on his moped. She couldn't help smiling when she saw his face loom into her eyeline, framed by the helmet.

'I'm not in uniform,' he said anxiously, kicking down the moped's stand and pulling off his helmet.

'So I see,' Gemma said, grinning at him.

'I mean, will I be in trouble?'

'Nah. There wasn't time, and you've phoned in a CAD. Don't stress about it. Mavis is trying to trace Meredith's phone, but just when you rang I remembered something – I persuaded her to give me her Apple login a few days ago, in case anything like this ever happened, and I could use Find My iPhone. She wasn't keen but I said it might be an idea, as a precaution. Let's try it now. Hop in.'

Emad opened the passenger door and climbed in, clutching the helmet on his lap like a pet, as Gemma slid behind the wheel and started logging into iCloud. She tapped in Meredith's details and waited a moment, tucking a long strand of curly hair back behind her ears. When she looked up, Emad was staring at her profile. When he saw she'd caught him doing it, he flushed briefly and looked away, embarrassed.

Something pinged on the screen and Gemma exclaimed, 'Oh! Her phone's still at Minstead. That's not good. Why isn't she answering the door then?'

Then she frowned and zoomed into the map with two fingers. 'Wait – it's not in the cottage. It's in an outbuilding somewhere in the grounds. Fuck. This is not good. Looks like it's about ten minutes away from the house. Let's get down there.'

'Should we call it in?' Emad paused. 'Sorry for the stupid questions. This is all still so ... new.'

She smiled at him again. 'It's not a problem, Emad, honestly. No-one expects you to know everything straight away. It took me a good couple of years before I started feeling like I had half a clue about how it all worked. So, yeah I think we should – better safe than sorry. At least they'll know where we are. And then we can see what's going on – maybe she just went for a walk, you never know...'

They glanced doubtfully at each other, as Gemma radioed and left brief, calm instructions with the control room as to their whereabouts, in case they might need assistance on the hurry-up. Then they set off across the dark lawns, towards a copse of trees due south of the house and Meredith's cottage, Gemma holding her phone out in front of her to see the map coordinates, while Emad lit the way with his torch app.

An owl hooted softly above them, making Gemma jump. For the first time, she felt the deep twitchy pull of fear, as if it was something physical inside her body, running around inside the nerve endings. She recalled the photos on the whiteboard of Ralph Allerton's bloated corpse, and then what Emad had reported the mental nurse saying – the one who'd shown him Catherine Brown's room with its Blu Tack pockmarks on the wall: how the staff thought it was funny that the woman had so many photos of a band she hated.

A woman so violent that she'd been considered a serious risk to herself and others for the best part of thirty years, with a rap sheet of violence as long as her arm. Not someone you'd want to have hating you.

'Not gonna lie, Emad,' Gemma admitted softly. 'I'm a bit scared.'

There was a pause, then Emad replied, 'Me too.'

'She's a nutter, this Brown woman, isn't she? Sounds like she might've been responsible for the attack on Meredith last time, if she's got someone on the outside helping her.' Gemma felt a huge pang of worry for both Meredith and Pete. If it really was Brown, going to the trouble of escaping, presumably for the sole reason of having another pop at Meredith, they could be in serious trouble.

'Sounds like,' agreed Emad. 'But all this might not be anything to do with her.'

'Really glad you're here.'

'Me too.'

They walked fast in silence for a couple of minutes, the only sound their panting breaths, until the lawns ended abruptly at a wooden fence. There was a gate set into it a little way along.

'Through here, I think. Shit, look.' She pointed the phone at the gate, where a padlock had been sawn open and was swinging by its hasp. 'This isn't looking good...'

They broke into a run, down a narrow gravel path twisting through more trees, until suddenly they arrived at a small, detached single-storey mock-Tudor building.

'Round here,' Emad whispered, and they tiptoed towards the entrance, trying to silence their laboured breathing.

Gemma could feel her heart banging so hard in her ribcage from both exertion and fear that she thought it would be audible for miles around. The heavy Victorian iron door, set with stained-glass panels, was ajar, but all seemed dark and silent inside.

They crept in.

'It's an old swimming pool,' Emad said in wonder. 'Wow. No idea this was here. Why is it so far from the house?'

Gemma didn't answer. She shone her torch around. 'Hello? Meredith? Are you there? Are you hurt?'

No reply, just a faint scuffling from somewhere around the edge that made them both jump again.

'Mice,' whispered Emad.

'Or rats,' said Gemma darkly. 'I hate rats.'

'So this is definitely where it says Meredith's phone is?' Emad began to explore around the edge of the pool. When his torchlight picked out the tiles on the bottom of the pool, he gasped. 'Fuck – look.'

In the middle of the empty pool's bottom was a small but clearly-recognisable puddle of blood, so dark in the dim light that it looked black.

'Oh God. And – here. Clothes. What the hell's going on?' Gemma had found a pile of men's clothes on the tiled side – shorts, boxers, T-shirt. Like someone had decided to have an impromptu skinny dip, without noticing that the pool had no water in it. No shoes or socks though, she noted.

'More over here,' said Emad. 'Looks like dungarees.'

'Meredith was wearing dungarees earlier. Let's see...'

She joined him and examined the pile, feeling through the pockets for Meredith's iPhone. Nothing, except a scrunched-up tissue and a Minstead House-branded cherry lip balm. 'They're hers, I'm sure. Those are her flip-flops. I wouldn't recognise her underwear, obviously, but that bra looks about the right size. I don't remember what top she was wearing, but the dungarees...'

'So how come her flip-flops are here, but there are no shoes by the guy's clothes?'

Emad shone his torch near Gemma's face. 'We're assuming they're Pete's, aren't we...?'

'Let's get back-up,' Gemma said. 'This is too weird.'

'Is the app still saying her phone's in here?' Emad asked.

Gemma immediately scrolled to it. 'You call it in, I'll check.'

Emad rang the control room and was just reciting his CAD number to the desk sergeant when Gemma exclaimed again and jabbed a finger at her screen.

'Phone's showing as *moved*. It's now there. Looks to be about—'

She was interrupted by the deafening and unmistakeable crack of a gunshot, from what sounded like very nearby.

'Send backup, air support and ground unit, out to beyond the old pool house on the Minstead Estate, south of the main house, NOW!' Emad yelled down the phone. 'Gunshot heard. Hostage situation likely,' and without hesitation or consultation they both ran out into the black night in the direction of the sound.

52

Meredith

By the time Caitlin had forced them off the grass and onto a small dark path through the woodland, dimly lit by Graeme's torch, Meredith had changed her mind; acceptance had evaporated and was replaced by a nugget of something small and determined. Her bare feet were studded with small stones, her thighs scratched by brambles, whippy twigs snatched at her face, and it felt as if the universe was telling her to get a grip. She didn't want to die. And there was no fucking way these two psychos were going to hurt Pete any more than they already had.

'Down the next hill, head for the far side of that field,' Meredith heard Graeme mutter to Caitlin.

Right, she thought. By her reckoning the far boundary of the Minstead Estate was at least another five minutes' walk. Graeme had obviously done his homework. Meredith felt her newfound survival instinct wobble. It couldn't be more remote. If Caitlin shot them, cleared the pool house of their clothes and left their bodies by the fence down there, it could be weeks before they were found.

But that's not going to happen, she thought, gritting her teeth, welcoming the pain in her toe as a sharp stone pierced it. There'd be nothing to fear anymore, because if she survived, it would mean that Caitlin and Graeme would either be dead – Meredith's preferred option – or back in prison.

She, Meredith, would finally be free.

If – *when* – she survived this, everything would change. No more paranoid hiding away, pretending to be someone else, moaning to herself about being lonely. She'd travel. Cambodia, Vietnam, Australia – she hadn't even been on a plane since the days of touring with the band. Maybe even try and meet someone, have a relationship finally...

As she limped along, she felt the hard moulded plastic of the knife's handle in her armpit, reminding her that she had to seize her moment, and soon.

How to do it? *Think, Meredith.*

Caitlin. She had to go for Caitlin, get the gun off her, before Graeme had time to react and pile in. It would be two against one, because Pete wouldn't be able to help.

Pete was staggering along next to her like a zombie, worryingly glassy-eyed and silent, just the rasp of his laboured breath and the fact that he was still just about upright convincing her that he was still with them. His arm hung at a weird angle away from his body.

'Stay with me, Pete,' she muttered.

'Shut it,' snapped Caitlin.

The moon suddenly came out from behind a cloud, illuminating them in a chiaroscuro of shadow-dappled branches. Meredith had a flash of an image – a pencil drawing of two naked children, a boy and a girl, hand in hand, walking into woods that welcomed them and whispered encouragements in the breeze lifting the leaves. Minstead was embracing all the ghosts of everyone who'd ever loved the place like she did.

Graeme and Caitlin were still behind them, the torch illuminating their own feet but not Meredith and Pete's – but this was good. It meant that Meredith could discreetly pluck the penknife tool out of her armpit and flip it open. She turned to try and catch Pete's eye, and to her astonishment, he flashed a stare back, first at her and then down at the knife, his focus sharpened for the first time since she'd seen him curled up on the pool's tiled floor.

His eyebrows shot up and in the moonlight she was sure he gave her a tiny complicit wink and a nod of his head – nothing that anybody else would ever have caught, but magnified by their twin telepathy. At that moment he was the spitting image of their father, how Meredith remembered him on the sidelines of her numerous races at sports day, smiling a smile just for her, not jumping up and down and almost aggressively urging her towards the finish line like the other dads did, but a calm, encouraging presence that gave her that final burst of strength – that helped her to give it her all; to not quit, to stay focussed on the goal.

And now Pete was giving her that signal.

This was it.

She was about to turn and run at Caitlin and Graeme, yelling, hoping that the element of surprise would give her that split-second advantage, but before she did, Pete suddenly groaned, stopped walking and collapsed on the roots of the pine tree they'd been passing beneath, lying motionless. Everything in Meredith instinctively wanted to run to him – but then she remembered the wink. He'd done it on purpose as a distraction.

Graeme was slightly behind Caitlin, holding the torch. Caitlin's arm – the one holding the gun – dropped very slightly as she exclaimed with surprise.

'Oh, for—' she began irritably as Meredith spun a hundred and eighty degrees on her heel and charged her, holding up the curved tool like a claw, screaming a banshee-like howl and launching herself at her, stabbing blindly with the claw until she saw the gun slip out of Caitlin's hand. Caitlin too sank to the ground, growling with pain and fury.

Meredith and Graeme simultaneously lunged for the gun, but luck was on Meredith's side – it had dropped very slightly closer to her than to Graeme. She was able to grab it and aim it right in Graeme's face, stopping the confused, angry man in his tracks.

Graeme and Caitlin must have both assumed that they would meet no resistance from the twins, Meredith thought; that she would be just as fearful as she'd been the time before in the van. A moment of triumphant adrenaline surging through her as she backed away towards Pete's prone body, to get out of reach of Caitlin's arms, where the woman lay flailing like an upended turtle.

In the moment before Graeme switched off the torch, Meredith saw that Caitlin was covered in blood: face, chest, head. For a moment she couldn't believe that *she* had done this; she didn't remember being that frenzied, but the preceding moments had been a blur of rage and self-preservation. She'd floored her, and it felt good.

Then they were plunged into darkness, and Meredith's bravado faltered. The woods were silent, a briefly complicit enemy, the still-ness only broken by Caitlin's bubbling breaths and Graeme's furious curses. For a moment they were caught in a tableau of hunters and prey, although it wasn't clear who was which. Meredith forced her frozen hands to grip the gun, finger on trigger; the cold iron centre of her world, determiner of who lived and who died.

She heard a rustle, footsteps stealthily approaching in the darkness, the same footsteps that had creaked up her staircase all those years ago and kicked a hole in her door, in her psyche, in her future.

Not this time.

'FUCK YOU!' she screamed hoarsely, and fired in the direction of the footsteps. The noise sent sleeping birds flapping skywards in panic, and in the split-second flash from the gun Meredith saw Graeme's body jerk up as if it wanted to join the birds, before hearing it crash to the leafy floor.

'Pete,' Meredith croaked, and heard his whispered, 'Here,' in reply.

At that moment, the almost-full moon came out from behind a cloud and cast the scene in shocking, ice-blue light, both Graeme and Caitlin lying motionless, Caitlin's neck glinting with the blade of the gardening tool still sticking out of it.

'Jesus,' Meredith said, dropping to her knees and crawling over to Pete, wrapping her shaking arms around his cold, naked body. 'I killed them both. Fuck, Pete, I killed them.'

'You saved us,' he whispered. 'You saved us, Mez.'

From somewhere up near the house, they heard a faint shouting – a woman's voice, drifting on the night air: 'Meredith! Pete! Meredith! Pete!'

'Thank God. I think that's Gemma,' Meredith mumbled. 'She must have heard the shot. I can't shout back. I'm too tired.' She held on to

Pete's back, wrapping her arms gently around him, not knowing where or what – or how bad – his injuries were.

Another sound superseded the shouting; the whump, whump of helicopter blades, shortly followed by the sweep of a searchlight beam. 'You won't need to,' said Pete, with effort. His voice was becoming fainter. 'Not sure how much longer...'

'Don't say it,' Meredith said fiercely. 'You have to hang on. I'm not going through all this to lose you now. Don't even fucking think about it. Promise me, Pete. They're coming for us.'

53

Gemma and Emad

Gemma would never forget the sight that greeted her when she and Emad finally reached the spot where the shot had come from. Her chest was heaving and her breath coming in pants as they crashed through the woods, trying to avoid roots and trunks, the light from her and Emad's phone torches both illuminating and wrong-footing them as the dual beams jogged up and down confusingly.

One shot, she thought. One person dead, possibly. Why only one? Had Catherine Brown killed Pete in front of Meredith, part of her extended revenge plan?

Oh God, she thought, *stop speculating and just get there*. Emad was ahead of her, fleeter of foot and more agile. He'd been like that at school too, she recalled, a flash of a sports day memory coming to her. Sweet, doe-eyed Emad.

For the first time it occurred to her that they too were in serious danger, running full pelt through dark trees towards an insane person with a gun, their only weapon the handcuffs that she'd clipped to the belt loops of her trousers earlier. *Two* insane people, most likely, as Brown must have an accomplice. She didn't escape until the morning after Pete went missing, so someone else must have taken him. And she'd had a getaway driver.

If anything happened to Emad, she would feel responsible. He was a rookie; this was his first life-and-death shout – and he wasn't even on duty.

'There's the chopper,' Emad panted over his shoulder. 'Looks like they've found them with thermal imaging.'

'Straight ahead then.' Gemma felt like she'd gone into a sort of trance, her whole being focussed on getting there, like the time she ran a half marathon; one foot in front of the other, keep deep breathing ... 'Nearly there.'

What the hell do we do when we actually get there? she thought.

Even though she'd seen their clothes lying by the empty swimming pool, it was still a shock to see the twins stark naked, lying under a tree like two overgrown fairy-tale characters abandoned in the woods. Hansel and Gretel, Gemma thought. They'd been siblings too. There was something so primal about the sight – and that was before Emad's torch beam landed on the bloodied body of who Gemma assumed was Catherine Brown and a bulky man lying motionless next to her a few feet away, like two harpooned whales.

'Jesus,' Emad yelped.

Catherine Brown had a number of visible stab wounds all over her face and torso, and an odd little curved blade sticking out of her neck, whereas the man was completely covered in blood from what looked like a shot to the chest. That must have been the shot they'd heard.

'Meredith!' Gemma called, running over to her, peeling off her stripy cotton jumper and laying it over the middle of Meredith's pale torso.

⊓⊔

Emad wished he hadn't left his leather jacket in Gemma's car – he was only wearing a shirt, but he stripped that off too.

Meredith was still clutching the pistol, her whole body shaking so much with cold and shock that Emad worried she might accidentally pull the trigger again.

Gemma was cooing at them in an unsteady voice. 'It's OK, love, you're all right; you're both safe now. Help's on its way. Pete, can you hear me?'

'He's badly hurt,' Meredith managed, her own voice bubbly with panic. 'I don't know how he managed to walk this far. I think he's got a broken arm and bad concussion, maybe a fractured skull. Please, help him.'

Gemma gently removed the gun from Meredith's grip, holding her hand instead, stroking it as Emad draped his shirt over Pete's motionless frame. With Gemma's help, Meredith slowly pulled herself up to a seated position and tried to lay the stripy jumper over Pete as well, but Gemma stopped her. 'You're freezing. You put this one on.'

Meredith ignored her. 'He's passed out. Don't let him die,' she begged.

'Shhh,' Gemma soothed, while Emad hopped uselessly from foot to foot. 'Just a few more moments. The helicopter crew will have life-support equipment and a stretcher for Pete. They can get him straight to hospital. Lift your arms up for me...'

Finally, Meredith permitted Gemma to help her into the jumper, raising her arms like a submissive child, and Emad couldn't help the relief he felt that Meredith's breasts were now covered. He knew he shouldn't be having such puerile thoughts, but he also felt very self-conscious that he was standing there without his shirt, and relieved that Gemma had been wearing a bra – it was weird enough to see her in just that. He wasn't sure he could have coped with seeing her chest completely bare as well as Meredith's.

⊓⊔

The police helicopter was noisily landing in a paddock a few metres away, rendering further conversation impossible.

Thank God it got here so fast, thought Emad, glancing at Pete's lifeless body. *And thank God I didn't have to try and immobilise either of them.* The dead guy was built like a brick shithouse.

He was just looking at his phone to call through to the station with an update, when a sudden movement caught his eye, illuminated for a moment by the chopper's lights shining through the trees. Unnoticed and not heard over the din of the chopper's blades, Catherine Brown had managed to stagger to her feet. She was pulling the small curved knife out of her neck and brandishing it over her head as she lumbered towards Meredith, who was seated with her back to her. Brown was about to bring it down...

Shit! Emad thought in panic. Why hadn't they checked that she and her sidekick were actually dead? Mavis would kill him. And then the adrenaline kicked in and he no longer had any conscious thoughts other than protecting Meredith and Gemma where they sat. With a yell he dropped his phone and threw himself with full force at the bloodied woman, just as she started to plunge the knife down, knocking her to the ground sideways, relieved to see the weapon fly out of her blood-slick hand.

Brown screamed with weak fury as Emad tried to roll her onto her front and sit on her, but she was so large and heavy, he couldn't shift her before she managed to headbutt him, his nose exploding with pain and blood that he could feel running down over his mouth and neck and making a sticky, matted nest in his chest hair.

Gemma had leaped up and run across to him, yanking at the handcuffs attached to the waistband of her trousers.

'Get her feet,' she barked, kicking Brown over onto her front and holding her down with her foot until she could wrench the woman's arms behind her back and cuff them together.

Emad kneeled on Brown's thrashing feet, trying to ignore his busted septum, every movement she made under his shins sending pain stabbing through his skull.

They finally managed to incapacitate her, Gemma pressing the woman's face into the loamy forest floor, harder than was strictly necessary. Lights and shouts could be seen and heard through the trees. Backup was here.

Meredith, bare-legged with Gemma's jumper just about covering her hips, had got to her feet and made her way over to where the three of them variously sat and lay. She crouched slowly down next to Catherine, reaching out and pushing Gemma's hand away from the back of the woman's head, replacing it with her own, seeming to not care that she was still naked from the waist down. She grabbed a handful of Catherine's hair and yanked it, until Catherine's doughy, bloody face was revealed, now covered with rotting leaves and soil, looking as though she had just been dug up.

Meredith locked eyes with her as the footsteps and bobbing lights grew closer. Catherine's glare didn't flinch away, a last gesture of defiance. Meredith smiled, slowly, her voice sounding stronger and more menacing than Emad had ever heard it.

'You failed, Caitlin. Again. What a waste of your life, eh? What a waste of Ralph's life, Andrea's life, Andrea's baby's life. But you still failed. You didn't get me, and you didn't get Pete, and now we're going to be free of you forever because you'll never be free again, not now your little puppet is dead. You spent the best part of thirty years trying to make my life a misery, and it hasn't worked.'

'It was all for Sam,' Brown whispered, all defiance extinguished, and Meredith laughed bitterly.

'Sam never gave a shit about you, or me. And I don't think you believe that, anyway. You just wanted someone else to blame for your psychopathic behaviour, and so you decided it was all *my* fault.'

The armed-response team crashed through the trees, at the exact moment Meredith spat in Brown's face. 'You're pathetic.'

A year later
Meredith

The plane was poised at the top of the runway, at that specific moment in time where it seemed that the thrumming anticipation of the passengers was all that would propel it into the sky. Meredith had forgotten what this felt like. Last time she was on an aeroplane had been on the final tour Cohen did in Japan, in 1994. She wasn't nervous, though. She was looking forward to it so much that she felt she could probably fly unaided.

'Welcome to Flight BA352 to Ankara,' intoned the captain over the tannoy.

'Look at us, going on holiday like normal people,' she said to Pete, whose long legs were sticking out ahead of him in the bulkhead.

'About bloody time, too,' he said. 'Can't imagine anyone's ever needed a holiday more than we do.'

They'd had to wait until after Catherine Brown's murder trial, although her three life sentences without parole back in Rampton had been worth it.

The trial had been gruelling in the extreme. All sorts of details the twins had been unaware of had been produced: including Graeme's van, found parked near the spot in the woods at the back of Minstead, equipped with plastic sheeting, spades and shovels, part of the preparations to bury Meredith and Pete's bodies. They'd had to listen to Andrea's parents sobbing in the public gallery behind them, day after day, their Hungarian translator muttering the horrific details quietly into their ears throughout.

Paula had pushed past Meredith in the corridor after the session in which she gave evidence. She hadn't spoken to her, and her son, Jackson, at her side, had hissed, '*Slag.*'

Unfortunately, a passing hack had overheard. Next thing, Paula had sold her story to all the papers, and for a couple of weeks Meredith had been featured in numerous tabloid articles with headlines such as 'My Ex Rockstar Best Friend Shagged My Husband Right before His Murder'. Paula had sold the house and moved away, to live closer to her sister in Norfolk, so at least they weren't likely to bump into each other.

Meredith wrote her a long and heartfelt letter of apology, to which Paula never replied; but it was closure, of sorts, for Meredith at least. She hadn't expected Paula to ever forgive her.

Her colleagues at Minstead House had been astonished to learn about her fling with Ralph, as well as her colourful past as Cohen's punky lead singer, but, to a tweedy man and twinsetted woman, they had been kind and supportive. The Earl begged her not to resign every time she tried to, and in the end they agreed she could have a year's sabbatical to recuperate and do some travelling. By the time she got back, hopefully the not-inconsiderable numbers of Cohen's fan club who kept showing up at the shop and the cottage, asking for her, would have lost interest again. Meredith had moved in with Pete on the boat, partly to escape the curious tourists and partly to help him recuperate from the operation on his arm.

They'd moved the *Barton Bee* to a different mooring though, in Kingston, to be nearer the hospital and away from the marina in Minstead, which held so many poignant memories of Andrea and Ralph.

At least Meredith had had the chance to thank Gemma properly for finding them in time. She hadn't seen her since the days after the attack, when Gemma visited Pete in hospital. Six months on, with her braces off and her hair cut into a more sophisticated shoulder-length style, Meredith thought she looked much older, in a good way. More self-possessed, less gauche. They caught up for coffee in a café round the corner from the court.

'It wasn't just me,' Gemma had said. 'It was Emad, really, who did more of the important stuff. He's the one who figured out the link between you and Catherine-slash-Caitlin. He was the one who stopped her from killing you after we'd assumed she was dead. I couldn't have done it without him.'

'Well, please tell him how grateful Pete and I are, to him too,' Meredith had said, and to her surprise, Gemma had blushed, the pink stain making her resemble her younger self again.

'I'll tell him this evening,' she said, fiddling with the sugar bowl. 'We've actually been dating for a few months now.'

'Ha! That's lovely,' said Meredith, with only a slight trace of wistfulness.

Pete too had a new relationship – with Lucy, the physiotherapist who'd been helping him post-op. She was lovely, petite and pretty, with a dry sense of humour that made them both laugh a lot.

It felt amazing to laugh again.

Lucy didn't have enough holiday entitlement left to join them in their villa for the whole three weeks of their holiday, but she was flying out for the last seven days. Meredith was looking forward to it almost as much as Pete.

During the week after Catherine Brown's sentencing, there was one final surprise. The new Minstead shop manager received an email with the words 'Please Forward to Meredith Vincent' in the subject line.

When Meredith read it, it didn't take her long to reply, giving only the address of the boat's mooring, and a date.

At the appointed time, two late-middle-aged women turned up on the dock, both dressed in sensible matching holiday clothes: sturdy jeans, walking boots, some sort of Gore-Tex jacket, little backpacks, both with short iron-grey hair. Meredith had to do a double-take, but as soon as she saw the face of the taller of the two, she knew.

'They're here,' she said to Pete, who was resting on the sofa with his feet up. She stuck her head out of the door, and waved them over.

'Samantha! Come on in.'

Samantha immediately hugged her tight, and for a moment the years and all the resentment fell away.

'My God, Meredith, what you've been through. And look at you!'

– she pushed Meredith gently away and scrutinised her at arms' length. Her midwestern twang was even stronger than it had been last time they'd met, Meredith thought. 'You look amazing, honey ... Oh, and this is my wife, Shelley!'

They all shook hands. Shelley was short and cheerful; older than Samantha with deep laugh lines around her eyes and furrows on her forehead.

'You look just the same,' said Meredith, which made Samantha laugh. 'Oh sure. Thirty-five years later, with grey hair and flab! Thirty-five years, can you believe it?'

'Is it really?' Meredith asked, although she remembered well. 1983, the year she dropped out of her A levels, lost Dad, abandoned Pete and her mother.

Samantha had been the architect of so much destruction in her life, and for years Meredith had only been able to focus on that. But now that Samantha was finally standing in front of her, Meredith was able to remember the positive things too. Love, passion, the boys in the band. Creativity, and the success that followed. Her first love.

After all, it hadn't been Samantha's fault that Caitlin was a psychopath.

Later, over mugs of tea and a plate of biscuits, Samantha leaned forwards.

'I just needed to apologise to you both,' she said. 'You and Pete. I was a total bitch to you both that night. I know it's, like, decades ago, but I'm so sorry. And then when I learned what sparked Caitlin's first breakdown, I felt even worse. I had no idea she'd even seen us on that silo. Or that she was so crazy about me. I'd just thought it was a casual thing.' She had the grace to look sheepish. 'I was pretty promiscuous back in those days,' she added.

Meredith remembered the girl with the short black curls who'd been at Cohen's first ever gig, and who Pete had seen Samantha kissing. The fist of jealousy and grief in her belly when he told her about them. She smiled ruefully. 'I think we were both unlucky to have encountered Caitlin,' she said.

'She found out that I was teaching at KU – the University of Kansas – and wrote me, you know,' Samantha said. 'A few times, in the nineties. I feel bad about that, too. I ought to have passed the letters on to the police and then she might have been stopped, but at the time I just thought they were the rantings of a lunatic. She kept going on and on about you, and how we'd ruined her life, and that she'd make us both pay. She would "sort you out" first then come for me. But I knew she was locked up, so I just never took it seriously. Then that time the police interviewed me about a blackmail attempt, I was mortified that you might think the letter really had been from me. If they'd told me about your attack, I could've helped, but I didn't know. I just thought it was about the blackmail. I'd have known it was her doing, straight away. She was lucky to have found that guy who'd do anything for her.'

'Or we were unlucky,' Pete contributed from the sofa.

'That too,' Samantha said, looking as if she was going to cry. 'Can you ever forgive me?'

Meredith smiled at her. 'Yeah. It's not your fault. Thanks for taking time to come and find me.'

'Couldn't come over to show Shelley your beautiful country and not see you, could I? We're going walking in the Lake District next week.'

'Lovely,' Meredith said. 'Pete and I are off on holiday next month too. My first holiday in over twenty years. I can't believe it.'

⊓⊔

And now here they were, on the plane, and Meredith did finally believe it. She looked down at her hands, one grasping each armrest, the skin on the backs of them both now of a uniform colour and smoothness. Pete wasn't the only one who'd had surgery in the past year.

Pete saw her smile and grinned back. 'They look so great. Funny, isn't it? I'd pretty much stopped noticing your scar, but now it's gone, I can't stop looking. They're just hands, but...'

'I know, me neither,' said Meredith. 'Although I still do have a scar.'

She traced the edges of a silvery hairline scar around the skin graft. 'I like this one, though. It's like a map showing new roads.'

Pete laughed. 'That's poetic. You should put it into a song.'

The plane's engines thrust and roared, and the overhead lockers rattled as they left the ground with a lurch, neither of them speaking for a moment until the tension eased and they were above the clouds.

'Maybe I will,' said Meredith.

Acknowledgements

I owe huge thanks to all the following people:

Simon Alcock, Franco Ianelli and Chris Phillips – I definitely couldn't write anything involving any sort of police procedure without all your invaluable help. Sorry for the random text questions and thank you so much for your patience and wisdom!

James Law, for giving up an afternoon to sit in a New Forest pub with me and help me brainstorm the plot after I got stuck.

John Freestone, for tidal information, and Pete Sortwell, for crucial research help back in the book's early days.

Martin Toseland, for trying to help me work out my character's motivations. With wine.

Karen Cocker, for giving up her time to help me with FLO procedures – any inaccuracies are either necessary for the plot, or are my own mistakes...

Helen Russell, for inspiration and background information on the life of the manager of a busy gift shop (and all the funny stories!).

Suzy Aitcheson, for planting the seed of inspiration that became Minstead House.

Elaine Burtenshaw and Marisa Rosato, for important plot assistance and hospitality over (top-quality) dinner on the Isle of Wight.

Amanda Hills, for assistance with boat terminology and insight into life on the river.

Phil 'Agent Phil' Patterson and the folk at Marjacq for being supportive and encouraging.

The Slice Girls, for support both practical and emotional: Susi Holliday, Steph Broadribb, AK Benedict, Alex Sokoloff (and the

Hon Member, Harley Jane Kozak). My other lovely author friends, especially Marnie Riches, Amanda Jennings, Kat Diamond, Caroline Green, all the Killer Women, all the Team Orenda authors and of course all of CS, you know who you are...

The powerhouse that is Karen Sullivan, and everyone else who makes Team Orenda tick: West Camel, Max Okore, Anne Cater, Liz Barnsley, Cole Sullivan, Sophie Goodfellow and Mark Swan.

Thanks to Simon Mattacks, audiobook narrator extraordinaire and buddy, for narrating the audiobook without taking the whole accent thing too literally.

Finally, to all the amazing bloggers who have been so incredibly supportive and dedicated – your work is very much appreciated. And to anyone who's ever read and enjoyed my books!